KU-339-137

THE AMERICAN LIBRARY

10, RUE DU GÉNÉRAL CAMOU
75007 PARIS

WITHDRAWN

13708

17-264

· T * H * E ·
ARGUS
GAMBIT

Éliane BENISTI

Agent Littéraire

80, rue des Saints-Pères

75007 PARIS - Tél. (1) 42.22.85.33

·T·H·E·
ARGUS
GAMBIT

THE DREAMERS OF THE DAY
BOOK ONE

David D. Ross

AMERICAN
PARIS
LIBRARY

ST. MARTIN'S PRESS
NEW YORK

THE ARGUS GAMBIT. Copyright © 1989 by David D. Ross. All rights reserved. Printed in the United States of America. No part of this book may be used or reproduced in any manner whatsoever without written permission except in the case of brief quotations embodied in critical articles or reviews. For information, address St. Martin's Press, 175 Fifth Avenue, New York, N.Y. 10010.

Design by Glen M. Edelstein

Library of Congress Cataloging-in-Publication Data

Ross, David D.
    The Argus gambit / David D. Ross
        p.   cm.
    ISBN 0-312-03287-0
    I. Title
    PS3568.084317A74   1989   89–30421
    813'.54—dc20   CIP

First Edition
10 9 8 7 6 5 4 3 2 1

DRAMATIS PERSONAE

In Washington, D.C.

President Jeffrey Shefferton
Senator Archer McClaren of Oregon
Senator Charles Ellsworth Macadew of Colorado
Secretary of Space Sheridan Mayfield
Percy Shelley Manners of Illinois, Senate Majority Leader
Secretary of State Randolph Harmon

The Cops

Inspector Mel Hardrim, Greater Washington Police Department
Deputy Assistant Director of the FBI Roger Ferdinand
Lenore Lippman of the U.S. Justice Department, Computer
    Division
Deputy Inspector Kirsten Fale
Inspector Alexis Moran, Detroit Field Division

The Capitalists

Adam Scott, maverick industrialist/inventor
Jason Scott, Adam's son and founder of Prometheus
    Enterprises
Horatius Krebs, owner of the Python Corp.
Jacob Kane, engineer, and Krebs's lieutenant
Rita Holcombe Duce, owner of the Tectonics Corp.
Bethany Williams, Rita Duce's executive assistant

The Scientists

Dorian Nye, Nobel Prize-winning physicist and adviser to the
    President

Alfred Strubeck, physicist, creator of the Strubeck equations
Sherlock Michlanski, Nobel Prize-winning physicist for his
    discovery of antigravity
Philip Norrison, astronomer
Noah Chambless, botanist, head of the team investigating the
    Santa Bella blight
Ralph Ferman, biologist on the team investigating the blight

In the Unified Soviet State

First Secretary Peter Brasnikov
Marshal Antonine Mikhailovich Tiomkin, Commander of the
    Strategic Spaceborne Forces
Colonel General Erwin Wolff, the Institute of Magnetic
    Propulsion
Colonel Pavel Orlov, Tiomkin's aide and former pupil
General Wen Chin, another protege of Tiomkin's

Any technological device that deprives a man of his job is evil; any scientific advancement that changes society without the permission of that society is criminal; any achievement that produces benefits without equally distributing those benefits among all people is antidemocratic.

—Senator Archer McClaren

. . . the first great crisis of the Republic ended with the Civil War, the second when she took up world leadership at the end of World War II . . . and the third great crisis began when she cast it aside.

—Grenoble Milner, *America: The Third Century*

. . . Americans never really ceased to be isolationist in sentiment, nor did they feel comfortable with the role of global power. As chaos spread: Paris in flames, London gutted, European civil war, the Ukraine in revolt, Tokyo occupied by Neo-Samurais, mass suicide in the Middle East; America recoiled to her ramparts, safe under her laser umbrella, while her robot subs mined the rich sea beds . . .

—Avery Fienstein, *Red Midnight, Black Noon*

PART

* 1 *

BLOOD
OF
THE LAMB

Chapter

* 1 *

"*The lines of Demarcation shall be Meridian 30 degrees West and Meridian 169 degrees West, including all oceans and territories north of the Panama Canal. Within these boundaries no merchant or military craft of foreign origin, neither land, sea, nor air, shall be permitted, except those member nations of the Pan-American Pact.*"
—*Thirty-first Amendment to the Constitution of the United States of America.*

1

In the dying fire of afternoon Flight 104 returned home.

For most of the journey from the People's Republic of England to Neil Armstrong International, the HST Lockheed Pegasus was scanned by the picket line of missile patrol airships extending from Greenland to Patagonia. An escort of four navy F-60s joined her at the invisible frontier of Fortress America, then she dipped into the low cloud cover to make her long gliding approach.

Five minutes out her running lights were visible from the deck of the nuclear USS *Oakland*, where surface-to-air missiles were targeted to fire if the aircraft deviated from her recorded flight plan.

She popped out of the fog. The setting sun broke into view, as if to welcome home the envoy of the president-elect, the first American to visit Europe since the last marines were evacuated from the United States embassy in London twenty-five years earlier. On Armstrong field, a man-made island resting on pylons fifteen miles from New England, Flight 104's flaming engines created a false dawn.

Ear-wrenching vibration climbed the acoustical ladder from basso profundo to piccolo. The plane's wheels sang as she touched down and taxied the length of the runway to a glass-steel tower, which impaled the island where the waves pounded patiently against its massive stilts.

This flight was extraordinary. It had required an executive order of the lame-duck president to allow Dorian Nye, Nobel Prize-winning physicist, to return from his mission. Airport security had been called out to restrain the newsmen while Nye's entourage disembarked.

Naturally all these precautions translated into delays and red tape for the average airline passenger. Despite over a hundred and fifty years of civil aviation, some things never changed.

Mel Hardrim, inspector of the Greater Washington Metropolitan Police, had joined Nye in London. As they emerged from the tunnel onto a platform overlooking the main floor of the terminal, his eyes moved over the crowd, which squirmed like a giant millipede recoiling on itself. Overhead, an immense holocube displayed a three-dimensional advertisement for a household detergent with bioengineered microscopic biobots called "stain eaters."

As they followed a ramp down into the crowd, Hardrim was uneasy. He disliked crowded lobbies, even when they were cordoned off. Nye coughed at his side.

Dr. Nye's tweed overcoat was draped over his left arm while he hefted an attaché/computer with his right hand. It was cold but sweat beaded on his shiny dome. He was small, flabby, and wore a look of eternal chagrin. His otherwise entirely nondescript face was distinguished by beetling brows and a firm mouth.

Hardrim smelled fear. Perhaps Nye was just nervous about the hearing, but Hardrim's warning intuition was blazing red.

He saw several people in the crowd with computer interface implants sprouting from the backs of their necks. 'Faces, they were called by the prejudiced and fearful. Hardrim counted himself in that group. Any of them could have been a potential assassin, as far as he was concerned.

Nye shielded dazzled eyes against the holovision lights. Hardrim squinted and guided him with a hand on his elbow. Tonight Nye would meet with the president-elect. Tomorrow he would testify before Senator Macadew's Special Committee on the World Famine. Until then, Hardrim was nursemaid to a sixty-year-old man.

A man burst between two security men. Swiveling, Hardrim saw a glint of metal and moved to shield Nye. The scientist instinctively stepped back, covering his face with his hand. It was the last gesture he ever made.

Hardrim saw and felt a white flash and searing wind near his temple. Dorian Nye's head exploded, splattering him with brains and blood and bone. Another shot! Hardrim reeled to his knees. Through a red haze he saw the assassin on his face in a pool of blood. His own hand gripped a revolver. He had instinctively shot the killer.

A guard cautiously rolled the assassin's body over.

"Clean through the heart."

The guard said something else; then, for some silly reason, his head started expanding like a balloon. Then the fake marble floor jumped up and slugged Hardrim in the face.

2

Somewhere a kid was beating a toy drum. Hardrim wanted to tell him to stop, but whenever he tried, the tattoo increased. He swallowed at the cotton lining his throat and squirmed under maniac dwarves wielding needles.

He sat up suddenly and was rewarded by a lance of agony in his head. His torso was swathed in bandages and he was in an infirmary. The air was pungent with antiseptics.

"Are you feeling better?"

Startled, Hardrim was hit by a wave of pain. When it subsided he saw a man in the brown and black security uniform squinting at him. The man was middle-aged, late seventies, Hardrim judged, although it was getting more difficult to tell whether someone was in his fifties or approaching his second century.

"No," snapped Hardrim, "I'm not feeling better."

"Just a little nick in your side. You could hurt yourself worse opening a can of tuna."

"How did I get this?"

"Fella you shot got off one more before he croaked. You remember now?"

Hardrim shook his head and was sorry.

"I don't remember shooting him."

"Well, you seem okay. Better get up. They need you in Control."

"Who are 'they'?"

"They is him. That is to say, Mr. Lin, the director of security on the island."

"I guess I'll have to see him sooner or later."

"Sooner would be better, sir."

Hardrim swung his bare feet to the cold floor. He looked around helplessly. "Where're my clothes?"

"Getting cleaned. They got blood and puke all over 'em."

Hardrim glanced at his bony legs, "I can't go to airport security looking like this."

"Your looks I can't do much about, but I can rustle you up a spare uniform until your suit is cleaned."

The outfit was tight in the waist and loose in the hips.

He was led down a corridor, past a poster with a stylized portrait of Uncle Sam pointing a finger at him with the admonition: I WANT YOU! TO HAVE A BABY. At the end of the corridor was a reinforced steel door with raised lettering that warned: AIRPORT SECURITY—NO ADMITTANCE.

Inside was a paranoid utopian novelist's dream, or nightmare, come true. The walls were lined with monitoring holocubes, computer consoles and techs with earphones and implanted interfaces. Images changed constantly, enlarging to focus on individuals, shrinking to embrace crowds. They spied on every conceivable spot: snack bars, ticket dispensers, information desks, and restrooms.

A tall man with short blond hair, scarred hands, and muscles that rippled with each movement, stood at the center. A small personal computer was holstered at his side. He turned abruptly. His icy eyes were unreadable; his mouth was a line set in stone.

"Inspector, glad you could make it. I'm Alain Lin." He didn't offer his hand.

"I didn't seem to have much choice, Mr. Lin."

"No," Lin's mouthed twitched into a smile. "We all admired your heroics this afternoon, but we have some very sticky questions that need answering. The inconvenience is regrettable, but as a police officer I'm sure you understand. Now—"

"What is your exact status here?" Hardrim interrupted.

"Status?"

"Do you have police powers? Who has jurisdiction over this matter?"

"Matter?"

"I acknowledge you control airport security, but this is a homicide."

"The island is outside state jurisdiction. Until federal authorities arrive I have protolegal status—"

"Protolegal? No such thing."

"Quasilegal then."

"You'll have to do better than that."

Lin struggled to be pleasant. "An important man has been killed in my airport. When the FBI arrives I'd like to give them a little information. Would you please answer a few questions?"

"Since you phrase it that way, of course."

Lin breathed out and nodded. He signaled a tech and a large screen came to life.

"This is the tape of the shooting." Hardrim relived the event from a dispassionate perspective outside himself. He was amazed how short the episode was—seconds, really.

"There's no question about your actions. You moved when you saw the threat and almost took the fatal bullet yourself. Most exemplary, though ineffective."

"Yeah. Sorry I screwed up on that final little detail, Lin."

Lin ignored the sarcasm. "Do you know this man?" The assassin's face filled the screen: pale, drawn, tortured from within; the body emaciated and frail, yet strong enough to throw two security men aside like tenpins. He was in his late fifties or early sixties.

"I've never seen him before today."

"Too bad," said Lin tonelessly. "We have a positive ID but no background. We're checking the main computer in D.C."

"How'd he sneak that gun past you guys? I thought you had metal detection down to a fine art?"

"That is an embarrassing question, Inspector, but now I have one for you." He looked at Hardrim with predatory glee. "When did you discover that the man you were escorting was not Dorian Nye?"

"What the hell—?"

"Or did you know it all along?"

"Dammit!"

"Did you plan his disappearance?"

"What are you talking about?"

Instead of answering, Lin sat at a console. "Project the FBI file fingerprints of Dorian Nye on a split screen with the victim's fingerprints." Two sets appeared. Hardrim stared, dumbfounded.

"Interesting, isn't it?" Lin's fingers played rapidly over the keyboard. "If you're not convinced, here are the two retinal patterns. There's no doubt. The man you escorted was altered surgically to look like Nye."

"That's impossible!" said Hardrim. "London police delivered Nye to me personally at Heathrow. His identity checked—"

"We'll verify that with the English authorities, but even if it checks, you're not off the hook. You could have made a substitution before you left London. The possibilities are many and we'll explore them all before you leave. I won't have an international incident laid at my door. I will find out who's responsible. From where I sit, you're the prime suspect. For now, the island will be sealed off. If Nye's here, we'll find him."

"Like you found the gun?"

Lin didn't answer, but a muscle twitched in the crook of his arm.

"Until things are settled, consider yourself under arrest."

"I want to contact my superiors," said Hardrim stiffly.

"Of course. Don't delude yourself. They can't help you. A plane from Washington will land shortly with federal investigators who'll be very interested in talking with you. You may go."

3

Deputy Assistant Director Roger Ferdinand had the moral air of a Torquemada, the smoothness of a Borgia, and a reputation for doggedness rivaling that of the defunct Royal Canadian Mounted Police. Hardrim knew his reputation, and that Alain Lin was mistaken if he thought anyone but Ferdinand was going to run the investigation.

When Hardrim was brought back he wasn't surprised to see Lin deferring to the federal cop like an obsequious maître d'. Obviously he hadn't told Ferdinand yet about the slain impostor. Hardrim wondered why. He decided that maybe the deputy assistant director hadn't stopped talking since his arrival.

"I think," (his favorite two-word combination) "that the bureau will give this assassination a triple-A priority." Ferdinand paced like a caged animal, his red velvet cape billowing against his tailored three-piece sharkskin suit at every turn. "The director called me from a three-day leave to deal with this and the damned stunt pilot he hired almost rammed into that blasted metal radio antenna you have sticking out of the ocean."

"That's a Tesla tower," volunteered Lin, "connected to the Omar Trench core tap. It provides a third of New England's electricity."

"Whatever." Ferdinand dismissed the unwanted information. "Too bad this mess blew up so quickly. Bad luck, having two hundred newsmen on the island. We find out anything, somebody will leak it and we'll read about it on the cube before we can send it to Washington."

He stopped pacing and stared at Lin coldly. "I don't like stepping off a plane to have some newsman tell me who the suspect was and give me more background on him than I have. I don't like that at all."

"That was no leak," said Lin evenly. "A reporter remembered him from twenty-five years ago and made the connection."

"I heard the plop-plop-plop of something soft and messy hitting the fan. My God, we've got to live with the new president the next four years! It's different for those TEA baboons. He's pledged to dissolve their stupid organization when he takes office. I knew it was a mistake for the bureau to take over technology enforcement.

"What will we say? 'Gee, Mr. President, we're sorry we let out the man who murdered the patron saint of your party twenty-five years ago. We're sorry he plugged your science adviser and special envoy to Europe, but accidents happen! We thought he was in a sanitarium.' Sanitarium! That SOB, uh—I mean our great leader—will be down on us like a ton of nuclear waste. I hope I didn't offend any fellow Progressive Nationalists with that remark."

"You're a Progressive Nationalist?" said Lin incredulously.

"I joined after the election and had it back-dated two years." He smiled at Lin. "You have to learn how to deal with politicians."

"I have some information that may help with a particular politician." Lin looked at Hardrim, who realized why Lin had been holding back. Lin began talking quietly to Ferdinand, whose eyebrows shot up while a smile formed on his lips.

Hardrim felt himself taking on the attributes of a sacrificial lamb.

Chapter

* 2 *

NOBEL LAUREATE VANISHES
AMIDST BIZARRE ASSASSINATION

Jan. 10—Washington—Dorian Nye, Nobel Prize-winning physicist, vanished yesterday somewhere between London and Neil
Armstrong International Airport. Although first reported as shot
to death reentering the United States, Nye is now listed as missing,
and the man who was shot in his place is unidentified.

Nye disappeared from the custody of Washington Police Inspector Mel Hardrim sometime before 4:30 P.M. EST when American Atomics Flight 104 landed. Hardrim denies that Nye was taken
from his custody, maintaining that the man delivered to him in
London was an impostor. The Scottish embassy in London, which
acts as the American representative in Europe, reports that English
officials deny the allegation.

Nye, 58, a specialist in the field of quantum mechanics and

energy conversion, was perhaps best known for his lifetime association with the late Alfred Strubeck, the father of the fusion space drive.

Nye returned yesterday from a speaking tour of socialist bloc nations, including Red Britain and United Europe. He was the first American scientist to legally cross the Atlantic since the establishment, twenty-four years ago, of the Lines of Demarcation.

Nye reported receiving threatening phone calls before he left. The trip was vehemently attacked by radical organizations opposed to East-West rapprochement. Nye made the trip at the request of President-elect Shefferton, who has pledged to end American isolationism.

Nye's disappearance caused widespread speculation. . . .

Jan. 11—Washington—The disappearance and attempted assassination of Dorian Nye was lent a macabre twist by the discovery that the killer, Lloyd Hunning, was a key figure in the death of industrialist Adam Scott twenty-five years ago. Scott's death was cloaked in mystery when one billion dollars (old standard) remained unaccounted for out of his fortune. When Technology Enforcement Agency agents, led by Hunning, forcibly entered Scott's metal works in Los Angeles, an accidental explosion resulted, killing Scott, his wife, and several TEA agents. The subsequent scandal destroyed the power structure of Senator Archer McClaren, probably denied him his party's vice-presidential nomination, and led to his censure by the United States Senate.

Until two weeks ago, Hunning was confined to a sanitarium in Red Bluff, California. He was released through an administrative error. . . .

Jan. 12—Washington—Key aides in the Shefferton transition team are demanding that the Allen administration explain why Lloyd Hunning was released from a sanitarium. . . .

Jan. 13—Washington—Former Senator Archer McClaren, (D, Oregon), once described as "the most powerful man in Washington, not excluding the president," died in Portland today after suffering a massive coronary. He was 78 . . .

Senator Charles Ellsworth Macadew turned a corner into the corridor that led to his office. Several media people were clustered at the door.

He straightened from the stoop he had been falling into lately and propelled his portly body forward in a confident stroll.

"Mornin', boys and girls."

The reporters cheerfully returned his greeting. Senator Macadew was a popular, friendly, open legislator who had always provided colorful copy during his three terms in the Senate. Few Capitol Hill figures were as canny, few did their homework as thoroughly, and none was closer to the new president.

He chatted and told a few ribald Capitol Hill stories, raising a storm of laughter over an Idaho senator who had found an uncalled for call girl in his Senate office seconds before he was due to receive a delegation of the D.A.R.

"Okay folks," he said, when the laughter had waned, "What can I do for you this morning?"

"How about a couple of pictures, Senator?"

"Certainly." The senator beamed what was known in political circles as Macadew's killer smile, a beatific expression more suited to a cherub than a senator. It was a favorite of cartoonists and had adorned the cassette cover of *Time* twice.

"Senator, has Dorian Nye's disappearance caused difficulties for your Committee on the World Famine?"

Macadew fished a long, hand-wrapped Cuban maduro from his vest pocket, applied a flame from an ancient lighter, and puffed it into life. A young woman, new to his press entourage, was horrified by the open flame and his flouting of convention.

Macadew pretended not to notice. "We were anxious to hear Dr. Nye, but we'll continue our work as before."

"Do you believe a conspiracy is involved?"

"I doubt it."

"Senator Jerome, the ranking minority member on your committee, said the disappearance is part of a Communist conspiracy. Do you disagree?"

"Wal," said Macadew with his exaggerated Colorado drawl, "Senator Jerome has been known to see a Communist behind every bush in Washington. I don't wish to contradict my colleague from the great state of Saskatchewan, but he is a member of the opposition and dedicated to torpedoing the president-elect's dreams of achieving understanding with the outside world."

"Sounds like you see Senator Jerome behind every bush in Washington!"

Macadew puffed appreciatively. He looked kindly at the woman who had been alarmed by the lighter.

"Did you have a question, young lady?"

She jumped in eagerly.

"Archer McClaren died this morning. Do you have a comment?"

His smile faded and he sucked the cigar as if meditating. "You're wrong," he murmured. "Archer McClaren died twenty-five years ago."

"Say that again?"

"Adam Scott killed him."

In the babble of voices, one of the older reporters, a columnist for the *Post*, made himself heard.

"You're saying that McClaren had been politically dead for twenty-five years and that Adam Scott's famous news conference is what did him in."

"Bull's-eye."

"That news conference was a watershed in American political history, Senator. It's been said you broke with McClaren because of it."

"Check your records, son," said Macadew. "I quit working for the Committee on Un-American Technologies *two weeks* before."

The columnist held up an old news clipping. "Not according to this. It shows you quitting as majority counsel the day after."

"It's possible my resignation wasn't announced until then," said Macadew lamely. "Those were very busy times, if you recall. A month later several thousand of us formed a new political party in the Astrodome."

"At that convention you said this about Scott's death: 'In a nation of cowards, he was a hero. Surrounded by compromisers, he stood firm. While all around him voices said, "Yes, we will!" he said, "No, I won't!" ' "

"That sounds like something I'd say."

"What would you say about McClaren?"

"Our present state of national affairs is his epitaph. Few men had his gifts of oratory, his intellect, his drive. None used them with greater skill. He was the supreme demagogue of our time."

"Senator," said a UPI reporter, "a lot has been made about the connection between Adam Scott's death and this Dorian Nye thing at the airport. Do you blame the administration?"

"Each time we probe deeper into the Allen administration it's like we've upended an old stump. We keep gettin' bigger shovelfuls of creepy-crawlies the deeper we go. But I haven't seen any of 'em accused of murder . . . yet."

"One more question?"

He beamed like a doting uncle. "Shoot."

"How will you vote on the core tap bill?"

"Let's see what shape it's in when it gets out of committee. I'll most likely vote no. I believe core taps are safe in areas of low seismic activity. I'm against discontinuing them. If that's all, I'll bid you good morning!" He gave a backhanded salute and disappeared into his office.

He passed his secretary with a perfunctory greeting and closed his inner office door. He slumped at the edge of the desk, pressing his fingers into the wood. If they knew how serious Dorian Nye's loss was, they'd be baying at his heels. His assurances would hold them a while, and maybe a solution would be found before he had to provide answers.

He chided himself for getting tripped up on when he had broken with McClaren. He should have known better. Williams of the *Post* always did his homework.

At the far wall was his personal filing compartment, behind an oil painting of Colorado's first senator. He tried to whistle it open, but his lips were dry from the cigar. He rummaged in his desk until he found his pocket synthesizer. The compartment slid open to the first notes of Bach's Brandenburg Concerto no. 2.

The old-fashioned tape was in his haphazard collection, unplayed for many years. Now he wanted to remember. He had been a guest at Archer McClaren's Washington penthouse twenty-five years ago. The columnist was right; Macadew had decided to break with the senator that night, because of what he had seen on McClaren's television.

The cassette slipped into the player on his desk. The cube darkened and a two-dimensional picture appeared . . .

Adam Scott stood full in the glare of the TV lights. They sculpted his angular face into brutal highlights. His forehead was high with hair retreating at the sides, but his prematurely white mane was a banner of defiance, uncombable and intractable.

His hands were thrust into his pockets and his lips were pressed together impatiently as he waited for silence. Someone adjusted the lights. His face softened. When it was quiet he spoke, without notes.

"Ten years ago, I began Scott Enterprises. I had little money, no backers, and only my own knowledge of chemistry and physics with which to start my business. Seven years ago I married Christine, my chief of chemical research. Today our company, privately held, is the eighteenth largest in the nation and the largest research and development firm in the world. I say this by way of introduction. . . ."

A ripple of expectation moved through the crowd. An ironic smile flirted on Scott's face, then he continued.

"Recently I appeared before the Board of Essential Technologies, populated by Senator McClaren's stooges. Their job is to 'protect' the environment from change and the economy from overstimulation, and to shield society by 'rechanneling' industry toward essential services and defenses for our new Fortress America."

Scott spoke calmly, unemotionally, with an almost Olympian detachment.

"The board summoned me so it could rule whether to allow me to patent a new discovery: a metal I call Osirium, whose properties include extremely high tensile strength, a high melting point, and low density. In short, an alloy making possible the advancement of the fusion industry, which has waited ten years for such a metal.

"Most people don't know that the board has the power to defer patents until it decides to let the product be manufactured.

"The board, created by Archer McClaren's legislation, has deferred thousands of patents. Scott Enterprises, due to my strong criticism of the senator, has often been the target of its actions.

"It's also no secret·that the TEA is behind court action to prosecute us under the McClaren amendment to the Sherman Antitrust Act. That is just an excuse to break up the corporation and confiscate its property." Scott looked at his watch. "What *is* secret is that at this moment TEA agents are moving in advance of a court order to shut down my research facilities."

Several reporters slipped away to telephone booths.

Scott's voice became edged in steel. "Ladies and gentlemen, we are in an age of technological stagnation, which might become another dark age. In these times, the fate of Scott Enterprises is unimportant, my fate is unimportant, but our discoveries are not. That is why at nine o'clock this morning we shut down our facilities and dismissed our employees with our regrets and two months' pay. That is why I called this news conference. Any profits to be made from Osirium after waiting five years are outweighed by the necessity that it and other discoveries be produced now!

"I'm releasing the formulas for Osirium, and all our other deferred patents, to the public. Where special expertise is required, my wife and I will help those who request it.

"I urge others of conscience to take similar actions. Revolt now may yet save our nation. Senator McClaren's servants cannot stop the flow of information if we have the courage to resist!"

The television's sound faded as a network commentator explained that copies of the formulas had been left at hundreds of newspapers and business rivals of Scott Enterprises. Senator Archer McClaren stood in front of the screen and smiled at his guests, who included congressmen, senators, and a cabinet officer.

"What a dangerous fellow I must be if Mr. Scott must go on network TV to vilify me," he chided like a loving, amiable father speaking of a wayward child. "You see what I mean. Free press, yes; irresponsible press, no."

He dominated the room effortlessly. He looked trustworthy. A father figure, yes, but definitely a young one; the kind who plays touch football with his son every Saturday and attends PTA meetings. He was in his fifties, but boyish good looks shaved fifteen years off that. His early checkered career as campus radical, underground writer, and gadfly politician were behind him. Now Congress moved at his touch, gutting NASA's budget so that a nearly completed L-5 space factory now hung uselessly in orbit. Even the president, who secretly hated McClaren, deferred to him. The nation was grateful to have a good man watching out for its interests. After all, he had been right. The SunSat One Disaster proved that. That he was perfectly positioned to take advantage of a trillion to one catastrophe proved not that he was an opportunist, but that he was a realist.

His enemies still called him the Chameleon, but they couldn't fight the evidence of a Midwestern village charred by microwaves misdirected from space. They couldn't combat a man whose actor and singer wife could put his message on an album and sell a million copies.

Fate had thrown him a skyrocket and he'd ridden it to stardom.

His influence waxed until a troubled president who had been a good astronaut but a poor chief executive almost begged him to be on the national ticket next summer. Such was McClaren's power that he hadn't made up his mind to accept.

McClaren played his audience like a violin. "Mr. Scott is a perfect example of an irresponsible capitalist, whose kind almost ruined this nation before we instituted sane policies of economic restraint and safe progress," said McClaren. "He is right about one thing: We've taken steps to render him harmless. In his paranoid ravings he accused the government of plotting to steal his property. I assure you that we plan nothing illegal. He will be compensated at fair market value. Such power cannot be allowed in the hands of one man who cares nothing for the public good.

"Someday we will also strengthen the libel and slander laws so that networks and newspapers will think twice before they give pulpits to every disgruntled businessman with outlandish accusations against his government."

He smiled modestly as applause interrupted him. He saluted with an upraised glass of sherry.

The cabinet secretary stood with his own upraised glass.

"Let me be the first to offer a toast to the next vice-president of the United States!"

"That's a little premature, Herbert," said McClaren deftly. "But I'll drink to the next vice-president, whoever that is," he paused, and supplied the inevitable, "as long as he's a Democrat!" to polite laughter.

A guest at the penthouse was Charles Macadew, the hottest corporate lawyer in Colorado until recently, when he had come to Washington to head up the stable of legal experts working for the Un-American Technologies Committee.

Normally loquacious, he had been quiet all evening, nursing a glass of Jack Daniel's and water, while all around him Washington society eddied and swirled. He drank as though the whiskey were bile. He was no innocent, God knew, and he had drunk deeply from a well of cynicism all his life; yet he gagged at using the law to destroy a man whose only crime was disagreeing with the almighty Senator McClaren.

A servant informed McClaren that he had a call.

"I'll take it in the next room."

The acoustics enabled Macadew to hear him in the next room.

"Where's Scott now? Contact our informant and say I'll keep my promise. Tell our men to take it easy. If Scott resists, don't hurt him. Better if he escapes. . . . Why didn't they wait for my instructions? Who's in charge of it? Not him! The man's not stable. He's a fanatic. Don't they call him the Gaucho? Don't tell me it's too late. Do it. Call me back when you have news."

A sheen of perspiration clung to his forehead as he emerged. He caught Macadew's eye and motioned him over.

"Possible trouble, Charles. Scott is up to something. He's at the Beta foundry. God knows how he lost our men. He might do something stupid when the TEA takes over the building. They sent that banzai fanatic Hunning but I called him off. We'll let Scott stew until morning, then I want you to get a court order so we have the law behind us when we occupy it."

Macadew nodded and the senator went back to his guests.

These events Macadew knew directly; others he could only speculate about.

That same evening Christine Scott turned off the delayed broadcast of the press conference as Adam Scott entered the control room of the Beta foundry.

She brushed a stray wisp back into her blond pageboy and nodded. They communicated almost subverbally, virtually reading each other's thoughts.

"That's the first step," he said.

"You cut it very close." Her mannish face was pinched with concern.

"Then let's not waste more time. They'll guess what we're up to before long. By then we'll be gone, I hope."

The Beta foundry was several miles outside Los Angeles, where he'd made the broadcast. A meticulously planned exit, with five switched cars and decoys, had bought some time. It was so bold and foolhardy to return to the foundry when a warrant for his arrest was due any time that perhaps it wouldn't occur to them until it was too late.

"They're probably still in shock," she said with a sharp-toothed grin.

"Don't bet on it," he snapped. "The escape route? Raymond?"

"I just spoke to him. It's prepared." They continued to use the code name for the close family friend, the only one privy to their escape plans.

"The boy?"

"Safe with his grandfather."

"The only thing left is to set the charge." He inserted a key and the console began pulsating with a malevolent red light. He took her hand. "Let's go."

The metal door closed behind them. They stood on the landing of an aluminum staircase fifty feet over the floor of the experimental foundry. The heat hit them like a wall. Six enormous vats cast an orange incandescence over the space, which was large enough to house a jumbo jet. The vats were filled with molten Osirium, heated many hours by remote control after the last employees left. Even several hundred feet away, the heat was uncomfortable.

A charge was set at the base of each vat. When they exploded, the metal, nearly as hot as the earth's core, would spill, destroying everything. Adam Scott's valedictory would be a defiant gesture at the government that had stolen his life's work.

They descended the steps and started for the door leading to a maze of underground passages used to maintain the plumbing and electrical systems. The plan was to follow them to a service entrance outside the complex, where a vehicle waited.

Suddenly the screaming of metal echoed through the cavernous space and the nearest door was flung open violently. Men and smoke poured in. They saw Adam and Christine. More doors wrenched open. Others rushed in.

"The fools!" said Scott, "When the charges go, they'll be incinerated!" Indecision was written on his face in orange light. The intruders couldn't block their escape, but he hesitated. He took several steps toward them, waved his arms and shouted.

"Back! Go back! You're in danger! The vats are going to explode!" His shouts were swallowed up by the space. He clenched his fists in anguish.

"I can't let them die."

"You can't surrender. They'll kill or imprison you."

"We don't know that."

"Don't we?"

He looked at her a long moment. "You're right. But I have no choice. I'll not murder them, even indirectly. You can still escape."

"No. Whatever we do, we do together. As always."

He looked at her again. No words were spoken but a world was said.

They ran toward the nearest vat, shouting and gesturing. In a few minutes the charges would blow.

Then the shooting started. . . .

Half in shadow, half in light, Lloyd Hunning's face was like a painted Halloween mask. He crouched at the foundry's main entrance and molded a wad of plastic explosive onto the electronic lock.

An avid student of commando and guerrilla warfare, Hunning planned his TEA operations like military coups. To his chagrin he had been too young for Vietnam, but he'd made up for it ever since. Some called him manic-depressive and lunatic. Others recognized him as a superior man. To them he gave unswerving, canine devotion. His own men followed him anywhere because he never asked them to go where he wasn't willing to go first.

·Archer McClaren was his personal god; his Satan anyone who sold the country to its enemies and put people out of work for his own profits.

At some point the fact that the TEA was a legal organization enforcing technology regulations became blurred in his mind. Sometimes he felt that he was fighting a war, though he was uncertain precisely who the enemy was or what he was up to. Hunning's superiors recognized this confusion and used it to their advantage.

He was tireless. It was as much in awe as in ridicule that they called him the Gaucho. Even his superiors knew the strain was getting to him to an unprecedented degree, but they postponed a scheduled rest when word came that a special man was needed to take over Scott's factories. A man like the Gaucho.

He hadn't expected trouble, although with smartasses like Scott you couldn't be sure. Then HQ informed him that Scott was planning something tonight. Hunning hoped so. His nerves twitched with anticipation. He'd taken Scott's measure on television. Such a looter and rapist of the public would never give up his property without a fight . . . yes . . . the enemy troops wouldn't surrender without a fight . . . Hunning shook his head to clear it.

After the main gate was broken, the squad divided into five groups. Each would plant charges at assigned doors, blow them, and all rush in at the same moment. His second-in-command Jack Buckman beside him, Hunning knelt behind a maintenance shack and set off the explosive by radio control.

His blood pounded. Smoke stung his nostrils. His eyeballs seemed to expand against their sockets and the ground slammed against his feet as he zigzagged into the building. It was hard to see in the orange light. Explosions! Shouting! He saw two figures, a man and a woman, standing together. They looked like—by God, it was! Hunning's lips pulled back like a death mask.

"Fan out! Don't let them escape!"

They moved to encircle the fleeing figures.

Buckman was panting beside him. He held a walkie-talkie to his ear.

"They've ordered us not to occupy the building!"

"Nonsense!" grated Hunning.

"Honest to God!"

"Traitors," said Hunning evenly. He ground the set into the floor with his heel.

"We can't disobey orders."

"This is a field operation. I have command discretion—"

"What the hell are you talking about?"

"Disobey me in the field and I'll shoot you where you stand." He pressed the muzzle of a .45 automatic pistol against Buckman's sternum.

He heard shouting. He turned. The man and woman ran toward him, shouting and waving. . . . The Vietnamese woman grinned toothily and offered a fruit to the young G.I. It was a grenade. The explosion threw blood everywhere. . . . It was a trap! Hunning started firing.

Their escape was blocked. Someone, then everyone, started shooting. A spent bullet skittered across the floor in front of Scott.

"They mean to murder us," he said incredulously. He took his wife's hand.

"Run! We might be able to make the control room."

Their pursuers, unsure of their mission, followed hesitantly. Only Hunning was sure of himself. He emptied his pistol at the fugitives and slammed in another magazine.

They reached the stairs. A bullet whanged off the aluminum. Christine gasped and sat on the first rung. Her hand covered her stomach; blood seeped through the fingers. Scott looked at her. It was hopeless. His eyes raged with hate.

"Blow, damn you, blow!" he screamed.

The six explosions were ridiculously small in the immense space as they went off in rapid succession. The sounds that followed were not. First came a tearing and wrenching of tortured metal, like the mightiest beast in the universe howling out its death agony. The center of gravity shifted in each giant vat as its supports gave way. Rivets popped like guns firing and a high-pitched squeal drowned out all other sound.

Hunning and Buckman were closest to the stairs. Hunning jerked around like a snared bird. They retreated.

Adam Scott cradled his wife in his arms as her life drained away.

The screaming agony of ripping metal was overwhelmed by the sudden hissing, roaring waterfall multiplied tenfold as molten Osirium began to spill. Rivulets of metal coursed like obscene glowing worms. One burned through a wall to a tank of water, which exploded, sending razor-edged shards whirring through the air. One man was split from skull to crotch; another was pinned to the floor like a moth.

Electricity leaped across the atmosphere of smoke, steam, and deadly gases and ignited into a sheet of flames. Hunning saw Buckman catch fire and flail like a paper marionette. He looked back. Adam Scott was in the center of an inferno, his wife's head in his lap, liquid metal tendrils creeping toward him. Then steam hid him forever.

Hunning had almost reached the door when an explosion lifted him and hurled him into the air. He hit something. He knew his arms and legs were broken, then he blacked out.

Most of the senator's guests had gone in deference to his well-known habit of retiring early when his wife was on tour. He had told his aides to stay. The amiability he had worn was cast aside. Only the hard, hungry politician, who'd had things very much his own way for five years, remained.

"Our friend Herbert has been talking with the horse's astronaut in the White House, I see. That was a not-so-subtle presidential nudge, in case you didn't notice." His voice was heavy with irritation.

Macadew set his glass on the coffee table and slipped out of the penthouse.

The phone rang. This time McClaren snatched it up before the first bell had died. He listened with growing horror. Things had gone badly. The foundry was a charnel house. Another Scott factory had been occupied, but turned out to be filled only with useless equipment. Worse: Adam Scott had died in the conflagration. The phone fell from numb fingers and swung like a man dangling from a noose.

"Take it away!" McClaren slumped in the chair, mentally flogging himself to come up with a strategy. A martyr in the enemy camp was bad no matter how you looked at it. They would make hay out of the missing equipment and no doubt accuse him of stealing it to prevent its use. Scott couldn't have done more damage if he'd planned his own death.

He looked around for Macadew, but he had left.

A servant brought the phone in again.

"I told you to take that damned thing away!"

"I—I can't!"

"Why not?"

It was the president. . . .

Macadew rode the elevator to the street. He'd had enough of McClaren. Already he had begun to formulate a plan to fight him.

* * *

A mile from the gutted foundry red flames reflected off the face of the man Adam Scott called Raymond. He'd waited in his car long past the time agreed upon for Scott and his wife to rendezvous with him. Obviously they weren't coming. Things had gone the way Raymond had planned, and for a time the senator had thought things had gone the way he planned, too. But he would never know it was Raymond who had sent Hunning on his final mission. McClaren would never think of Raymond as anything but informant and betrayer of Scott's plans— certainly not the initiator of his own. It was ironic, Raymond thought, that the senator would be rewarding him for betraying them both.

A stiff breeze began to blow smoke from the blaze toward him. He inserted the key in the ignition and drove away.

For a long time after he had put the old-style cassette away, the old senator sat at his desk, lost in thought. He had never actually met Adam Scott, but across the gulf of years he had felt himself grow closer to him, and mourned the fact that he had been denied the opportunity to know him better.

"My God, together we could've given 'em so much hell." muttered Macadew, bowing his head. He blinked his eyes rapidly to clear them of moisture and took a deep breath to banish the empty feeling in his chest.

It was time to get back to work. He checked his appointment calendar, consulted his watch, and pushed himself to his feet. He just had time to make his next committee meeting.

Chapter

* 3 *

Jan. 15—Washington—President Theodore L. Allen began removing his personal effects from the White House today, saying he wanted to let the new president get an early start. "After all, he's not a bachelor like me," he commented. "I'm sure Mrs. Shefferton would like to begin putting her own charming touches on the place." The president divorced his own wife Edna a year and a half ago, the first American president to do so while in office.

Jan. 16—Washington—No clues have been uncovered in the disappearance of physicist Dorian Nye, who vanished a week ago.

Jan. 17—Peking—The government of Greater Asia has decided, in an effort to cut down on bureaucratic red tape, to execute 50,000 civil servants.

Jan. 18—New York Hourly News—The "Oxy and Up Club" announced plans today to join with more than a million members of the U.S. Federation of Centenarians in a monster rally outside Washington during the inauguration. The organizations want to pressure the new president to raise the mandatory eighty-five retirement age . . .

Jan. 19—Editorial, The *Sun* . . . We near the end of a disastrous era in our nation's history. It may be said almost without fear of contradiction that President Allen will be the last chief executive of either the Republican or Democratic parties. He will be remembered as the last isolationist, a living political fossil. Nor will the scandals of his personal and private lives, too numerous to list here, go unrecorded. It was once said of Warren G. Harding that he was not a bad man, just a slob. So may it be charitably said of President Theodore L. Allen, who leaves office tomorrow amid a sigh of relief from our beleaguered republic. . . .

Jan. 19—Editorial, the *Post* . . . a wise man, a far-sighted man, who sold his own political future for a golden vision of peace and prosperity. We now enter a dangerous era, fraught with the perils of Jeffrey Shefferton's internationalist policies. We believe that four years from now the nation's verdict will be a firm nay! and that Shefferton will be the only president to spring from the Progressive Nationalist party. Next election year the people will return to the sane policies of the Democratic party. Tomorrow we bid sad farewell to a man who joins the ranks of great . . .

Jan. 20—Washington—Jeffrey Shefferton was sworn in as 51st president of the United States at noon on the steps of the nation's capitol by Chief Justice Oliver Irvine. . . . The new president followed tradition, placing a wreath at the Ground Zero monument in San Diego. He wore radiation resistant clothing. . . . Shefferton attended evening ceremonies at the Deseret Space Center in Colorado as units of the lunar-based space fleet created a light display 150 miles up visible over much of the Southwestern United States.

The fleet included battleships *Republic* and *Thunderer*, the battlecruiser *William T. Sherman*, corvettes *Geronimo*, *Crazy Horse*, and *Cochise* . . .

1

Sheridan Mayfield touched the top of the holocube and the words of the micronewspaper faded.

Outside it was snowing heavily, as it had for two days. But a blizzard couldn't have spoiled the inauguration.

He wiped his plate clean of egg with a slice of toast and topped it off with a sip of real, though tepid, coffee.

He shaved, checking for what he whimsically thought of as his vital signs. His puckish, bulldog face was well into middle age, with irrigation ditches under eyes and cheeks. Thin hair was carefully combed over an extensive bald spot. His stern, stubborn mouth was as unlikely to form a compliment as a compromise. Only the eyes suggested that the stoic might be a strenuously cultivated show. They were the true vital signs, sparkling with wit and humor. Sheridan Mayfield was not the crabby old monster he pretended to be, though he was monster enough.

He grinned to himself, a private smile, reserved for a few. One had been a girl he loved, before she moved away or married or died, or perhaps merely grew up; he didn't remember which.

His memory was somewhat selective. He vividly recalled a wasted semester before he'd met the man who gave his life purpose, whose destiny grew with his until it overshadowed it. That destiny enveloped him now, because the man was Jeffrey Shefferton, the new president, Sheridan Mayfield's best friend.

He preened before the mirror, something he normally scorned. He was going to the White House for the first time—not that opportunity had been lacking. But he had promised himself, that first night in Washington, as the city lay reflected in the Potomac, glowing with charm and innocence that belied the pulsating power and corruption that lay under the ivory patina—standing at the White House gate, bathed in its light, he had sworn a silent oath never to set foot inside until he could go in with Shefferton as president.

It was a ridiculous oath, made by an outrageous young man ignorant of national politics. Now, so many years later, he wondered that he had had the gall even to think it. Yet now it had come true.

The holophone broke his reverie.

"Yes, Ruth?"

"Sorry to disturb you at home, sir, but I thought I should remind you of your appointment with the president this morning," said his secretary.

Mayfield smiled. As if he would forget that. "Thanks. Have my car sent over in half an hour."

He poured a glass of orange juice and enjoyed the last moments of solitude left before he began his first day as Secretary of Space Exploration and Development.

2

Since the election, Mayfield had felt misgivings that his special relationship with Shefferton might change. Men elected to the highest office soon see themselves in a different light. Sometimes they isolate themselves spiritually and morally. All presidents are tempted; many had succumbed, among them Theodore Allen.

Allen's conduct in office, while not exactly criminal, had left a bad taste in the collective mouth of the electorate, who turned him out of office virtually by acclamation. Everyone prayed for Shefferton to be the healing draught after the pain of yet another lousy president. Mayfield thought he had the potential.

Mayfield had been with Shefferton at the start, that first assembly election where they'd squeaked by so narrowly. Two unsuccessful congressional bids followed, and political oblivion was almost the result. They survived a razor-thin party nomination fracas and then Shefferton made the fateful decision of his career. In mid-campaign he announced he could no longer support his party's platform. He renounced his nomination, sought and got the nod from the fledgling Progressive Nationalists, and went on to win despite every prediction that his cause was hopeless. Twice elected to Congress, then the Senate, finally governor of his state, and Shefferton didn't change. He was always forthright, candid, with integrity seemingly sheathed in titanium steel, yet humble and unpretentious. Now he was president, and Mayfield wondered if now he would change.

When Mayfield was escorted into the Oval Office, he knew all was well.

Shefferton spent what seemed like five minutes pounding his back, enveloping him in a powerful bear hug and almost shaking his hand off. Mayfield was always astounded by the grip of the huge man, who stood grinning like a boy who'd just won a wrestling match.

Shefferton was the largest man to occupy the White House: taller than Lincoln, though not as wide as Taft. His gray eyes, set dramatically under wide, sweeping brows, crackled with intelligence. Youthful blond hair, shaved close to the skull, denied his sixty-two years. His comparative youth could have lost him the election if many other factors hadn't been on his side.

Mayfield was prejudiced, but with Shefferton he felt close to greatness. He saw the figure of a good, sincere, genuinely talented man, with nothing but the best interests of the nation at heart. A man who would do great things, if allowed to. At such times, Mayfield felt proud and sad. Proud, because he'd helped Shefferton get there; sad, because he feared that a good man couldn't be president without losing his decency or his life. Washington had killed too many heroes.

The president's talonlike grip on his shoulder brought him back to reality.

"I'm glad you're here, Sheridan, to share it. I want and need your help. There must be at least one trustworthy man in my administration."

"Two, damn you, Jeff!" exclaimed a deep gravelly voice that Mayfield instantly recognized. The rotund, balding senior senator from Colorado was sunk in a luxurious leather chair, shoes off and stocking feet planted on a priceless coffee table. A rooster ruff of white chest hair sprouted from his unfastened collar. He raised a tumbler of bourbon in mock salute.

"Mornin', Sheridan."

"Kind of early, even for you."

"It's never too early for me, son," Macadew growled, sitting up. "Anyway, Jeff, what's this horsedump about there bein' only one trustworthy fella in your administration? Why, I know for a fact that our lordly Senate Majority Leader, Percy Shelley Manners, loves you like a 'brother!"

Shefferton and Mayfield smiled. If that was so, Manners had used Cain and Abel as his role models. The Wonder Boy of American politics despised Shefferton for "stealing" the nomination, robbing him of the chance (which had been slim at best) to be the the youngest president at thirty-six, and for ignoring Manners during the campaign, studiously avoiding giving even tacit approval to the state machinery he controlled.

"I would have two trustworthy men," said the grinning president, "except you are so falling down drunk on the Capitol steps they have to cart you home every night."

Shefferton enjoyed the repartee. Macadew antedated even Mayfield as a crony. Mayfield stopped calling his chief by his first name after the election, but not Macadew. Mayfield knew Shefferton expected him to do the same, but he couldn't bring himself to address the president of the United States as "Jeff."

Despite appearances, Macadew was no rube. He was as manipulative and crafty a politician as Mayfield had ever known and the president prized him as a master strategist. His country boy accent might come and go as the occasion demanded, or as his liquor consumption varied, but his political judgment was consistently brilliant.

"Let's cut the corn pone, Charley," said Shefferton. "We have work to do. You senators may not work, but I'll be up until midnight."

The senator splashed more whiskey in the tumbler. "God-damned bastard Allen!" he spat the name.

Shefferton smiled ruefully. "I'm afraid Allen was a worse president than even we suspected. The entire government bears the scars of his ineptitude, but he gave special attention to the Defense Department."

"Worse than we thought?"

"Much worse. Many warships on the active list are really mothballed. Two of our twenty divisions are little more than exercises in juggling figures. The air force is dangerously overloaded with obsolete aircraft." He punctuated each point by poking his palm with his index finger. "But that's not the worst. I've just finished an intelligence report on a breakthrough in railgun technology by the Unified Soviet State. With that they could launch enormous payloads directly into space, without shuttles. They could launch heavily armored warships to challenge our lunar fleet, eliminating the strategic value of the moon. Our ABM laser system could become obsolete. It was built to counter reaction-drive ICBM's, not missiles launched at fractions of the speed of light. The report is dated July of two years ago.

"We aren't researching the system ourselves. None of the Joint Chiefs have ever heard of the report."

Mayfield felt outraged by Allen's monstrous neglect. The Soviets could theoretically regain the initiative they'd lost during the revolution and civil war.

Shefferton warmed to one of his favorite themes: that the isolationists were unrealistic, naive, and contemptuous of the technology that let America maintain its position as a loner behind an invulnerable curtain.

"They'll vote money for bullets, warships, or dirigible missile boats to patrol the Lines of Demarcation, but they don't understand how vitally important research and development are, or how big a threat the Soviets can become again if we allow them to project their power into space."

"Wal," said Macadew, "Lots of folks thought Russia wouldn't be a threat for a hundred years after the Genetic Commies went picnickin' on the White Russians, Czarists, and Theocrats. When the Chinese came barrelin' through Siberia we thought, 'That's the threat!' Then the Japs and Drangs jumped their ass an' we thought the threat was reborn

Japanese militarism. When the Europeans quit shootin' each other and invaded the Ukraine, presto! they became the bogeyman. The Chinese and Japs cozying up to each other with that corporate communism was so bizarre and scary that they became the threat."

The Russians had surprised everybody by trouncing their invaders and taking back much lost territory. The smaller Russia became a rejuvenated, lean and mean Unified Soviet State, minus the detenteniks. Premier Kurtzov dealt with them as brutally and effectively as he ate his eggs in the morning.

The president shook his head. "Confusing times require coherent policies, Charley. I sincerely believe we ignored an opportunity unprecedented since the end of World War Two. The great powers prostrate, mired in civil wars or unwinnable wars of conquest. Only America was strong and at peace—"

"Precisely because we didn't get involved," said Macadew.

"But you opposed isolationism."

"True."

"We could have imposed peace."

"Or become embroiled in someone else's war."

It was hard to dispute his logic. America had emerged once again as the most powerful nation on earth, with Asia broken and bleeding, Europe feeble, and only a reborn Russia to worry about.

"You advocated intervention, Charley."

"True."

"If we had we might not have Red Britain, Socialist Europe, Greater Asia, and three-fourths of the world in chains. You said we were shirking our duty to freedom."

"True."

"You're an old hypocrite, Charley," said Shefferton fondly.

"Jus' a politician, Jeff, able to see all sides of every issue, an', if needs be, argue for or against 'em all. Which may be why I'm in my chair and you're in yours."

"Well, it's time someone lost sleep over this mess," said the president philosophically. "No bankers' hours for this administration."

Macadew drew out a cigar and regarded it thoughtfully before putting a flame to it.

"You've got your work cut out for you, Jeff. You've got to change folks' attitudes! In some cities I could get arrested for lightin' this stogie or for carryin' a box of matches. Arson's still a capital offense in most towns. Hell, I'm old 'nuff to remember watchin' TV an' seein' the

Millennium riots an' the 82nd firin' on the looters in Atlanta. A lot of people have forgotten that, but everybody remembers what happened to San Diego. You ask 'em what caused it, they'll say 'foreign influence'—dealing with the outside—that let the terrorists in the country to begin with." He closed his eyes and sipped the cigar. "Maybe they got a point."

"Your famine committee could help turn public opinion around, Charley. Americans are a humanitarian people. We'd rather help people than fight them."

"My committee may be finished without Dorian Nye," said Macadew bitterly. "We're stuck with the same solutions that added up to zero last month, last year, and twenty years ago."

"Is one man that important?" asked Mayfield.

"Sit down, Sheridan," said the president. He fingered a tiny device on his collar. "Send in a glass of milk for Secretary Mayfield."

Mayfield sank into the leather chair next to Macadew, who sloshed his own glass half full again. When it arrived, Mayfield sipped the milk.

"You weren't fully briefed on this. I thought you had enough to worry about with your confirmation hearings." Shefferton sat at his desk.

"Dorian Nye was more than a goodwill ambassador to Europe, although that was the story. We gained a tripartisan character for Nye's mission by persuading Al Ames to endorse it and President Allen to allow it while he was still in office. Allen was originally a problem."

"I blackmailed him," said Macadew happily.

"How?"

"Long story."

"Correct." Shefferton looked uncomfortable. "Nye's mission was to arrange a cooperative effort with the Europeans to deal with the famine and other mutual security concerns—"

"You mean the Soviets?"

"Yes. We've only contacted the Europeans by intermediaries previously. But they are concerned. The Russian bear is growling at Poland. They're undermining the Croats, and the Serbs may pull out the of Illyrian League to appease them. The Europeans are definitely concerned.

"Nye was also going to consult with scientists in Europe and Britain about something called the Strubeck equations."

"You've lost me now."

"Here are some facts: Three years ago the greatest scientist of our time died. It's generally accepted that Strubeck ranks with Einstein, Newton, and Hawking." The president, a passionate technophile, was in a pedagogical mood.

"Shortly before he died, Strubeck told colleagues that he was on the verge of a discovery that would end famine on the earth. He didn't elaborate. Everyone assumed he failed. But his notes and diaries contain references to a process for artificial photosynthesis.

"It was always assumed that he never carried his theory beyond the brainstorming stage—but I wonder; such a great man. He gave us fusion space flight, isolated the first faster-than-light particle, and led the team that drilled the original core tap, thus solving our energy problems into the next century. Would such a man give us hope, if none existed?"

"But the problem with feeding the world's hungry isn't that we don't have enough food; it's that we don't have an efficient way to distribute it," said Mayfield.

"My understanding is that Strubeck's process would produce a highly concentrated and therefore easily transportable food product."

"What's the connection between Nye and Strubeck?"

"Nye was Strubeck's closest associate during his last years. Nye said Strubeck never mentioned a process for artificial photosynthesis, but they didn't see each other for several months just before Strubeck died. He said Strubeck often encoded his notes with a complex formula involving two multidigit prime numbers known only to them. So if Strubeck left notes, Nye could decipher them.

"He said he wanted to confer with scientists in Europe that Strubeck had contacts with before tackling his notes.

"So we have a puzzle: Strubeck claimed to be able to end famine on earth. Dorian Nye could decode whatever secret notes he left behind, if we hadn't lost him."

"Why not put our code breakers to work on Strubeck's effects?" asked Mayfield.

"Our cryptographers tell me it could take fifty years to break the code without knowing which prime numbers we're dealing with, even if we knew which papers or molecule chips to start on.

"Nye cut short his visit at Charley's request. Whether he returned, or never left London, depends on whom you believe. We do know that the man shot at Armstrong International wasn't Nye."

Shefferton opened a portfolio and fit a pair of glasses on his nose.

"This is an intelligence report from Brasilia." He squinted at it. " 'Two days ago a grain blight was reported several hundred miles south in the village of Santa Bella. The disease attacks and destroys cereal crops. It is moving outward in all directions from its point of origin. It has spread fifty miles.' " He looked up, "Does that suggest anything to you?"

"Many things, none of them good," said Mayfield.

"This is my private nightmare," Shefferton dropped the portfolio. "What if someone knew in advance about the Santa Bella blight and kidnapped Nye to keep the Strubeck formula out of our hands so they could manufacture a catastrophic world famine?"

"Is that what you think?"

"Seems like a fair assumption." Macadew sucked the rim of his whiskey glass.

"What are you going to do?"

"Send a team to Brazil to analyze the germ and find out if it threatens us. It may be localized and attack only South American strains. North American grains are mutated cousins and may be immune. We may be safe. But I must know now. At the rate the virus moves it will be here in a few weeks, just when our own planting season begins. We can probably protect our underground crops and the tiered hydroponics farms, but most of our farmland is still cultivated under the sky. If our plants aren't immune we must take measures immediately to protect our existing reserves from those within and those without."

Shefferton's face said that the double meaning was intentional.

"Sounds like Fortress America is being rebuilt before we had a chance to begin tearing it down," said Mayfield softly.

"We do what we must, Sheridan," said Shefferton sadly. "Reality is the great destroyer of ideals."

"Jeffrey," said Mayfield quietly, relieved at himself, "You know I'm behind you. I'll do whatever you say."

"Good. I want you to coordinate the investigations of the FBI and CIA into Nye's disappearance—"

"I'm not a policeman."

"But I trust you. In this case loyalty outranks expertise. Use their knowledge as a tool—"

"To find Dorian Nye."

"Or the equations, if they exist." Shefferton looked out the window. "If we have them it won't matter if Nye is in enemy hands, dead, or insane." He turned back and held out his hand. "Good luck, Sheridan. And God help us all."

"Thank you, Mr. President."

Chapter

* 4 *

"I smashed the blue gun metal across his jaw, bashing him to the floor. 'Okay, transistor head. You're dealing with Max Flynt and I've had it with your 'face friends and your conspiracy to take over the world. You've got one chance to talk before I format your memory!' "
—*Rocky Dillon,* 'Face to 'Face

1

Mel Hardrim put the thriller down on the sheets, blinked tiredly, and watched cigarette smoke curl over his bed until it was speared by light from the window. His shorts and undershirt hadn't been washed in days, but he didn't particularly care.

His wound made him move carefully. The bed was as good a place as any to avoid looking at unpaid bills. He'd tired quickly of nursing beers at the local bar, of getting the same answers at the station, and of brooding in his backyard. So he decided to try bed until he got tired of that.

There wasn't much else to do. Commissioner Flaherty had been sorry, he said, but until Hardrim was cleared or crucified by the investigation, he was suspended without pay.

Flaherty was following the book. So had Lin, although Hardrim hated him for the relish he took in his single-minded persecution. Even Roger Ferdinand, smooth, corrupt bastard that he was, was merely doing his job with his best suspect. And a thorough job he had done! Hardrim couldn't remember anything comparable to the eight hours of questioning by the deputy assistant director. A Drang needle and silk session would have been paradise by comparison, he thought.

He was angry. He did hate. Someone had engineered a setup that left him holding a bag with the word *sucker* on it. He would give a lot to find out whom. Perhaps it was Nye himself.

Ignoring the twinge, he strolled into the den, shaking with frustration. For a man who relied on direct action, it was excruciating to confront a problem that couldn't be reduced to its simplest terms and dealt with.

From the ceiling flowed an argent stream of liquid light, installed by his last live-in girlfriend. He hadn't had the heart to deactivate it. Crossing to his water sofa his feet stirred the gurgling surface into muted chiming. He activated his holocube with a voice command.

The night before he had watched the Met perform Roth's *Lord of the Ring*, Part 1, distinguished by the voice of Placebo Arauenez, the first chemically altered castrato. He'd found its harkening to the lush romantic era somewhat overripe and preferred the brassiness of Holsum's "The Galaxy" and the mathematical atonality of Takagawa's "Rashomon" Suite, which followed. He skipped the United States Symphony Orchestra concert originating from seventy-seven cities; he'd had his fill of Williams's *Star Wars* Symphony. The rest of the program was an unexciting mix of Rachmaninoff and Beethoven.

He scanned the index: Someone was putting on a conference-line performance of Moliere's *Tartuffe* with actors providing their own costumes. A space was open in a role-playing mystery set in Sherlock Holmes's London. There was a tour of the San Francisco Metropolitan's sand painting exhibit and a reairing of William Hurt's definitive portrayal of President Franklin Delano Roosevelt. Something caught his eye: A documentary next week entitled "Billion in Bullion: The Mystery of Adam Scott's Missing Fortune."

Idly, he requested Dorian Nye's biography from the central network. Words rolled by: birth date, education, career, an update of his disappearance. It was straightforward, brief, to the point. All too brief. And the point, it seemed, was to drain every bit of moisture, leaving nothing but the bare husk of Nye's life. As a measure of that life it was useless. It told much about Nye the great man, little about Nye the man. No emotions, no motivations, no desires, no prejudices. He knew what Nye had done, but not why he did it.

Hardrim sighed. It was a bit much to expect an X ray of a man's soul from a computer bio. When that became possible, men like him, specializing in the more violent motivations and emotions, would become obsolete.

He stretched and made a decision. He wouldn't sit and wait; he would break the rules and investigate on his own. He didn't expect to find anything, but what the hell? It was better than waiting to get canned.

Where to begin? Unlike in a robbery or shooting, there was no corpse, at least not of the victim. Nor a certainty that there was a victim, or that any crime had in fact been committed.

Perhaps the news might give a clue to the investigation's status.

The *Washington Post* appeared in the cube. He scanned the headlines:

NYE DISAPPEARANCE CONTINUES TO STUMP POLICE

SENATE COMMITTEE CONVENES WITHOUT KEY WITNESS

ROGUE CANCER EPIDEMIC IN MEMPHIS

SOMNUS MACHINE MALFUNCTIONS, MAN STARVES TO DEATH IN SLEEP

MINISTER CALLS FOR END TO GENETICALLY ENGINEERED HYBRIDS

SANTA BELLA BLIGHT SPREADS TO AMAZON

One headline piqued his curiosity:

MICHLANSKI SPEAKS IN NYE'S PLACE

Washington—IPI—Sherlock Michlanski, friend and one-time pupil of missing scientist Dorian Nye, will speak in his place at the 14th annual American Conference on Physical Sciences today at 11 A.M. at the Sheraton Hotel.

Nye, who vanished Jan. 10, was to have delivered the convention's keynote address. Michlanski, a Nobel Prize-winning physicist and former chairman of the American Scientific Union, is dean of physics at the Michigan Institute of Technology. He studied under Nye at Columbia University. News of his scheduled address drew mixed reactions from delegates.

Despite impressive scientific credentials, Michlanski is considered a maverick because he advocates a national program to develop faster-than-light travel. In a recent speech at Stanford University he declared "FTL is not only important to the human race, it's the only thing that can keep us from blowing ourselves up!"

Faster-than-light travel has allegedly been proved impossible by the work of Christopher Falcan, and, to a lesser degree, by mathematical proofs offered by Sam Houston Teddiwitz ten years ago.

Michlanski's address is expected to be controversial.

Michlanski had been Nye's friend. Hardrim decided to attend the conference and talk to him.

2

Michlanski in Washington! Sheridan Mayfield ached to talk to him. He tilted his chair back precariously as the article faded from the ten-foot office holocube, replaced by a 3-D analogue of the solar system, with America's possessions in blue.

He often gazed at it while meditating on the challenges of his department, what many jokingly called the department of the exterior.

Topography dictates the locations of great cities. In space, "topography" dictated the locations of man's outposts.

It dictated that most of the effort to hurl a spacecraft into the void would be spent reaching low earth orbit, a mere sixty miles above the surface. It takes less than half that energy to travel from low earth orbit (LEO) to geosynchronous orbit, 22,300 miles in space, or to an orbit around the moon. It takes even less effort to go from geosync orbit to a lunar orbit or to one of the Lagrange points.

So topography mandated that the LEO stations be a few miles above the last wisps of earth's atmosphere. Here the LEO shuttles, the sumo wrestlers of the fledgling space economy, hoisted themselves with great effort a tiny distance. At the LEO stations they were relieved of their burdens by slimmer, more graceful cousins, ships much too delicate for the atmosphere.

The next level of settlement was geosync orbit, a ghetto swarm of spy satellites, antimissile defense stations, communications satellites, the Soviet warship base station Cosmograd, and the American hotel-metropolis-warship base Midway. Here, too, would be America's new solar power satellite. Metaphorically speaking, physicists like to think of space as a fabric like a rubber pool table top, which sags in with the masses of celestial bodies. Earth is at the bottom of an incredibly deep "gravity well" and Luna is in one about five percent as deep. Off to the sides, where gravities of the unequally contesting worlds cancel each other out, are the five Lagrange points. Two—L-4 and L-5—are stable dimples in the fabric of space, where you could put a space station and with laughable effort toss payloads from the bottom of Luna's laughable gravity well to rendezvous with it.

In fact such a space station had been built, about the time of the famous SunSat One disaster. In the resulting clampdowns, with Senator McClaren in the ascendant, SunSat was dismantled, and L-5 was only saved from destruction by a veto from the astronaut president, who was weak but not completely craven. Even so, Congress, dominated by the antitechnology parties, cut all funding, and the president—using contingency funds Congress couldn't touch—was only able to maintain a crew of caretakers.

For decades L-5 was a battlefield between the McClarenites and their foes. Neither side won a decisive victory. McClaren's adherents couldn't marshal the power to destroy the station; followers of Adam Scott and the Progressive Nationalists couldn't reactivate it. Under President Allen even the skeleton maintenance crew was recalled. Then Shefferton won the presidency.

Yet in the overall scheme of things, finally activating L-5 was simplicity itself. Mayfield had other problems to tackle. Some were logistical: supplying space stations and bases on Luna, Mercury, the asteroids, and Jupiter's moons. Some were theoretical: gauging the importance of a computer study that predicted an independence movement for territories beyond Mars's orbit within a decade, unless faster modes of space travel were introduced to make them more accessible (and easily controlled) from earth. Others were more grandiose: planning expeditions to the outer planets and the future expansion of man (or America, at least) to the stars. The main obstacle to that dream was the supposed impossibility of traveling faster than the speed of light.

Sherlock Michlanski believed in FTL and loudly declared it. But only his undeniable credentials as one of the great minds of physics kept him from being dismissed as a fool. His colleagues sneeringly tolerated him, hoping no one would take him seriously. But how do you not take a winner of the Nobel Prize seriously?

Mayfield buzzed his secretary.

"Yes sir?"

"Find out what room at the Sheraton Professor Michlanski is staying in and put through a call."

"Yes sir."

Mayfield leaned back, humming softly. Michlanski's relationship with Nye could prove useful. Perhaps Nye had discussed the Strubeck equations with him. He might have a clue what they contained or if they were feasible. Besides, Michlanski was one of the most brilliant men of the age and Mayfield had always wanted an excuse to meet him.

"Secretary Mayfield?"

"Yes?" He sat up and adjusted his tie.

"Hotel management couldn't find him. Shall I try again later?"

"I suppose so," he said irritably.

"Yes sir."

"Uh, Ruth, wait a minute."

"Yes, Mr. Secretary?"

"I've decided to attend the convention. Make the arrangements."

"Yes sir."

It would be hard for the keynote speaker to avoid a few words with him. Then Mayfield intended to arrange a longer chat later.

3

A banner was unfurled in the hotel lobby: WELCOME PHYSICISTS!

Conventioneers were the same all over, Hardrim thought. Taxidermists, truckers, or physicists, all welcomed the chance to escape the everyday, to cut loose and run wild a little. The hotel bar was doing a thriving business in mute testimony to that fact.

The lobby was packed but it was not an unruly crowd. Hardrim blended in well. There were few flashy capes or bizarre headdresses to contrast with his brown business suit, although a few men wore grouchos.

He drifted with his ear open and learned a lot about the keynote speaker; a lot of opinions anyway.

"The man's a crackpot! I've known it for years."

"Now look, you can't get the Nobel Prize without knowing a few things."

"Boy genius! Maybe when he grows up he won't be such a pain in the neck!"

"I don't know why he doesn't stay on that island of his and leave respectable people in peace."

"Frankly, I think he's a breath of fresh air among all you stodgy know-it-alls!"

"Why did Nye have to go and get himself kidnapped?"

"Michlanski's talking? God help the theory of relativity!"

The man didn't draw neutral responses. An hour before his speech the lobby was buzzing with talk of him. Hardrim glanced at the rostrum where technicians were setting up equipment. The news services liked the rotund scientist. He always made colorful headlines.

Hardrim sat close for a better chance to talk to Michlanski after the speech. He found himself behind a man whose skull bore the unmistakable scars of a recent thalamic interface implant. Hardrim was always vaguely uncomfortable around interfaced humans, or 'faces, as they were called by the vulgar.

He changed seats, took out a cigarette, and allowed himself the luxury of observing people without mentally frisking each one. It was a hard habit to break. When he heard a commotion at the main entrance his hand crept to his shoulder holster. He relaxed; it was just a bigwig politician—a secretary of something or other, and his aides. They sat a few seats from the front. Two, Hardrim noted with professional interest, were bodyguards.

Their charge was an uninteresting specimen, but Hardrim knew he must have some unusual quality. Perhaps he was rich, certainly he had influence, maybe talent, possibly genius. Something had made the president of the United States choose him.

Hardrim started to suck his cigarette into life but a man several seats away gave him a dirty look. Not wanting to attract attention, he put it away.

The seats filled. Michlanski might not be liked, but he could attract an audience. Soon there was standing room only and not much of that.

A ripple stirred the audience, becoming a roar as Michlanski entered from a side door and approached the podium. His supporters made up for their lack of numbers with sheer volume.

He acknowledged the applause with a wide grin and a wave and bounded up the steps, a remarkable feat for a 250-pound man. He looked across the auditorium, and beamed with childlike pleasure.

Hardrim was startled by his youthful face. The Polish scientist was in his thirties, but looked ten years younger. He had petulant lips, a turned up freckled nose, and unruly blond hair that flowed into a wild, unkempt beard that encircled his head like a wreath of wheat. Darting blue eyes were buried in ample cheeks. A garish checkered tie angled over the podium from his collar. His coat looked as if it had been folded in a suitcase. He resembled a juvenile Santa Claus traveling incognito.

He adjusted his glasses and riffled through his papers until the noise died. Then he began.

"It's an honor to address this distinguished assembly, especially since I missed the first thirteen conventions. I speak to you under sad circumstances. We all mourn our friend Dr. Nye, whose absence makes this gathering poorer." His voice had a fine musical timbre, of surprising strength and range.

"I read in the newspools that I'm to give a controversial speech. That surprised me. I didn't know I was controversial." He paused. "I thought everyone in the scientific community agreed I'm nuts!" He acknowledged the laughter.

"Don't worry, I won't disappoint you this morning. In fact, you may leave here more convinced of my foolishness than ever. Well, so be it."

A middle-aged, almost entirely bald man leaned over to Hardrim, "I hope he enjoys himself. It'll be his last chance to talk to a sane audience." He obviously liked the prospect.

"Today," said Michlanski, "my subject is one most of you will find disagreeable and some heretical, if I may use such a religious term to a body of scientists.

"The subject, as you may have guessed, is faster-than-light travel."

A restless wave passed through the crowd. Several laughed, some were angry, the majority appeared embarrassed. The man next to Hardrim grinned like a satyr and rubbed his knees gleefully.

"The fool's cut his own throat!" he chortled.

"Why don't you hear him out before you bury the body?" snapped Hardrim, thoroughly irritated. His neighbor threw him a withering stare and returned his attention to the podium with a huff of indignation.

"Faster-than-light travel—FTL—is the lost orphan of modern science," said Michlanski. "No one admits to its parentage. Everyone associated with its early research can claim to have been doing something else at the time. It has become the Larmarckism of latter-day theoretical physics; almost a term of abuse. Today nobody likes to remember that at one time sober men of science, many of them sitting in this auditorium, looked at FTL as a real possibility. But today the men of that time are labeled simpletons and fools and FTL is a theory searching for a theorist—a homeless waif in a pantheon of legitimate ologies.

"Ladies and gentlemen, I don't accept that! I refuse to consign FTL to the reject pile, joining in oblivion the Silly Putty 'sciences' of astrology, numerology, and phrenology.

"I don't accept it, Dorian Nye didn't, and neither did one of the greatest men who ever lived, Dr. Alfred Strubeck.

"So, why am I here, expounding my oddball theories before a hostile audience, on holovision, making a laughingstock of myself and possibly you?

"For the shock value! I expect that portions of this speech will be available to every family in America, that a few open-minded people outside the scientific community will give the theory some thought. Perhaps, in view of my not unknown achievements, I may be heard where it will count most, in the halls of government."

Hardrim saw the politician sit up very straight.

"There is no other way. FTL must be researched thoroughly to be proved or disproved. A program to take us to the stars will cost more than any space research ever cost before. It will dwarf the moon project, the Mars project, and all the interstellar probe projects. It will be like a war effort.

"Like a war it will be risky, because there are no guarantees that FTL is there to be found.

"But eventually we have no choice. We must find FTL. We must escape the solar system. For too long we've sat in the womb of old Mother Earth. Her ability to nourish us has reached the limit. We feel the birth pangs. It's time to reach outside. Like all births it will be unpleasant. But pain is no excuse to avoid life. We must be born, or die."

Chapter
* 5 *

1

When Michlanski left the rostrum, Mayfield jumped up and chased after his quickly vanishing figure.

The scientist disappeared into a side door. Mayfield opened his mouth to call after, but the swelling applause was too loud. He reached the door. It opened on a corridor. At its end he saw Michlanski enter an elevator.

"Doctor Michlanski!" he yelled.

A mischievous grin flashed on the doctor's face and he gave an ironic little wave as the elevator door closed.

"Damn it!" said Mayfield, breathing hard from his sprint.

2

When Michlanski vanished from the stage Mel Hardrim realized he could never cut through the milling crowd to catch him. He would have to locate the man's hotel room later.

He made his way to where refreshments were being served. His old friend the bald man was in a heated debate with another man. They had attracted a growing circle of onlookers.

The other was in his early forties, lean and dark, with a sharp, cadaverous face framed by raven hair. His hands, resting halfway in his coat pockets, displayed crisscross scars. As Hardrim drew near, the man laughed; an unpleasant sound like a rasp of a metal file.

"Laugh, Kane," said the bald man, "but Michlanski is through. No one will take him seriously again!"

Kane looked at him with contempt.

"That's ridiculous, Randall. It would take more than an ill-advised speech to destroy his standing in the scientific community."

"Merely ill-advised?" brayed Randall, "You mean you believe FTL is possible?"

"Yes."

"Then you're as big a fool as he is!"

Kane reddened and moved toward Randall, then reconsidered and reached for a glass of punch.

Randall had attracted reporters. That made him puff up like a pouter pigeon. He talked even louder while Kane listened, cynicism chasing across his face like frost on a dark pane.

"Benlavi proved beyond doubt that the force needed to propel mass faster than light is infinite, therefore impossible to achieve. Falcan expanded on that work and Teddiwitz's proof took in the space around singularities and neutron stars to show that the so-called warped space effect could not be used to jump the light speed barrier. If that isn't enough, we have Einstein, father of us all, who would have scorned such theories."

Kane whirled and viciously elbowed past Hardrim to the canapes. "The ass!" he muttered, "He's ignoring tacyons and Swycaffer!"

"Michlanski cast himself from the company of reputable scientist this morning," Randall continued. "He's a maverick; irresponsible, irreverent, undisciplined, with no respect for more experienced colleagues. Tonight I'm offering a resolution condemning Michlanski for his ridiculous address. I don't wish my name associated with his remarks. I'm sure my colleagues don't either."

The reporters drifted away and Randall held court with his admirers, talking, laughing, pouring champagne.

Kane, deadly calm, went up to him.

"Randall," he said slowly, "You're an irritating ass. I'm amazed that the government put a cretin like you in charge of a fusion research facility."

Randall splashed wine on the table.

"You can't talk to me like that, Kane!"

"There are two kinds of people in the world: those who are laughing at you behind your back and those who are in the same boat with you. You'll never be on a mental plane with Michlanski, or me for that matter." He smiled wolfishly. "Why not accept your inferiority instead of attacking your betters?"

"We'll see who's inferior tonight!"

"It should be much more entertaining than Michlanski's speech. Pamela and I will love it, I'm sure."

An electric shudder passed through Randall.

"You wouldn't dare! Everybody knows that she—that I—that you—you'd actually flaunt—"

"It's hardly a singular accomplishment."

"But I can't make a speech with her and you . . . and everyone—" His voice trailed off. Sweat trickled down his cheeks and he began hyperventilating.

"You don't seem well," said Kane. "Pamela told me you have heart trouble and a bad back too."

"You bastard!"

Kane patted him on the back. "Remember, Pamela and I will be right out in front to cheer you on."

Randall choked down an answer as he became aware that people were smiling. The smiles became chuckles when he threw his glass down with a snarl and stalked off. Kane's eyes followed him, then he turned to regard those who had laughed.

"You enjoy his discomfort, but most of you agree with him. That makes you no better. Someday Michlanski's genius will be proven and that will make a lot of you into fools. Then those who fought him will lionize him and pretend they knew it all along." His laugh rasped mirthlessly and he disappeared into the crowd.

A waiter passed on his way to the kitchen and Hardrim collared him. "Who was that man?"

"Mr. Jacob Kane, chief engineer for Horatius Krebs." He saw Hardrim's blank look, "You know, the Python Corporation."

"I got you. Kind of an unpleasant guy."

"Right, like Vlad the Impaler was unpleasant."

"You seem like a literate fellow," said Hardrim.

"I'm working my way through college."

"Of course."

"Really! I pulled a lot of strings to work here during the convention."

"You sound like a man who could tell me a few things."

A wide grin appeared, "I didn't think you were a guest."

"How about it? I'll buy you a drink. When do you get off?"

"A couple of hours. Meet me at the Puce Palace. Near the university." He looked at Hardrim's figure critically, "Oh, and dress casual."

3

"With their victory over the Terminator City Quicksilvers the Tycho City Craters are one step closer to facing the undefeated Midway Floaters for the Inner Planets League championship. The winner will square off next month against the Ganymede Icemen for the Universe Cup of Weightless Soccer VII. As usual, this season our earth teams didn't have a chance—"

"Secretary Mayfield," Ruth's voice overrode the cube's audio. "The gentlemen have arrived."

"Right on time, too," said Mayfield, glancing at his index finger. "Have them wait forty-five minutes, then show them in."

"But—"

"If any of them get up to leave, buzz me immediately."

Mayfield leaned back, grinned, and tapped the armrest to play the rest of the sports report. Then he previewed an upcoming network documentary on the mystery surrounding the billion or so in money and equipment that had turned up missing from Adam Scott's estate twenty-five years ago.

A heavyset actor with a salt and pepper beard and a resonant voice stood on a windswept hill overlooking a large factory.

"I'm standing in front of the Omega factory in Dayton, Ohio. On that fateful night this was one of the factories seized by federal agents. They reported a virtual Potemkin village; a factory of facades and fake equipment. The Beta foundry in Los Angeles was so thoroughly destroyed in the catastrophe that killed Adam Scott and his wife that it was impossible to judge how much equipment was functional and how much, if any, wasn't. The raids themselves, and all of Senator McClaren's acts, came under such sustained attack in the days and weeks that followed that subsequent statements by federal agents involved in the seizures were discounted."

The actor displayed his profile and his voice deepened dramatically.

"Yet the fact remains that when the Alpha, Delta, and Omicron factories are taken in account, over a billion dollars in old-style reckoning turned up missing. Were federal agents in on the take? Was Archer McClaren? If so, why did he die a poor man? Or is there another, more sinister explanation?"

And later:

"Why did many high-ranking Scott Enterprises employees and TEA agents who might have been involved in the scam turn up missing or suffer peculiar accidents since that night?"

And finally:

"What is the entire truth about Adam Scott's death? Was Archer McClaren the biggest victim of a fabulous caper? Or did he deserve to account for much, much more? Is there . . . another explanation?" Long pause, followed by an extreme close-up.

"We may never know."

Mayfield turned it off in disgust. The damned thing asked more questions than it answered, which was only fair, since no one really knew what had happened to the billion dollars.

"I'm showing the gentlemen in now, sir," said Ruth.

Mayfield put on his sternest face.

He knew the five men personally or by reputation: Alain Lin, security director for Armstrong International; Samuel Delcro, assistant director of the CIA; Vice-admiral Enrique Jose Campbell of the DIA; Roger Ferdinand of the FBI; and Edward Tark, federal marshal for the Territory of Selene. Of these, only Tark dealt with Mayfield in his capacity as head of SED.

Mayfield had intentionally put the extra chairs in the next room; so they had to stand. During the moment of confusion and discomfiture he studied each reaction. Lin was cool, amused. Delcro, too, had played power games before and took this one in stride. Campbell obviously thought admirals ought to be above this sort of thing, and was irritated. Tark was confused. Ferdinand's camel's hair suit and cape, and his teak briefcase, contrasted nicely with his deepening crimson face as he fought to control his temper.

"I think—"

"We'll find out what you think in due course, Mr. Ferdinand," snapped Mayfield. "Gentlemen, nice of you to come. Marshal Tark, glad you happened to be in Washington."

"My pleasure, I think."

"You're here because you each head an investigation of Dorian Nye's disappearance for your individual bureau or agency. The president wants me to coordinate your efforts. I wanted to have this chat to outline the chain of command and information, so there's no doubt in your minds whom you are responsible to."

"This is very irregular, Mr. Mayfield," said Ferdinand. "The normal chain of command would have each of us report to our superiors, who would, in turn, report to you."

"I want to make one thing crystal clear: During this investigation I am your superior. You will report to me and *no one else*. This is a signed presidential order to that effect." He held up a plastic document electronically sealed to prevent tampering. "Your superiors have been notified that you are detached from their authority for the duration.

"Furthermore, this investigation takes exclusive priority over other matters you have pending. You'll have to put all your other investigations on the back burner."

"You can't—" said Ferdinand.

"Can't I?" Mayfield handed him the order.

"It's like being drafted!" said Admiral Campbell.

"I'll expect daily reports from each of you," said Mayfield. "I think that's all. You may go."

After another moment of confusion they started to file out.

"One moment, Mr. Ferdinand; I'd like a word with you in private."

"Certainly!" The FBI man's aplomb returned. "I thought you'd probably want to assign most authority for this investigation to me. Perfectly logical under the circumstances—"

"Nothing of the sort," said Mayfield curtly. He took a document from the desk. "This is a copy of your voter's registration. Someone has backdated it two years. That's very serious, tampering with a notarized document. I suggest you take care of it."

"Yes sir, I will."

"Good-bye, Mr. Ferdinand."

4

The bar was a foggy maelstrom of light and shadow, of colors ripped from a thesaurus, of sounds taken from a carnival, of smells that assaulted the nose like a chocolate shop, greenhouse, opium den, tannery, soy plant, and pizza parlor.

Hardrim entered the dark, cloying atmosphere and blinked at the fluorescent dandelions his eyes made of the buglights and blacklights that guttered along the walls. Dimly he distinguished individuals: At a table an Arabic figure smoked a hookah and played chess with a pale obese man in a G-string; a man in a one-piece leather jumpsuit was stretched out at another table, snoring quietly; at the bar two men with half beards were breathing from transparent bubbles. Hardrim was drawing certain inescapable conclusions about the place when a young woman wearing horizontal silver stripes drifted by like a barge in the fog. At his elbow a man reading *Campus Life* threw it aside and came to his feet.

"I said to dress casual." He came into the light. Blacklights made his purple leotards and dark red snakeskin hip boots glow. A bright yellow groucho curled disdainfully over his lips.

"For me, a black turtleneck and slacks are casual."

"You're adversely affecting the ambiance."

"Gee whiz, I'm sorry."

"People are looking at you."

"If they're lucky I won't look back."

"Let's take a booth."

The booths, closed and airtight, gave new meaning to the term singles bar. The air was smoky yellow, sparked by little electrical fireflies. The piped-in boom-boom music was laced with subsonics that tickled Hardrim's reptile brain. At hand on the table was an autobartender. He took out a cigarette.

"Please!"

"If I order a gin and tonic what will happen?"

"Laughter."

"Well, what's good?"

"This is primarily an inhalant bar."

"I offered to buy you a drink, not a sniff."

"That's very angular of you. Try broadening your horizons."

Hardrim ordered a Pink Turnip, the gaseous equivalent of a Shirley Temple, sort of a mild laughing gas. His dad had told him of getting similar reactions as a boy from sniffing whipped cream cans. The young man ordered something in a large tulip-shaped bulb. When it popped from the slot he inhaled deeply and leaned back with closed eyes. Hardrim caught a whiff of a dizzying rose fragrance.

At length he came down. "Ah, now what do you want to know?"

"That scene between Randall and Kane—what was it about? What's the background on the scientific argument between Michlanski and everyone else? . . . What's Michlanski's room number?"

"All that for one bulb?"

Hardrim stacked a handful of small denomination gold coins (he'd just cashed his unemployment check) on his side of the table. He was still giggling a little from the Pink Turnip.

"That seems adequate compensation—" The stack moved across the table.

"Hee-hee! In economics, hee-hee, don't they teach you not to charge more than the traffic, hee-hee, will bear?" He pulled back all but one coin.

"The technical information I'll give gratis, since that's my field and you could look it up. The scene between Randall and Kane is worth more. It would take you a lot of digging to find out what I've picked up listening to all those private conversations." He picked up two coins. "Michlanski's room is the real problem. He's given strict orders not to be disturbed, so it involves a risk to my job." He moved two more coins. "And the management wouldn't look kindly on a nonguest snooping about the guests—if I told them." He moved the rest of the stack.

"It's police business." said Hardrim, putting his badge on the table. He picked up all but two coins.

"In poly sci they teach us to keep up on current events, *Inspector Hardrim*. I recognized your face." The stack moved back. "My name, by the way, is Dexter Grue." He started sucking a Popsicle shaped like a girl in a bathing suit. Presently the suit began to fade.

"Okay, Dexter, we seem to have a deal," said Hardrim glumly. "Now tell me, what did Kane mean when he said that Randall was ignoring tacyons and Swycaffer?"

"Did he say that? How interesting," said Grue. "He was referring to two schools of thought about how faster-than-light velocity might be achieved. First: Benlavi's disproof of FTL rests on the assumption that a tacyon—a faster-than-light particle—is a charge without mass. That is the most widely accepted theory, but it's unproven. What is true is that as mass approaches the speed of light it becomes infinite. Michlanski says that light speed is a barrier that cannot be breached but might possibly be leaped around.

"The second is more complex: that the light speed barrier can be disregarded entirely by harnessing a process known in particle physics as the quantum leap. In quantum mechanics it is impossible to predict or establish where a subatomic particle may be at a particular nanosecond, but it can be assigned a probability, which generally means it could be anywhere in a spherelike area around the nucleus of an atom. However, it is theoretically possible for a particle to be anywhere in the universe at a given moment, although extremely improbable. When a particle ends up in a new place it seems to do it without traversing the intervening space. It disappears in one place and appears in the other. That is a quantum leap. As I said, such leaps are normally made within extremely tiny parameters but theoretically could occur at much greater distances.

"So, it is quite possible that particles of matter are popping in and out of existence even as we speak. An entire galaxy could suddenly come into being."

"But you said that was extremely improbable."

"True, but in a universe of infinity, anything that can happen, will."

"This is related to going faster than light?"

"If it is somehow possible to influence probability then theoretically a large collection of particles, the mass of a spaceship for example, might be moved from one point in the universe to the other without touching the intervening space."

"The old space warp concept?"

"The same effect. Of course, if you calculate the energy needed to move one electron one meter, it's almost impossible to conceive."

"So, it's impossible."

"Except that at the turn of the century a scientist named Swycaffer developed mathematics for what became known as Swycaffer's threshold. He established that if a certain very tiny percentage of particles in a molecule were disturbed out of their normal probability, they would tend to *influence* the surrounding electrons to follow, like a chain reaction."

"Like atomic fission?"

"A family resemblance. The idea was quite popular for a while after Swycaffer came up with it. Even Strubeck embraced it, though he remained silent when researchers gave up on it. Most people assume he too gave up but was too stubborn to admit it. Now the only man of stature who believes is Michlanski."

"You sound like a fan."

"I am indeed. I arranged to work at the Sheraton to hear his speech. If he is right—a mighty big *if*—he will become one of the two or three men who entirely changed our perception of the universe. Newton was first, then Einstein expanded upon him, without destroying his basic truth. Sherlock Michlanski stands in the same relation to Einstein. If he's right, the secret of FTL will be part of the Unified Field Theory, an expansion of all that has gone before."

"Unified Field Theory. I've heard that term before."

"I imagine you have, Inspector," said Grue drily. "The philosopher's stone of modern science. Sought for over a century; glimpsed occasionally, like some unicorn seen dimly in the mists, almost, almost touched, but before eager fingers could seize it, prancing off again.

"A Unified Field Theory would unite the basic forces of the universe. At one time, scientists thought they were very close to bringing electromagnetism, gravity, and the forces that bind atoms together into one all-encompassing equation. But then they discovered that there were more than just those forces. They discovered hypercharge, which is a subatomic force. Michlanski discovered antigravity and later macrogravity, which is a force observable only between immense masses, like galaxies. The search for unifying fields was becoming like the search to find the universe's smallest particle, a search without an end. If you can't identify all of the basic forces in the universe, it's hard to unify them in one set of mathematics.

"Michlanski believes that it's not necessary to understand or even identify all the basic forces—that they are in fact infinite. But that without knowing them all it is possible to construct a unifying equation that will predict each force for whatever level of reality you care to check. I don't pretend to understand his math. Few people do. But Michlanski hypothesizes that once we understand this unifying equation, we can use it to set up a field where probability could be altered; that such fields in fact exist in black holes and neutron stars. If Michlanski finds it, nothing will be the same again."

"Sounds nifty. What about Randall and Kane?"

"Jacob Kane stole Randall's wife. Randall is proud and extremely vain. If Kane walks into the auditorium where he's speaking, arm in arm with his wife, Randall could have a heart attack. He came close this morning. The hotel management was asked by a delegation of physicists to ask Kane to leave. They declined."

"Why?"

"One does not war with Horatius Krebs's lieutenant without mighty hosts at one's back. Neither is a man to offend lightly."

."Why does Kane care if Randall gives a speech condemning Michlanski?"

"I haven't the dimmest notion."

"Let me put it another way. Why does the scientific establishment care what sort of opinions Sherlock Michlanski has? I always thought that scientists weren't into politics; that truth was their goal."

"It may also surprise you to learn that scientists like to get drunk and occasionally to have sex."

"No need to get snotty, Grue."

"Scientists have never been divorced from politics. In the last century there was a big debate over whether the technology existed to shoot down incoming nuclear missiles. Some scientists said it would work, others said it would not. Coincidentally, those who said it wouldn't work were also those who were philosophically opposed to an ABM system and politically wedded to disarmament. There were others who believed it would work, but didn't dare say so because they were afraid of being labeled as prowar. So politics does influence scientific 'truth.' In fact, many of Michlanski's enemies are earth-firsters, and some, like Randall, are part of the group of establishment scientists who collaborated with McClaren and the government to keep technology down. They sincerely believe man must use all his resources and intellect to deal with problems on earth, and that the space program is a tragic waste of energy."

"Thank you." Hardrim stood. "When can I expect that room number?"

"This afternoon."

"Good. Now, if you'll excuse me, I think I'll get the hell out of this Chinese cathouse!"

5

Mel Hardrim left the elevator. Room 395 was at the end of the hall. Through a window near the door he saw the white obelisk of the Washington monument jabbing the afternoon sky.

He knocked.

"Who is it?" said a voice from the door speaker.

"Mel Hardrim."

"I don't know anyone by that name. Good-bye!"

"I need to talk to you, Professor Michlanski. It's very important."

"Not to me!"

"I wish you'd talk to me. I'm a police officer investigating Dorian Nye's disappearance."

"Horsefeathers! I've talked to the police already. What a transparent ruse on your part."

"I'm not acting officially, Doctor," said Hardrim. "But the case is very important to my career."

"Wait a minute! Are you the police inspector who lost Dorian Nye? The one who was shot at the airport?"

"The same," said Hardrim, wincing.

A click and Michlanski was in the doorway, holding what looked like a chocolate malted. His clothes were even more disheveled than they had been in the auditorium. He had removed his tie and unfastened the top buttons of his shirt.

"Come in. I'll give you a few minutes. You sound as if you might be interesting." He shook the malt in his face. "But I warn you, the moment you stop being interesting, out you go!"

Hardrim barely suppressed a chuckle. Sherlock Michlanski was a very unusual man. He acted like a roadrunner. He couldn't keep still. He sat a moment, all the while crossing and uncrossing his barrel legs. He sucked on the straw until it made an empty sound, tossed the malt, and reached for a candy bar. He leaped up and went to the window. It was very disconcerting.

"What's on your mind, Mr. Hardrim?"

"What can you tell me about Dorian Nye?" he said lamely.

Michlanski clucked and shook his head.

"Come now, sir! Certainly you can be more specific! We don't have all day, you know. At least I don't, though I imagine you unemployed people do."

"I can't be specific," said Hardrim slowly.

"Eh? Why not?"

"Well—I don't know exactly what I'm after. Let me explain—"

"Please do. Tell me, young man, do you have any notes?"

"Notes?" Michlanski's use of the term *young man* disturbed him. Their age difference was not that great.

"Yes, notes. Questions. An organization of your thoughts. Really! You are quite disorganized for a police person!"

"I'm sorry. Look—I'm trying to find out what I can about Dorian Nye—his life, work, everything, anything. The central computer wasn't very helpful."

Michlanski chewed his candy bar thoughtfully. "I don't know how much help I can be, Inspector. I've known him for many years. I was his assistant at the university. But I've seen little of him since then. Most of what I could tell you can be found in *Who's Who* or the computer you've already consulted."

"Anything will be helpful. I need to know about Dorian Nye the man. Tell me about your friendship."

Michlanski ran fingers through his beard and sat down.

Pulling up a chair beside him. Hardrim plumbed his coat pocket as if for a cigarette and fingered a recorder whose microphone was a button on his sleeve. It could pick up a pen scratching across a room.

"I entered college at age sixteen. It was a traumatic experience. I was the smallest, youngest student in every class, but also the brightest. I had nothing in common with my classmates. They avoided me. Regardless of my intellect, emotionally I was a child. So I was a loner.

"He was my professor the first year and one of my few friends. Another was Sammy Teddiwitz—"

"The founder of Gigatex, who disproved FTL travel?"

"He thought he did. He'll be remembered more for developing the zero resistance generator and molecule chips. But in those days he was more interested in getting drunk and arguing theoretical physics than in becoming a computer tycoon.

"But that's another story. Nye liked me. I helped with his experiments and graded his papers and tests. Our relationship was like uncle and nephew, but closer in many ways because, at its best, the friendship between tutor and pupil can be one of the most profound."

"How long did this continue?"

"A couple of years only. We drifted apart. He rose in the administration of the university; I branched out into other subjects besides physics. I became socially acceptable. I learned lessons the highly intelligent must learn if they want normal friends: to talk to people on their level without condescending."

Hardrim looked at him. "You learned to do it very well, Doctor."

Michlanski laughed and patted his knee. "Perhaps you're brighter than you think." He sat back and scratched his chin.

"After graduation I went to Stanford. Our paths rarely crossed. We remained friends, spoke and wrote frequently, but that's not much when you come right down to it, is it?"

"I had hoped you might have talked to him before he went to Europe."

"I first heard about the trip on the newstapes. I was surprised. He was always so nonpolitical."

"You don't think he defected?"

"What an absurd notion! He well knew that America is the only place for a scientist. We may be emerging from an antitechnology kick, but the rest of the world came so near to destroying itself that they can't provide decent research facilities for their scientists."

"Haven't the Russians made great strides?"

"They have a lot of catching up to do. Dorian's too independent to work for them anyway. He'd go bonkers in a month. It's just too silly!"

Hardrim stood, sighing. That demolished his main theory.

"Thanks for your time, Doctor. I'm sorry you couldn't tell me more."

"A pleasure." Michlanski smiled jovially, extending his pudgy hand.

"That's an interesting ring."

Michlanski looked down.

"Oh yes. A fraternity ring."

"Really? It doesn't look like one."

"Well, it is." He handed it to Hardrim. It was black enamel with a pattern of eyes etched in silver.

"What sort of fraternity?"

"Astronomy," said Michlanski. "My major before I settled on physics. The eyes are the symbol of the fraternity. 'Eyes upon the Universe' was our motto. Kind of a repulsive thing but it appeals to my bizarre nature." He slipped it back on.

"If you think of any more questions, call me in Michigan." He guided Hardrim toward the door. "It gets pretty lonely on my private island. I can use the diversion."

Michlanski immediately closed the door. A digital clock glowed amber on the nightstand. He touched the top and it changed to red. It had gone yellow earlier, indicating he was being taped. He drummed his fingers on the wood. Why had Hardrim taped him? Perhaps he didn't want to take notes. But then again . . .

His eyes wandered to his index finger and he frowned. The ring! He snatched it off and threw it into his suitcase, which he began to pack. He was canceling the rest of the visit.

Something had come up.

PART

* 2 *

WELL
OF FIRE

Chapter

* 6 *

Feb. 5—Miami *Sun*—Severe earthquakes along the mid-Atlantic ridge threaten to halt construction of the Challenger core tap in the Puerto Rico Trench, the deepest point in the Atlantic Ocean. Deep fissures in the sea bed wall around the metal bore could force up magma and crush or melt the tube, bringing white hot rock in contact with sea water. . . .

Feb. 6—*Washington Post*—Debate continues in the Senate on the core tape bill, which passed the House last week. A close vote was predicted but yesterday's events at the Challenger core tap boosted support of the bill, which would ban government-guaranteed loans for core taps, make it illegal to finance them at less than six percent above the prime rate, and institute tough new construction standards. . . .

1

Charles Macadew woke up covered with sweat as someone shook him insistently.

"Senator!"

He sat up abruptly, realizing he was in the steam room and recognizing the masseur, Bernie. He shook his head like a wet retriever and groped for his drink, now nothing but a tumbler of tepid water.

"You were in here a long time, Senator," said the wiry little man, with a disapproving look at the drink. "There's two calls for you. One's the White House and the other—"

"Thanks, son." Macadew heaved to his feet, his mind still cloudy. "Would you tell the other caller to hold his water till I finish talkin' to Jeff?"

"Sure thing, Senator."

Macadew stumbled into the locker room. He roughly toweled himself, combed his hair into wet order, slipped a sweat shirt over his head and climbed into a pair of baggy trousers. He went to the nearest call booth.

"Macadew here."

"Hi, Charley." President Shefferton peered over his reading glasses from his desk. "You look awful."

"Fell asleep in the steam room."

"Did you see the news about the Challenger tap?"

"Yeh."

"What on earth is Percy Manners thinking of, trying to push through anti-core tap legislation at a time like this?"

"He's thinking of himself, as usual. How he can embarrass you and chalk up points. It's perfect. You haven't taken a stand yet and it'll make him look good with the antitechnology crowd. Have you seen that holocube spot Percy paid for? Shows a hot, dusty cowboy stoppin' for a drink at a well that's belchin' smoke and flames. Then Percy comes on, real solemnlike, and says 'A thirsty man doesn't need to drink at a well of fire.' " Macadew snorted. "Make a hell of a cocktail!"

"That's not funny, Charley. Now the damned press is starting to refer to the tap as the well of fire. Once they latch onto a simplistic nickname like that they never let it go. Mindless propaganda could kill the entire core tap industry just the way nuclear power was killed by the link with atomic bombs. This bill has got to be stopped."

"Veto it."

"I can't afford a brawl with Congress this early, Charley. The party must present a united front until I push my programs through. Unfortunately, the biggest crack in that front is on ecology. And the core tap issue squats dead center over it. Core taps must take up the slack on our energy production until we can begin construction of our power satellite network."

"If it wasn't for Archer McClaren we'd have had that puppy working for thirty years."

"The environmentalists will fight us even harder on this issue, Charley."

"I take it I'm bein' asked to run interference fo' the president."

"Do what you can. I'm not asking the impossible."

"Unless the Tectonics Corporation fixes up that problem damn quick you may be askin' the impossible."

"Do what you can, Charley." The president's image vanished.

"I'll take that other call now, operator," said Macadew.

"I held my water as long as I could, Charles," said a feminine voice.

"Rita, my dear! I am mortified!"

Rita Holcombe Duce remained the one woman who could intimidate Charles Macadew. She was formidable. Painfully thin, with severely cut gray hair, a face like Nefertiti's, and cool green eyes, she regarded him with stern affection. She had been beautiful once and calling that beauty to mind sometimes made his heart ache. It was uncomfortable for a man his age, conveniently settled in a dull marriage, to be reminded that once there had been such a thing as passion. She was hard to like, but easy to fall in love with. Yet it was only in the years since their romance (curious word, it didn't even begin to describe the ramifications of their relationship) that mutual respect had matured into friendship.

That friendship was cemented by a political alliance when the presidency and controlling interest in the Tectonics Corporation passed from her brother, a tycoon but not a scientist, to Rita, who was both. Under her leadership (or dictatorship) the Tectonics Corporation became aggressive and innovative. Now she was struggling, perhaps fatally, to complete her most ambitious project: the mammoth Challenger tap, destined ultimately to provide the energy needs of the old Confederacy.

Characteristically, she came to the point: "Charles, I need your help."

"That's the prevailing trend today," he drawled, absentmindedly patting his pockets for a nonexistent cigar. "What the hell's goin' on down there?"

"The quakes caught us by surprise. Our Nares Plain seismic station gave us a ninety-eight percent probability of no tremors for a month.

That would have steered us through the most critical stage. We've just penetrated the Moho discontinuity—"

"Moho what?"

"—we've pierced the crust into the upper mantle. We were about to cap the magma when the quakes opened vertical cracks near the bore, forcing mantle material toward the surface. Normally, it would seep slowly through the sea bed or give birth to a volcano. But horizontal fractures have opened and the magma threatens the bore's upper section. At that level we don't use Collapsium shielding. If the magma isn't stopped it could destroy the bore and turbines. An explosion at that depth would bring tremendous volumes of sea water in contact with the mantle material—and that could be tragic."

"Puerto Rico's just a few miles away," breathed Macadew.

"The whole Caribbean, Charles. When Krakatoa blew off its cone sea water rushing in, caused an explosion equal to a dozen hydrogen bombs and tsunamis a hundred feet high—"

"My God, will that happen?"

"The potential is there. Before I'd let that happen I'd destroy the tap by plugging up the bore with explosives. But I mean to save her. The board of directors wants to cut our losses and get out. That's the most dangerous course of all."

"Why?"

"They want to salvage equipment right up until the critical moment, then blow the tap. But it's impossible to make predictions—we don't entirely understand the forces involved. I'll save the Challenger outright or blow her up!"

"You'll ignore the board?"

"It's the first time they've been unanimous about anything. I must be right."

"Against such logic I am defenseless."

"But I'm stymied if the core tap bill passes. No one will give me credit for extra equipment. I'll have no choice but to blow her up, and five years' work and several million ounces of my investors' gold and all hopes for cheap Southern energy. The entire core tap industry will be doomed. The bill makes financing new ones prohibitive."

"Tha's the whole idea. Look, darlin', at last count there's a hundred and one votes for and maybe fifteen against. As long as it looks like you're going down for the count we're stuck in a bear trap!"

"I need time, Charles. Time to show that the tap is safe. Time to save her." A definite note of pleading was in her voice, something he had never heard before.

He chuckled slightly and a wide smile appeared.

"Wal, time is one thing I can get you a little of. But the rest is up to you."

2

Drain the Atlantic and the ocean floor's most striking feature would be a spectacular mountain range, shaped like a fat sine wave, slashed repeatedly with deep fractures across its entire length from Iceland to Antarctica. This is the Atlantic Ridge.

A deep rift runs down the center. Here continental plates meet and great forces well up through the crust, thinner than on the continents. Magma oozing up and pushing out is the elemental force behind that immensely slow process known as continental drift. This is the breeding ground for earthquakes and volcanoes.

West of this rugged backbone the floor is deeply gouged. The deepest wound, the Puerto Rico Trench, is 27,500 feet below sea level. From that depth only three miles separate the floor from the boundary of the earth's crust. Here Rita Holcombe Duce had sunk the Challenger tap. The term *core tap* was a popular misnomer; in reality it was a mantle tap. The iron-nickel core lay 1,700 miles and many years of drilling deeper.

Five miles up floated a ten-acre helicopter landing platform and submarine bay. Resting on enormous pontoons doubling as living quarters, the platform barely swayed in the high waves, last remnants of a winter storm. Chal-Surf One was a small community staffed with meteorologists, oceanographers, engineers, and workmen on rest leave.

Six red circles with X's marked the helipads from the bright yellow platform surface. Several hours before, a Tectonics Corporation jump-jet had dropped off two people: Rita Duce and a stranger.

He looked to be in his midthirties but might have been older; a streak of pure white cut a swath through his unruly reddish mane, giving him the air of a prophet or a madman. But his eyes were twin pools of reason in a calm face. His features were etched sharply. The overall impression was one of determination.

Rita Duce, bundled in a flannel jacket under a bright orange slicker, squinted at the cloudless sky. She looked back at him.

"You haven't said much, Mr. Scott."

"When I've seen everything I'll have more to say," said Jason Scott. His jumpsuit was open at the neck and glistened with salt water. He reveled in the chilly spray that made her so uncomfortable.

Two specks appeared in the cobalt sky to the sound of rhythmic thrumming.

"My creditors," said Rita with distaste. "Or partners, depending on your perspective, I suppose."

Scott raised an eyebrow. "You don't seem the kind of woman who easily abides partners."

"I don't." She looked at the growing shapes as though they were vultures. "But these days few companies could build the Challenger tap alone." She awkwardly stuffed a hand in her slicker pocket. "I retained final say on all matters pertaining to the tap's construction—at a price. Now I'll pay that price if they decide to call in my loans."

"You financed the Challenger tap with notes payable on demand?"

"It was the only way." Her sun- and wind-burned face crinkled into a strangely sweet, almost motherly, smile. "I'm sure you, of all people, can understand. What was it? Three brilliant successes before you were thirty and you went bust three times."

"Each time more spectacularly than the last!" He laughed deeply, unreservedly. Rita Duce found herself joining him, laughing for the sheer triumphant joy of it.

"I understand a man like you, Mr. Scott," she said after catching her breath. "Anything worth doing, or grand, or imaginative, or visionary, or daring, is done by people like you and me. Unfortunately, nature didn't equip us to deal with"— she looked up again—"the bankers."

"Bankers?"

"Not actually, but their minds have deteriorated until they think only of interest rates, tax shelters, and avoiding risks." She made a noise halfway between a sigh and a snort. "Many years ago they called the biggest petroleum producers the Seven Sisters. For the past decade the Seven Sisters have been the producers of minerals and energy from the oceans. The Tectonics Corporation is one of the sisters. Those helicopters carry five others."

"And the seventh?"

"Python," she spat. "Like me, Horatius Krebs doesn't like partners, but he can afford to do without them."

"You don't have to tell me anything about Krebs."

"I can tell you that if he didn't have a total monopoly on Osirium metal my Challenger tap would be safe."

"Krebs legally stole the patent for Osirium from my dead father's estate," said Scott mildly.

"I had forgotten. You've as much cause to hate him as I do."

"Hate is a useless emotion."

"I find it concentrates the mind wonderfully."

The helicopters hovered over the platform, whipping spray into their faces.

"I'm afraid you must make up your mind now if you want the job. All my advisers are against trying to save the tap. That's why I called you."

"There was never any question of my not accepting. I've made arrangements to take leave from my Andean project, for which you will pay Condor Industries a princely sum each day."

"No conditions?"

"One. Total control."

She stiffened. "I'm not used to people telling me what to do with my company."

"It's the way I operate. Ask Señor Mendez."

She frowned and for a long moment their gazes locked, until she realized that the only will being tested was hers. Scott did not yield, he did not push, he merely maintained. She laughed again.

"Dammit, Scott, I like you!"

"The feeling is mutual." He enveloped her in a hug.

"I accept your conditions," she said. "Small price to pay for the twenty-first century's Renaissance man."

"That's a silly thing to call me, Rita. Today's microtechnology and mental disciplines make it possible for almost anyone to be the kind of hands-on engineer-manager technocrats used to dream about. My notoriety is undeserved in this field. I adapted existing techniques to my own methods."

"Yes, and Columbus crossed an ocean anyone could have crossed before, if they had only tried."

Further words were drowned by the roar of the choppers landing. Then the engines cut out and the only sounds were the sea, the soft swishing of the rotors, and from half a mile off, the low moaning of a freighter's horn.

"The S.S. *Anaconda*, property of Horatius Krebs, of Brazilian registry, bound for Lagos, Union of Black Africa," said Scott softly.

"Illegally, of course."

"Of course."

"What are you up to?"

"Remember my conditions," he said with a grin.

Five men ranging in age from early fifties to late nineties climbed from the helicopters. The companies they represented or controlled were Transnational, Minerva Enterprises, Bore Reaver, Global Dynamics, and Ottawa Engineering.

"The ones to watch are Alban Tupper of Minerva and Henry Nab of Transnational," whispered Rita. "Henry's senile, but when he's lucid he's more than a match for the rest. Tupper's a bitter, mean-spirited scrooge."

"The others?"

"—would make acceptable bookkeepers. They'll follow Nab and Tupper."

Rita Duce, aristocratically polite and charming, made the introductions.

"Gentlemen, my new chief engineer, Jason Scott."

"Fired the rest of 'em, heh?" cackled Nab. He had a disconcerting habit of sticking out his tongue slowly and pulling it back, like an ancient monitor lizard.

"Scott," said Tupper with a weasellike smile, "Any relation to Adam Scott?"

"His son."

"I'm not impressed."

"Would you follow me, gentlemen?" said Rita quickly.

The sun reflected off Henry Nab's glasses as he looked out over the ocean. He pointed with his cane. "There's another chopper."

"Who else is coming?" asked Tupper with narrowing eyes.

Rita looked at Scott with an upraised brow.

"A representative of the Python Corporation," said Scott.

"What in hell for, Rita?" said Henry Nab shrilly.

"Why bring in outsiders?" demanded Tupper, "Particularly that outsider?"

"I'll leave all explanations to my chief engineer, when he chooses to make them," she said.

A large black helicopter bearing the coiled serpent emblem of the Python Corporation settled next to the others. The pilot, a lean, tall man in black pants and turtleneck, stepped lightly from the teardrop cockpit. He saw Scott and his dark face smiled crookedly.

"Jason Scott! I would have bet my soul you'd be here!"

"Rita Holcombe Duce," said Scott quietly. "I'd like to present Jacob Kane of the Python Corporation."

Chapter

* 7 *

Feb. 7—*Science Review*—The leader of the biological team sent to investigate the Santa Bella blight is not a patient man, or one who bears fools gladly.

Dr. Noah Chambless halted a news conference to tell reporters the difference between a virus and a bacterium.

"You reporters have a duty to your readers. Santa Bella blight is a serious, even catastrophic threat to agriculture along the equator. Average citizens need to be informed about it. I trust you wouldn't confuse fission and fusion, so don't confuse viruses and bacteria." The tall, spare Texan spoke as if he was teaching a class of freshmen. He used a pointer to indicate a rice-shaped illustration labeled "Santa Bella blight," which was shown to be point zero two five micrometers, about one hundredth the size of the grain cell it was attached to. "Note our third illustration, a common bacterium. Note the difference in size. Can you all say micrometers?"

For eons it was part of the great Brazilian rain forest, green, dark, wet, primeval, and immortal. Then men cut down the trees, ploughed furrows, and sent the uprooted giants to sawmills to make lumber for the nation's young cities. Through hard work the loam had yielded abundant crops. That was yesterday. Today the healthy plants were powdery ash; the undulating golden ocean of grain was a deathly lunar landscape.

Hernando Perito was no ignorant peasant. The state university had taught him to use the land without raping it as his ancestors had done. For them there was always more rain forest at the edge of the clearing. He had no such luxury. He had learned to renew the land, to pamper it with the science at his disposal. He was a modern agricultural scientist; but now, kneeling in the gray dust that was his farm, he felt close to his primitive forebears who were so helpless before nature.

A rustling behind him made him turn away, ashamed to be seen with tears in his eyes.

It was the North American, Ralph Ferman, of the scientific team sent by the American president to combat the blight. He was young, short, and slender, with an amiable manner, unlike the aloof Dr. Chambless who led the Americans. Sensing Perito's sorrow, he drew back to avoid embarrassing him.

"Hello, Hernando."

Together they surveyed the blasted land. A breeze stirred the gray wisps. The Santa Bella blight had moved like a curse, so quickly a man's eyes could watch the grain shrivel and die.

"You must think me morbid to come here every day."

"A man has a right to mourn a loved one, even a crop of grain."

"I do not mourn, I pray."

"For what?"

"For God to stop this terrible thing before it destroys my country."

Ferman sighed. "God may be the only one who can. There's no indication it will stop before it reaches North America."

Perito's dark compassionate eyes fixed on his friend.

"You fear for your own country. I will pray for you too."

Was Perito too naive to realize that the team's main purpose was to protect the United States, that Brazil and all of South America were expendable to that purpose?

"I'm not a spiteful man," said Perito, as if replying to that silent question. "I do not wish this—this on anyone."

"I do have some good news," said Ferman. "Your land will bloom again. Tests show that the blight didn't permanently damage the soil. That gray stuff looks bad but it's sterile."

"Excellent news, my friend. That was my worst fear. If I can grow other crops, things are not so terrible. No worse than a flood or fire or drought." He smiled for the first time.

"I've got to go. I'm due in Chambless's tent to make my daily report."

"You look worried. Have you discovered a serious thing?"

Ferman shrugged. "A puzzling thing. I'm not sure what I've found, if anything. It's a peculiarity in the virus samples. I'm going to tell Chambless about it."

"What will he do?"

"Probably nothing. It probably means nothing and he'll have an explanation, something I haven't thought of. Chambless is the foremost man in the field and I'm just out of college."

Perito caught his arm above the elbow in the intimate friendly way of Latins.

"Never underestimate yourself, my friend. Never assume that someone is right because he is older or more educated. Age brings rigidity to some rather than wisdom. And this Dr. Chambless, him I do not like."

"That's no criterion for judging a man's opinion. His brilliance is undeniable. Yes, he's cold and aloof. I don't warm up to him myself. He reminds me of a med school instructor who dissected cadavers. But he's fair and impartial." He smiled. "Why not fly to Brasilia tonight for a few tall ones, eh? If I'm not assigned extra work?"

"Of course. Tonight then."

They separated, Perito to his ranch house, Ferman to Chambless's tent.

The camp was laid out like a small town. Rows of tents for workers and junior scientists radiated from the administrative hub. The setup was portable on an hour's notice and had been moved twice since arriving in Brazil. They followed the blight—now twenty miles north. Two days ago it was a hundred yards.

As Ferman went inward on one of the spokes he was passed by jeeps loaded with scientists and equipment, going to collect soil and plant samples, take photos and holographs and observations. As each jeep flew by he was enveloped by dust. He waved. He knew them all by sight and most by name. Some of the women he knew very well, but he kept that sort of thing to a minimum in camp. Rio and São Paulo, well, they were different.

Ferman always felt the urge to wait for the butler to answer when he went to Chambless's tent, although everyone had standing orders simply to go in during daylight hours.

"Good morning, Dr. Chambless." He squinted in the green gloom of canvas-filtered light before a card table the chief used as a desk. The interior was like a small mobile library. Chambless traveled with hundreds of books, a personal computer, and several hundred pounds of delicate instruments. It was a headache for those who did the lifting, but he hated microfilm books and insisted on doing most of his own lab work.

Chambless was scrunched up in his chair like a very long, spindly light fixture that was folded and bent into a small space. He unfolded himself and linked his hands behind his back.

"Did you discover anything interesting yesterday, Mr. Ferman?" The ritual greeting. Ferman presumed he used it with everyone.

Chambless's soft Texas drawl was soothing if one wasn't used to it, or to his technique of putting people at ease, then pouncing on their theories and shredding them. His rapier analytical powers were so keen that victims often didn't discover what had happened until they turned to leave and fell apart in several places.

"Nothing in my area, sir. Santa Bella didn't react to any of the new agents. So far, nothing affects it even slightly without also destroying its host victim."

"I see. You said nothing in your area—"

Ferman took a deep breath.

"Well, sir, I've been doing some extra lab work on my own."

"Very commendable, Mr. Ferman," said Chambless softly. "I wish other staff members displayed your fervor. But I suppose most feel they deserve to relax at night after a hard day's work. I'm gratified you don't share their attitude."

Ferman blushed. He was almost certain Chambless knew he'd spent many off hours in some of the wildest night spots in Brazil. But his face, a block of stone carved with that damnably superior smile, betrayed nothing.

"If you are impelled to do extra work, why not confine it to your assigned field?"

"Well, sir, since it is my free time, I used it on something that interests me." Mistake!

Chambless's eyebrows formed scornful arches.

"I'm sorry your present assignment doesn't interest you, Mr. Ferman. Perhaps if you—"

"I didn't mean that, sir!" He was rapidly losing any control of the conversation. "I love my work but I've pursued other study in my spare time for curiosity's sake. That's when I came across something that may be valuable. I thought I'd better bring it to your attention."

"Quite right," said Chambless. "Anything germane to our mission here interests me. Take a seat, Mr. Ferman, and tell me what you've found."

Chambless remained standing, putting Ferman in the uncomfortable position of looking up to him. He swallowed hard.

"Let me provide a little background, sir, so you won't think I'm entirely off base with this notion. In graduate school I did a paper on mutated diseases, specifically effects of hard radiation on bacteria in space. As a matter of fact I paid an enormous amount to take the Earth-Mars transport to study, firsthand, the bacteria you proved were actually a mutated terran strain and not native Martian." He caught his breath. Was his flattering reference to Chambless's famous work too obvious?

"You also found time to backpack to the foot of Olympus Mons and join an expedition to the summit." An icy smile crystallized. "Actually, Mr. Ferman, I'm quite familiar with your background. I read the academic records and resumés of people who come to work for me. But please continue."

Flustered but not yet routed, Ferman plunged ahead.

"I think I've established my ability to talk about this subject. It occurred to me that the Santa Bella blight is probably a mutation since its like has never been encountered before. Also that it might be a disease brought to earth from a space station or colony after exposure to high radiation. I studied it under the electron microscope with that in mind."

"What did you discover?"

"I did a nucleic acid analysis. I believe it's a mutation, but not an accidental one."

Chambless sat slowly and folded his hands on the table. "What exactly do you mean?"

"I believe it is man-made. The chromosomes bear evidence of manipulation, or so it seemed to me. I realize it's hard to differentiate between man-made manipulation and gamma-ray mutation. But I came up with evidence of human tampering: I analyzed the genetic code with the DNA molecules and found that the blight is almost perfectly constructed to do what it does. It is an almost perfect grain-destroying organism. To use an analogy, it was like looking at a lawn mower blueprint. A lawn mower bears a family resemblance to a motorcycle, but everything about it is built toward its goal of cutting grass. That is rare in the biological world. A virus may cause sickness in a human, but it does so because the human system reacts against it or because its by-products create a bad environment in the host. A virus never exists solely to annihilate humans. Santa Bella exists solely to destroy cereal plants. Its genetic structure is 'engineered' toward that goal. It differs radically from other grain-killing blights. I have to assume that if it's a mutation, it must have been blasted by a tremendous amount of radiation to account for so much of its DNA structure being altered. If it were, probability dictates that some of the changes wouldn't be related to its grain-destroying characteristics. Some ought to be harmful to it. A virus with that many DNA alterations shouldn't exist, unless it is manufactured.

"If two bricks are stacked together, it might be chance. A wall of bricks must be erected by an intelligence."

There was a long pause. "Did you feed your data into the computer?" asked Chambless.

"Yes."

"And the probability of the mutation being entirely natural, given your other assumptions?"

"The odds are several thousand to one against."

"Very interesting." Chambless rubbed his lips with his index finger. "We know that the disease is a mutation. The suggestion has been made that it is from outer space, an alien form. We also considered that it might be an altered earth virus. That we might be dealing with a man-made plague was foremost in the president's mind when he sent us." He sat back, contemplating the tent's ceiling and pulled a timeworn briar from his coat pocket. He filled it from a pouch smelling faintly of wintergreen, and vainly looked for something to light it with.

"You wouldn't have a lighter, would you?"

"I'm sorry, I don't smoke."

"How can a man think without a pipeful?" He rummaged in the rear of the tent, gave a cry of triumph, and resumed his seat with a small, elegant lighter of black enamel etched with a silver design of eyes. Applying the heat element, he puffed contentedly.

"Your theory is interesting, Mr. Ferman, but pardon me if I don't jump in the pond with you just yet. I want your notes, software, and holographs taken with the electron microscope so I may double-check your data. I hope you are suitably honored." He smiled the warmest smile Ferman had seen him exhibit.

"Yes sir, as long as I can have them back."

Chambless looked as if he had made a faux pas of a ridiculously juvenile nature.

"Really, Mr. Ferman, you may rely on me to handle your work with care. Try to remember that this is a unified effort. You used government equipment in your nocturnal investigations.

"Now, I'll expect the things I asked for as soon as possible this morning. You're excused from your regular duties to gather them. Time is our vital element. Santa Bella moves ten miles a day and waits for no man."

"Yes sir," said Ferman doubtfully. He started to leave.

"I really didn't thank you, did I?" said Chambless. "Your zeal is most exemplary. Believe me, it won't go unrewarded."

Chapter

* 8 *

1

"**P**oint fourteen, honored colleagues, is this," said the junior senator from Puerto Rico, Jorge Luis Maria Vega de Santiago.

His eyelids almost shut, yet sitting in an attitude of rapt attention, Charles Macadew half-listened and half-dozed. Stirring himself, he glanced slyly at his watch. Senator de Santiago had gone on for an hour and was probably good for another ninety minutes.

Macadew gloated. If the Senate leadership wanted to ram the core tap bill through with a minimum of debate, they had picked the wrong floor leader. The feisty little senator was many things: vain, flamboyant, eloquent, courageous, and intense, but he was never brief. To him, the legislative process was a form of single combat and he was its Don Quixote.

Macadew, who always made it a point to know his adversary, had turned the core tap debate into a personal duel with the Latin senator. He challenged every point, every fact, every fraction, and the Puerto Rican felt honor-bound to respond to each objection.

On point sixteen, Macadew padded out of the well of the chamber, pausing outside the big doors to take a deep breath. He was thirsty! He started for the Senate cloakroom.

"Senator!"

The majority leader had followed him. At thirty-seven the youngest majority leader in Senate history, Percy Shelley Manners was impressive. Macadew barely came up to his broad shoulders. An aristocratic profile carved on a massive head topped with curly black hair, and baby blue eyes, combined with a rich and silky voice to produce a campaign manager's dream.

"What can I do for you, Percy?"

"I want to congratulate you, Charles, for foxing me so completely!" Manners smiled broadly, coldly. He wrapped a big arm around the shorter man.

"Why, whatever do you mean?"

"Don't kid a kidder, Charles. We both know I made a tactical error choosing Jorge to be floor leader and you've brilliantly exploited his weakness. But I know, and you know, we have the votes to pass it handily—"

"I don' know any such thing!"

"I didn't think he'd waste time replying to every niggling objection of yours in detail."

"You'll pick these things up when you've been aroun' a few years, Percy. And I fully expect you to be here fo' many productive years—" He smiled his killer smile and disengaged himself.

"How can I persuade you to drop your delaying tactics so we can get on with the business of the Senate?"

"The business of the Senate *is* talkin'."

"A great man like you, Charles, shouldn't make light of the legislative process."

They didn't call him Perfect Manners for nothing, thought Macadew.

"Come now, Charles, we're both members of the same party."

"Wal, I know that, Percy, but I'm not sure you do."

"If you feel that way, why did you help elect me majority leader?"

"'Cause I'm a politician who stays bought."

"Implying?"

"Implyin' nothin'."

"Why did you agree to the deal in the first place?"

"To keep Harmon from leadin' us to a third defeat. I was willin' to hand him the State Department to make room for you and to give the veepship to Teresa St. Clair to make the conservatives swallow the deal."

"You were willing to do anything but let me have the nomination."

"Jeff's my man, son."

"I had the delegates."

"You had your chance to beat Harmon—you failed. Dark horses happen. That's a fact of politics."

"I've admired you since I was a boy," said Manners bitterly. "I don't comprehend how you can be so blind. Shefferton's radicalism will destroy the party. We've stood for peaceful internationalism, for less restrictive technology regulations, for a clean, healthy economy. Shefferton stands for adventurism, an arms race, for science and technology unfettered by common sense or common decency; for wasting our precious resources building pie-in-the sky dreams in space.

"You accuse me of disloyalty! Yet I've never publicly opposed the president since he took office—"

"The year is young."

"That's how loyal I am! But on core taps I've made my position clear, unlike Shefferton."

"You know he's against the core tap bill."

"Let him say so publicly."

"He won't fight a losin' battle this early."

"If he takes no stand, I'm free to lead the Senate as my conscience leads me. I'm honor-bound to do so—"

"Your honor has a way of lookin' out for number one, Percy."

"You question it?"

"Le's jest say that your ethics could be put on a pretzel without seriously deformin' it."

"I won't trade insults with you. I admire you too much."

"I like you, Percy. You're a good boy. Someday you may even make a good president. But you're a hypocrite. You 'n' me, we're both tomcats—I know it, but you refuse to accept it. Tha's the difference."

"What do you hope to gain by playing for time?" Manners looked at him piercingly.

"Why, to defeat the bill, of course!"

"Nonsense. We have more than enough votes."

"So you keep tellin' me."

"If you're going to be stubborn, I guess I must work on some of your supporters."

"You might give Jorge a try," he said with an impish wink. "You know, that was truly a blunder of epic proportions."

"Yes," said Manners unhappily, "I know."

2

Jacob Kane's smile was suave.

"I'm here as a go-between if you choose to ask Python for a financial arrangement."

They sat in the conference room. On the bulkhead was a computer projection of the Challenger tap. For reference it showed Chal-Surf One free-floating on the surface of the ocean. Miles below it, resting on the ocean floor, was the glassteel dome that held air like an overturned bowl. The bore grew out of the dome, so the whole structure was shaped like a round-headed nail with the point cut off. The head was the dome, the nail was the bore, sunk two and a half miles into the basalt. From the terminus dozens of needle lines, representing individual drills, extended into the mantle.

"You mean you're here to spy for Horatius Krebs!" said Alban Tupper.

"What if he is?" said Rita Duce calmly. "The whole country knows our problems in general terms. I don't care if Mr. Krebs knows them in their particulars."

"I don't want him here!" said Tupper.

"I'll be happy to step outside until you're done," said Kane.

"No," said Rita Duce firmly, "I wouldn't ask even Horatius Krebs to lend me money without all the information."

"You would consider taking money from Krebs? On his terms?" cackled Henry Nab. "Gad! You are determined, girl. I believe you would deal with the Devil himself!"

She looked at Kane and a grim smile played on her lips.

"Yes, I would."

Tupper laughed cynically. "I think you're smarter than that. You want to intimidate us into extending the loan. You know we can't legally stop you from fighting to the end, no matter how hopeless your chances. You're betting we'll back you to save our investment." He gave Kane a black look. "To hell with it! Let him stay! I'll not be intimidated."

"The aim is not intimidation," said Jason Scott, "but to demonstrate that we will save the tap, by whatever means, even if we must deal with Python."

"It's too late for that." A string of drool ran down Henry Nab's chin.

"Not so." Kane leaned with folded arms against the bulkhead. "I'm authorized to offer Mrs. Duce an immediate line of credit for equipment and materials, delivered by the fastest means."

"You've got two, maybe three days at the most," said Tupper. "The only thing holding up the core tap bill is a filibuster by Macadew and a few diehards. When they cave in, you're finished. I say call in the loans and cut our losses."

"Dammit!" Nab seemed to pull himself together. "I didn't come here on a joyride. If I'd made up my mind I'd have stayed home. Let's hear what Rita has to say before we decide."

Alban Tupper glared but the others nodded in agreement. He inclined his head with mock humility.

"By all means, let's hear every side."

Rita Duce walked briskly to the computer projection and faced them. When she began to speak it was with the assurance of a gambler who knows that no game is over until the last card is turned. As she spoke she manipulated the projection to rotate, enlarge, and identify the points she wanted to illustrate.

The four energy executives opened their attachés, so their personal computers could record the data as Duce presented it, and so they could consult them from time to time. Kane leaned against a bulkhead and casually took notes on the lightpad of his holster-sized model.

Vivid crimson crazes appeared as Duce described how the earthquake had opened a vertical vent and subsequent quakes had produced horizontal cracks that were widening, threatening to intersect the main shaft of the bore.

"With some warning we could have taken precautions that would have reduced or even eliminated the danger to the tap. We could have sunk shafts parallel to the Challenger to give the magma safety vents to the surface, or, with less warning, erected heat shields around the vulnerable sections of the bore. But our early warning seismic station failed us."

Standing at the back of the conference room, Scott became aware of Jacob Kane next to him when Kane's hand clamped down on his arm, nails biting flesh. Kane's breath was cold in his ear. He spoke so low that his voice was almost subliminal, yet Scott heard each word clearly.

"Don't answer. Don't give a sign that I'm talking to you. Listen— get out of this while you can. I won't insult your ridiculous sense of honor by asking you to betray Mrs. Duce, but it should be obvious that this is a charade. She can't win. Those men don't want to save her. They want to destroy her. They hate her. I'm here to pick up the pieces. Whatever deal I offer will be loaded. You can only destroy yourself by staying involved."

Scott pondered this. When he looked back, Kane was now standing at the other end of the room, seemingly absorbed in note taking. Had he imagined it? Kane matched gazes with Scott and a cynical grin formed. He hadn't imagined it.

Rita Duce described the topology of the area of the tap, the known faults, the rills and canyons of the ocean floor. She explained that the area had long been known for seismic activity. An extinct volcano shaft was several miles west of the bore, but it had shown no significant activity in the last century.

"We face a political and an engineering problem," she said. "We must restore the tap's integrity quickly and convincingly enough to stop the Senate from passing the core tap bill."

"Which you will never do," said Tupper.

"I'm not right on top of the state of the art," said Henry Nab with a dry chuckle, "but I believe the only way to protect the bore in the short time left is to install a heat shield of Osirium." He cocked his head. "Am I right?"

"Possibly," said Rita Duce. "This precise problem has never been encountered before—"

"So the real question is will Python provide it to you." His eyeglasses flashed as he looked at Kane. "Will it?"

"Under the proper circumstances."

"Which are?"

"Between Mrs. Duce and myself," said Kane smoothly.

Nab laughed again. "Well, I'm not half the pirate Horatius Krebs is, but in his position I'd make you pay through the nose—hell! I'd make you hand over half the company." He stood and leaned on his cane. "Rita, girl, the way I see it you've been hosed. As much as I like to agree with a pretty woman and disagree with Alban, I'm afraid I'm calling in my chips. I'm sorry this will ruin you, Rita, because you're one of the great creative people left in this business. But I'm too old for risks anymore." He sat, staring ahead and seeming to sink into himself like a slowly deflating balloon.

"Good, that's settled!" said Tupper gleefully. He glanced at the others, as if ready to fight them all, but they nodded and, with finality, closed their attaché computers in unison. He turned to Rita. "That makes it official, Mrs. Duce. We are required to give you twenty-four hours' notice. If you don't come up with the amount stipulated in our agreement by then you'll be in default." He paused at the door. "Good day."

The others followed. If Rita Duce was stunned or depressed she gave no indication. She exhaled slowly with her eyes closed.

"So this is what it feels like to be free. I'd forgotten." She looked at Kane. "Let's talk business, Mr. Kane. Try and be brief; Mr. Scott and I don't have all day. What are your terms?"

"Hardly piratical," said Kane. "You seem confident that you can deal with the problem in a short time, say three days?"

"With Osirium metal we could. If we take longer the Senate will end our problem for us. You agree, Jason?"

"Yes."

"Very well, Python will put all its resources at your disposal; all its equipment, unlimited credit on materials, guaranteed delivery by whatever means you stipulate. If, in three days, a federal inspector gives the tap a clean bill of health, you will have five years to pay us back, at the standard rate of interest. If not, Python will get sixty percent of the combined assets of the Tectonics Corporation and complete operational authority over the uncompleted Challenger tap."

Rita Duce paled.

"You *did* say you could do it in three days."

She looked at Scott. He nodded.

"We have a deal, Mr. Kane."

Kane's eyes gleamed as he took a plastic document from his attaché.

"All it requires is your signature. I have authority to affix the seal of Horatius Krebs."

"The chancellor with the signet ring of the prince," said Scott.

"The analogy has some validity, my friend." He gave the paper to Rita Duce. She signed with a flourish. He affixed the seal.

Kane bowed, a gesture that, on him, conveyed insolence. "Thank you, madam. If you have quarters for me, I will await your instructions."

"I'll have a list of what we want from Python in about an hour, Jacob," said Scott.

"Your quarters are on C deck. The steward will show you, Mr. Kane." said Rita Duce, indicating a man who had just entered. When Kane had gone, she turned to Scott.

"I hope you know what you're doing."

"I know exactly what I'm doing."

A telephone on the bulkhead chimed. She picked it up, listened a moment, and hung up.

"The workers in the bore have gone on strike," she whispered. "They claim they're in imminent danger."

"A little too convenient, wouldn't you say?" Scott smiled.

"Dammit, Jason, how can you be so calm? How can we erect the heat shields if the men refuse to work?"

He grasped her shoulders and looked into her eyes. "Rita, it's time to let me do my job. It's time to trust me. Believe me when I tell you this doesn't surprise me. *Trust me!*"

"All right."

"I'm taking over your office."

"But I need my office! It's the nerve center of the organization. Bethany Williams, my executive secretary, runs everything from there!"

"That's why I'm taking it over." He looked stern. "Besides, you won't need an office for a while. You're taking a jump-jet to the mainland. You've given me complete authority, now let me use it. I can do that best with you gone. Do you agree?"

"Yes."

Chapter
* 9 *

Bethany Williams greeted Scott at the door of Rita Duce's office.

"I have several reports for you, Mr. Scott." He was somewhat taken aback by her efficient adaptation to a radical change.

Bethany was a tall, handsome woman whose only concession to originality in personal appearance was a stylized helmet-shaped hairdo, with strands dyed a shiny bronze, whipped into the consistency of dessert topping.

In a short time her efficiency, tact, and organizational ability had so impressed Scott that he easily believed Rita Duce's assertion that she ran everything from her office. So brilliant was she that Scott felt she was wasting herself as a mere executive secretary. She was leadership material, and Scott despised wasting such talent.

By lucid management of data flow, Bethany helped him hook into the decision-making network of Chal-Surf One and the bore operation in what was, even for him, record time.

Scott sat at Rita Duce's desk. Two deep connectors embedded in his ears fed him seismic data from sensors on the ocean floor. Two small holocubes on the desk displayed rows of figures and equations. His eyes roamed back and forth between the cubes. With his right hand he took notes on a lightpad.

A red light blinked in the corner of one of the holocubes, announcing that someone was waiting to see him. He was interviewing as many key personnel as possible in the short time he had before it was necessary to act.

So far he had met the security chief; the surface operations officer; and the strange, lisping leader of the cyborg "gill" men, who had been caught topside, isolated from his people when the revolt struck at the base of the bore.

The door opened and the computer chief, Ron Qwale, entered. He was skinny, with an egg-shaped head, and was almost crossed-eyed. He wore blue jeans, a western shirt, and a string tie. Twin pigtails hid shaved interface patches on the back of his skull. His smile was simple and strangely childlike as he absorbed the sight of Scott being fed information by three different sources.

"Are you an interface, Mr. Scott?"

"No, I have an ability to process data from several sources at once," said Scott. "Excuse me a moment, I think I missed something—" After a moment he removed the deep connectors and shut off the monitors. "Sorry to keep you waiting, Mr. Qwale."

"Not at all. Very fascinating. Are you interfacing with the system to your satisfaction?"

"Yes, but I won't waste your time with that," said Scott curtly. "I have a specific problem and you may be able to help."

"Anything, of course."

"I have reason to believe there may be a security leak that helped someone take advantage of Mrs. Duce at a time when she's especially vulnerable. That suggests a high-level leak. Also that someone has access to the project's data network. Any suggestions where I should begin looking?"

"I guess I would head the list, Mr. Scott." Qwale smiled ingenuously. "Add to that list most of our administrative staff, the bore foreman, and the superefficient Bethany Williams."

"You don't trust Miss Williams?"

"Well, as a cybernetics man, I really don't care for people all that much. I'm rather fond of the gill people; they are so delightfully twisted and deformed by their strange new natures. 'A sea change, into something rich and strange,' as Bill the Bard said. But I am particularly uncomfortable around anyone, woman or man, who is that confident and efficient without being connected to a computer."

"Then you must find me quite disturbing, too."

Qwale merely shrugged and smiled.

"Prepare a report by the end of the day detailing all who have access to the network. I also want a report on how Chal-Surf One gets data on probable tectonic activity on the sea floor."

"Is there a problem with that?"

"Don't try to second-guess me. Just do it. If I have questions, I'll talk to you again."

"That will be a long report. Should I boil it down?"

"No, I'm a very fast reader."

"That figures. Good day, Mr. Scott."

When Qwale had left, Scott buzzed Bethany. She entered his office almost immediately.

"Get the foreman of the bore crew on the horn."

"That would be Arkady Kazan." She put a portfolio with the man's holograph on the desk in front of Scott.

Kazan's face materialized in the cube.

"What's the situation?" said Scott.

"Who the hell are you?" demanded the graying fortyish man with a wrinkled, squashed-down face and bulging forearms.

"Your new boss."

"Jason Scott? But we just heard about your appointment—"

"Don't waste my time. Why have the men stopped working?"

"They're scared. They know about the magma cracks. They think Mrs. Duce is lying about the danger. They've taken over the dome and demand transport topside immediately. All except the gill men, that is. They fled at the first sign of a mutiny."

"Have the mutineers taken over the subs?"

"No, the assistant foreman got to the sub pens first and sealed the airlock. Damned stupid stunt—"

"Can you patch me into him, Kazan?"

"No sir, I can't."

"Try to calm the men. Tell them I'm on my way to talk to them."

"I can't do that, sir. They're a mob. They'd tear me to pieces."

"There doesn't seem to be a whole lot you can do, Kazan." Scott ended the conversation. He looked at Bethany. "Can you reroute the call to the assistant foreman? He seems the only man down there with any initiative."

"I think so, let me try." She put on a headset linking her brain to the system computer. She closed her eyes and her lips moved slightly, as if recalling a distant memory. She opened her eyes. "Try it now."

A dark, almost bluish black man in his middle or later thirties, with craggy features and woolly white hair, appeared in the cube. He spoke with a mixture of Southern and French accents that Scott recognized as Creole.

"You Jason Scott?"

"I am."

"I'm Matt Taylor. You better get down here damn quick if you want to prevent a mut'ny or worse."

Scott smiled at his commanding tone. "I'm doing my best to do that, Mr. Taylor. Is that why you took over the sub pens?"

"Damn straight. When you comin'?"

"As soon as I get a sub, Mr. Taylor."

"Name's Matt. Well, better make it soon." Once more a command, not an appeal. Scott liked his attitude.

"Are you in danger? Can they blast the locks and get inside?"

Taylor smiled contemptuously. "If they want to bring five miles of water down on 'em. This is no place to play around with explosives."

"What about leaving through the waterlocks on their side and swimming in from the ocean on your side?"

"Nope. Gill men are the only ones who can operate this deep without a sub. Even if they could the gills wouldn't let 'em."

The gill men—cyborgs altered surgically with special skin grafts that made them at home under water—were clannish and close-knit. It was tempting to call them a "race" since they shared common interests, prejudices, and habits, and made no major decision unilaterally without consulting the whole clan. Although they had fled, they were within hailing distance of the dome. They abhorred violence—but they would stop sabotage of the dome from the sea.

"Good. I'll be there directly. Oh, I hope you don't mind some added responsibility. You're replacing Kazan as foreman."

"Okay." His image faded.

"He seems a man of few words. What can you tell me about him?"

Bethany slid another of the ubiquitous portfolios under his nose. He shook his head. "I said, what can *you* tell me about him?"

"He's quite a man. He worked a three-barrel slusher on the moon, mining ilmenite ore for oxygen to toss into low earth orbit for shuttle fuel. An electrical explosion of some sort killed everybody in the little operation except him. He walked back to Tycho, a thousand kilometers. He pushed a little oxygen refiner in front of him on a jury-rigged tread wagon and managed to keep himself in oxygen until he got there. But the worst part is that he walked the whole way in the lunar noon. The ordeal turned his hair white at the age of twenty-five. Oh, yes, he keeps a freezer full of alligator tail roasts."

"You *do* know a lot about him."

"He's sort of a Kit Carson figure. Larger than life." She crinkled her eyes a little. "Like you."

"I see I'm being set up for something. Go ahead, spill it."

"I told Mr. Haggard, the security chief, your intentions. He wants to go with you with a squad of men. There's nearly a thousand men down there. We don't know who's armed or how many are part of the strike. He's worried about your safety."

Scott shook his head. "If I can't keep order without company goons at my back, I'm not much of a manager. You can't gain a man's respect by threatening him."

"Aren't you going to be armed?"

"What's the background of these men?"

"Well, the work is highly technical, with some heavy physical labor. They're a mix of heavy construction people and softpalms. And about two dozen gill men."

"Probably a few toughs whipped the rest into striking. They don't sound very intimidating. My men in Bolivia are ex-convicts, former mercenaries, dock workers. They work dangerous for big money. They'd take these gentlemen apart."

"And you're tougher than they are?" She looked skeptical.

"They won't work for someone they don't respect."

She crinkled her eyes again. "That's an important thing to you, isn't it? Respect. I get the feeling you wouldn't mind if someone thought you were a complete bastard as long as he didn't question your competence."

He fixed his water blue eyes on hers with complete frankness. "You're right. Part of the reason I'm working for Rita Duce is my respect for what she has done. I approve of her values. My father died to uphold values like those. The least I can do is risk my life occasionally when I believe in the cause. I sense a similar motivation in you. Obviously you're qualified to be more than Rita Duce's executive secretary."

"Perhaps I'm an underachiever."

"If I believed that, we wouldn't be having this conversation. I think you're drawn to work for Rita because you are like her. You're both creators. Doers. In fact, I doubt you'd be comfortable working with anyone less. You're serving an apprenticeship, whether you acknowledge it or not."

She laughed. "Stick it, Scott! I'm not interested in your psychoanalysis, and I don't need job counseling."

"I think I'm right," said Scott quietly.

The holocube buzzed. It was Kane.

"I just heard about your problem. Nothing serious, I hope."

"I can handle it, Jacob. Your sources are excellent, for you to have learned of this so quickly."

"I must protect Python's interests."

"I'll bet. I have a list of things I want delivered here."

"So soon?" The list was faxed to his terminal. He read with growing interest. "You surprise me, Jason. A submarine mole and industrial fission bombs? I'm afraid this may take a while."

"Our agreement is that you will provide us with whatever equipment we require by the means that we stipulate."

"You must allow for physical impossibility. We have no submarine moles or industrial nukes we can deliver on such short notice."

"I think you do. It's just slipped your memory."

Suspicion dawned on Kane's face. "What do you mean?"

"Your ship S.S. *Anaconda*, is a few miles from here."

"That's an oil tanker, if I recall."

"Taking oil to Nigeria? Don't be silly, Jacob."

"As you know, it would be extremely illegal for an American ship to go anywhere near the African coast—"

"Ships have been known to change flags and alter their structures in mid-ocean to deceive the authorities. The navy was alerted several hours ago. If the *Anaconda* doesn't change its heading soon, they'll intercept. The government might wonder what a load of nukes and a submarine mole are doing heading for Lagos and the dictator of Black Africa. If they found out your master is supplying Juba Aman Dana's nuclear arsenal it might stir up trouble even Horatius Krebs couldn't buy his way out of."

"A clerical error, I assure you." Kane smiled. "I'm sure there won't be a problem for the *Anaconda* to change course and dock with you."

"I didn't think there would be."

"But I still don't see how you can put Osirium shields on the bore using those products."

"I never said that was what I need them for," said Scott. "You did."

Chapter
* 10 *

Feb. 9—Baltimore *Herald*—Senator Charles Macadew's one-man filibuster against the core tap bill continued as he read a volume of chili recipes into the record, discussed roping and branding steers, and scorned entreaties to end his lonely battle. The bill's opponents pack little support in the Senate, but Macadew has great personal influence. Colleagues have resisted his pleas to change their votes, but also refuse to support the Senate leadership in imposing the cloture rule to end debate.

1

It took several hours to reach the inky bottom of the Puerto Rico Trench. Scott made good use of the time on a computer connected by relay to the Chal-Surf One system.

On board the only sounds were the five crewmen talking quietly, eerie groans and wails of metal under almost unimaginable pressure, and sonar moans as the equipment registered the strange luminescent inhabitants of these depths.

At the controls was Needle, the gill man. Wiry, muscled as tightly as a steel cord, he was so short as to almost be classifiable as a dwarf. Artificially induced fur covered his body and bioengineered membranes pulsated over his eyes, ears, nose, and mouth, and under the lymphatic glands of the throat where his artificial gills were surgically implanted. When he spoke at all it was in a soft, lisping singsong, as if conversation in dry air was uncomfortable.

Jason Scott was content to let the cyborg pilot them to his home. He was absorbed in his search. He had brought his own terminal on board. Its special modifications—integrated molecule chip circuits he had designed—gave it the power of a much larger mainframe.

He jacked into Chal-Surf One's network. It was time to go hunting. He booted a search program designed to combat wormhole and virus programs, significantly modified by him to be a search and destroy program for network moles. He called it Bloodhound.

The terminal holocube created an analogue of the Tectonics Corporation network, a 3-D "map" with symbolic representations of various functions and entities within the system. It looked like a very orderly, multitiered, pyramidal spider web.

Bloodhound quickly identified a number of entities that had every business being within the system. He noted that at the moment Rita Duce was calling Chal-Surf One, demanding another progress report. With a chuckle, Scott reached out and cut off her link in mid-sentence. That would teach her to keep her word!

After noting and cataloguing various protective programs at the edge of the system, Scott rode Bloodhound deeper into the thick body of mainframe programs. Here was a tangled growth like a serrated flower: the program monitoring life support in the dome. One of its petals was bent and discolored—it had been hours, apparently, since the dome's air ducts had been serviced. Things were getting out of hand down there.

Scott began looking under the surface for the less than obvious. There!

A bluish, fuzzy presence near the intersection of several vital service nets. Scott smiled. "Hello, Jacob!" His old friend's signature was unmistakable. He reached out to zap the spy. Wait! Kane was never obvious. Look below the surface. Ah, there it was! A purplish strand, interwoven so tightly with a communications link that it might have remained undetected forever. Scott quickly wove a blocking net around the intruder and set it to play a three-day loop of false information. Then he let Bloodhound devour the decoy. Kane might believe that his decoy had been found, but that his real mole was intact. He might be fooled for several days.

Scott quickly located another mole, much less sophisticated, belonging, if he recognized the electronic signature, to Minerva Enterprises, Alban Tupper's company. Another, cheaper, almost laughable spy belonged to Henry Nab's Transnational. It had wormed into a zone it couldn't escape from, and fed a steady stream of data about waste disposal aboard the floating island.

Then, like a ripple on a pond, Scott sensed something else. Subtle, virtually undetectable—yet it was there, just under the surface. Bloodhound couldn't quite focus it. It was there and it wasn't. Then, with an explosion and a broadcast emotion that was nothing other than blind rage, the mole self-destructed. He had gotten too close. So close he might have been able to identify the intruder. Now, that was interesting!

Scott looked up from his terminal. They were near the end of their journey.

The dome sat like an overturned bowl on the ocean floor. As they approached it, the water changed from black to deep purple to dark green. Light was as alien to this universe as the bubble of air or the men inside.

The submarine entered a dark tunnel at the base of the dome and surfaced in an immense chamber lit blindingly by hydrogen lamps lining the ceiling.

Matt Taylor stood on the quay, cradling a submachine gun. Scott joined him.

"'Bout time you showed, Mr. Scott."

"Glad to meet you, Matt." Taylor was shorter than he had imagined, but very fit. His knuckles were rubbed raw.

"Have to fight your way out, Matt?"

"Yeah. There's a few ringleaders of that crowd who think they're pretty tough. They stirred up the rest."

"Do you think there could be outside influence?"

"Might be. Hadn't thought about it, but might be. That would explain a lot."

"A lot of what?"

"Why we've had so many accidents, why there's always rumors floating around that the bore ain't safe."

"Or why the strike began at such a convenient moment."

"You call this convenient?"

"Convenient for someone, Matt." He patted Taylor on the back. "Let's go."

"What you got in mind?"

"To talk to the men."

"You takin' these guys with you?"

"No. They've got work to do. Needle's got to contact his people."

"You goin' without a gun?"

"No gun. You can stay here if you want."

"No, I'll go along."

"Then you'll have to leave your gun too."

Taylor reluctantly put the weapon down. "If they get past us, they'll get to the subs."

"If they want to go after I've talked to them, let them."

They reached a large airlock, which separated the submarine docking area from the main dome. Taylor had secured it from the inside. He turned a wheel to open it. Inside, a crowd of men resting at the entrance scrambled to their feet. Several were armed with pipes and wrenches. A few had guns.

"Where's your spokesman?" Scott rested his hands on his hips and surveyed the growing congregation. Only a few faces were hostile. The rest showed conflicting emotions: uncertainty, fear, confusion. They were not yet a mob. If Kazan had been stronger or more decisive, Scott thought, he could have nipped the strike in the bud. It could still be done, but only with care.

Three men stepped forward. Again, only one looked hostile. He was bald, muscle-bound, with a split lip and bruises that Scott suspected matched raw patches on Matt Taylor's fists.

"I'm Jason Scott."

"The new boss?"

"Down here?"

"You nuts?"

"I'll be damned."

The bald man thrust his jaw out like Mussolini. "We want out!"

"Anyone wanting out can take a sub upstairs with no problem from me. Collect your pay and we'll fly you home on the first available jump-jet."

"We're not quittin'! We just want out of this tomb!" snarled the bald man. "We know it's getting set to be buried by lava."

"Then why am I down here? Whatever you think you know, you're mistaken. The magma flow problem will be solved in twenty-four hours."

"You can't without us! We have to erect the heat shields."

"I don't need you for anything, mister. I have men in Bolivia who can replace you in hours."

"You're lyin'!" He lunged. His blow to the head never connected. He was thrown off balance and face down to the pavement with a smooth motion.

"You seem to have bad luck with fighting, friend." Scott released the back of his shirt. "I'd give it up." He turned to the other leaders.

"You've been lied to, men. I won't ask you to put up shields to protect the bore. It would take too long. We must pass federal inspection in forty-eight hours. We've just taken delivery of ten excavation fission bombs and a submarine mole topside. We're going to plant the bombs and create an escape vent to an extinct volcano shaft west of the bore."

"What do you mean 'we'?" said one, to cynical laughter.

"Very well, 'I.' " A smile flickered on Scott's lips. "Craziness runs in my family." He held up his arms. "Now listen! If any of you want to go topside and give up the highest paying job in the business, I won't stop you. But this bore will be safe once the safety valve is created."

"We got to trust you?"

"That's right. But ask yourself why you've been led into a strike when Rita Duce needs you most? Who has something to gain? Not you! But if some of you are in the pay of one of her competitors, they might have a lot to gain. Think about it.

"You all know Matt Taylor. He'll be in charge here from now on. I'm sending Kazan upstairs. Any objections?"

The men laughed and jostled each other. They started to disperse and get rid of their weapons.

"Good," said Scott. "I'll meet the submarine mole at the dock."

"Pretty sure of yourself, ain't you?" said Matt Taylor.

"Pretty sure of my men." Scott turned to leave. Two shots rang out in rapid succession. He whirled as the bald ringleader collapsed, a bloody hand on his chest, a gun on the ground.

Matt Taylor slipped an automatic pistol back into a coat pocket. "Don't be too sure about this man followin' every one of your orders," he said with satisfaction.

2

The submarine mole, with ten mini-fission bombs, arrived several hours later. As Scott gave the boat and its deadly cargo a final examination, Rita Duce called from the mainland. Interference at that depth was too great to send a 3-D image, but her voice was loud and clear.

"I just found out what you're doing, Jason." The concern in her voice was obvious.

"I hope you won't try and talk me out of it." Scott double-checked gauges on the sub's control console.

"No, I—I just want to thank you. You're doing far more than I could ever ask."

"You'll get my bill."

"Dammit! Won't you even let me thank you?"

"For doing my job? No."

"I got word from Senator Macadew. He's still talking up a storm. He's asked the navy to keep an eye out for you."

"Not much they can do if I get into trouble down here. But I appreciate the sentiment." He began loading the bombs, each about the size of a medicine ball, into the ejection tubes. "One thing you can do for me—"

"Anything."

"I'm sending you a list of facts to check, like the background of the head of the Nares Plain seismic station—"

"Harold Peron? He's worked for me more than a year, since he was fired by Horatius Krebs."

"Sometimes you are a little too predictable."

"He's a good man, Jason."

"He might be. I've already done some checking. His station reported a ninety-eight percent probability of no earthquake for the next few weeks two weeks ago. The two government facilities in the area, Conception and Texas Hat, both recorded fifty percent probabilities in their areas, just a few miles away. I'd like to know why the disagreement. And why our own computer showed Conception and Texas Hat agreeing with Nares. I had to call the directors of the two stations to get their actual figures."

"That's a lot to digest, Jason."

"Chew on this: I'm sending another list of your employees to check with the FTC and see what their investment portfolios look like."

"Jason, be careful. We're not talking on a protected band."

"Then I better watch what I say. You will do as I ask?"

"Very well."

"I must go now."

"Good luck."

Minutes later, the submarine mole was immersed in nearly absolute darkness, broken only by the powerful beams of her lamps.

As the name implied, the submarine mole had two functions: underwater travel and excavation. Although normally used to excavate sea bed mines, it was admirably suited to the task at hand. Scott's only worry was the pressure. The mole didn't normally operate at such depths, although it was built to. He kept an eye on the pressure gauges for the first sign of a leak or potential rupture.

He had plotted where to plant each bomb so he merely had to allow the boat's automatic pilot to find its way to the first point.

That happened an hour later. The craft upended until it was perpendicular to the bottom and began to dig.

It was very tedious. The only indication of digging, aside from the instruments, was an occasional bump. No sensation of sinking. Visibility was nil.

A bell clanged. The first point had been reached. He ejected the first bomb.

The craft turned again. From now on it would travel horizontally. The passage was smoother for being inside a fault, which Scott intended to widen into a safety valve for the magma threatening the Challenger bore.

The journey continued. He planted explosives at each point until only one remained, on the inside wall of the extinct volcano. The mole broke through the wall. He ejected the charge. The craft started up the shaft. When he was far enough away he would detonate the ten bombs in sequence.

As he climbed the radio began to crackle. Faintly he made out Matt Taylor's voice.

"Jason Scott, can you receive?"

"This is Scott. Go ahead, Matt."

"Jason, there's been another minor quake. Did you feel it?"

"No."

"Sensors show the magma being pushed faster toward the bore. We have less time than we thought."

"Send me the figures, now."

"Roger."

The equations appeared on the ship's computer. Scott stared at them for a long moment.

"Jason, you there?"

"Roger. I got the figures. I'm going to blow the bombs in two minutes. Even that may be cutting it too close."

"Where are you?"

"Inside the volcano."

"Damn."

"When I reach the rim, I'll detonate."

Sonar showed the mole to be at the rim of the shaft. He pressed the detonator. He heard none of the bombs but the last. Suddenly the craft was seized as if by a giant hand and flung away like a toy. Outside the water boiled and the ship's air-conditioner whined with strain.

Hanging upside down in his webbing, nursing a bruised lip and a wrist that felt broken, Scott smiled. The explosion was far enough away. Now the trick was to get away from the volcano before it came alive, because the mole wasn't built for speed.

As it plodded along, two blips appeared at opposite ends of his sonarscope. He had company. And five miles beneath the ocean's surface was not where you expected a lot of traffic.

He changed course. Both blips changed course too. He began to sweat. He couldn't outrace or outmaneuver them. He started to dive. The only chance, a slim one, was to reach the floor and dig, and hope he didn't encounter any lava.

A third blip appeared. One of the subs had fired a torpedo. About a third of the way to the mole, the missile began to waver. A burst of static made Scott rip his earphones off. The torpedo zigzagged, changed course, and began to chase its parent, which tried to outmaneuver it. When the smaller blip intercepted the larger, both vanished from the 'scope.

He put the earphones back on. Interference from the explosion made reception bad. Finally—

"Do you read us, Jason Scott? This is the U.S.S. *Anchorage*, do you read?"

"*Anchorage.* This is Scott. Thanks for saving my life."

"Our pleasure, Mr. Scott."

"What was that other sub?"

"We thought you could tell us. We didn't mean to destroy her, just to deflect her torpedo."

"Uh, *Anchorage*, I advise a quick retreat from this area. Things are going to get hot."

"We noticed the explosions, Mr. Scott. Many thanks for the warning. Roger and out."

3

"The operation was a complete success." Rita Duce had flown out from the mainland. "The Feds will be here within the hour to inspect the Challenger." She peered at him. "You look tired."

"I haven't slept in about forty-eight hours," said Scott. "Before I do I must clear up a few things."

Bethany Williams entered the office. "Mr. Scott, the security chief is here."

"Send him in."

Haggard looked like his name today. He was unshaven and his uniform looked slept in.

"Sir, we tried to arrest Peron, but when we got there he had already left Nares Plain station."

"By submarine."

"There's no other way."

"I have a pretty good idea what happened to him." Scott looked at Rita. "Peron's stock portfolio is very damning. When you penetrate the dummy fronts set up to hide his interests, he turns out to own hefty chunks of stocks in a high-tech coolant firm."

"How does that implicate him?"

"The only company that buys that particular product is a solar energy firm owned by Alban Tupper."

"So Alban wanted me to fail all along."

"The rest of his portfolio is made up of stocks in Python."

"Alban is working with Krebs to destroy me?"

"They have a mutual interest. But Peron's guilt doesn't explain it all. True, he doctored the data from Nares. He also tried to murder me a few hours ago, and paid the ultimate penalty. But he needed a link aboard Chal-Surf One; someone to alter the data from Conception and Texas Hat; someone to alert the plant in the dome when we signed the agreement with Python so a strike could cripple us at the perfect moment." He turned to Bethany Williams. "He needed you, Miss Williams."

She returned his look with cool defiance.

"If it's any comfort to you, you didn't make any major mistakes. You covered your tracks admirably. I found your mole in the computer network, but you destroyed it before I could examine it closely enough to identify it. The weak link was Peron. There really was no way to hide the discrepancy in the readings from his station and the others, which forced you to go to extraordinary lengths to cover his tracks. Even so, I only had circumstantial evidence against you—Peron foolishly rose to the bait and tried to kill me. Tell me, was he your lover, or were you simply partners?"

"Why do you care?"

"Actions are not important in and of themselves. Motivations are. I'm a student of human nature. It interests me why people behave in the ways that they do. Indulge me. I think you owe me for betraying my trust. At least an explanation."

A single tear formed in the corner of her right eye. "I loved him." She wiped the tear away. "But we also stood to gain a great deal of money. You can't do anything without it, Jason. No matter how noble your dreams."

"Dreams are ashes if you cut corners and cheat to achieve them, Bethany."

"How does it feel to have a philosophy that puts you at odds with the great majority of mankind?"

Scott didn't reply to her question, but just shook his head sadly. "I'm gravely disappointed in you, Bethany. You were meant for great things."

"Yes, I still am."

"If you will, Mr. Haggard. Escort her to the mainland."

"Don't you want her arrested?"

"As I said, the evidence against her is circumstantial. Good enough for me, but not for a jury. She's not worth our trouble." She didn't resist as she was led from the office. They passed Jacob Kane at the entrance. He leaned against the bulkhead.

"You seem none the worse for wear," he said to Scott.

"I suppose you came to tell me you didn't have anything to do with the attempt on Jason's life," snapped Rita Duce.

"I didn't come to tell you anything, Mrs. Duce." Kane folded his arms insolently. "Believe what you want and be damned."

"I know you didn't, Jacob," said Scott. "Just as I know, but can't prove, that you're behind most of the mischief I just cleaned up after. You wouldn't try to kill me. You're not—"

"I'm not stupid. Peron was stupid. Why kill someone after he already has the goods on you and has passed them on? I, on the other hand, have no interest in your death, even though you outmaneuvered Python, this time, and beat me. The stakes were high, but the risk was small. And, win, lose, or draw, we still get interest from the enormous loan we made you. Besides, tomorrow is another day."

"Kindly get off my property as soon as possible, Mr. Kane." Rita Duce was livid.

"With pleasure. The accommodations are abominable. Are you heading back to the Andean project, Jason? May I offer a lift?"

"I'll be here for several days more, Jacob."

"When you do go, take it from an experienced world traveler: Go by air. Underwater transport is very unreliable these days."

When Kane had gone, Rita Duce sat down heavily. "Now all we have to do is sweat out this federal inspection."

"You sweat. I'll sleep."

"It looks as though we just might pull through with saving the Challenger before the Senate vote and you're going to sleep before we get the verdict from the inspector?"

"When there was something I could do to influence that decision, Rita, I did it. There's nothing else I can do. I'm going to sleep. Good night."

PART

3

A THOUSAND
EYES

Chapter

* 11 *

The possible fall of Western Civilization has been discussed in Spengler's Decline of the West *and as recently as Baler's* European Götterdämmerung. *It is certainly possible for a civilization to fall while believing itself healthy, as Rome did. But is it possible for a culture to believe in its own destruction and live?*
— *Avery Fienstein*, Red Midnight, Black Noon

Feb. 9—*Washington Post*—The core tap bill was narrowly defeated in the Senate today after a three-day filibuster by Senator Charles Macadew, and after federal inspectors pronounced the Challenger tap safe . . .

Feb. 10—API—. . . American scientists have been unable to arrest the progress of the grain blight north and south. The Agriculture Department denied that it expects the blight to spread to North America. Precautions are being taken . . .

March 6—Houston *Star*—. . . Hydrofoil gunships and spotter planes from the carrier battleship *Farragut* forced the Soviet submarine to surface after a ten-hour duel off the coast of Brazil, a hundred miles inside the Lines of Demarcation. . . .

March 15—*Le Monde*—. . . crossed into Venezuela. It was noted at 12:55 A.M. (Paris time) a kilometer inside. This places the blight almost on the banks of the Orinoco River. . . .

March 18—*Washington Post*—Congressman Hussein Ben Yami (R–Los Angeles) called for a resolution of the House condemning President Shefferton's meeting with the three members of Greater Asia's ruling families . . .

March 23—*Los Angeles Times*—A mysterious arrest in the blight's southern progress baffles scientists gathered in the Brazilian hamlet of Mundo Azul, twenty miles northeast of São Paulo. The southward spread of the disease has been slowing, but it continues unchecked in its invasion of North America, where two more cases were reported north of the Panama Canal. . . .

Eleven o'clock on a Monday morning and Sheridan Mayfield was a few degrees from boiling. His fuse was short at the best of times and as one disagreeable thing piled on another his aides braced for an explosion of awesome magnitude.

Unaware of the anxiety he caused, Mayfield smouldered in his lair. The day had begun badly with the morning newspools' evaluations of Shefferton's first sixty days in office. To Mayfield it looked as if all the editorials were penned by the same isolationist sonofabitch. The president was condemned in varying degrees for his willingness to deal with the outside world. Most editorials barely gave him a C-minus for effort in dealing with the economy. The antitechnology rags called him an ecological criminal for wanting to build more fusion reactors and for not moving to kill core taps, and attacked his proposed spending increases in the space program.

The criticism wasn't confined to Shefferton. Criminal collusion between Mayfield and the aerospace industry was hinted because of news that Rockwell, Boeing, Harley-Davidson, General Dynamics, Python, American Atomics, and Gigatex expected whopping gains for the first quarter. Restrictions on the manufacture of spaceship hulls and propulsion units had been lifted in January, consistent with Shefferton's campaign pledges. These policies addressed the reality that American companies were in space to stay. If they couldn't use American products they would use De Ruyter, Tigre, Mitsubishi, Parsi, or, heaven forbid, Volga.

Mayfield's administrative skills had also been scathingly attacked, which he thought woefully unfair since no one had noted the awful state of his department when he took over. Two months wasn't enough to chop the deadwood, but the media thought it was. It wasn't comforting to remember that they had dumped the same load on all previous administrations.

More bad news followed. Preliminary reports offered few leads in the Dorian Nye case. The man shot at Armstrong International was an English actor, Arthur Vinius, a player of minor roles (his most notable was Charles III in the BBC's "Life of Quinn Halliday") until he got to play the most realistic death scene of his career. Who had hired him, and why, were unknown.

Few leads, but lots of theories; brainchildren of the game theorists, computer freaks, and astrologers inhabiting the dark corners of the FBI, CIA, and DIA. For those who wondered what happened to Dungeons and Dragons enthusiasts who didn't grow up, Mayfield had an answer.

No progress, and the president was breathing down his neck. No, that was unfair. Shefferton made polite inquiries, and looked wistful when told there was no progress. That expression tore Mayfield's guts. Better that Shefferton threw things instead of being so patient. It made Mayfield love him and hate himself.

In his despair he had called Sherlock Michlanski many times, first at the hotel, then at his Wolverine Island home, only to be told by the caretaker that he hadn't returned. Now he was the only tenuous link to the Strubeck equations. Mayfield had to talk to him.

In Washington the pressure was felt but unspoken. As Santa Bella's tentacles drew closer—soon, very soon, Strubeck's equations might be man's only hope. And no one even knew if they really existed!

His desk holocube buzzed. He slapped it savagely.

"Yes?"

"Sir?" Ruth's voice was small.

"What is it? Speak up!"

"Sir, you asked me to tell you when Mr. Grant called."

"Grant? Yes! Put him on!"

The cube cleared to a thickset, curly-haired man in a red flannel shirt. Behind him was a large body of water, studded with small craft, overhung by threatening thunderheads. He was in a calling booth.

"Mr. Mayfield, he finally showed up."

"Michlanski's on his island?"

"We've been watching day and night. This morning a chopper landed. It was him! He won't leave without us knowing."

"Excellent!" Mayfield's good humor returned. "Keep me posted. If he leaves, tail him, even if you have to commandeer a VTL. But don't let him know he's being watched."

"That's easy. The lake is covered with people. It's fishing season." He signed off.

Mayfield sat back, smiling. He touched the cube.

"Ruth, my dear, please connect me with Dr. Michlanski's residence on Wolverine Island." He beamed at her surprise in his change of moods, then amiably caused her to disappear.

It might actually be better to have Michlanski working on the Strubeck equations, he thought. Only Nye's intimacy and knowledge of Strubeck's secrets made him desirable. In other ways he couldn't compare with the brilliant, albeit erratic, Michlanski. He wanted both, but he had to have Michlanski.

"I'm sorry, Mr. Secretary. I can't complete your call."

"Why not?"

A long pause—then: "Dr. Michlanski refuses any calls from this office."

"We'll see about *that*! I'm authorizing a first-level override of his holocube. If he won't talk to me voluntarily, I'll drop in on him without permission."

"We need phone company clearance."

"Get it."

The authorization was not long in coming.

"Proceed." Ruth's image was replaced by a light pink dial tone, which suddenly became a crazy kaleidoscope of colors. A high-pitched sound lashed out at him, until agony throbbed behind his eyes.

The whine was intolerable. His ears felt about to explode. He punched the holocube.

"Dammit, Ruth! What's happening?"

"I'm sorry," she wailed, gripping her temples. "He must have an override jammer."

"Damn your eyes, Michlanski!" Mayfield held his hands to his ears. "All right, turn it off."

The gyrating colors and penetrating whine faded. Mayfield bent over his desk until the pain began to subside.

"Ruth?"

"Yes sir?" said a faint voice.

"Are you all right?"

"I'll be fine in a minute, sir."

He smiled wanly. "Listen, I'm not letting our Polish friend have the last laugh. Get the technical director of the phone company. There must be a way to override that confounded jammer."

In minutes a man in the phone company uniform materialized.

"I'm Jim Travis, technical director of Atlantic Holophone for the Washington area. May I be of service?"

"I just tried to override the holophone of a Sherlock Michlanski and almost had my brains fried by his jammer."

"Yes, jammers are perfectly legal. Very expensive. Creates a feedback of the holo wave signal. Very disturbing, I understand."

"You don't need to explain that. I want to know how to get around it. Don't you need a license to own something like that?"

"It's all quite lawful. Our records show he built it himself. He has a generator on Wolverine Island, so there's no way to cut his power.

"Of course," he smiled conspiratorially, "it could be overridden by pouring so much power into it that it overloads. But I need authorization from the highest authority and we cannot be responsible for the results."

"I am the highest authority you'll ever talk to. I'll be responsible."

"Will you sign a release?"

"Yes, dammit! Hurry up!"

A plastic copy popped from a slot in Mayfield's desk. He affixed his signature and fingerprint and electronically sealed and stored it in Central.

Travis nodded. "That's fine. We'll begin in a moment." His image vanished. "We're starting the procedure *now*!"

Once again he heard the whine, though much subdued. This time there was no light show.

"We're applying more power. The jammer is highly sophisticated." The whine jumped an octave and Mayfield's head vibrated with it. He gritted his teeth.

"Well, Mr. Travis?"

"We're applying still more power. It seems to have no effect. I've never encountered a jammer this powerful. We may blow our own system."

"Pour it on."

"I won't take responsibility. You could cause a blackout."

"I've already taken responsibility. Do it!"

Mayfield clasped his head and opened his mouth. He couldn't take it much longer.

The silence was explosive. Mayfield looked up to see Sherlock Michlanski staring at him as though he was an insect. He wore a brightly hued caftan, and his hair and beard were freshly washed and combed. He said nothing.

Finally: "Well, I assume you want to talk to me about something."

"We seem to have overridden that jammer of yours."

"That's incorrect," said Michlanski calmly. "I turned it off to keep you from plunging the East Coast into a blackout."

"He's telling the truth," said Travis's voice.

"Get off the line!" barked Mayfield.

Michlanski put his hands in his pockets and smiled slightly.

"Please talk, Mr. Mayfield. I'll give you five minutes."

"Five minutes, hell! Who do you think you are, dictating to the United States government? I'll talk to you until I'm finished."

"I hope you're finished in four and a half minutes. I should cut you off now since you've violated my right to privacy under the Thirtieth Amendment. But, what can I do for you?"

Suddenly Mayfield was embarrassed. "We need your help. I don't know why you've avoided me, but you must know that with Dorian Nye missing or dead your scientific genius is vital to us. You're the only one who can help us solve the riddle of Strubeck's equations."

"That's flattering, dear fellow, but I'm afraid I must disappoint you. My energies are engaged in a project—the most fascinating I've ever attempted."

"What's more important than the survival of millions of human beings?"

Michlanski balanced restlessly on the balls of his feet.

"Is that a rhetorical question or am I expected to answer? You and I have different value systems, I think, sir. I consider what I'm doing far more important than anything you can offer."

"You don't realize the extent of the calamity—"

The scientist shook his head. "Poor little man, how you underestimate me. You think that because the public is denied facts, all remain ignorant. I know you can't fight the blight and I know what that means. Mass starvation. The great nations forced to open their stores to feed their neighbors."

"That information is classified."

Michlanski was delighted. "Really? You forget the power of the human mind. Some intelligent men do exist. I am one of them. Despite censorship and your childish efforts to keep the people uninformed, I, Sherlock Michlanski, know better!"

"You know all this and you won't help us?"

"No, I won't."

"Don't you feel any responsibility to your fellow men?"

"I will ignore that juvenile appeal to my emotions, Mr. Secretary. Oh dear, your five minutes are up."

"Please listen! There's no one else. I believe Dorian Nye is dead. Without one of you we will never find Strubeck's equations. The world will starve to death."

"Don't be pessimistic. Perhaps your chances of finding Nye aren't quite that bad. Of course, even if you do there's no reason to believe his equations will be of any use to you."

"You haven't seen the papers. You don't know."

Michlanski shrugged. "Just as you say, Mr. Secretary. Good-bye." Before Mayfield could open his mouth to reply, Sherlock Michlanski had vanished.

Chapter

* 12 *

"Flynt, I want you!" she breathed. The way she looked, that cleavage gnawing away at my will power, made me want to smash the muzzle of my automatic into her lying teeth. It was an effort to remember that she was an interface. "You miserable slut, I'd rather make love to a rubber dolly. Now hand over the molecule chip or you're history."
—Rocky Dillon, 'Face in the Crowd

1

Hardrim hated the streets.

At ground level he plowed into lunch-hour pedestrian traffic. He neatly sidestepped a fat lady and her small black fidex. The hybrid barked screechingly and arched its back. Avoiding it, Hardrim pushed aside a music tube hawker who tried to peddle him the latest in the intravenal hit parade. The idea of injected music made him sick.

Years on the beat had made him hate the streets and their people, their ways and dress: young men in G-strings and body paint, dandys in pink top hats and purple grouchos, young women dressed like Hester Prynne in *The Scarlet Letter*. His skills had finally moved him off the streets, promoted to detective and then inspector. Being back reminded him how much he wanted to find out who had set him up.

His unsatisfactory interview with Michlanski spurred him downtown.

He parked his hovercar in the hangar under the New Justice Department Building. Not feeling generous, he primed the booby-lock with hangover gas. An amateur locksmith would wake up in jail suffering from the world's biggest headache.

He took the elevator to Criminal Justice, then to Violent Crime and finally to the office of Lenore Lippman, director of section C of the computerized data bureau of the United States Department of Justice. That was a big title for such a little woman, so he had always called her Lenny.

Would she be glad to see him? He visualized her: one-quarter inch over five feet; short black hair, round, tempting face, and small mouth like a ripe cherry tomato; quick to laugh, but just as quick to sneer. She was slim and lithe.

They had met when Hardrim was at the federal crime college. He'd believed his lurid lectures on violent crime to be unsuccessful unless, by hour's end, at least one student fainted or was forced to go throw up.

That night Lenny was the one.

She had sat in front, pert and sexy and somehow challenging. Soon he found himself playing to her alone.

He related the lurid case of Dr. Gilbert Voltare, a generous human-itarian to his neighbors, who preyed on young women, luring them off the streets, and for kicks, performing abortions.

Her hand shot up. "What is an abortion?"

"You mean you don't know?" he asked innocently.

She hadn't known, nor had anyone else, so he told them.

Dead silence. She rose slowly, unsteadily, and her shoes beat a rapid tattoo to the end of the corridor.

Hardrim bought her some tea and apologized, but also chided her for obviously not reading her sociobiology texts, or skipping the part about the discovery of the universal male contraceptive.

He admitted it was a dirty trick. "But necessary. In our business we can't have illusions. The world is mean and dirty and evil. Some evils we hide from the public, but we can't afford to hide them from ourselves."

Her color was returning, so she challenged him briskly. "That's a grim view. Why are we here, if not to improve things?"

"To keep them from getting worse. We maintain the equilibrium. When someone, a criminal, throws the system out of sync, we restore the balance."

"God, an existentialist cop!" Her laugh was husky. "And I thought you were just a cynic!"

"That too, and a seeker after truth. Most of all, a seeker after truth, I think."

"That's a pretty heroic role you've chosen. Mel the titan holding back the hordes of darkness!"

"I've seen them up close," he said. "They're worth holding back." He started to light his cigarette, and realized he'd left the lighter in the classroom. "I almost dropped out of this job when I first started."

"Mel not a cop? I find that difficult to picture."

"I was in vice. I couldn't get worked up over boxing or other banned gladiatorial sports. What's hilarious is that I got hooked on cigarettes from busting all those butt parties. Thank God they repealed the tobacco laws or I'd probably be smoking two packs a day. My problem is, I've got to respect laws I enforce or I can't function. Only part of that job I liked was nosing down the snuff pimps." He smiled at the memory. "What saved my soul was getting transferred to homicide."

"Your soul?"

"Hallelujah, sister."

"You're like a character out of *Atlas Shrugged*, my favorite movie." She rested her chin on her hands. "What's yours?"

"*Casablanca.*"

"You are immersed in ancient history!"

"That's why I like it. It has nothing to do with now. When I want entertainment I don't want an added dose of philosophy."

"What kind of music do you like?"

"Old-wave classical, baroque rock, nonsequitur, oblivionist, atonal, jazz, impressionistic, even opera. I'm also learning to play the sitar."

"You're not schizophrenic at all, are you?"

"That's what I keep telling myself."

"I play the zynthecon." She arched her eyebrows. "Perhaps we can practice together sometime."

They began a strange courtship. He took her to expensive restuarants, to the premiere of the opera *Trial of Socrates*, to ballets. None of which he could really afford. They were an odd pair: He was cynical and hardbitten, she was bright, loving, optimistic. He was cultured, yet with some prejudices Lenny found disturbing, including his intense dislike of those with computer implants.

He constantly feared that she found him boring, so one night he suggested a new technical entertainment, the Surroundee.

"You don't have to spend money on me, Mel."

"That's what it's for," he said quickly. "Surroundees are like the feelies in *Brave New World*. Complete sensual immersion. You can experience an opium den in Delhi, swim the Great Barrier Reef, or float in space." He laughed nervously. "They're supposed to have sex surroundees too."

She grinned impishly and squeezed his hand: "I think I'd rather experience the real thing, wouldn't you?"

So they did.

Today she gave no indication she was glad to see him again until they were past her secretary, when she turned and gave him a very satisfactory welcome kiss, with all the trimmings.

"That was nice." She stood down from her tiptoes and let out her breath. "You've still got the knack."

"You never lose it." He was pleased. "It's like sky-flying, you never forget how. I've had lots of time to perfect my technique, being out of a job and all."

"I heard, Mel. I'm sorry."

"I don't need your shoulder to cry on, though you can keep it handy in case I come up with some other use for it."

"Always the joker, aren't you? No matter what hard knocks life deals you, you always have a wise remark." She softened. "I meant to call you. I really did. But work piled on me and, besides, a girl likes to be called sometimes."

"Yeah, well, I didn't exactly come to renew old friendships, though we can do that too, if you like."

"Not exactly flattering, but I'm listening."

"I need your help. I don't have privileged access anymore and Central's no help."

"Are you in private investigation, Mel?" Her eyes betrayed concern.

"I'm into getting the bastard who set me up! That includes investigating the life of Dr. Dorian Nye. Heard of him?"

"I don't live in a convent. Matter of fact, I did some work on him for the CIA and FBI."

"Then you know it's classified."

"Where did you get that idea?"

"All I got from Central was basic stuff. I figured the spooks put a hush order on the rest. Not so, I take it."

"You take it correctly. Dorian Nye's life is an open book—"

"With all but the chapter headings cut out."

"Why would they classify it?"

"They don't need reasons."

"Look, Mister Know-it-all!" She put a finger in his face. "I read that data. I'll admit it's spare but there isn't that much available. Nobody put a damned hush order on it. Do you copy?"

"Yes," he said sourly.

"I'm sorry to be short with you, Mel, but they gave me a hard time for the same reason. Wanted to know where the rest of it was. As if I knew! They implied Justice had classified it!"

"What if someone not in the government classified it?"

"You're talking about tampering?"

"Yeah."

"That's in deep space, my friend. The sophistication required to tamper with the memories of every major computer in the nation is mind-boggling. The equipment, the time, the expertise—"

"Is it possible?"

"Theoretically—"

"Is it possible?"

"Y-yes."

"Assume someone tampered with the computer network to keep people from finding out something. How could it be done?"

"Look here, Mel," she said briskly. "Before you go off on improbable tangents, we've tried to do that kind of thing to the Soviets for years and they've tried to do it to us. But as far as I know, no one has ever been able to remove a piece of data from circulation for long. Outsiders have been able to order computers to forget things and for a while they would be lost. That happened a lot in the old days. But now we have almost instantaneous duplication—because we can store so much, we store it in triplicate, quadruplicate, and quintuplicate!"

"Isn't it risky having vital secrets lying around like that?"

"They're on molecule chips. Nobody but the computer can read them and it won't tell anyone not authorized to know where to look for them. It's almost a fail-safe system."

"Someone got around it."

"Maybe, maybe not. Maybe all this is just a lot of paranoid thinking."

"Lenny, sometimes you're a real bitch!"

"Yes, I know." She grinned.

"Okay, I give up. Nobody's been tampering with our national net-work."

"That we know of."

He exploded. "What the hell are you saying? I thought you were trying to convince me otherwise!"

"Nooo," she said innocently, "I just want you to realize it's fantastically absurd. It's not impossible."

"Can I prove it one way or the other?"

She sat primly on the desk, allowing her dress hem to rise like a barometer to just below her thighs. "If you can find a fact in a newspaper, journal, or family record that contradicts the computer's summation, you might be onto something. You see, someone could tell a computer to forget something, or file it where none could find it. But he couldn't track down every newspaper, or everyone who knew Nye, or destroy every court record. There's simply too much unrecorded junk lying around to wipe it all out."

"That sounds like a lot of work. I might not find out anything."

"It's your time, Mel. You do have plenty, though offhand I can think of better ways for you to spend it."

He looked at her silky legs and nodded glumly.

"Yeah, I could too."

"Now's as good a time as any to see if Dr. Watson knows more about Dorian Nye than Central."

"Who's that?"

"Our crime computer."

"Why would a crime computer know anything about Nye?"

"Dr. Watson is an omnivorous reader, although he's mainly concerned with collecting and dispensing data on brutal crime. In fact, we have more on rapists, axe-murderers, cutthroats, quirks, sados, and garden-variety thugs than any system in the world."

"It should be like old home week for me."

"Watson reads other things, too, to cross-reference and file facts that might bear on our cases. That's why he might have info in his innards that wouldn't be in Central. Want to try?"

"Why not?"

2

The large room housing the mainframe was equipped with a ten-foot cube and horseshoe console.

Lenore Lippman walked in and whirled with her arms spread.

"Mel Hardrim, meet Dr. Watson."

"Does he talk?"

"If I want him to. Sometimes I spend days talking to no one but Dr. Watson. Usually I don't even notice I'm alone."

"Girl," he slipped his arm around her waist. "I fear you are sadly in need of immediate attention from a member of the male species."

"Sad but true." She firmly removed his hand. "We can fool around later. Now to work! We must save your career. That's the trouble with you men—you never know when it's time to concentrate on work."

She sat at the console and donned a headpiece. She caught his wince in the corner of her eye. "Mel, that's a ridiculous prejudice. Quit reading that Rocky Dillon trash! An educated man like you! Besides, I'm not acting as a true interface—"

She ran her fingers over light-sensitive keys. Hardrim couldn't find a safe place to lean so he retrieved a chair and sat next to her. He was enthralled by the swift play of her fingers, chilled as she communicated on another level with the computer. Each flickering eyelid, sigh, and intake of breath was a clue to the exchange of data as she gave commands and took information faster than two humans could verbally exchange thoughts. He understood perhaps ten percent of what she was doing. That probably partially explained his fear.

She looked up. "What do you want to see first?"

"Biography." He took from his pocket the personal trideecorder he had used to record Michlanski and set it on the console.

She touched a key and the cube filled with rolling type. Hardrim sat back, letting it interplay with his thoughts, stir his brain, inspire. When the last line crawled to the top and vanished, Lenny leaned back and ran a hand through her hair.

"Was that significantly different from Central's information?"

"It was more detailed. But the blank spots are in the same places."

"Funny, that was the FBI's complaint," she mused. "What part could have been covered more thoroughly?"

"Mainly the period after his doctoral thesis up to his appointment to Columbia to assist Dr. Alfred Strubeck."

"Okay, let's run that again."

DORIAN NYE WAS AWARDED HIS DOCTORATE AT AGE 24 BY STANFORD UNIVERSITY CALIF USA. SIX MONTHS LATER HE CHANGED RESIDENCE TO HILLCREST MICHIGAN USA TO ACCEPT TEACHING POSITION AT HARRIET BEECHER STOWE COLLEGE DETROIT MICHIGAN USA. HE BECAME DEAN OF SCIENCES AT AGE 40. AT AGE 42 HE WAS INVITED TO BE A MEMBER OF THE FACULTY OF COLUMBIA UNIVERSITY NEW YORK CITY NEW YORK USA. THERE HE ASSISTED ALFRED STRUBECK (SEE STRUBECK, ALFRED)

IN HIS FORMULATION OF THE PLANER DIMENSIONS THEORY.
THIS ASSOCIATION LED TO MUTUAL RESEARCH WHICH LATER
RESULTED IN ISOLATING THE FIRST FASTER THAN LIGHT PAR-
TICLE. THIS RESEARCH BEGAN JULY . . .

A detailed account of the search for the tacyon followed.

"Eighteen years of a man's life brushed aside with a dozen words but
the rest of his life covered in great detail," said Hardrim. "They used
two thousand words just about the tacyon."

"It's not unheard of for someone to remain obscure for half his life,
then suddenly become famous."

"It's so damned sudden! An obscure professor of an obscure college,
who takes sixteen years to become dean of sciences. This same man wins
a Nobel Prize in physics seven years later. Previously, he published no
books, gives no important speeches, does nothing noteworthy in any
way. Then he becomes associated with the great Alfred Strubeck and
suddenly starts appearing in *Who's Who*!"

"Unusual perhaps, but not unheard of," she said doggedly.

He drummed his fingers on the console. "Dammit! I wish I knew
what he did those eighteen years."

"He taught! Why are you so sure you have something with this
'missing' eighteen years?"

"Because it's all I've got and I have to start somewhere." He scratched
his lower lip thoughtfully. "I have an idea. Call up Strubeck's bio; let's
see what he was doing then. Maybe there's a connection."

There wasn't. According to Dr. Watson, Dorian Nye and Alfred
Strubeck might never have heard of each other until they met at Columbia.

"Are you ready to run the pictures?"

"I suppose. That shouldn't take too long. I don't want to steal you
from your work and get you into trouble."

"I'm very independent. As long as I produce. I'm free to use my time
as I please."

"By all means run the pictures."

He was surprised by the volume of holographs taken of Nye. Many
flat photos were in the collection also, of a young Nye before the advent
of mass holography. The sources were newstapes, holovision recordings,
and magazines. Most came from the last decade. The earliest was from
a high school yearbook. It showed a thin, owlish adolescent whose hair
was already receding.

Each was identified with a date; a source, when known; and the location of the shot, if possible. The last showed him shaking hands with the president of Europe, at his official residence at Versailles. The date was January 8, two days before Mel Hardrim met him in London, or met a man he thought was Nye.

Nye looked relaxed and cheerful. President Gernais didn't look quite so happy. Did he know something or was he suffering from too many escargots?

Hardrim sat up.

Nye was wearing a ring on his right hand. He hadn't worn one when Hardrim met him. He was sure because he always made mental inventories of people he was assigned. There had been no ring.

"Could you enlarge that ring?"

The outstretched hand grew to fill the cube. An advantage of holographs was that they could be enlarged many times without losing resolution. Tiny finger hairs were easily visible; minute lines crossing the joints stood out like canals.

It was the ring that interested him. The design was unique and he had seen it before.

"Sherlock Michlanski! His had the same eye pattern engraved in black enamel! See if Nye ever belonged to an astronomical fraternity in college. Michlanski said it was a frat ring."

NEGATIVE

"Can we identify that design?"

Lenny pointed a green pencil laser at the ring.

IDENTIFY

THE SYMBOL OF ARGUS, A GIANT OF GREEK MYTHOLOGY WHO HAD 100 EYES. HE WAS MADE GUARDIAN OF IO AND WAS LATER KILLED BY THE GOD HERMES.

"Argus." He rolled it over his teeth. "I've heard it used before but I don't know where."

"This will be easy!"

PRINT ALL ENTRIES FOR WORD: ARGUS

The cube opaqued, then:

ARGUS BOOKS LTD.

ARGUS CONSTRUCTION CO.

ARGUS OPTICALS INC.

ARGUS PAINTS

ARGUS HOLOGRAPHIC SUPPLIES INC.

ARGUS FRICTIONLESS AIRCARS CO.

ARGUS RETAIL CO.

ARGUS SOCIETY

ARGUS TEXTILES

ARGUS VAN LINES

"That's quite a list." Hardrim sighed. "I suppose I'll have to look into every one. I notice there's no astronomical fraternity listed by that name. I wonder why Michlanski lied?"

"Find that out and you may solve your entire mystery."

"Let's finish looking at these holographs. I'm particularly interested in those taken during Nye's cryptic period."

"His what?"

"His cryptic period. What's wrong with that? It is a big enigma. Eighteen totally blank years."

"Have it your own way, Mr. Bond. But before we do that, why not take a break and get something to eat?"

Hardrim looked at his watch. Three hours had passed. But he was reluctant to abandon his first solid lead, even to eat.

"Couldn't we go a little longer?"

Lenny brought him to his feet and placed his arms around her waist. She looked up at him.

"The trouble with you men is that you don't know when it's time to stop working."

Chapter

❋ 13 ❋

1

The conqueror marched north.

All known antiviral agents had failed to stop it. Experimental serums from secret germ warfare labs in the American Southwest had failed. The infested crops were bathed in radiation and incinerated by powerful X-ray lasers from orbiting American warships. Nothing worked. Santa Bella continued its maddeningly regular pace north, devouring all crops in its path.

While one team puzzled over the mystery of why the blight had stopped moving south, Chambless and the original expedition followed it first to a Nicaraguan field, then to a still smouldering, charred rain forest of several hundred square miles.

Desperate for any delay, they erected a barrier of ultrasonic broadcasters of a type used before against some viral forms. In the narrow isthmus they might have had a chance, but now all anyone hoped for was to slow it down. To slow *them* down.

Them! Ferman smiled to himself. Everyone said *them*, as if the blight was a sentient being, or an army.

Ferman remembered reading *Empire of the Ants* as a child and being so terrified of H.G. Wells's image of an intelligent insect horde that for weeks he squashed every ant he saw. This was a similar feeling, only worse because it wasn't fiction.

He walked back from the broadcasters, which spanned the horizons like a marching column of giant windmills. It was time to report to HQ. He passed new tents. The camp's size had doubled as a frightened United States government recruited every available scientist, even from foreign nations. A second village grew outside the camp as editors sent their ace reporters to cover what might be the biggest story of the century.

Dr. Chambless looked up as Ferman entered.

"Ah, Mr. Ferman. I trust you are well today."

The omission of his "Did you discover anything interesting yesterday?" litany startled Ferman.

He was wary. "Quite well, sir. Thank you."

"Good. Sit down." Chambless looked over the bridge of his nose. "I suppose you're curious about your report?"

"Yes sir, I am."

He had almost chewed his fingernails to the knuckles worrying about it.

"I must compliment you on the quality of your work—"

Ferman sighed with relief.

"But I'm afraid it contains a fatal flaw that renders your entire theory inoperable."

Ferman's jaw dropped.

"It's not really your fault. Anyone could have made the same mistake."

"What mistake?" he whispered.

"The other morning the crux of your argument for a man-made origin for the blight was your belief that there are no viruses with a similar structure. So if the blight was a mutation, it must have been bombarded by a huge dose of radiation, which would have destroyed it. From this you theorized that the virus was man-made, not a random mutation. Am I correct in my interpretation of your ideas?" Chambless lit his pipe and puffed meditatively.

"Yes."

"Good." He folded his hands on the card table desk. "Your theory is sound if you are correct about there being no other virus with a similar background. But such a virus exists. Its structure is only slightly different from our blight. Instead of cereals it attacks only wild grains native to Central Asia. Apparently cultures of it were aboard a Soviet space lab and subjected to deep space radiation. The Russians are being close-mouthed in the extreme. Nor can I blame them. Who would want to accept blame for the Santa Bella blight?"

"But Dr. Chambless, I found no mention of such a virus in the computer. What did you call it?"

"The yellow rot." Chambless held up a scientific journal with a five-year-old publication date. "There's quite an interesting article. Recorded observations go back as far as Herodotus. Ancient Chinese chroniclers tell of Hun migrations caused by its destroying their horses' forage. Some careless person in Washington didn't read the journals carefully, I suppose, so it didn't get into the computer. Such things happen. Usually they don't cause such damnable mischief!"

Ferman took the magazine cassette.

"Is the yellow rot's DNA structure in this article?"

"No, I found that out when I double-checked your findings. Sorry, Mr. Ferman, such things happen to the best of us."

"And I'm far from being the best."

"No, no, no, Ferman, don't underestimate the merits of your effort. It's not your fault the data was incomplete and it doesn't detract from the high quality of your work. No, Mr. Ferman, you should be proud, as I am, to have such a dedicated, talented young man working under me. Believe me, there are good things ahead for you in this field."

"Thank you, sir."

"And sooner than you thought. Mr. Ferman, would you be interested in assisting Bill Wendell? He's working on genetic engineering to mutate a natural enemy to attack the blight. Such work would challenge you more than your present assignment. Bill needs a good right hand and you've shown your worth. How about it?" He leaned forward, a benevolent expression on his normally cold face.

Ferman hesitated. He was good at his work and enjoyed it. Besides, the genetic engineering angle seemed likely to be the cavalry riding to the rescue of the dead settlers, while some hope remained at the chemical end. He was reluctant—yet Chambless thought mutated viruses had a good chance to defeat the blight. Who was he to question it? Chambless was the foremost authority in the field . . .

"Mr. Ferman, I asked how about it?"

"C-could I think about it? Until tomorrow morning?"

"If you think you need to." He obviously thought it was a waste of time. "In the meantime, continue your present assignments. We can't afford to waste time or manpower. Santa Bella waits for no one."

Ferman winced at Chambless's favorite cliché.

"Sir, I wonder if I might have the data back? Since you have no use for it, I thought I'd keep it."

"Mr. Ferman, why must I keep impressing on you that no data connected with this project is personal property? You used team resources. The information is not yours." He rustled some papers on his desk. "Good day to you."

2

Had he sabotaged his chances for promotion? Chambless had looked angry and his mercurial temperament was well known. Tomorrow he might come up with a reason for Ferman to stay exactly where he was.

Which wouldn't break my heart! thought Ferman as he worked through the afternoon testing agents on various culture slides. Shortly before mealtime he finished. He was satisfied with himself and his work and had just about decided to stay with it, even if it meant turning down more money and prestige.

He didn't dine in the common tent. He wasn't in a social mood. He needed to think. As he ate in the tent, darkness fell. He lit a hydrogen lamp and hung it from the center crosspiece.

He made up his mind to refuse Chambless's offer, if it still held. Instead of waiting for morning he would talk to him now, while he still had the guts. Courage had a bad habit of melting just when he needed it.

Outside the tent he almost collided with his roommate, Tony Chapel, who installed ultrasonic broadcasters.

"Ooops! Hi, Tony."

"Have you heard the news?" Chapel demanded.

"What news?"

"Traces of the blight have been found two miles north of the picket line. We've been outflanked!"

"When did you hear this?"

"Just now." Chapel's clenched jaw stood out in sharp relief. "Somebody really blew it! There's no way it could have spread so soon unless some boob forgot to get decontaminated after working in the afflicted area."

"I suppose so."

"Where you going? I'm hoping for some chess before sacktime."

"Later. I'm going for a walk. I'll be about half an hour. Why don't you set up the men?"

"You okay, buddy? Anything wrong?"

"Nothing. Chambless has me a little rattled, that's all."

"He's a changeable son of a bitch for sure! But he has a lot on his mind. Everybody's edgy. He broke up a fight today—"

"Himself? You're joking!"

"Imagine a stork in a dogfight."

"What was it about?"

"One of the foreign scientists, a Turk, I think, but definitely an Epiphanist, riled our Arab. You know the one; his uncle's the grand mufti of Los Angeles. Anyway, the Turk said the blight is God's curse for the world's religions remaining divided and that it would destroy all who don't embrace the 'Triad Vision.' The Arab tried to carve him with a dagger. Chambless is sending both of them home. Damned towelheads!"

"Take it easy with that towelhead stuff—I'm from L.A. I grew up with Arabs. You can't blame the poor guy—a lot of his relatives committed suicide after the Epiphany. I know Orthodox Jews and our Catholic friends in the next village who would pull knives too—"

"Let 'em feud elsewhere!" He snorted with disgust. "We have enough to worry about. Boy, am I burned up! Now we'll have to move the line again. What a day!" He disappeared into the tent.

Ferman walked slowly, his hands in his coverall pockets. Most tents were still lit, but soon they would be dark. By now news of the disaster had spread. Everyone knew that tomorrow would be busy.

Near Chambless's tent he slowed to a crawl. He was reluctant to confront the prickly scientist.

Light from the tent formed a faint bar on the ground. He breathed deeply and moved toward it. He heard Chambless's soft Texas twang. Three silhouettes blocked the lamp hanging from the center of the tent and he smelled wintergreen pipe smoke.

He moved closer.

"I want you to keep an eye on him. He's too smart not to be suspicious after that fish story I sold him this morning."

Ferman couldn't hear the other's reply.

"I'm not going to do anything—yet," said Chambless. "After morning I'll tell you exactly what I want done."

The third man said something high-pitched and stammering, but once again Ferman couldn't make it out.

"I understand your concern," said Chambless. "We'll have you home in a day or two. After that trip I'd think you'd look forward to a few hours' rest."

The third man laughed nervously. The other spoke.

"No," said Chambless, "He's too cautious to do anything before then . . . maybe too cautious for his own good."

Ferman didn't wait to hear more. Stunned, he moved away, and by luck, escaped detection when the first man suddenly emerged from the tent. He stood, framed by the light, facing inside.

"Wait," said Chambless. "I'll go with you. I think the three of us should look into that."

Ferman hid in the enveloping dark as they left and headed for the data and communications tent, which housed the main computer. When they were out of sight he slipped into the tent.

His heart pounded. If he was wrong he would spend the rest of his life regretting it. But he had little choice. Chambless had tightly sewn up his bag of options.

He extinguished the tent light. It wouldn't do to be given away by his shadow. Using a light pen he searched for the data Chambless had wanted so much to keep. It was on the desk. Perhaps he had planned to destroy it. Ferman tucked the manila envelope under his arm and stuck his head outside. No one in sight.

He half considered returning to his tent for his things. But Chambless was bound to return soon. It wouldn't take long to figure who had taken the data.

He walked rapidly toward the field where the aircars were parked. Stealing an aircar wasn't brilliant but it beat hiding in the jungle. He smiled when he remembered that Tony was waiting to start a chess game. He would have a long wait.

Alec Shaffer, camp security director, guarded the aircars. He was tall, burly, in his late forties, with bristly iron gray hair. He grinned, obviously glad for the company.

"Howdy, Ralph! How's it going?"

"Fine, Mr. Shaffer. Did you draw guard duty tonight? I thought you command types escaped such menial jobs."

"Dream on," said Shaffer. "What are you up to? Going to Mexico City for a little cerveza and senoritas?"

"A little programmer from Tecate. Very user friendly!"

"Uh-huh." He was unimpressed. He checked his clipboard. "I don't see your name. What are you trying to pull?"

Ferman's chest tightened. If he couldn't bluff his way through this, he'd never fool anyone else either.

"Come on, Mr. Shaffer! This is a special night and I have a special little woman waiting for me with a pitcher of tequila. Couldn't you make an exception? Just this once?"

"Just this once!" mimicked Shaffer. "You're breaking my heart! I suppose it won't hurt. Nobody's taking out cars tonight anyway because we're moving camp tomorrow. Most smart people are in bed, but I guess you don't fit that category." He jerked his thumb toward the nearest aircar. "Be back before dawn."

Ferman climbed into the twin seater hovercar. Moments later he was speeding north as the camp lights sank under the hills. Unobserved now, he banked east, toward the coast. He would ditch the aircar, hike to the nearest fishing village and charter a boat to a seaport with an airfield where he could fly to the States.

Time was imperative, but he figured a small delay caused by his evasive tactics might put Chambless off his trail until he got his information to the authorities.

About four in the morning he left the aircar at the bottom of a rocky, treacherous creek bed—a trick that almost got him killed.

Dawn found him walking toward the rising sun. Below was a village. The sun danced on an empty bay. Fisherman leave before dawn.

Chapter

* 14 *

Galveston *Sun*—Possibly the richest discovery of gold in history has been made by the Tectonics Corporation's Challenger tap. Corporation president Rita Duce announced today the discovery of an extremely rich deposit of platinum group metals. Geologists are swamping Tectonics Corporation with requests to visit the site. The discovery may be larger than deposits in South Africa and Alaska. . . .

1

The elevator door hissed open and Deputy Assistant Director Roger Ferdinand of the FBI stepped into the San Francisco field division headquarters. A secretary detached herself from a row of computer terminals.

"Sir!" She scuttled to keep up with him. "Two messages came for you on the wires."

"Fax copies and bring them to the office." He walked to the door at the end of the office, into an auxiliary office maintained for the convenience of visiting officials.

He stepped to the window. The view from the top of the Hemispheric Trade Center on Alcatraz Island was superb. Morning sunlight danced off the Golden Gate Bridge. From the jutting balcony he saw the crystal span of the glassteel Oakland Bay Bridge shrouded in mist. Below, hydrofoils skimmed between the island and peninsula, where the new Gigatex pylon, looking alien next to the familiar Transamerica pyramid, dominated the skyline.

The secretary brought the fax sheets. He dismissed her with a curt nod and sat in a leather chair. He was a speed reader. Finishing the sheets, he rose abruptly and paced for a moment before activating the nearby terminal.

"Broadsword Ivy Pudding Hershel."

"QUERY," said a pleasant contralto.

"Dictation mode."

"PROCEED."

"To Sheridan Mayfield, Secretary of Space Exploration and Development, John Glenn Building, Washington D.C.

"Secretary Mayfield, Judge Louis Crown in Sacramento finally issued the warrant we need to open the files of the Sandstone Sanitarium in Red Bluff and question Dr. Jeremiah Xerxes and staff. Xerxes was able to delay us because of the hospital's obscure status. It is operated for the Central Intelligence Agency, Defense Intelligence Agency, National Security Agency, and the Technology Enforcement Agency. Because TEA was once entrusted with extraordinary legal powers, many of its agents, including Hunning, possessed privileged information.

"I have concluded that evidence vectors no longer place Inspector Mel Hardrim at the apex of the wave function of the guilt or innocence matrix and have therefore deactivated the investigation of him. Computer interface personal note."

"PROCEED."

"Remind me to recommend to Commissioner Flaherty of GWPD not to reinstate Hardrim. His stubbornness is not conducive to good discipline. Such an individualist could taint a whole department. Note ends. Interface with existing dictation. Wait!"

"WAITING."

"Interface personal note: Check to see if there is an undercover bureau operative now working in the Greater Washington D.C. Police Department. If so, assign to a soft monitoring of Hardrim's activities. Perhaps we can catch him at something. Note ends. Interface with existing dicatation."

"PROCEED."

"The key to the Dorian Nye case is hidden in the strange circumstances of Lloyd Hunning's release. Xerxes is hiding something, unless his delays have simply been a bureaucratic knee jerk against a perceived encroachment of his territory.

"Be assured I will spare no efforts to obtain every bit of information about Xerxes and his establishment.

"Other less encouraging information may relate to our investigations. Our Montreal field division reports intercepting messages indicating that a long dormant deep cover agent, code-named Bengal, has been activated by Europe. He was placed as long ago as before the Unification, possibly as an agent provocateur by the French DST (Direction de la Surveillance du Territoire) to encourage Quebec separatism. When the DST merged with the West German Federal Information Service (Bundesnachrichtendienst) to form the Service Europeene d'Intelligence, they inherited Bengal. This corroborates other sources indicating that the Europeans believe we faked Nye's disappearance to embarrass them. The 'sleeper' was apparently activated to form an organization to investigate this, a daunting task in view of our hostility to foreigners, and prohibitive travel restrictions.

"I strongly suggest an intensive search to locate this Bengal before he runs for cover. I would so recommend to the director if I were free to communicate with him about any matters relating to this investigation.

"Enclosed with this communication are related documents and my agenda for the day. Message ends. Execute."

"EXECUTED."

"Terminate Dictation Mode."

"TERMINATED. WAITING."

He went onto the balcony, shutting the glass doors behind him. The salt air stirred his thick hair and he was glad he had worn a warm herringbone tweed suit. He was reasonably sure no spy devices were installed on the balcony, but he held his body to provide maximum blockage from spying eyes as he took a small leather-bound book from his coat.

"March 26, 0900 hours," he wrote with a gold pen. "Just sent off my daily report to Mayfield. We have the go-ahead to invade the sanitarium. Mayfield was so weary of proper channels that he wanted to send in a squad of agents and I almost agreed. A shoot-out between our men and the spooks would have been interesting. I think we would have cleaned house. Maybe next time. I'd especially like to terminate some of those TEA baboons—What is Xerxes hiding? Too bad I had to drop my case against Hardrim. He was the perfect fall guy to take pressure off us, since we are still responsible for the TEA. He has great character, but in this instance that quality doesn't serve the state, it merely annoys. Hardrim is a cipher—beneath my notice. Yet, I intuit that a little extracurricular spying on him might pay off.

"On to other matters—I am tired of reporting to Mayfield. He brought me to heel; I admire his use of force. He is a Machiavellian prince in the rough, but too much the ideologue. Ideology, doctrine, dogma, contaminate the pure object of power: to rule. Men with causes are dangerous, to themselves, ultimately to the state. Tired of never-ending circus of men with causes. Don't they know people will surrender anything—honor and liberty—to be secure in their homes, well fed, and entertained? I feel kinship for police in Unified Soviet State or even G. Asia. At least they understand power."

His desk holocube was buzzing. He pocketed the book and went to the desk.

"What is it?"

"Dr. Jeremiah Xerxes is on the line, sir."

"Interesting." He was pleasantly intrigued. Did Xerxes know about the warrant already? "Hello, Dr. Xerxes, what can I do for you?" For now the game of cat and mouse amused him.

Steady blue eyes returned his intimidating stare. Chagrined, Ferdinand looked down. Remember, he's a trained psychiatrist, he thought. He looked up. The eyes were embedded in a deeply bronzed face, framed by white curly ringlets, and a kinky spade-shaped beard. A prominent nose hooked over sensuous lips, pointing to an equally sharp, dimpled chin. But he was drawn back to the eyes. He'd seen eyes like that before, in the faces of mortally wounded soldiers, and once, the eyes of his own father, shortly after his retirement from the police, just before he ate the gun.

"Nothing," said Xerxes. "There's nothing you can do for me, Mr. Ferdinand." He had a faint accent. Ferdinand recalled that he was a Balkan immigrant. "But perhaps I can help you."

"A little late for that, isn't it?" His smile was triumphant. "You spared no effort to deny us your files. Now, as I'm sure you've learned, we have a federal warrant. What can you possibly offer me that I can't take anyway?"

"The only records that will help you—those in my mind."

"You'll talk, Doctor."

"I was an intelligence attaché with the Drangs, Mr. Ferdinand. I saw them peel away a man's skin without killing him. I was trained in the needle and silk technique. To me you are an amateur. You can't threaten me."

"I think you are a bit paranoid. I certainly wasn't threatening you with physical harm."

"Good cop, bad cop, and harsh lights. It's all the same, and they were practicing it in Old Cathay a millennium ago."

"Jail has a way of concentrating a man's mind to his true priorities."

"So does death."

"What do you mean? Are you in danger?"

"Almost certainly."

Ferdinand pressed an intercom button. "Get the special agent in charge of the Sacramento field division on the line at once."

He looked at Xerxes. "I can have agents at the sanitarium in half an hour."

"They'd find a corpse. Come yourself, with no fanfare, and I may still be alive. I'll tell you what I can."

"I must say you are taking this calmly, Doctor." Ferdinand reached for his briefcase.

"I've lived with the reality of my own death for some weeks now, Mr. Ferdinand."

"What do you mean?"

The line went dead.

2

Dr. Jeremiah Xerxes's study was dark and cool, rich with smells of fine woods and leather, the friendly scent of old books.

As Ferdinand's image faded, Xerxes slumped forward and rested his face in his hands, feeling the bristles with his palms. He breathed deeply and stood. He was so tired. But that would soon end. He could sense that. He had taken the last fateful step in a life whose steps had led through many a dark maze. Now he would come into the light, whatever that was.

A white form darted across the floor.

"Ciao," said Xerxes.

"Meow," said Ciao, arching his back sinuously, inviting the inevitable stroking. The psychiatrist buried his fingers in the angora's thick fur and rubbed. The cat's throat vibrated with pleasure.

The vibration stopped.

The curtains behind Xerxes rustled. He didn't turn. An ironic smile flickered on his face.

"You're finally here."

"Yes." The male voice was strangely sterile, strangely cruel. "You were expecting me?"

"Yes."

"Then you know it's no good fighting me."

"Yes, I know that."

"Acceptance?" The voice sounded disappointed.

"It's my karma," said Xerxes. "May I sit?"

"Certainly. But careful, very careful."

As Xerxes slowly turned he sensed the mass of the other, shifting, gliding, staying behind him. He sat.

"Surely you don't fear me?" said Xerxes.

"I respect you. Your thinking is not entirely Eastern. You might decide to resist your karma. That would be inconvenient and painful."

"Do I know you?"

"The general's army was small. The number of Europeans smaller. We met."

"You had no trouble with the guards, the sensory devices? I'm not prying, you understand. It's professional interest."

"I was water. I was air. I was all-seeing. You know the training."

"Alas, I was not an adept, just a scholar. May I ask a question?"

"Always."

"Who is killing me? Who in the agency gave me the orders concerning Hunning? Why did they order him released?"

"What you never understood was that your contact in the agency— wasn't part of the agency."

Strong hands grasped Xerxes's vertebrae and broke them with a loud crack.

At the sound Ciao arched its back, spitting like a demon. Xerxes's head lolled onto the desk. The man regarded the aroused feline with amusement. He took a small camera from his coat pocket and shot the corpse from various angles. The rapid white bursts created little instants of disjointed time.

He replaced the camera and paused, savoring the moment. Then he left the room through the same window he had entered.

Chapter

* 15 *

1

The discovery of the Argus symbol on Dorian Nye's ring was Mel Hardrim's first real break. Not spectacular, but he felt like a man who had been pounding on a boulder with a sledgehammer. Any cracks were welcome.

Armed with Dr. Watson's list, he set out to make a canyon from that crack. He checked each name with every state, federal, and local agency available. That was a lot of fingerwork, combined with personal interviews. Luckily he was at the center of the bureaucratic spider web. A tug at this strand or that often brought results.

By week's end he had eliminated all but one entry: the Argus Society. The rest checked out as genuine businesses or active organizations. The Argus Society had a funny smell.

The society's own pamphlet, wrangled from a friend at the charitable organizations office, told little, but more than other sources had. He suspected that about ten copies existed and rated his acquisition on the same scale as finding a First Folio.

It described the Argus Society as ". . . dedicated to disseminating knowledge, and promoting scientific thought and reasoning throughout the world. To this end the Argus Society supports colleges with scholarships, encourages new ideas with grants to research, and helps spread these ideas by promoting publication of scientific works of merit."

Quite a mouthful. A worthy goal, if carried out. But when he checked with accredited colleges and universities all over the country he found that no student had attended on an Argus Society grant in ten years. No books had been published with an Argus Society honorarium during the same period. Just what had the society been doing for the past ten years?

He wondered if the society wasn't liable under the law for not carrying out its avowed purposes, but found that since it didn't ask for contributions it could use its money for any purpose.

Its membership rolls were secret, although a list of its officers was available. All were scientists, and alive, but that was about all you could say about them. Not a distinguished name. Yet men like Dorian Nye and Sherlock Michlanski wore the society ring. Something very odoriferous was going on. Something very strange. Something bad, all his instincts told him.

He looked up. His holocube was ringing. It had malfunctioned all week, sending gonglike shock waves through the apartment instead of a soft chime.

The caller was Ed Flaherty, commissioner of police for Greater Washington, and, until recently, Hardrim's boss.

"Where have you been? I've been calling for two days!"

"I've been watching the pigeons crap on the Roosevelt memorial."

"Yeah, and while you were watching pigeons you got in a few visits to federal agencies in town. What, may I ask, is prompting all this activity?"

"You may ask."

"Dammit Hardrim!" Flaherty's bulldog face turned brick red. "Don't be a smart ass! I want to know what you've been doing. I want to know now!"

"I was under the impression that I am suspended, about to be fired. Under the circumstances what I do with my time has ceased to be your business." He matched stares with Flaherty.

"That's not fair, Mel. I did my best to keep your tail out of the grinder. Is it my fault I failed?"

"No. You're a nice guy, but don't expect me to hand over the combination of my vault to Nice Guy Ed."

"Mel, I thought we had a nice working relationship. I thought we were friends."

"You give orders well and I follow them well—but that doesn't make us Damon and Pythias."

"Look Mel, be reasonable. You can get your job back."

"You mean I didn't kill Dorian Nye? I'm thrilled!"

"We checked your story with the Brits. It holds. We tried—I mean Ferdinand tried—to link you with Lloyd Hunning, and failed. You're clean."

"So why did you start the conversation like Ivan the Terrible?"

"I apologize. But I've been trying to get you for two days. You know how that irritates me."

"Lucky for you people don't get ulcers anymore or they'd be using you for a lawn sprinkler. Now, a key question: If I get my job back, can I stay on the Dorian Nye case?"

"There is no Dorian Nye case for us. It's completely in federal hands."

"How about loaning me to them as a show of intradepartmental cooperation?"

"Hardrim, are you being deliberately perverse?"

"No, I just like to know the ground rules before I make an agreement. No deal. Keep your job."

"Keep my job? Are you nuts?" Flaherty almost howled. "What's so important about this Nye thing that you'd give up—"

"All this?" finished Hardrim. "It's become important—more than anything right now. Sure, I like my job but I like my self-respect more. I'm not somebody's dog. When I get kicked I don't come whining back with my tail tucked down. I got kicked hard, by Alain Lin, Ferdinand, the department, and whoever engineered Nye's disappearance or murder, or whatever the hell it is! I'm not going to settle for 'good dog!' and my box back. I want to know why. There's a purpose behind all this. You guys are standing under a mountain of crap a mile high and you don't even know it! It's so big it may end up burying me, but I'll chance it to have a crack at finding out what it's all about. Can you understand that?"

"No. But I never did understood you." Flaherty sighed. "Tell you what, Mel, I'll give you three weeks to wrap it up. If you've got your answers then, I'll welcome you back. That's to show that I'm not one of the ones doing the kicking."

"That's fair, Ed. Thanks." Hardrim smiled. "I'll be seeing you."

Flaherty had barely faded from the cube when the gong reverberated again.

"I've got to get a repairman in here!" Hardrim winced.

"Hi Mel, I'm just returning your call—you look terrible."

The caller was Todd Wheeling, an estimator for the Smithsonian Institution. Wheeling examined artifacts and documents acquired by the museum and estimated their worth. His nose slalomed down from receding blond hair and between pale blue eyes. He used his job to justify all sorts of sunny junkets, so he was always tan, even in the depths of winter.

"Thanks for calling back, Todd."

"I just got into town."

"I know. You were evaluating Alfred Strubeck's estate."

"Okay, I know what you know, but what I don't know is what you don't know."

"I know," said Hardrim. "What are my chances of seeing some of the documents Strubeck bequeathed to the Smithsonian?"

"Not just documents! He left us the whole bloody ball of wax. He had no heirs. It's enough to make your tongue hang out! By the way, Mel, I want to show you my newest Hemingway letter next time you come over for tennis, and a Gertrude Stein I got in Montreal—"

"What are my chances of seeing the Strubeck stuff?" he repeated.

"Nada. Nil. No can do. Zero. Smaller than infinitesimal. Would you like to see the crown jewels of the late theocrat of Russia? That'd be easy—"

"Why not?"

"Because it's out of our hands now, that's why! Some jelly bellies from the Federal Uppity Bureau of Expectoration took over. It was tragic! Science isn't my specialty, so I brought in some buddies from the Natural History Museum and we were having a ball. You think a night on the town with some broads is fun? You haven't lived until you've stayed up all night trying to estimate the historical value of correspondence between a man and his podiatrist. How do I do it? I use dice."

"Did they give a reason?"

"Do they ever? Damned feds! What did you want to read? I saw a lot of things and my memory is great. What did you say your name was?"

"I'm interested in anything that Strubeck might have written to Dorian Nye, or about him."

Wheeling blinked owlishly. "I never saw anything like that—but we were only into a couple of weeks. I suppose your best bet would have been his diary—" he leered, and broke into a series of giggles. "I gotta tell you a story. If there's one thing you learn, it's how creative and devious some people are." He hunched forward, his blue eyes protruding like marbles.

"We were doing a routine dating of all his papers—everything he didn't commit to disks. You take minute ink and paper samples and expose them to chemicals and lasers. We found that several volumes of his diary, which he kept for fifty years, were not as old as the dates indicated. The books and paper were, but the ink wasn't! Isn't that great!"

"You mean somebody forged volumes of Strubeck's diary?"

"It's better than that! Strubeck himself redid some of the passages. Talk about having the last word. It was his handwriting. He bowdlerized his own diary! He went back ten, fifteen, sometimes twenty-five years, and rewrote entire six-month entries. He was really clever about it too. I guess he hunted down blank books with the right manufacturing dates. Where he slipped up was on the ink's drying time. Knowing an ink's original moisture content, you can determine when it was put on paper. It's only by the oddest coincidence that we even made the test, and made it on the right passage. If we'd first done it on an unchanged passage we wouldn't have tried anywhere else. Old fart! I bet he had a really perverted sex life and didn't want his biographers to know. Probably like something out of *Tropic of Capricorn*! Speaking of Henry Miller, I managed to grab—"

"Did you make copies of anything?"

"Yes, but the FBI confiscated everything. . . . Oh, I do have one copy. A letter from Strubeck to another scientist—I don't know why he put it on paper since he probably sent it by computer—discussing a formula he was working on to convert pure energy to sugar molecules, or something like that. Very dull technical stuff—I still have that. Do you want to see it? I could dig it up."

"It doesn't sound important—unless you stumble onto it, don't bother."

They exchanged good-byes and Wheeling's image turned to gray nothingness.

2

Ralph Ferman was hungry, tired, dirty, and very pleased with himself. He had eluded capture and survived his adventures on a Nicaraguan fishing scow and an ancient charter jet that had buffeted him every minute of a fifteen-hundred-mile trip to New Orleans.

It was late afternoon, in the spring, when New Orleans is at its best, fragrant, moist and bright. Anything seemed possible to Ferman. He was downtown, standing in one of the neutral zones between the two lanes of traffic on Canal Street. To his left, a narrow, cobblestoned street named Decatur disappeared into the French Quarter toward the river. To his right, the same street was called Magazine, and a large commuter tram was parked at the corner, loading passengers.

He had enough money to get to Washington, where he was sure he could get Chambless arrested as a traitor to humanity.

From a curb he hailed a cab. New Orleans taxis were still mostly human-driven. It was part of the city's charm. A cab stopped, floating, and he opened the door. Too late he saw someone in the back seat. A large hairy hand hauled him in. The door slammed shut.

"Hello, Mr. Ferman," said a cheerful voice.

· He shook his head and sat up. His traveling companion was husky with rough features and a gristly, unshaven look. His grin was not unpleasant. He held an anesthesia gun.

"You're right." His grin widened. "You could make a break for it without seriously risking your life. But since the taxi is moving briskly, the most you can hope for is a sprained arm or leg and a doozy of a headache when you wake up. Why not save yourself the trouble? Sit back and enjoy the ride."

Ferman let his breath out raggedly.

"Who are you?"

"First name's Sebastian. That's all you need to know. I work for a man you know very well."

"Chambless," said Ferman tonelessly.

"Yes indeed."

"How did you find me?"

"We never lost you. You were given an aircar with a transmitter. We tracked you to the fishing village and followed the boat to the airport. Our people saw you hire the plane and I was waiting to pick you up."

"You let me waste all that time?"

"It saved us the trouble of guarding you. We wanted you in the States anyway."

"What an idiot I turned out to be."

"Not an idiot. Just not a very good conspirator. I'm afraid you've read too many adventure stories, Mr. Ferman. The good guys don't win any more often than the bad guys. And how can you be sure you're one of the good guys?" He smiled roguishly.

"What if I stick my head out and call for help?"

"Assuming I let you do that, you'll be arrested for aircar theft. Your name was sent to every police force in the nation.

"You'll have me jailed on some trumped up charge while Chambless carries out his damnable schemes!"

"You make him sound like Fu Manchu. If we wanted you in jail we would have taken your evidence and handed you to the police. It's no trumped up offense; you did steal an aircar. I think you're better off with me, don't you?"

Ferman sat back glumly as they left the city on a highway. He never saw anything of the driver but the back of his head. Never once did he speak. He tried to identify a landmark as dark shapes whipped by at 200 miles per hour.

They took a narrow road into darkness, true darkness, not the semi-twilight of the freeway. Ghostly cypresses leapt out at them as the road narrowed again. They slowed. Spanish moss enveloped them, then reared back to reveal a small cabin with a single light in the window.

They climbed from the hovercar, which vanished into the darkness. It was humid. Night birds called shrilly. Something disturbed a pond. Wind moved the tops of the cypresses.

"When does the voodoo dance start?" said Ferman.

Sebastian laughed. "Good for you. You're keeping your sense of humor."

"Yeah. I'll laugh all the way to the grave."

"You think I'm going to kill you?"

"You kidnap me, bring me to a cabin right out of *Huckleberry Finn*. What should I think?"

"Think what you like." He covered him with the gun. "Go inside. You'll find it more comfortable than it looks out here."

He was right. The one room was furnished like a bachelor apartment, with two water beds, a holocube and two monster speakers, a well-stocked refrigerator, a microwave, and a muscletoner.

"The holocube only works for incoming calls. I hear you play chess. Maybe we can have a few games."

"How did you know?—Oh, Chambless." Ferman looked around. One door. It would be hard to escape. Of course, Sebastian had to sleep sometime . . .

"Help yourself to the food." Sebastian walked around the room. "Feel free to listen to the cube. Personally, I like classical rock, but my tastes are flexible. It's getting late; if you want to skip a meal and go right to sleep, that suits me. Let me know when you're ready. I'll give you a shot of the sleep gun and we'll both rest easy."

"If you're not going to kill me, what are you going to do?"

"Keep you out of circulation until I'm told to let you go. Then I'll take you wherever you want, even to the authorities. They won't believe you and will probably put you in jail. Or you can keep your mouth shut and do pretty much as you please. Simple, eh?"

"Devastatingly simple." Ferman planted himself on the couch. "Do you want white or black?"

Chapter
∗ 16 ∗

*. . . {T}he arts reflected the moral ambiguity of the new century.
Pessimism warred with uncertainty and fear, exemplified by the
Malibu Arabian school of painters. Zef Hanzel's monumental* Ice
Age *trilogy was supposed to chronicle the decline of the entire northeast
United States. This general sense of dread produced only a few rebels,
like the maverick sculptor-engineer Jonathan Hammer, whose great
statue* Triumph!, *outside San Diego harbor, was intended to be a
colossus of the West, a counterpoint to the rebuilt Statue of Liberty,
which, ironically, was delayed until many years after the completion
of Hammer's work.*

—Henri Partagas, Art and Discourse

Quietly, ominously, the fog crept in from every horizon. Wolverine
Island, rearing up from the cold gray of Lake Michigan, took on the
appearance of a verdant dream, an isle where Odysseus might have tarried.

The island was battered by chill winds and icy breakers. Currents
broke on the rocky base, forming a treacherous network impossible for
anyone not intimate with it to navigate.

The closest mainland was Charlevoix, thirty-two miles away. The small
town, supported by fishing and tourists, had shrunk from the days before
the great shift in population drained the Northeast. Of its island neighbors, the largest, Beaver Island, was a smudge on the horizon on a clear
day. To the north and east Lakes Huron and Michigan met to form the
Straits of Mackinac.

Barely a mile and a half square, covered with pine and maple, with
perpendicular cliffs seventy feet high on its west and south, Wolverine

Island was almost totally inaccessible. No landing field existed. The beaches were too tiny and rocky. The only way in or out was by helicopter or jump-jet, and a grid of sharpened steel poles in the sand discouraged them also. Sherlock Michlanski liked his privacy.

Each hour motorboats containing Sheridan Mayfield's spies completed a circuit of the island. They were trying to look like fishermen and failing miserably.

A week ago Michlanski had dismissed his servants and sent them to the mainland. A helicopter had landed on the roof to pick them up. The agents noted that the two-story brown brick house was lifeless except for an occasional excursion by the handyman or his wife, and when Michlanski walked along the edge of the cliffs. The lights often burned past midnight.

Inside, Sherlock Michlanski was thinking. He reposed on a curious couch of his own design. It kept his head higher than the rest of his body no matter what position he fell into, assuming many unlikely shapes to accommodate the restless scientist.

He was engaged in a mental exercise that had intrigued him for a week: to visualize a six-dimensional cube. It had been easy to construct a tesseract, a four-dimensional cube. The next step was harder but his mind overcame the petty limits of physics and the pedestrian bounds of normal human imagination. He imagined a five-dimensional object.

He prepared for the next step, keeping the image firmly in his mind's eye. He could see it! It existed, at least within the steel-bound limits of his great brain.

The final step—extending his five-dimensional cube into the sixth dimension. It was like drawing a square on paper, he thought. That was two dimensions. To make it actually three dimensions, you reached out and folded the paper. His mind reached out to fold the five-dimensional paper . . .

The image exploded into a thousand fragments of shattered crystal. The soundless detonation reverberated from the back of his mind to the front.

His eyes opened and he addressed some Polish swearwords at the screaming alarm. He lunged at the computer console in the center of the room. The scream died in midwail.

Michlanski knuckled his eyes.

"Okay, Leonardo, what's wrong? You've just obliterated a five-dimensional mental image that will take me hours to reconstruct."

"My apologies," said the computer in the voice of one of his old math professors. "One of the circling boats has capsized. Two men are being swept toward the island."

"Zerrk!" Michlanski went to the picture window overlooking the shoals. He saw only mist and water. "Where? Show me on the holocube."

The opaque box lit with gray light. In the waters beyond the cliffs two men struggled against the powerful undercurrents that were carrying them toward the rocks.

Michlanski rested a finger on his chin. "This is terrible. Those two chaps will be pounded into ground round." He sighed philosophically. "I suppose we must save them, eh Leonardo?"

"That would be the most socially acceptable solution."

"And bring them here, too. How much time to save them?"

"Outside estimate: three minutes, if they continue to struggle. This takes into account the speed of the current and that they will beat their arms an average of—"

"Pipe down!" said Michlanski. "Send the Ro-boat to pick them up. When they land have Gerald bring them to me. I want to talk with these intruders."

"Completed as ordered."

"Good. Shut off the cube." Confident the Ro-boat would carry out his orders, he lost interest in the scene.

He dropped onto the couch, which squirmed. He rested his chin on his hands. His beard tickled his wrists. "This is most unfortunate. It couldn't have come at a worse time. The last thing I need is snoopers rambling about."

"You have considered the possibility that this was planned?"

"I'm way ahead of you. I think Sheridan Mayfield may have ordered them to sink their boat. Well, they will get to observe me firsthand. Just so I keep them out of the basement. We couldn't have that, could we?"

"No." The computer didn't understand rhetorical questions.

Gerald escorted two men into the library. Their wet clothes created small rivers on the Persian rug as they took in their surroundings. Michlanski was used to incredulous reactions from strangers. His home was unusual, to say the least.

Strange abstract paintings shared wood-paneled walls with a leopard skin and rhinoceros head. Opposite the fireplace a rough wood shelf supported statues of people and unidentifiable objects in electric plaster, a sculpting medium that hardened instantly or became soft depending on whether a positive or negative electrical charge was applied. The main curiosity was a six-foot glass pyramid suspended a foot over the floor, supported by nothing.

Michlanski studied them. They were muscular and darkly tanned. Their blue jeans and shirts were basically the same as Gerald's, but the contrast between them and that sinewy bag of chicken bones couldn't have been greater.

They tore themselves from their surroundings. The thick-set, curly-haired one stepped forward with a smile, displaying white, evenly spaced teeth. He was about thirty. The other was shorter and chunkier, blond with a square face. As they rubbed their hands to restore circulation, Michlanski saw thick karate calluses. These were not harmless boys.

"We're grateful to you, sir," said the first. "If you hadn't sent your robot ship we would have been killed for sure. Those rocks looked sharp to me."

"Very sharp. You're lucky to be alive. You have my computer to thank for spotting you in the first place."

"You're welcome," said Leonardo.

"We had no idea anyone was at home, ah, Mr. . . ."

"Sherlock Michlanski." He chuckled inwardly at the charade. "And yours?"

"I'm Chuck Grant. This is Jack Smith. Are you the Sherlock Michlanski who won the Nobel Prize and invented antigravity? The one the news calls the greatest genius since Einstein?"

"Yes I am." Michlanski felt himself warming toward them already. "Of course, whether I invented or discovered antigravity is something else again. The fine line between the physicist as creator and as technician becomes blurred in my field. Can you create a law of nature? Did it even exist before I conceived it?" He shrugged amiably. "I don't know. I do admit being mentioned in the news. I have a unique name. Papa was an Arthur Conan Doyle fan, otherwise I might have been cursed by a typically Polish name when I escaped from the motherland. He thought Sherlock was good English name."

"This place is something, Mr. Michlanski." Grant poked his companion. "Isn't this place something, Jack?"

"Yeah."

"Do you really think so?" Michlanski smiled like a delighted child. "I'm proud of my little estate. I always wanted a place to let my imagination run wild. Would you like to see more?" He glanced at them sidelong. A sly, half-formed smirk tugged at his thick lips.

"Sure thing!" Grant looked meaningfully at Smith.

"We'll start with my living room, proceed down the hall to my playroom, then go downstairs to the—"

"Laboratory?" said Grant hopefully.

"Eventually. But first indulge me and let me show you the more mundane aspects of my hacienda." He sailed out of the room, with Grant and Smith in pursuit. Gerald waited until they turned the corner, then walked rapidly down the hall in the opposite direction.

"This is my special room, where I keep my favorite books, paintings, statues, toys, games, whatever." Michlanski pointed out objects as he named them.

"Toys?" Jack Smith spoke his second word since arriving.

"Certainly. We never outgrow toys. We are all children at heart, constantly learning, adding to the sum total of our minds; reaching out and exploring. A toy is a device to expand the mind. But toys must be fun." From a white marble table littered with colorful objects he picked up a pink rubber ball. "This is a toy." He tossed it to Grant. "Catch!" Grant automatically reached where the ball should have been, but in mid-flight it swerved, evading his frantic groping, looping and spinning like a thing alive.

It hung suspended, mocking capture. Michlanski's pudgy hand effortlessly closed on it.

"How do you like it?"

"Some toy," said Grant. "What is it?"

"A sphere of rubber containing an antigravity impeller, controlled by this box I hid in my hand when you weren't looking." He opened his hand to reveal a matchbox-size object. "A toy."

"That's fantastic, professor!" said Grant. "Why don't you use it in space ships?"

"It only works on small masses. Anything more than a few pounds uses thousands of watts of power. To lift a spaceship would drain every nuclear plant in the country."

"Too bad."

Michlanski looked shrewdly at Grant. "Are you in the space industry?"

"No, I'm a department store salesman." He looked around. "Where did you get the paintings and statues?"

"I made them."

"I thought scientists weren't interested in that stuff."

"I'm afraid four hundred years of Newtonian thought created an unfortunate schism between the right and left halves of the brain in our culture that is only just being mended. Linear reasoning led us to believe that the universe was a giant logical machine, but intuitive leaps tell us it may really be made of puff balls of nothing. Einstein was an artist more than a logician. It may be that theories that explain existence are more real than what they try to describe. Answers may depend not only on how the questions are asked, but on who is asking them. Is reality discovered or created? How could I not be interested in art, young man?"

"Some of it is pretty good. A few of the statues are weird, but that's because I don't know what they're supposed to be."

Michlanski went over to the paintings. "These are my interpretations of extra dimensions. I believe that when we have intuitive insights, our subconscious is working in other dimensions."

"You think the fourth dimension looks like this?" Grant focused his eyes with difficulty.

"To me it does. It may look different to each human who sees it, if any have. By painting I try to give substance to my vision. It's a human failing, I'm afraid, to want to name that which you don't understand. It's an attempt to comprehend the incomprehensible. Now, let's proceed to my workshop."

It was the largest room so far and the messiest. The floor was strewn with metal shavings, sawdust, screws, solder, and things dropped or ignored. A wooden table dominated. On it were innumerable and unnameable objects; inventions or models to illustrate theories; some half-finished, others not properly begun.

Michlanski delighted in Grant's questions, neglecting to mention that the workshop was an auxiliary to a larger, more sophisticated laboratory in the basement.

As he explained the workings of a meter to measure gravity, there was a frenzied rustling on the worktable and a white and yellow form leapt expertly onto his shoulder. He acknowledged the dwarf cat's presence with an upraised brow.

"This is Schrödinger. Pay him no mind for he adores attention." The hybrid feline, about the size of a hamster but fully mature, regarded them with disdain, then fell to licking its paws. Something startled it and it vanished from his shoulder.

Michlanski continued his inventory of inventions, demonstrating a spray that preserved perishables without refrigeration and a device for neutralizing calories in sweets.

"That's not perfected yet, I assume?" said Grant.

"That's right, but how——" His scowl was only half-fake.

"What's in this thing that looks like a coffee percolator?"

"Coffee. Like some?"

Gerald appeared in the doorway. "Sir, is the cat in this room?"

"Schrödinger? Maybe yes, maybe no."

Gerald, used to this sort of behavior from his employer, shrugged and examined the room until he located the cat. Holding it by the nape, he said, "Sir, there are two Coast Guard cutters. They are signaling—"

Michlanski nodded to his guests. "If you'll excuse me. Gerald, keep them company."

"We'll just look around," said Grant.

Michlanski strode into the library at full tilt. "Console on!"

"Operational."

"Why didn't you tell me the Coast Guard is signaling?"

"I was not instructed to monitor that source of communication as per your orders—"

"I knew you'd figure a way to wriggle out of it somehow."

"That is physically impossible. Wriggling is—"

"Be quiet! I suppose they tried the radio before they started using blinkers?"

"Affirmative."

"None of that! I programmed you to talk like the rest of us. You can be replaced, you glorified thermostat!" He paced, rubbing his hands. "Put a call through to one of those ships."

A voice crackled from the speakers. "This is Captain James Sylvester of the Coast Guard cutter *Lancer*. Who is this, over?"

"The man you're conducting naval operations against."

"You are professor Sherlock Michlanski?"

"The same."

"We understand you rescued two men whose boat capsized. We came to pick them up."

"Peachy. The Seventh Fleet was tied up, I presume."

"Are the fishermen unhurt?"

"They're fit. I've been giving them a little tour."

"We'll send a launch to pick them up directly, sir."

"That will be easier said than done. I advise you to let me send them out in my Ro-boat."

"That won't be necessary. We are quite capable of landing on the island. We are the Coast Guard, after all."

"Captain, I insist. There is no safe landing place. I made sure of that. I won't have you people smashing yourselves against my rocks. It is too much to ask me to rescue two boatloads in one day. So if you will kindly, ah, heave to about two hundred yards off my west coast, I'll send them out. Is that clear, sir?"

"Message understood. *Lancer* out."

Michlanski returned to the workshop. "You'll be happy to learn that I just spoke to the people who will take you home."

Grant and Smith struggled to look happy.

"Gerald will take you to the Ro-boat. It will take you to the cutter. It's been very pleasant." He smiled innocently. "I hope you learned a lot."

Five minutes later Gerald returned to find his employer working on a project with a laser cutting tool.

"Well?" Michlanski raised his eyebrows expectantly.

"They're gone. The talkative one tried to lose me once, but he was never out of my sight. I saw another ship further off signaling to the first two. They've made no move to leave."

"They'll have an admiral commanding this business before they're through." Gerald exited and Michlanski resumed his work.

"Are they gone?" asked a slight man standing in the doorway.

"Yes. It went well. I gave our visitors a guided tour. They found out nothing."

The other nodded, rubbing a bony hand through a patch of hair struggling to survive on the back on his head. He frowned, shaggy brows crouching low as he struggled for the right words. "We-we'll have to be careful now, w-with everything. I can't have them interfering with my work. I w-won't have them."

"Don't worry, old chap. This is just more harassment from Mayfield. In his primitive way, he's very persistent."

"This can't go on much longer. According to your computer, someone has been making inquiries about the Argus Society."

"Argus Society! That is very serious. It may be time to proceed to the next step of the plan. You agree?"

"Y-yes."

"I'll check with the others. We don't want anyone caught flatfooted by the change in the timetable. I'll talk to Noah Chambless first. Can you be ready by midafternoon?"

"Yes, I can," said Dorian Nye.

PART

4

THE
STRUBECK
EQUATIONS

Chapter

* 17 *

1

When Boris Edvard Baptiste closed his antique store that night, it was for the last time.

His call had finally come, in a violet envelope sealed with red wax. Only in Montreal were such civilized amenities still possible. It read:

> Tuesday, 11 P.M. 1140 Rue de Pontchartrain. Ask for Emil.
> —Puvain.

Puvain was his control. Over the years there had been at least five Puvains. The latest had been in place two years.

Baptiste was in his late forties, dark, with wavy thick black hair; what his mistress called "greasy good looks." In excellent shape, he fenced, played racquetball daily, and practiced religiously on the firing range.

He had been set up in business years ago. He was a deep cover agent, a "sleeper."

The government that had planted him no longer existed. Its heirs maintained him. An established sleeper was valuable in Fortress America. After half a lifetime, his time had come.

Eleven hundred and forty Rue de Pontchartrain was a small warehouse near the airport. Standing at the entrance, with an attaché case at his feet, snapping two-inch-thick wooden dowels with his fingertips, was a man who introduced himself as Emil.

His manner and personality were peculiar and Bengal soon had conceived a distinct distaste for him, like something sticky and unpleasant you accidently get on your hands, and because you can't identify it, you run to the lavatory to wash it off.

Emil's voice was whispery and dry, devoid of inflection. It reminded Bengal of the whiskey-laden voice of an ancient, rich pederast who had pursued him as a child and about whom he had never dared tell his parents.

But no one would mistake Emil for an old man. He had a fine physique, far more so than Bengal's, who worked at it. His taut chest and arm muscles coiled and uncoiled as he casually snapped the thick wooden sticks.

Pale, with finely chisled features set in coarse, pocked skin, Emil could have been a child of all races, or an outcast of them all. His hair was wavy, almost translucent in its whiteness.

They entered the tomblike dark of the warehouse. At a touch from a remote control unit hydrogen lights flamed into life.

It was empty save for two dozen wooden boxes. Emil casually inserted his fingers under a lid and pried it open. He brought out a military issue rifle and tossed it to Bengal to examine.

It was one of the newest issue Kalashnikov rifle/laser combinations. Made from hardened plastic, glassteel, and ceramic, it was deadly, easy to use, simple to assemble and disassemble, and impervious to most weapons detectors.

Other boxes yielded radiation grenades from Israel; Black African antipersonnel mines; antitank weapons from the Illyrian League's elite Werewolf Brigade, with the snarling wolf's head still emblazoned on the sides; knives, ammunition, explosives, handguns—enough to equip a force of urban guerrillas.

"Impressive," said Bengal. "What are we going to do with them? Sell them to a third party?"

"We'll use them," said Emil. "It's amusing how often people fail to realize that their purpose is to kill. I sold weapons to a SoHi dealer in Atlanta. He operated a boutique in Peachtree Plaza by day, and dealt by night. He had hundreds of rifles and grenades in an underground fortress. Electrified barbed wire. Mines. He was ready for Armageddon. But when narcotics agents and FBI showed up, he surrendered like a kitten."

"You expected him to go down fighting?"

"Why else have weapons? 'Top of the world, Ma!' " He laughed a whispery laugh, leaned against a crate, and began snapping wooden dowels like vertebrae.

Bengal couldn't look into Emil's leaden eyes as he outlined a plan for Bengal to recruit men and women from French-speaking Quebec natives sympathetic to an independent Quebec, free of the United States.

"Patriotic cannon fodder?" said Bengal. "That may be hard. There's not much separatist sentiment any more. Most give it lip service, but it is romantic nonsense."

"Yet there are still many dedicated to it?"

"Perhaps enough fanatics for our purposes, if pay is good."

"It will be."

"Can you tell me what we will be doing?"

"I will train them, and you, to carry out terrorism and sabotage; to infiltrate; to act singly or in concert."

"Pardon, monsieur. I thought we were to gather intelligence about this Dorian Nye disappearance. Isn't Paris afraid the Americans will use it to embarrass the European government?"

"Don't second-guess Paris or Puvain," said Emil with a ragged smile. He reached swiftly as a moray eel and grabbed Bengal's wrist. The implication was clear: Wrists and dowels are not that different. "And don't, as you value your life, try to second-guess *me*. Unquestioning obedience is the wisest course."

"Just as you say. Your pardon," said Bengal as calmly as he could manage, although his spine felt like pulverized ice.

Emil indicated the attaché case. "There are lists of several caches of gold. Use it as needed. Recruit your force."

"All I can do is my best."

"Do more than your best. Succeed. I will contact you to begin training. The rent runs out here at the end of the month."

Shortly after midnight, Boris Baptiste stood across the street from the antique store. Emotionlessly he lit a joint and didn't flinch when the storefront erupted into white hot flames that rapidly consumed it.

Quebec separatists would take credit for killing a traitor to the movement. No trace would be found of Boris Baptiste. The time of Boris Baptiste was over. The time of Bengal had begun.

2

April 3—San Diego *Union*—The Mexican-American border has been closed. This order was transmitted to the Mexican provisional president by American commissioner Agnes Shears this morning. Units of the Mexican Home Guard have been placed under the command of Pacific Supreme Commander Lt. Gen. Albert Terry, USMC, in accordance with Article 10, Section 3, of the Pan American Pact. American nationals have until midnight to cross into the United States. Rumors persist that the Santa Bella blight was sighted in Tampico, Mexico, about 250 miles from the Texas border. All border towns have been evacuated until further notice. Texas Rangers crossed the border to implement . . .

"Checkmate," said Sebastian for the hundredth time.

His deadly combination of rook and knight had again toppled Ferman's defenses. He glumly acknowledged defeat by causing the floating 3-D chess board to vanish.

"Playing you is like playing the computer."

"Yes, but you'd be bored without my witty conversation."

Ferman couldn't help smiling, or liking Sebastian, the most congenial of jailers. Considerate, amenable to all his wishes but one: that he be freed. He went out of his way to make captivity as pleasant as possible. He stayed up as late as Ferman wished before resorting to his sleep gun. He was the perfect host, which made it all the harder for Ferman to plan his death.

But the Santa Bella blight would cross the border in days. The authorities had to be told that the man entrusted with stopping the blight was working to spread it. They had to be shown the documents from Chambless's tent. That meant taking them from Sebastian, and probably killing him.

But Sebastian was quick, tough, and clever. He had the only weapon, and made sure of no potential weapons. Eating utensils were plastic or paper. Nothing even faintly resembled the fabled blunt instrument of detective fiction. There were no glass or metal objects that could be detached and used in an attack. It would be Ferman's untrained, subbrute strength against Sebastian's cool competence. Ferman had always been the victim of the playground bully. His adult life reflected no change. Fighting was for punch-drunk middleweights or idiots, not thinkers.

This was the exception. To escape he must fight and win. His only advantage was in knowing when.

"How about another game?" Sebastian had an insatiable appetite for inflicting humiliating defeats.

"How about something to eat instead?"

"Sandwich do until dinner?"

"Fine."

"Something to drink with it?"

"Yes. Something hot. Coffee maybe."

Sebastian put two paper cups in the microwave.

Hot water.

Ferman rubbed his fingertips nervously. Sebastian removed the cups of boiling water and added coffee. Its hot, acrid odor filled his nostrils. Sebastian blew on the coffee to cool it.

Ferman threw the coffee in his eyes.

Sebastian screamed and fell backward, clawing for his gun. Ferman aimed a kick for his face but had to jump to avoid the flash of the sleep gun.

Ferman hesitated, then ran for the door. Sebastian heard him and tried to block him. Sebastian looked monstrous; pure hate made him a demon incarnate. Ferman dodged him, overturning a chair. Sebastian stumbled against it. Then the door was open and Ferman was in daylight. It was hot and as he ran, his shirt became damp and stuck to his skin.

"Ferman, you bastard! I'll find you!"

Ferman zigzagged into the thickest part of the forest, tearing his shirt, face, and arms a dozen times. After a while he stopped to listen. In addition to his furiously beating heart, he heard the birds and wind and nothing else.

Sebastian's eyeballs were on fire. He could barely see. He staggered to the holocube and overrode its command against outgoing calls. Chambless's stork figure appeared.

"Ferman got away!"

"How did he accomplish that?"

"He threw coffee in my face. Almost blinded me."

"Sorry about your face. You should see a doctor."

"Aren't you going to send someone after him? If I could get my hands on him—"

"Be calm. I was going to release him in a few hours anyway. He can't harm us now unless he has the papers."

"No, he didn't take them. The sneaking little coward rushed out of here so fast—"

"Then we have no problem. The authorities won't listen to him. Everything will go according to plan. A little ahead of schedule perhaps. You really should have medical attention. I'll send a hovercar. Be sure to keep the papers in your possession."

"Don't worry, I will."

Chapter

* 18 *

> April 5—Phoenix *Tribune*—The Santa Bella blight has definitely halted. After resisting the efforts of two scientific teams, it has contained itself approximately within the Tropics of Cancer and Capricorn and shows no sign of advancing. Most Central American crops are ruined, but apparently the disease does not flourish very far north or south of the Equator.
>
> April 12—API, Brasilia—The Santa Bella blight was a one-shot affair, say scientists winding up work on the cereal ravager. It dies quickly if its food supply is restricted . . .

Cabinet meetings were held in the New White House, a wing added at the turn of the century. The cabinet room was done in early twentieth-

century American. The walls were a subdued blue, the carpet a rich
eggplant interwoven with gold threads. Oil paintings of Theodore Roosevelt, George C. Marshall, and Albert Einstein hung near the great
fireplace and the door.

Mayfield arrived early with two hamburgers. The president's new
breakfast cabinet meetings were agreeable to him. He sat at the conference
table. His sandwich wrapper partially covered the presidential seal in the
center of the glassy top, a conceit from a more decorative age.

Shortly before eight, cabinet members began arriving. One minute
before the hour Vice-president St. Clair swept regally to her favorite
chair after quietly greeting each cabinet officer.

Teresa Evangeline St. Clair was, Mayfield had decided, a very attractive
woman at forty-five. Her tall, slender figure was set off by graying hair.
She was truly a member of the political aristocracy: On her mother's side
she was great-granddaughter of the first President Kennedy and a cousin
of the second. On her father's side, "Uncle Bill" was the president for
whom the Twenty-Second Amendment was repealed.

Following almost immediately was Secretary of State Randolph Harmon, twice the standard bearer of the Progressive Nationalists, now their
senior statesman. Elegant in a silk morning suit, his wavy blue white
hair superbly coifed, he looked like an elderly deity, or at least a high-
ranking seraphim.

From opposite ends of the party coalition, they were twin crosses
Shefferton had borne for a unified party in the last election. Of the two,
he loved Harmon less. The vice-president, at least, was a shrewd horse
trader and wily tactician (it ran in the family). Harmon was self-righteous
and patronizing. His rank was a tribute to nostalgia, not ability.

But they were both skilled at what Mayfield hated most. He liked to
work alone and was at his best in intimate conversation. In groups his
tongue wrapped around his teeth.

At five past eight the chief of staff appeared.

"Ladies and gentlemen, the President of the United States!"

Shefferton, flanked by bodyguards, took his place at the head of the
table.

"Sorry I'm late, but I suppose that's the president's privilege. I had
a call from the Speaker on pending legislation to increase Bureau of
Colonization appropriations. Mr. Saratoga was adamant about a substantial increase."

Everyone smiled. The strong-willed Speaker Melvyn Fitzgerald Saratoga was devoted to expanding American space colonies. If true to form, he wouldn't rest until he rammed such a bill through the House. It was hard to say no to Mr. Speaker Saratoga.

"With the colonies in the Speaker's hands, we'll proceed to more pressing matters." Shefferton picked up his fork. The morning's business passed quickly. He took up the economy and polished off his prune juice, dealt with a threatened Tubeway strike and his English muffins, discussed the appointment of the next envoy to the pope in Buenos Aires and ate a sliced tomato, finished a report on the armed services and mopped up his fried egg with a piece of toast. He leaned back, loosened his belt, and had the plate removed.

The CIA director, Colonel Farley, was recovering from a new set of implanted teeth. Presenting his report was a deputy, Benedict Probst, a man of limp flesh, droopy eyelids, weak posture, and a handshake like cold ham. Even his hair, flaccid and dangling, seemed anemic. Mayfield found him repugnant, a personification of the word *spook*, but his brilliance in interpreting satellite data was undeniable.

His voice was like an early-days computer simulation. "We have new evidence of Soviet railgun technology, which we discussed a few weeks ago. We think we've found traces of an experimental track ten miles long. It was disguised, in an area avoided by civilians: the Kyshtym district, where a nuclear accident occurred many years ago. It is abandoned now. But there is unexplained traffic in and out of the Himalayan military district, near the Greater Asian border. This may indicate heightening tensions; perhaps a planned armed incursion. But much of the traffic is unmilitary: civilian technicians. The Himalayas are a prime location for a railgun track since the high velocity of a projectile dictates minimum atmospheric resistance."

"You've found no evidence of railgun construction?" inquired the president.

"Negative. However, five years ago we detected a series of seismic disturbances emanating from the Himalayas. Probably underground nuclear explosions, possibly to excavate a cavity for an underground installation. The abandoned rail may indicate also that the Unified Soviet State is further along than we thought. We must also consider the possibility of tracks that we haven't found."

"Is that a high probability?"

"Affirmative."

"Well, keep on it. I want periodic reports."

"Yes sir."

"We have several reports on the famine. I've invited Senator Macadew to listen in, since his people and mine have worked closely on this."

"Thank ya, Mr. President, I'm sure," drawled Macadew.

"The secretary of agriculture will report on the Santa Bella blight."

The secretary, blunt, no-nonsense, unimaginative, a farmer for twenty years and a former Alberta congressman, was an agrarian encyclopedia. He was obviously horrified by the blight.

"We can thank God we were spared, because our team was powerless. We still don't know what stopped it."

"Does Chambless think the blight was a gift from our Soviet friends?" asked Shefferton.

"He believes it is a natural mutation."

"And his staff?"

"They agree."

"Hardly surprising. To be safe, interview some of them privately. They might be more frank."

"Yes sir."

"Are we taking action to isolate sources of contamination?"

"Yes, but Greater Asia and Black Africa are suspicious. They aren't cooperating fully—"

"That's unnecessarily stupid of them," said Shefferton. "I better call Chairman Tua and that maniac Juba Aman Dana."

"Th' Leopard might not return the call of a mere mortal, Jeff," said Macadew.

"Then we'll have the secretary of state talk to him." The president grinned. Harmon chuckled but his eyes were cold.

The next report showed that U.S. grain reserves had increased enormously, thanks to two very productive seasons and many new tiered hydroponics and underground farms. Improved storage had allowed the reserve to grow to ten times the annual consumption of the nation.

"We're in a good position," said the secretary of agriculture. "Even if we had been hit hard we could have fed our people. Now we should consider ending our boycott of grain sales. We could make some very lucrative deals with South America."

"It would be immoral to profit from this situation," said Harmon stiffly. "This is a splendid opportunity to build a reserve of good will in exchange for our grain reserves."

"Give them the grain?"

"We have plenty."

"That decision will be made later, gentlemen," said the president. "Senator, we'll hear from you now."

· Macadew cleared his throat, a sound akin to a bellowing water buffalo, and bestowed his beatific smile.

"Thank ya, Je—eh, Mr. President. As you know, we've been studyin' the possibility of global famine for months, since the opposition set up the committee, but not much got done." He chuckled. "This year we compiled a barrel of info about countries where we believe a famine of disastrous proportions is imminent.

"They are the Union of Black Africa, Greater Asia, most of South America, the Aryan Empire, much of the Middle East, Egypt, Turkey, and the Philippines, in short, the nations unable to curb their populations. Asia's problems were compounded by the civil war and India's population, which is now two billion. The Rulin' Families have tried forced sterilization but Chairman Tua fears a revolt. Old bushwhacker knows a grim situation when he sees one."

"I got that impression when I talked with representatives of the Ruling Families," said Shefferton thoughtfully.

"For two years," said Macadew, "crops have been below average for lack of rainfall. The vote isn't in yet on this latest batch. If it's normal or better, the problems won't be aggravated. If not, we may see a catastrophe.

"And that was the situation before the blight. It's a whole new rat in the wood pile—throws our calculations off. If the blight spreads from South America—" he shuddered. "Three fourths of the world lives in those places. Ten billion starvin' folks. All moral arguments aside, I don't think we need our military experts to tell us what a threat they could be."

"Thank you, Charles," said Shefferton. "We recently discussed the Strubeck equations and their possible bearing on our situation. As you know, I assigned Sheridan Mayfield to find Dorian Nye or the equations. Sheridan?"

Mayfield's collar tightened. He swallowed, tasting the bitterness of failure.

"I'll begin by detailing the progress of our attempt to locate Dr. Nye, who is reputed to have the equations."

"I guess that means you haven't found him." Secretary of the Treasury James Griffin led a chorus of chuckles.

"That's correct," said Mayfield patiently. "Our information boils down to this: Nye left for Paris December twentieth. This is documented by retinal and fingerprint evidence. He toured Europe until January ninth when he arrived in London for a three-week lecture series. The same day he canceled to fly back home at Senator Macadew's request. Sometime between then and the landing of his flight at Armstrong Field, Dorian Nye vanished, replaced by an actor, Arthur Vinius. This is our concrete evidence. We know Vinius was murdered by Lloyd Hunning, whose release from the sanitarium may be part of a larger plot because the sanitarium head, Dr. Xerxes, was also murdered. We also know a deep-cover spy ring has been activated here by the Europeans to locate Nye."

The president leaned forward. "Do you think one of the other powers has him?"

"We know Nye visited CERN physics research facility, among others. Europe lost many scientists in the war. Nye would be valuable to them. But the secret services of Europe, England, the Unified Soviet State, Black Africa, the Aryan Empire, Greater Asia, and the ISAFTA Alliance are all looking for him. They seem to believe we have him but are pretending we don't.

"That burns me!" said Macadew. "We'd damn well know if he's in the country, wouldn't we?"

"Our surveillance technology is such that if he is, he would have to stay indoors to elude it. But if he does, he could escape us indefinitely.

"We're fairly sure Nye didn't escape off planet, even to the moon. He has a synthetic heart, powered by a radioactive pellet. He couldn't escape detection at L-5, Midway, or Tycho Brahe Base."

Harmon smiled icily. "That narrows it down. All we have to do is search a haystack of ten billion people for one needle!"

"Succinctly, that is correct."

"I don't appreciate pessimism," said Shefferton. "Failure I can accept, but this evidence proves nothing yet. If Dorian Nye is alive or dead, the evidence exists and we'll find it. Am I correct, Sheridan?"

He wouldn't be pushed. "I don't know. He may have engineered his own disappearance. We may be matching wits with a genius who doesn't want to be found."

"Sheridan, you need more time. But it is a precious commodity. What other options are you exploring?"

"We searched Strubeck's and Nye's papers and data for references to the equations. Negative on both. That leaves one possibility, an . . . unlikely one."

"Explain."

"It might be possible for Sherlock Michlanski to reconstruct the equations. If it can be done, he would be the one to do it. But he refuses."

"I'm sure we can persuade Michlanski of the great service he would be performing if he helps us," said the president. "Perhaps you used the wrong approach. You aren't the most diplomatic of men. I'm sure he's a loyal American. Such a great mind couldn't be so selfish as to refuse to help alleviate a world famine."

"I'm afraid he is." He remembered the holocube incident and winced. "I have his house under surveillance. I ordered two agents to gain entry by a ruse, since I can't request a search warrant."

"I will call him personally. In these times there can be no such thing as noncooperation with government. Individualism can be taken too far."

"He won't listen." Mayfield was bitter. "He has no respect for higher authority. You'll compromise your dignity if you lower yourself to appeal to his nonexistent higher nature."

"My dignity isn't so fragile it won't survive a brush with Professor Michlanski," said Shefferton gently. "I'll crawl up the cliffs of his island if it will make a difference in fighting this menace."

An aide entered and gave Shefferton a note. As he read it the color drained from his face.

"You all better hear this," he said. " 'The Ecuadorian steamer *Santiago* today was impounded for gun-running in the Nigerian port of Calibar by Black African officials. Among items confiscated were grain sacks spoiled by a grayish mold. The sacks were taken ashore and had not all been destroyed before one was stolen. Several hours later the first case of rot was reported at a nearby plantation. It bears a striking resemblance to the Santa Bella blight.' " The president dropped the note. He was remarkably composed. "Ladies and gentlemen, we're screwed again."

Chapter
✳ 19 ✳

1

At the knock on the door of his photography studio, Karl Chapin peered through the night scope mounted in the door, satisfying himself of the caller's identity before admitting him.

"Ah, Mr. Fain, good evening."

"And to you, Mr. Chapin." He moved with the grace and economy of a cat. His voice, Chapin had noted before, was curiously neutral, or, if it had an inflection, it was cruelty.

"No one has ever requested to watch my darkroom work before, Mr. Fain. But since you are willing to pay—"

"I'm a history buff. Some play with eighteenth-century muskets. I like old-style predigital photography, and you are an acknowledged master. I looked all over Los Angeles before I located you here in the middle of the Arab district—"

"I was here before there was an Arab district. I'm glad there are still those who appreciate the subtlety of flat photos. Do you have the roll?"

"Yes." They entered the darkroom.

Chapin turned on the red light, and, working swiftly, ran the film through the three-step bath to develop it.

"How did you get into the field, Mr. Chapin?"

"It was a hobby for a long time. Then I worked for the government. I got fed up with bureaucracy and set myself up in business. I've never liked holography, so—"

"That would be a perfect attitude for a member of the TEA."

"That's amazing! Or did I tell you—"

"I'm a good guesser. A talent I have."

Chapin held the film up to the light. "But these people are dead!"

Fain lashed out. He held the other's face in the stop bath while he thrashed. His struggles grew feeble, then stopped. Fain held his face under longer than necessary, then let the body fall to the floor.

He dried the film and made several prints. He turned on the light, took a camera from his pocket, and photographed the body several times before leaving through the back door.

2

Roger Ferdinand stood near the entrance to the photo studio, barely containing his fury.

"Please stay out of the inertia field, sir. We're still taking air samples."

"Do you know who I am?"

"You're not my boss. That's who you are."

The tech elbowed past. Ferdinand sneered impotently. The police and county coroner's forensic technicians were incredibly impertinent. They were in league against him.

The officer in charge, Lt. Armando Valdez, ambled over with his assistant, Sgt. Hassan. He wore a porkpie hat and juggled a steaming burrito between his fingers to keep it off his stained trench coat.

"Tha's really a lovely outfit you're wearing this evening, Mr. Ferdinand. You keeping yourself entertained?"

"Your baboons are keeping me out, Valdez."

"We baboons are very territorial. Besides, until the air samples are taken, the temperatures and disturbances recorded and the static electricity measured on furniture and rugs well, you know. Standard operational procedure."

"Then give me a static suit."

"On my budget you expect me to have spares?"

"Then order the damned coroner's office to issue me one."

"I wish I had the authority you give me credit for."

"Look, Valdez, I don't know what you have against me, but it's infinitesimal compared to what you will have. This is the second potential witness I've lost. I must know if the killer has the same MO. This is a federal matter—"

"What did the killer do, violate Señor Fain's civil rights?"

"I don't have to give you explanations. But if the killer escaped south to the contaminated zone, that's federal jurisdiction."

Ferdinand wasn't about to tell the local police about his investigation, which had been given a whole new dimension by the death of Dr. Xerxes. The sanitarium director had dropped a clue when he spoke of the needle and silk treatment, a torture perfected by the Drangs—soldiers trained in psychodynamic combat by the maverick Chinese General Lao Tse. The general had invaded mainland China with 30,000 men and came within a cat's whisker of toppling the Communists.

Ferdinand had learned that Xerxes had been an observer in Lao's army, where he'd picked up a taste for things oriental. After Lao's defeat, many caucasians in his employ became agents and assassins for secret services all over the world, including the TEA and CIA.

Xerxes's death had been a textbook case of a Drang assassination.

Because Lloyd Hunning was connected with Adam Scott's death, Ferdinand had decided to flag the names of all former TEA agents implicated in that death, plus people who were known to be close to Scott.

When Fain, formerly of the TEA, was found dead, his name was immediately brought to Ferdinand's attention. Luckily, he had been in the neighborhood.

"Hey, cabron," Valdez was saying, "we've sent squads after crooks in T.J. before without you guys gettin' interested. Why assume this particular killer hotfooted it for San Diego? If you want to take over jurisdiction for every criminal who escapes from Los Angeles, my brother, we might just let you."

Valdez pointed his finger in Ferdinand's face. "But until I get orders, you are nothing but an irritating civilian. As to what I have against you, señor, let's just say I don't like your tactics, how you tried to frame that officer in Washington—"

"Spare me."

"'I'm doing all I'm legally required, Ferdinand. You can review the evidence when I do."

"I have a long memory, Lieutenant."

The forensic technician spoke in a bored monotone. Behind him stood an electric blackboard with a floor plan of the photo studio.

"Residual carbon dioxide and heat and still-moving air currents were impossible to record in any of the rooms except where the victim was homicided because the murderer deliberately propped the back door open with a block.

"Ah, most of the static charges on the rugs and floor were destroyed—we had a Santa Ana condition last night. But rug fibers retained imprints of two sets of shoes. The killer wore a flat sole and weighed between one hundred and two hundred pounds."

"So he was either a child or a football player," said Valdez. "Can't we narrow it down more than that?"

"It's very strange," said the tech. "The killer had an unusual balance or equilibrium, almost like a ballet dancer—"

"Or a psychodynamic killer," said Ferdinand with satisfaction. "A Drang."

"Ah, the tile floor of the darkroom yielded little. But one interesting thing: Several very intense bursts of heat, quite localized, took place at the time of death."

"Someone lighting a cigarette?" said Valdez.

"No smoke."

"Since it took place in a darkroom, it might well be a camera flash," said Ferdinand.

Valdez glared at Ferdinand. "No doubt you will say that your other killer took flash pictures of his victim also."

Ferdinand never had any qualms about not being a gracious winner. "FBI technicians found that Dr. Jeremiah Xerxes's killer took flash pictures of him immediately after the murder. It's the same man, Lt. Valdez. This case is mine."

Valdez's expression was implacable. "So it seems, Mr. Ferdinand." Their eyes met. "Don't spit on any sidewalks while you're in L.A., señor."

3

It was a grueling morning; by noon, Sheridan Mayfield was ready to escape. The Genoan, a small Italian restaurant on the tenth floor of a building overlooking the Tidal Basin, was quiet, dark, and restful.

He sat in a corner, watching flames dance inside a red glass shade, waiting for his usual: ravioli and spaghetti. The chef sang from *Rigoletto* as he rolled pasta. Mayfield lost himself in subdued sensory impressions: the smell of tomato, the rasping baritone, the dark.

A clatter of crockery broke his reverie. A dark-eyed girl planted steaming food before him with a smooth motion, opened a bottle of Chianti, and poured his glass three-quarters full.

Halfway through his meal she returned. He was wanted on the holophone. Since he'd begun working with the FBI and CIA he was never able to lose himself, not matter how hard he tried.

He muttered venomously as he shut the soundproof door behind him, drew the lead-lined curtains, and entered his personal code. The passion pink dial tone faded to the golden bearded cherubic face of—

"Michlanski!" he said, as if he had been punched in the stomach.

"Glad you remember me, Secretary Mayfield." He smiled cheerfully. He wore blue jeans and a faded yellow sweat shirt.

"What kind of joke—" he caught himself, allowing a tiny hope to bud. "Why did you call, Professor?" he whispered.

"To help you."

"You've changed your mind? You'll help with the Strubeck equations?"

"Not exactly." Michlanski leveled his gaze. "Secretary Mayfield, I want three things from you."

"Three things? What do you mean? What are you talking about?"

"Three things," said Michlanski. "To meet with President Shefferton, today. This afternoon."

"Meet with the president? But, but, why do you?"

"I want a helicopter to pick me up at Wolverine Island."

"Helicopter?"

"And secrecy. Total, absolute secrecy. When the meeting is over I'll tell you what you can bring into the open."

"What are you talking about? A meeting with the president on such short notice—you must be insane!"

"Are you finished?" Michlanski's voice was icy. "Listen: Dorian Nye is alive. I know where he is. Tell the president."

He vanished. Mayfield stared blindly, then reached numb fingers up to enter a number.

"White House, good afternoon." said the operator.

"I want to talk to the president."

Chapter
* 20 *

That afternoon the White House press corps noticed that something was up. Tours were canceled. Secret Service details were doubled. No one got in or out without the say-so of the chief of staff.

Rumors multiplied: of an Asian plane violating the Lines of Demarcation, of another naval clash with the Soviets; that the president was ill; in a coma; dead. The White House was ominously silent. Knots of the media and the curious gathered at the gates.

A roar in the sky focused all eyes on a fleet of huge armored helicopters moving majestically toward the White House. Reporters spotted the insignia of the Third Infantry, the crack ceremonial regiment from Fort Myer, rarely seen except at inaugurations . . . and funerals.

The helicopters landed in a hurricane. Men in battle gear poured out, took positions on the grounds, and politely made the crowd move back from the fence.

The crowd became silent. From the west flew three more helicopters.

The middle ship, blazoned with the president's seal, settled on the lawn while the others hovered nearby.

Seven people emerged and were escorted inside as holovision crews frantically trained equipment on them. The chopper's rotors became a ghostly blur and it heaved itself up to join its sisters. All three turned west and vanished in the clouds.

In his study the president of the United States sat watching the news. The commentator, a white-haired father figure, was pontificating about the activity at the White House.

"Washington is inundated by rumors and theories at this hour," he said. "Many concern the president's health, which may have prompted summoning a specialist to treat the ailing chief executive—"

"If wishing made it so, right, Manfred?" The president laughed at the image.

"Dr. Brian Schubert, renowned heart specialist, and other well-known physicians were observed landing moments ago at the White House—"

The president chortled and stretched.

"This doesn't explain the deployment of two companies of assault troops on the White House lawn."

There was a knock at the door.

"Come in."

Sheridan Mayfield stuck his head in. "Am I disturbing you?"

"No. I'm enjoying America's number one ignoramus."

"You're watching Manfred's drivel?"

"I like to see how I'm being misrepresented to the nation." He shrugged. "When they stop, I'll know I'm dead. Are our guests settled in comfortably?"

"Yes, and anxious to see you. Michlanski is very insistent—"

"I'll see them in a few moments." He glanced at the newscaster and ran a hand over his jaw. "He looks more peeved than usual tonight."

"Whatever the reason," said Manfred solemnly, "we, and the rest of the nation, look to the White House tonight and ask 'Why?'" He looked up. "This is Manfred Grayson, wishing you a pleasant tomorrow."

"This has been the evening news with Manfred Grayson—"

Shefferton turned it off, stood, and smoothed the creases in his trousers. "I'll see our guests now."

The two men shown in by the Marine guard wore combat fatigues: Dorian Nye was a scholarly infantry major, Michlanski an unconventional mess sergeant.

Shefferton felt a frisson. He had always felt stage fright dealing with scientists the likes of Nye, who, after all, had isolated the tacyon. Compared to him, Shefferton was just a politician. Seeing him again after all these months was like seeing the dead revived. From his well-fed look, life in the underworld hadn't been too bad. Still, since the disappearance the physical Nye had so combined with the mental giant in Shefferton's mind that it was unnerving to see the small, ungraceful, painfully shy gnome with a protruding forehead instead of the Zeus of physics he remembered. In army fatigues Nye seemed physically smaller. The spell was broken completely when the professor said something in his hesitant, stuttering speech. At that moment the president felt himself master of the situation, or at least on equal terms with the two scientists.

"Welcome to the White House, gentlemen," He deliberately made his own voice booming and confident. "How was the trip?"

"Unique, Mr. President," said Michlanski coldly.

"Dr. Nye, it's a pleasure to see you alive and well."

"Thank you, Mr. President."

"I must compliment you on the originality of our security arrangements," said Michlanski with even more ice in his delivery, just to make sure everyone heard it. His hauteur was convincing, and Shefferton felt something of the trepidation toward Michlanski that he had derided in Secretary Mayfield.

"Don't you feel secure?" said the president more defensively than he had intended.

"What could be safer than being surrounded by an army regiment? I am confused by your definition of secrecy however."

The president grinned. "In this case I define it as completely misdirecting the media from our meeting. If we had brought you in by normal means, you would have been spotted. By bringing in four hundred soldiers we focused attention on the single chopper carrying some people easily identified as doctors. My people generated rumors of my needing a heart specialist. Besides, I've always loved ostentatious military displays. All my critics will tell you."

Shefferton motioned them to sit and looked sharply at Mayfield. "Don't hover, Sheridan." Mayfield plopped into his favorite stuffed armchair.

"Dr. Nye, you've had the entire nation on tenterhooks. May I ask why?" He regarded him keenly.

"It's a long, complex story."

"I've set aside the whole evening and no one has yet questioned my ability to absorb complex subjects. Please begin."

Mayfield smiled. Shefferton was being polite, but the powerful will under the silken exterior was obvious.

"Mr. President, w-when I left for Europe I h-had every intention of returning. But during my trip I pondered the threats against me."

"Dr. Nye, you assured me you were enthusiastic about my proposal for a joint effort of shared fusion technology with the Europeans, and that you supported an American-European interstellar expedition."

"I received three separate death threats about my diplomatic mission before I boarded the jet for Europe. Each time the threat came to a hotel or home where I was supposedly incognito. Whoever made the threats knew I was instructed to contact President Gernais and offer him American aid to resist Russia's destabilizing efforts against Poland and the Balkans."

"It hardly takes a crystal ball to divine our intentions toward Europe. I won't trivialize the fact that isolationists discovered your location. But we weren't in the White House yet, and dispite President Allen's assurances, we know some of his top aides were hostile to your mission. We could have provided more protection if you had asked for it."

"I-I'm not a brave man. No amount of bodyguards can prevent a truly dedicated assassin from achieving his end. I was not willing to die for my activities in Europe on your behalf."

"On your country's behalf."

"Many have different ideas of what is good for the country. I devised a plan to get home without exposing myself. I paid an actor to impersonate me while I returned by another route."

"What other route?"

"I'm afraid that must remain a secret."

"Not only did you vanish, Doctor, but you found a way to breach our borders—"

"N-not all doors are locked, sir. That is all I will say on the subject."

"A man died!"

"He would have been me—that is defense enough."

"Very well, but why did you hide for four months while the world searched for you? Why make us believe you were kidnapped, dead, or defected?"

"If someone tried to kill me once, he might try again. Your inspector didn't protect my double."

"He was a policeman. I think the Secret Service does an adequate job of protecting me."

"Mr. President," said Michlanski, "if you die, the vice-president succeeds you. If Dr. Nye dies, there is no one else."

Shefferton clamped his jaw grimly. "Very well, I'll accept that, too. I'm more interested in the results of your mission. Did President Gernais agree to a summit?"

"Y-yes. The sooner the better. He thinks a joint declaration of our two countries' guarantee of East Europe's integrity is necessary to keep the Unified Soviet State from attempting a coup in Warsaw before the end of the year."

"Where does he suggest the summit take place?"

"He said to ask if you remember the Atlantic Charter."

"I understand. In World War Two Franklin Roosevelt and Winston Churchill met secretly aboard a United States battleship in the middle of the Atlantic and formed the British-American alliance.

"Now, and most important. The matter we discussed before you left has risen to paramount importance. Do you have the Strubeck equations?"

"That brings us to our purpose in coming here," said Michlanski. "We wish to negotiate the terms under which you will receive what you call the 'Strubeck equations.' "

"Are you giving your government an ultimatum?" Shefferton's voice was deadly quiet.

"Terms. All are negotiable, save one."

"What are your terms?"

"We must ask that the discussion be held in private."

The president was puzzled. "You mean Secretary Mayfield? He is my most trusted aide."

"What we have to say is for you alone," said Nye. "L-later others may be told, depending on circumstances. But we insist on a few moments alone with you, the president. Do you agree?"

"Frankly, you're tantalizing me beyond all endurance." He looked at Mayfield. "We seem to be playing by their rules."

"I understand." Mayfield nodded to the others and left, passing the ubiquitous naval officer whose attaché contained nuclear missile codes, called the "football." He went to the elevator. As he reached for the down button the door opened and Randolph Harmon, Secretary of State, stepped out.

"What the hell is going on, Mayfield?" Above his faultless evening suit his face was constipated with blood.

Mayfield had never liked him, or the way he treated everyone like a flunky, but until now Mayfield had never gone out of his way to bait him.

"The president is in a private meeting."

"With whom?"

"If he wants you to know that, he'll tell you."

"Damnation!" Harmon was bitter. "That low-grade moron downstairs gave me the same runaround. Have you seen the news?"

"Yes."

"Well! What's the meaning of those troops? People think we've declared war!"

"It would take more than the Third Infantry to initiate hostilities, Randolph." Harmon twitched with annoyance. Nothing irritated him more than being addressed by his first name.

"Am I the only man who understands the delicacy of foreign policy? I'm on my way to a state dinner at the Aryan embassy. I'll have to explain this! You know how the foreign press loves to lambaste us!"

"Instead of apologizing for the harmless posting of some troops why not ask the ambassador what happened to those demonstrating students arrested in Teheran last month?"

"That's an internal matter. I should expect even you to realize that."

Mayfield started to step around him, "If that's all that's on your mind, you may as well go to dinner. The president will be a long time yet."

Harmon exhaled explosively, turned on his heel, and stepped back into the elevator, closing it in Mayfield's face.

When it returned, Mayfield rode down to the wing of the White House normally open to the public. For awhile he played the tourist, unconscious of time, until one of Shefferton's aides touched his shoulder.

"Sir, you're wanted in the president's study."

"Thanks."

The president sat with his chin resting on his right hand, looking into the fireplace as if it was the portal to eternity. He was quiet a long time, then he became aware of Mayfield.

"Sheridan, sorry to keep you waiting." His voice came from a great distance. "Have you ever wanted to see the future?"

"I can't say the desire has ever burned brightly. I don't want to know my future. I'm not sure I want to know our future. It would make the present so futile."

"Perhaps," said the president dreamily. "At this moment I want very much to know the future. I would give a great deal to see how our world turns out in a hundred years; if it's intact, or if our efforts are in vain."

"Some world will exist, even if we fail. Man is a hardy beast. If the Ice Age didn't do him in, he can survive anything."

"Once I was critical of my predecessors who feared history's judgment. But it's a heavy burden tonight. For the first time since taking office I understand the meaning of the presidency. It's nothing I imagined: power, prestige. It's responsibility; the pain of doing what you know is right, even if it ruins you. I understand why so many presidents feared the history writers. We serve two constituencies: the present and posterity. What one may praise us for the other may vilify. It's hard to know which to serve." He looked at Mayfield. "I must be boring you . . ."

"Not at all . . . Jeffrey. Do you want to tell me about it?"

"I—I can't tell anyone yet. That's why I feel so alone. Tell me, if you had your choice, would you be Hitler or Lincoln?"

"Lincoln, of course." The question astounded him.

"So would any sane man. That's why I'd like to know the future tonight, to see which way history paints me."

"I don't understand."

"You will, sooner than you wish. I know it's unfair, since you could go down as my Himmler or Goebbels."

"I don't share your fear. We're mortals. We do our best. If we succeed, good, if not, we know we tried. It doesn't matter what history says."

"Perhaps you and I are in the wrong positions. You seem to be the strong one."

"Strength is not the vital factor. Character is. Mr. Lincoln was sometimes crippled by intense depressions. We would put him under a psychiatrist's care today. But he saved the Union."

Shefferton smiled. "I hope you're right. Tonight I've committed myself to a course of action. I don't know if it's moral, it's probably illegal, and I'll be impeached for it if anyone finds out before it's done. But it's the right thing to do. I know that. God help me, I know it." He looked tortured. "It's a hell of a thing, asking a man to do that. But, what the heck? It goes with the job."

Chapter

* 21 *

"Ladies and gentlemen," said the announcer, "The president will address the nation at six P.M. Eastern Standard Time. The White House provided no advance copy of the speech, which will be simulcast around the world. . . ."

"What do you think he'll say, Mel?" asked Lenny. They were sitting on the couch.

"I don't know," said Hardrim slowly. "I don't know much about anything right now. After that news conference with Nye and Michlanski I don't know what to think or believe." He grimaced. "Flaherty called —wants me back right away since Nye isn't lost anymore."

"What will you do?" She snuggled closer, resting her chin on his shoulder.

"I don't know that either."

"But you'll have to make up your mind soon."

He grimaced again. "Yeah."

". . . in just a few minutes. An estimated five hundred million viewers will tune in on holocubes and televisions around the world. Please stand by—"

Holo cameras set up in the Oval Office focused on the president's desk. Technicians bustled about, adjusting lights checking meters, arranging the desk to best effect.

The activity stopped when the president entered. He looked relaxed and refreshed and endured the fussing of the makeup artist without complaint.

"You forgot the red nose!" he joked.

"I got some whiskey, Mr. President," said one of the techs. "That'll give you one pretty quick!"

"No thanks!" He held up his hands in mock horror.

"Two minutes, Mr. President."

"Thank you." Shefferton sat, snorting with amusement as the makeup man combed his hair again and adjusted his tie.

The chief technician made the thumbs up sign.

"Give it to them, boss!" he whispered.

"This time I think I will."

"Live from the White House we bring you an address by the president of the United States." The camera zoomed in on the presidential seal, then dissolved to Shefferton's face.

"Good evening, friends and fellow citizens. I apologize for barging in on your suppers, but I've heard that the best way to get people's attention is to interrupt their meal. Believe me, I need your attention tonight."

Senator Percy Shelley Manners wrinkled his nose with distaste. "He is spreading it thick tonight." He impatiently pulled a black curl from his eyes. He was breathing hard from a rough game of racquetball with his teenage son and was in his sneakers and sweatshirt.

"I wonder what his game is?"

"Many of you saw Dr. Nye's news conference and share our relief at his safe return. But you may not realize its significance for this nation and the world.

"As I speak, a great plague sweeps through Africa, destroying all grain in its path, leaving millions to starve. The Santa Bella blight has already wiped out most crops in Central America, and unchecked, will do the same in India, China, and the rest of Greater Asia, in the areas we call the Torrid Zone, about twenty-three degrees north and south of the Equator.

"Manpower and technology from all over the world are concentrated to fight the menace, but they may not succeed until too late. Three-fourths of the world faces death by starvation.

"This is surely the greatest potential catastrophe ever to confront mankind. What we do may determine the fate of civilization for centuries."

Senator Charles Macadew lounged on his couch with a tumbler of Bushmills. He was bleary-eyed with fatigue and alcohol (it was not his first of the day). He raised his glass in salute to his friend and muttered what, with an allowance for profanity, approached being a benediction.

"The time is past when we can look across the ocean, secure in our fortress, and disdain the evils of the world.

"We are not safe, we are not secure. How can we be when three-fourths of the world dies while we maintain huge stores of grain? We can destroy enemy missiles and sink enemy ships, but what do we do against an ocean of people who implore us 'Save us or we sink!'?

"We must end our twenty-five-year boycott of foreign markets. We must open our silos and let grain, not missiles, pour forth to save the world from death.

"Yet this may not be enough. If the blight finishes its hellish task, about five and a half billion will be without food next year. To save them will take a united effort by America, United Europe, the Unified Soviet State, and others who have escaped the blight. Together we can feed them until next year's crops are harvested.

"But what if next year's harvests are inadequate?

"The world has been balanced on the edge, and the Santa Bella blight has pushed it over. Unless something very drastic is done, even the generosity of the so-called 'have' nations may not be enough to save humanity."

At his dacha on the shores of the Black Sea, Soviet Premier Peter Brasnikov spooned a generous portion of caviar onto a rye cracker and ate it with relish. Tall, thin, swarthy, with aquiline features, sensuous and hedonistic, he was a most un-Russian Russian, at least in appearance.

The full moon and unseasonably mild weather had inspired a beach party. It was well after midnight. Most of the guests had passed out from the free-flowing vodka, but Brasnikov was watching a portable holocube set up on the sand.

After six months in power, he never missed the chance to study his American adversary. He spoke fair English, but kept an interpreter for complicated phrases.

"What was that last sentence?" he barked.

" 'Even the generosity of the so-called "have" nations may not be enough to save humanity.' "

"The fool doesn't expect us to give food to Greater Asia?" he growled. "Utter nonsense!"

"But the means of salvation exists," said the president, his eyes lighting up. "You have heard much speculation about the Strubeck equations. What I am about to tell you is not speculation. It is fact.

"The Strubeck equations exist. They are available to the people of the world. This formula, my friends, will realize a dream as old as science: the direct transformation of the sun's energy into food. At the same time another dream will be realized: the end of hunger. This process, called artificial photosynthesis, unravels the mystery of how plants create food.

"Dr. Nye has made the Strubeck equations available to this government, and outlined what we believe is the best way to develop a workable food factory.

"He calculates that the factory must be in space, twenty million miles from the sun. There this prototype of other space factories will test the equations. If successful, it will be the first of many sending food back to Mother Earth.

"I will ask Congress to fund what we call PH One by issuing new shares of United States common stock, and to fund future stations as needed.

"I will also ask Congress to authorize me to sell grain to foreign markets as soon as possible.

"Finally, and perhaps most important, I call on our neighbors United Europe, the Unified Soviet State, Argentina, Australia, South Africa, and others with grain reserves to join us in redirecting them to areas most desperately in need. To this end I am calling an international conference in New York at the end of this month. I invite all interested parties to send representatives.

"Once more, my fellow citizens, and friends around the world, I emphasize that we can't allow enthusiasm for the Strubeck equations to blind us to the danger of our situation.

"I do think we can look optimistically at the adventure of the coming months. We Americans can perhaps be forgiven if we indulge in a moment of pride. We remember that not so long ago President Kennedy exhorted his countrymen to land a man on the moon. Ours is the land of the possible and the impossible. We are the people who build canals, bridge chasms, construct deep sea tunnels, throw roads across the Rockies and build cities on the moon. We are the nation that tames continents and tears down tyrannies. If we set ourselves the task of saving the earth from starvation forever, we shall succeed. It is time we emulated our pioneer forbears by returning to the road to greatness.

"Thank you for listening and good night."

Chapter

✳ 22 ✳

1

He didn't know how long he had been running. His watch had smashed against a cypress. It seemed the sun had moved since then. How long was that? Hours?

He stopped, trembling, sweat stinging his eyes. A dull throb radiated from the elbow he'd hurt when he fell on a rock.

The forest seemed endless. He ought to have seen the highway by now. He looked back. Was Sebastian there or up ahead?

Ferman stumbled on, eyes half shut, more somnambulist than conscious man. Sometime later—was it just moments?—he was brought wide awake.

The highway. He gazed glassily at the artery and vein of New Orleans. He had to get there to get transport—to convince the authorities to listen. Once he showed them the proof . . .

He sobbed into his hands. Because of his cowardice, Sebastian had the proof. His breath came in hoarse gasps. Nothing to do now but push on—find someone. Make them listen.

He went to the highway, avoiding the knee-high lasers set six feet apart to keep small animals off a road where hovercars cruised at three hundred miles per hour plus.

Ferman had never hitchhiked but he had read about it. He soon found it was impossible with cars traveling that fast. By the time the driver noticed him (if he wasn't asleep or reading) and shut off the autopilot, he was five or six miles down the road.

In the late afternoon shadows he was still hoofing it south, footsore but determined. A speck grew into a rest station. He mustered as much enthusiasm as a man can who is dead on his feet, bruised and slashed, his mouth tasting like Vietnamese fertilizer.

The rest stop was a combined cafe, six-room motor inn, and bus station, run by a fat woman in plaid trousers and pink rolled up hair.

He still had money. The sign said NO FOLD, ONLY GOLD. He was tired rather than hungry so he laid out a ten milligram piece for a room, or more precisely, a closet with a bed. The pink-haired woman eyed him suspiciously but didn't ask for ID—fortunately, since he was almost certainly on file with the police by now.

Squirming into the room, he bailed out over the mattress. When he awoke his eyelids were sticky, his tongue thick, and he could barely stand, but it was a 200 percent improvement.

The contents of the fold-out sink made him feel even better: a disposable razor (it was assumed that guests of cheap motor inns couldn't afford dipilatory treatments), soap, mouthwash, and a toothbrush. When he emerged from the coffinlike shower he was human again.

The cafe's morning crowd had dwindled to two truckers drinking coffee. He decided to chance it instead of feeding at the "public trough"—what the well-to-do sneeringly called the automatic booths like the one across the highway, that dispensed free, nutritious, but deliberately tasteless food to the poor or anyone who chose to eat there.

Ferman sat a stool away from a short, dense trucker who looked as if he worked out every day. His head was a large rock set between two boulders.

"Howda." The man's voice was a rockslide.

"Good morning."

The waitress took Ferman's order: four fried eggs, bacon, and toast. The trucker followed her movements appreciatively.

"Nice gams."

"What?" Ferman understood well enough, but couldn't quite believe there were still people who used that word.

"Good-looking legs," said the trucker slowly.

"Very attractive."

"Where yawl goin'?"

"Nowhere now. My car broke down."

"Ya goin' to N'awlins?"

"Yes."

"They's a bus station over thah." He pointed next door.

"Don't like buses." Buses required ID. His order arrived and he began to eat.

"Ah'll give ya a lift if the price is raht."

"Five milligrams?"

"How 'bout ten."

"Okay."

"Ah'm leavin' in faav minutes. Mah rig's over thah." He pointed. It was big, a nuclear job, with Hazelton fans like the ocean-going hovercraft, a cabin big enough for a passenger jet, and thirty big wheels for city traffic. The kind of rig called "schooner of the highways" by the romantic press.

When Ferman climbed aboard, his host was strapped in, entering the start-up code. He handed over the gold piece.

"Name's Trapus—Herman Trapus." A brawny hand vigorously pumped Ferman's. He returned to the controls. The engine awoke: a volcano after a sleep of centuries. Monstrous fans roared into life, sounding like the explosion of the cosmic egg. Baffles moved into place and muffled them.

Trapus guided the behemoth onto the freeway, accelerating to 250 mph, then put it on automatic and leaned back. The world flew by, but so smoothly that it was like watching a three-dimensional film. Ferman hadn't known modern trucks were so comfortable.

"Relax an' enjoah the trip. We'll be thah in an hour."

"Are you going to sleep?"

"Ain't no job more cushy than drivin' a truck. 'Cept ya gots to know what ya doin'. Tha's what they pay fo', knowhow." Ferman watched the scenery. When he looked back, Trapus was snoring.

Sixty minutes later a bell rang. Trapus awoke and sat up. "We're here." In the intervening time they had crossed several medium-sized rivers and left the bayou country. They now crossed the Mississippi on the Huey P. Long Bridge into the city. From here the ancient Superdome still dominated the skyline, although challenged by two manifestations of the local cultural renaissance: the Marie Laveau Arcology and the Napoleon IV Memorial Tower. The latter celebrated the city's deceased, flamboyant, Creole mayor; the former was a self-contained colony of several thousand practitioners of voodoo. They rose almost as sentinels guarding the mouth of the Father of Waters.

They took a roundabout route on relatively narrow streets to the storage and warehouse district on the riverfront. New Orlean's population was a third less than a century before, but she was still a mighty port. Trapus expertly wheeled into an area where workers were emptying two other rigs. He shut down. "This is whah we get off, buddy. Been nice travelin' with ya."

"Thanks." For ten miligrams of gold it probably had been nice.

Ferman walked along the levee, toward the skyscrapers. He had no plans, only an ultimate destination: Washington. For the hundredth time his pockets yielded the same dismal contents: enough to eat once, cheaply, see a Surroundee, or take a taxi ten blocks downtown. He dared not use his credit card in a state that could nab a traffic violator when he used one, or registered in a hotel, or bought a plane ticket.

He approached the center of the old town, near the French Market and Jackson Square. Many new, tall buildings had sprung up here, and and tourists rubbed shoulders with well-dressed pedestrians, some of them socially conscious enough to have their hands dyed to advertise their politics, philosophy, or religion. Near the old United States Mint, Ferman felt the sidewalk vibrating. Ahead was a large flashing sign: TUBEWAY FREIGHT TERMINAL.

The main terminal was miles away at the airport, but even this loading terminal took up a city block. In front a line of people carried packages. In the rear, trucks and vans delivered larger loads.

The first Tubeway was built at the turn of the century by National Parcels Company after the post office was killed by computer mailing. Delivery companies competed fiercely to move freight faster, cheaper, with more convenience, but mainly faster, faster. In essence, the Tubeway was an incredibly long gun barrel and the freight-carrying projectiles were the bullets.

NPC's tubeways linked every city on the continent and they wanted to build one under the Atlantic.

He found himself inside, not sure what to do, but sure he must do something. He entered an empty elevator. When the doors pulled apart, he stepped into the Tubeway tunnel itself. Workers were loading the silvery smooth torpedoes. He looked into the open side of the closest one; it was silent. On its metal skin was written: WASHINGTON D.C.

It was too much like fate. No one was watching. The supervisor was faced away, lighting a cigarette.

He plunged into the black. He was surrounded by huge chromium containers, like vacuum bottles. They filled most of the large space. His vision adjusted and he moved his hand to uncover red letters: INERTIAL CONTAINERS. What were they? It seemed very important to know the answer.

He looked for a clue. Why were the containers attached to the sides of the torpedo as though part of it?

The door hissed shut, throwing him into an inky, bottomless lake. The floor moved. The projectile rolled into a launcher. Panic seized him by the throat. He clawed the smooth insides of the torpedo.

He took a mental grip on himself. He wanted this; it was foolish to panic. It was dangerous, but acting rationally he might reduce the danger. Obviously he was in the wrong place if the torpedo was about to be launched. He went astern and spread out against the bulkhead.

The torpedo moved vertically. Cold metal pressed against wet palms. Something clamped solidly.

Silence. Then sudden impossible pressure as the universe knelt on his chest. Then blackness, much darker than the physical dark that surrounded him.

2

Bart Huntly, assistant manager for incoming traffic for the D.C. Tubeway Terminal, was on one of his inspections.

His long legs ate up distance so that few could keep up with him, and he didn't encourage anyone to try. He was a graduate of the school of person-to-person contacts, and the peculiar angle of his prominent nose suggested that some of them had been violent.

He dropped in unannounced on unloading zone 81, and took in the scene: Men, not working, were crowded around a torpedo. Huntly plunged into them, liberally using his elbows.

"What's going on?"

His breath hissed.

The haggard but intact figure of Ralph Ferman appeared in the entrance, leaning on two workers.

"My God!" said Huntly.

"Is this Washington?" Ferman's voice was thick.

"Damn right it is! Who are you and how in hell did you get into one of my torpedoes?"

"My name is Ralph Ferman, and is my travel agent going to get a nasty letter."

"Somebody call the cops. Get this clown off company property!" He rampaged toward his office and Ferman sat on the ground until the police arrived and took him to jail.

3

Hardrim had been back at work in his old job as a police inspector for two days, but already he felt in the thick of things. They were always shorthanded, so as soon as he was certified, a caseload the size of a small car was dumped on his desk. And he was loving it.

The president's speech and Dorian Nye's press conference had convinced him to stop his vendetta. He had his job back and he had Lenny. He owed Nye for that. His apartment was converted for double occupancy, with benefit of clergy, which he'd never thought would appeal to Lenny.

Doubts remained. The investigation hadn't been entirely a vengeful crusade. He had turned up some strange things, like the Argus Society. But that wasn't his business. Too much evil existed in the world for him to worry about more than the small fraction that intersected his desk. Some hotshot could dig up the scandals. Someone always did.

That morning, as soon as he sat down at his desk they gave him a live one. His assistant, Lt. Jakes, walked into his office, laid a file on his desk, and then hung around while he read it with growing wonder.

"Unusual criminal, don't you think, Inspector?"

"I've never run into anything quite like it." Hardrim motioned Jakes to sit. "Let's see. Born Ralph Frederick Ferman. Birthplace Sacramento, California. Twenty-four years old. Caucasian. Protestant. Democrat. Graduated University of Cal at Berkeley. Assigned to Santa Bella blight team. Stole an aircar in Nicaragua, got to the states, and stowed away on a freight Tubeway torpedo. It's a wonder he's alive. How is he?"

"A few bruises. Medics say he'll be fine, but of course medicine is an inexact science except when it comes to computing hospital bills."

"Such bitterness. Just because the scalpel slipped during your vasectomy."

Jakes ignored the joke. "He's bandaged and sitting up in his cell."

"Is he on the drool, pumping Love Fudge or Royal Jelly?"

"No signs of a drooler or Royal Jelly. He doesn't have the vacuous lovesick stare of a fudgy."

"I suppose I'll have to visit Mr. Ferman. Sounds like too much fun to leave to a flunky. Of course, you can observe."

"What about your paperwork?"

"Goddammit Jakes, you know how to rile me." He picked up a report and made a rude noise. "Final judgment in the Fremont case: The judge finds that guilt is distributed in the following manner: fifty-seven percent between the bartender who sold Fremont three drinks before the murder; the city of Washington, which laid him off his construction job; his wife, who was having an affair; his daddy, who beat Fremont as a kid; and Fremont's victim, because he made a fuss when Fremont demanded money; and Fremont himself; forty-three percent. The bills for damages are in the mail. Who's the fudgepacker who writes judicial programs?"

"Are you finished fulminating, sir?"

"Yes. Come along."

4

Hardrim always steeled himself to visit the "Ninth Circle," as he called the jail block devoted to addicts, perverts, and hard cores. As he passed the cells his stomach tightened.

"Hey, it's the long arm of the law!"

Like a rattlesnake, Hardrim's fist closed on the man's collar and pulled his face against the bars. "You don't watch out, the long foot of the law's going to core you like an apple!" He released him so forcefully that his skull cracked against his bunk like a rifle shot.

Hardrim glared at Jakes. "Ferman has no business being with these effluvia. Put him with the white-collar offenders."

"You got it."

Ferman's was a ridiculous tale only a fool would listen to, much less believe. It was rotten with holes, devoid of motive, and fantastically melodramatic, but Hardrim believed it.

He didn't know that yet, and he was consciously calling Ferman crazy as he left his cell, but his subconscious was whispering that maybe the man was sane.

"What are you going to do with him?" asked Jakes, back in Hardrim's office.

"Don't know yet." He planted his feet on the desk and sipped coffee. "We can't hold him without charging him. I'm not sure what laws he's broken here."

"Trespassing on Tubeway property. A stolen aircar."

"He stole the aircar in Nicaragua, which hasn't asked to extradite him. Tubeway won't press charges, either. He'll be free soon."

"He's sure no hardened criminal. He's loony. They shouldn't let him use the can without a padded toilet seat."

"That's why I want him out of the Ninth Circle and on ice for his own safety. What if his story's true? Someone might try to kill him."

"I thought you didn't believe that malarkey!"

"I owe it to any citizen to check out his story."

"You're the boss."

Hardrim chuckled. "I see the wheels turning, Jakes. You don't believe that any more than I believe you believe it. But think what you like as long as you squeak when I pull your string."

"Thank you, sir."

"I want you to reserve a couple of hours on the mainframe."

"Captain won't like it—"

"You're not squeaking, Lieutenant! He won't find out because you won't tell him. Right?"

"Squeak!"

"Excellent. Now get lost! Let me know when we can get in."

Jakes disappeared down the hall, squeaking hysterically, drawing stares from some women at the water fountain.

He ambled back later in the morning and gave the high sign.

"Two hours?" asked Hardrim.

"And a half." He smirked. "God. I was magnificent! I sold Collins such a bill of goods—"

"Don't incriminate me with the details."

"You ordered me to do it," said Jakes sweetly. "Squeak. Squeak."

"Blackmail me later. Let's go. I don't know how to operate those things worth a damn."

"Should be part of every educated man's curriculum, sir."

"Why, when I can get an idiot savant to do it for me?"

5

Jakes sat at the mainframe's console. Hardrim set up his personal recorder containing the Ferman interview.

"Display a detailed map of the New Orleans area. Maybe we can locate where Ferman was taken after his supposed kidnapping."

He scrutinized it. "Okay, he left here," he pointed at downtown New Orleans. "Was driven north on the freeway for less than an hour. Display a radius, considering an average speed of two hundred and fifty miles per hour." A red circle formed around a relatively small area.

"Enlarge magnification." He pointed with a light pencil north of the circle. "That could be the rest stop he mentioned. Somewhere in there is a house and a pond in a middle of a wood, if he's telling the truth."

Jakes ran his fingers over the keyboard. Shading appeared on the map, embracing about ten square miles.

"Your forest."

"Interesting. But it only proves that Ferman knows the highway."

"Computer shows no houses in the forest. There are hundreds of ponds, bayous and lagoons. It's a preserve. No building has been allowed for years."

"He said it was just a cabin. Maybe it's been there a long time. Fax me a copy of that." He pocketed it. "Now play me the data on Noah Chambless."

Hardrim read. Chambless was another of the egghead types he had been encountering a lot lately. This one had skated through college and into a high-paying professorial chair after grad school. In ten years he was the acknowledged voice of his discipline. He had written several highly readable books for laymen and was a bit of a celebrity. Finally he was snatched up by the Agriculture Department and paid a ridiculous salary to run a Bureau of Plant Diseases. Another high achiever.

"Anything else?"

"Just pictures."

"Let's see them."

The holograms flashed by, one every five seconds. A few family shots, pictures from journals, newspaper . . .

"Stop on that one!"

It had obviously been taken many years ago. It showed a young Noah Chambless in a group. Hardrim recognized two others for sure: Dorian Nye and Alfred Strubeck. The rest he wasn't sure about. One looked like a teenage Sherlock Michlanski with short hair and no beard. Next to him were two boys: one husky with flaming red hair, the other slim, dark, and sullen. They were in a room. On its back wall was a bronze plaque engraved with a pattern of black eyes and one word: Argus.

"What's the source?"

"The Detroit *Star*. We got it a week ago from the Michigan State Library archives. The *Star* shut down twenty years ago but many copies were stored in the central computer."

"You couldn't get all the records, could you?" whispered Hardrim. "One was bound to slip past, sooner or later."

"What are you talking about, Inspector?"

"A case that's just reopened," said Hardrim. "And won't be closed this time until I have the truth!"

Chapter

✲ 23 ✲

The basic error of thought by our twentieth century comrades was the belief in the perfectibility of man as the first step toward achieving the collectivist triumph. The error was in the possibility of perfecting man as he is. The solution was simple. If man can't achieve his destiny in his present nature, his nature must be changed.

—The Genetic Communist Manifesto

A crisis of confidence in the eventual triumph of communism rocked the upper strata of Soviet leadership, precipitating rebellions that lost Russia her East European empire. The incompetence of the Orthodox theocracy that followed, and the intrigues of the fascist White Russians and Czarists, almost disintegrated the state. Horrible as Kurtzov's methods were, including the hydrogen bombing of Kiev to crush the Ukraine's secession, he and his Genetic Communists undoubtedly saved Russia.

—Avery Fienstein, Red Midnight, Black Dawn

Premier Kurtzov makes Joseph Stalin look like the Pillsbury Dough Boy!

—From a speech by Senator Charles Macadew

1

Three of the nation's most powerful men sat, drinking, around a table on a veranda in the afternoon sun.

The Speaker of the House, Melvyn Fitzgerald Saratoga, held a brandy.

Senate Majority Leader Percy Shelley Manners sipped a margarita. The host, Senator Charles Macadew, paid homage to his usual square tumbler of Irish whiskey.

"Wal, I'd say that speech put our boy Jeff pretty well into orbit, gentlemen. His policies are damn near coin of the realm raht now. The opinion polls show—"

"That doesn't impress me one iota, Charles," said the Speaker, sipping his brandy. He rested his thumb in his vest pocket, a characteristic mannerism. He was sixty, and to his own way of thinking, full of sagacity, craft, and skill: fruits of a life of hard knocks, hard choices, and hard fighting. He was short, with thick snowy hair, and a jutting jaw that boded ill for those who crossed him. He ruled the House of Representatives like the czar of all the Russias.

"Wal, don't you think the opinion of the American people is important, Melvyn?"

"Is that you or the president asking, Charles?"

"I'm sure your opinion is always important to Jeff—"

"That's why he gave that speech without consulting any of us. Well, he won. We're all inundated with calls to support him. But I'll tell you one thing. This legislation better be shepherded through both houses fast. Once the average citizen starts to think about it, he's not going to like it."

"Will ya support it?"

"If you mean, will I praise it, no. But the president deserves the cooperation of the leadership. I'll tell you plainly: I don't like giving away most of our grain reserves."

"Selling them."

"At ridiculously low prices." Saratoga's look would have charred cedar. "The rest of the package appeals to me. The space program's long overdue for expanding. This PH station, or whatever the hell you call it, sounds good. A bit farfetched, but if scientists like Nye and Michlanski back it, I'll buy it.

"I'm not sold on the rest of it. I'll push it through, but you can tell our friend he owes me. Tell him we'll be watching closely while he hobnobs with Brasnikov and Chairman Tua.

"He's tearing down twenty-five years of foreign policy in six months, and if he's not careful he'll throw away all the good that policy's brought. We run our hemisphere. We don't worry about world opinion. Once the public sobers up from the near beer he fed them, they'll wonder why we're suddenly worried about Africa and Asia."

"That's all part of the platform of the Progressive Nationalist Party, Melvyn."

"Your goddamned friend is the only one I ever met who thinks that a party platform is anything other than a toy for the delegates to play with until they vote the way they're told to. If the inefficient economies of those countries can't feed them, they should change to ones that can. Propping up tottering regimes isn't my idea of humanitarianism."

"Tha's hardly an objective analysis. The famine was caused by a grain plague."

"You're the chairman of the famine committee, Charley. You know better. That plague was just the last straw."

Manners, who had been quietly sipping his margarita, cleared his throat. "This is getting us nowhere. We must reach a consensus. Both measures must pass immediately. We can't allow the country and our opposition the spectacle of the party not uniting behind our leader on his first big test."

Macadew felt a compulsion to choke so strong that his eyes watered. He narrowed them into suspicious slits.

"The Speaker said he will help pilot these programs. I will do likewise, but I also intend to be an enthusiastic supporter, not a lukewarm fence-sitter."

"You can go to hell, Percy!" Saratoga thrust his face a few inches from Manners's. "I won't be lectured on party loyalty by you! I learned party loyalty before you were potty-trained!"

"I wasn't questioning your experience," said Manners pointedly. "If you are as loyal as you say, I'm sure the two bills will have no trouble."

"My loyalty," said Saratoga with deadly calm, "is to the country. I've seen a few presidents. I expect to see one or two more after Jeff Shefferton, if God and my constituents see fit to keep me here. Right now he's my president, my party leader, and my friend. But that wouldn't make me support those measures if I genuinely thought they were bad for the country. So don't push me. I'm giving my unenthusiastic but solid support. Take that and stick it in your pipe, or wherever else you want, and smoke it!" He sat down, still pale.

Macadew looked from face to face like a soldier who has survived a heavy barrage without being hit.

"Wal, that's fine! We're all agreed to support the president."

Before the argument could reignite he escorted them to the door. It hadn't been easy to ask support for a program he wasn't sure about himself—to ask them to take the president's word that it was best for the country. Macadew was doing something rare for him, putting his faith in someone else's judgment. Early in his career he had recognized that he had all the qualifications to be president but one: He was too truthful. Faced with keeping his honesty or advancing his career, he chose to be the conscience of the Senate, saying the necessary when others shrank from controversy. He paid the price: Percy Manners was majority leader. Teresa St. Clair was vice-president. Others held important chairmanships. Others had more power. Charles Macadew growled and thundered, fought the good fight, and kept true to himself.

But this time he was putting his faith in a man.

2

"We cross the Lines of Demarcation in five minutes, Comrade Premier."

Premier Peter Brasnikov favored the stewardess with a cold smile and returned to his briefing book for a moment before looking out the window.

The sky was clear and empty over Greenland except for his small jet and the escort of swingwing fighters (called Fabians by the Western press) from the carrier *Kurtzov*.

As they crossed the invisible border the Fabians peeled away in long eastern-bearing arcs, and red stars were replaced by the white of the American escort planes.

Far away over the dirty-looking tundra Brasnikov saw a glint that was probably the dirigible aircraft carrier serving as the American mother ship.

A shiver ran up his spine. He was in the power of his enemies. What would he do if the situation was reversed? So much time had passed since the last cordial relations with the Americans. How was diplomacy conducted in the distant days before the Civil War, and the invasions from Europe and Asia?

I must learn to curb my paranoia, Brasnikov thought. I'm safer in the center of world capitalism than in my own bed. Probably much safer.

Kurtzov had been paranoid. Paranoia and ruthlessness were his twin evil geniuses. Afraid of poison, he bought his own food in the markets, escorted by plainclothes goons, then cooked it himself.

He was eating a vile concoction of cabbage and badly burned meat that final day when he summoned Brasnikov for what he believed was his death sentence (Kurtzov liked to watch his victims squirm). The premier, built like a statue of an Aztec god, with little piggy eyes, had begun a brutal tirade of abuse when suddenly a piece of meat lodged in his windpipe.

While Brasnikov watched—stunned, fascinated, unable to move—the premier thrashed like a hooked fish until he was dead.

Ironically, Brasnikov's inability to act earned him a reputation for ruthlessness. His fellow Politburo members, overawed by the "regicide" in their midst, immediately handed him supreme power.

Brasnikov soon developed true ruthlessness as a survival skill. Those who knew the truth about Kurtzov's natural death suffered unnatural ones of their own.

But Kurtzov was always with him. He was the man who had tamed the dreaded Committee for State Security (KGB), virtually annihilating its top men, reconstituting it as his own creature under a simple name: the Committee, the K. His legendary decision to bomb Kiev; his uprooting and resettlement of virtually every family in the nation in order to eradicate, once and for all, any national feelings within the Unified Soviet State; his program of genetic engineering that was beginning to bear very strange fruit indeed: They were hard to live up to.

Yes, the old tyrannical bastard had planted the seeds, and Brasnikov would harvest them. He was flying into the outstretched arms of the naive Americans. They would trust him and view his own suspicions as wholly deserved by them for their past sins. He chuckled softly. It was silly to fear entering the den of his enemies, because they were just looking for the right opportunity—to surrender.

3

The International Conference on Famine Relief would meet in the old United Nations building in New York. Representatives began arriving several days early.

The first was Francois Gernais, president of United Europe. President Shefferton met his plane at Kennedy; Armstrong International still had too many unpleasant connotations. He spared no efforts to make the welcome lavish. Cannons fired a twenty-one gun salute, the Marine Corps orchestra played the European national anthem (the chorus from Beethoven's Ninth Symphony), and a squadron of warplanes thundered overhead.

Gernais, tall, white-haired, massive, embraced the equally large Shefferton and planted twin kisses on his cheeks. Then they mounted a rostrum and gave short statements.

."Don't look too glum," Shefferton told the press. "We'll have a lot to say after the conference convenes. Right now I'm anxious to get to know Mr. Gernais and help him to know our people." Then they were swept away by a White House limousine.

The same scene was re-created for each national leader. Sheridan Mayfield, who attended some of these events, noticed that Shefferton was enjoying himself enormously. His step was springier, he was more animated, his smile readier and more sincere. As he whisked about with firecracker abruptness, he seemed to derive strength from the pace.

On the afternoon of Chairman Tua Kau Feng's arrival, the president was whistling merrily as the Marine Corps Orchestra played "Ruffles and Flourishes" and "Hail to the Chief." He caught Mayfield's stare and grinned like a boy.

"Come on, Sheridan! What a gloomy gus you are!"

"I'm sorry, Mr. President. Did I do something wrong?"

"Don't play innocent! You think I'm enjoying this too much." He punched Mayfield playfully. "Being president can be fun, you know!" Just then several jets flew over, drowning every sound with a sustained roll of thunder. Shefferton laughed and pointed at the musicians struggling against the sonic boom. "You know, that's a mighty catchy tune! Isn't it?" He gave a little half skip and went to greet the Asian ruler.

Brasnikov arrived last, without ceremony, several hours ahead of schedule. That, and his flight in a small private jet, fueled rumors that he didn't really want to be at the conference.

The gathering of such a constellation of world leaders made the East Coast go wild with parades, fetes, parties, interviews, ceremonies, and special events. The great hotels and society families competed to offer the visitors suitably sumptuous accommodations.

One major world leader was conspicuous by his absence. Juba Aman Dana, the Leopard, ruler of the Union of Black Africa, condemned the conference as a charade and declared that his country would not beg for food while a prosperous, well-fed nation like South Africa flaunted its racial policies. A huge parade of military hardware in Lagos was broadcast worldwide. Holovision screens showed the African ruler watching it from his palace balcony. He was tall and straight as an assagai, and wrapped in a royal leopard skin. Young, visibly muscular, Dana was easily the most virile-looking world leader. He made pointed reference to this by traveling with a harem of 600 women of every race and nation, most of them there by choice.

"That young man is going to be a lot of trouble," observed President Shefferton that evening as he watched the news in his study. He had eaten tacos and frijoles for dinner and was now paying for it by nursing a glass of soda water.

"Trouble?" said Mayfield. "For whom?"

"Most anybody. That military machine he's been building accounts for half of his budget. He won't let it sit on its hands. It's fatal for a dictator to have a strong army with nothing to do. The idle officers start self-improvement projects, like installing themselves in his place. No, he'll use that army, all right, and pretty soon!"

"I was readin' Lambert Healey's column in the *Post* this mornin'," rumbled Senator Macadew, who had helped himself to a generous supply of the president's whiskey. "He points out that the cycle of world wars has run about one every fifty years since the Thirty Years War. He thinks we might be overdue for one."

"What the hell does he call that mess in Europe and Asia, if not a world war?" said Shefferton irritably. "It's only been a few years—"

"Yeh, but the world balance o' power was jarred out of kilter. We may get a war sooner than normal, like when World War Two followed on the heels of World War One because things were left so unbalanced—"

"This geopolitical theorizing doesn't take into account one thing," said Mayfield. "The last time the Africans tried to take on South Africa they got a bloody nose."

"Yeh, but that was over twenty years ago and they weren't hardly more than a loose-knit confederation. Naturally they got tanned by South Africa's crack troops. They were a rabble fightin' a real army in its home territory. But the Leopard's made his army into a first-rate bunch of hell-raisers. He's united his country, given it drive and purpose. That's the imbalance of power Lambert Healey was talkin' about, the sudden rise of Black Africa. It was tribes and petty nations before; now it's an empire, and it adores Dana. Fella's a durned African Napoleon, Bismarck, and Alexander rolled into one!"

"You admire the guy, don't you, Charley?" said Shefferton.

"Hell no! Just givin' the Devil his due. I'm scared to death of him! You're right, he's just waitin' for the chance to jump somebody. And I wouldn't want to be in South Africa's shoes if he picks them. They got a fine army, but numbers have got to count for something, and Dana's got 'em outnumbered ten to one."

"Dana is big trouble," said the president thoughtfully. "I just hope he doesn't use the famine as an excuse to attack."

"What could we do about it? It's an African matter," said Mayfield.

"When I ran for president I tried to impress upon people that there are no purely local matters anymore. If Africa starts a continental bloodbath, we'll be drawn into it. That's why we can't let it happen, and if it does, we must try and stop it."

"That's a tall order," said Mayfield. "Our constitution still contains an amendment forbidding foreign intercourse except on the smallest scale."

"This conference is the first step to repealing the Thirty-first Amendment. Its success will demonstrate how shortsighted it is for the United States to remain Fortress America. As a nation we proved our point. We were fed up with the world. It was a crappy world all right. But we learned just how truly crappy the world could get without us. Everyone turned to Russia and Asia, and our influence waned. Only the war kept us from being permanently stamped as a tertiary power. Now we have the opportunity to reassert our leadership."

"All I can say, Jeff, is don't trust anybody," said Macadew softly. "Be mighty careful. You an' me and Sheridan might have learned our geopolitical lessons well, but a good half o' my colleagues in the Senate are so ignorant that if you ask 'em who Franklin Roosevelt was they'd tell you he's the guy in the wheelchair in that exhibit in Disney World. Hell, most of 'em think we lost World War Two to the Japanese and that the terms of surrender were that we had to buy all the televisions, cars, and sewin' machines they could turn out. They don't know from internationalism. They expect you to fall on your ass, and they're licking their chops. You may have won on a platform of internationalism, but you haven't proved it to the big power boys, and it could still ruin you."

"My personal ruination is the least of my concerns. Too many presidents have put getting reelected above doing right. If I'm to be a one-term president, so be it. Most presidents are one-termers anyway because they don't do what they want until their second term." He set his soda water on the table. "Well, I don't know about you gentlemen, but I have a busy day tomorrow. I'm going to bed early. See you at the conference."

Chapter

* 24 *

1

The first morning President Shefferton called the conference to order with a brief welcoming address. Reciprocating speeches took up the rest of the morning. The delegates reconvened after lunch well fed (perhaps ironically) and refreshed.

The media were excluded at the insistence of the Soviets. Only delegates were allowed in the conference room, a relic from the days when the United Nations had occupied the building. It had a capacity of 100 and was about half full. A circular table dominated it.

The goodwill that collected like dew that morning had evaporated by afternoon. The famine victims were locked in hot debate with the producer nations who were supposed to be helping them. The main antagonists were the Soviets and Greater Asians.

"I will tell the chairman of the Ruling Families the facts again," said

Premier Brasnikov, livid after two hours of pounding tables countered by acid comments from the Asians. "The Unified Soviet State has no excess grain to feed the hapless billions of Asia, who cannot see fit to stop up the wombs of their women."

Chairman Tua, an exceptionally tall and wrinkled man of indeterminate age, smiled indulgently.

"Russians are perhaps motivated by altruism not to further pollute the world's gene pool," he said in English so perfect that only its precision suggested it was not his mother tongue.

Brasnikov, uncertain of the words, waited for a translation before growing red-faced. "It is well known that during their good crop years the Ruling Families collected great silos of grain, enough to feed several hundred millions for months."

"True, Asian diligence produced more good years than the Unified Soviet State can boast of. But this surplus can only sustain a small percentage of our population until next year's harvest."

Brasnikov gave a careless wave of his aristocratic hand. "But we have *no* surplus. We can barely feed ourselves. We cannot give any away, or our people will starve."

"Soviet starvation is Asian abundance. Soviet bare sustenance is Asian luxury beyond the most opium-laden vision. We think it interesting that Russia conceals her shortages to impress the world with her 'excellent' agricultural programs. Yet now she bewails her misfortune when in fact she has a surplus. This is vile hypocrisy." He pointed a long fingernail. "You would starve us if you could."

"Nonsense."

President Shefferton intervened. "Gentlemen, accusations can accomplish nothing—except end this conference. I suggest that each nation here prepare a report telling either how much it needs to stave off disaster, or how much it can contribute."

Brasnikov muttered under his breath, then nodded. "Mr. President. I suggest we adjourn until tomorrow to prepare the reports."

"Time is vital. We could take up other matters in the meantime, such as the means of distributing the relief supplies."

"We must first know who is going to get the food before we can discuss its distribution."

"Very well, we'll adjourn until tomorrow afternoon."

"Please remember one thing as you write your report, premier," said Tua Kau Feng gently.

"And what is that?" Brasnikov raised his eyebrows.

"We in Greater Asia have ten million soldiers and fifty thousand tanks waiting to cross your borders should you try to starve us into oblivion."

"And we have one hundred million bullets and five hundred thousand antitank shells waiting to greet them." Brasnikov said, then turned and left the auditorium.

2

"I think you and I are beginning to be friends," said President Gernais to Jeffrey Shefferton, his guest for a buffet of French delicacies.

"I believe so, Mr. President." Shefferton took a bite of an exquisite gallic pastry and closed his eyes. "Magnificent!"

"I fear," said Gernais, as if making a terrible confession, "That in spite of being president of all Europe I am still loyal to my native cuisine." He left unsaid that France dominated the confederacy because the war had been unkind to the two Germanies, reducing them to about the same level of devastation and loss of population as at the end of the Thirty Years' War.

"I can't say I blame you," said Shefferton.

"As I said, I believe we are becoming friends, so I would consider it a singular honor to be able to address you by your first name, and would be flattered if you did the same."

"Francois!" Shefferton raised his glass.

"Jeffrey!" Gernais returned the salute. "And now to the subject of our meeting, although I confess that I expected it to take place aboard one of our warships. But a luxurious American hotel is eminently preferable to a tossing deck."

"I thought the subject of our meeting was friendship and good food!" said Shefferton with a laugh. "But we do have much to discuss. I am sorry we weren't able to meet before now. But events have moved rapidly since the return of Dr. Nye."

"Jeffrey, you are aware that Premier Brasnikov is not being frank with us. My intelligence sources tell me that the Russians had a particularly good harvest and that they expect an abundant one next fall. If so, they are attempting to play us for fools."

"We haven't seen their report yet, Francois."

"It might be wise to make our plans in advance." Gernais poured himself another glass of wine. "Brasnikov made it clear that Russia doesn't have enough to feed itself. His report will undoubtedly reflect this."

"What do you propose?"

"United Europe will be honest and aboveboard in this matter. Our reserves are not large, but we offer them freely, in exchange for American friendship."

"Our friendship does not come with strings attached."

"All things come with strings attached, my friend. Before our unification we depended on American troops for protection and endured economic domination and military subservience as the price. Then great upheavals gripped the world and your nation left us alone to face the tide. We chose to swim rather than resist the waters. We accommodated the Soviets until they too were forced to retreat. The time has come for no more strings. We are independent, although not as 'united' as our name implies. We want friends and allies, not masters. Is America prepared to be our friend?"

"What are you asking for? An economic alliance? A military alliance? A lowering of tariffs?"

"Friendship, and all that word implies. A friendship that runs two ways. To establish this friendship I suggest that we unite to nip Soviet treachery in the bud."

"How? The United States has no leverage over the Unified Soviet State. We don't trade with them."

"Ah, but we do. We sell them sophisticated electronic technology— not as good as yours, but better than what they can produce, although, as we all know, they are catching up fast. If we cut off trade they may fall farther behind you in space, the one area where they fear American competition.

"Naturally, if we threaten this we place ourselves in great jeopardy. The Russians are already subverting the Polish government, and it may fall soon. The Illyrian League has fallen to pieces. Russia could conceivably gain control of Constantinople. We have our own problems with a religious war in Italy and brushfires all over the continent caused by the Epiphanists and their many enemies. We are in no position to resist a strong Russian push into Eastern Europe. If war comes, Spain will secede. She has always been a loose piece of our federation. She is unhappy because we abolished Catholicism and because we haven't been able to negotiate the Israelis out of the Gibraltar naval base they bought from the English.

"But if America applies pressure on Russia in space, and Greater Asia threatens action, that, combined with our economic boycott, might force her to cooperate with the food distribution and pull back in Eastern Europe—at least for a while."

Shefferton sat quietly a long moment, his lips on the rim of his glass. Then he smiled. "I think it's in the interests of world peace for us to cooperate, Francois. I accept your offer gladly."

Thus began a conversation that lasted well into the night.

3

"This is blackmail!" said Brasnikov furiously.

"You're absolutely correct," said Shefferton.

"Are the Asians party to this brigandage?"

"No, but if we put it to them I think they'll be happy to join in."

"It's not really that bad, Premier," said Gernais with false sympathy. "You are selling at fair market prices."

"I laugh at your fair market prices. Ha! No money will exchange hands, only worthless Asian credit."

"About as hard to collect as Russian credit," said Gernais.

Brasnikov turned on him with a snarl. "Why this treachery? Why are you siding with the imperialists?"

"The old slogans don't work anymore, Premier. We know you too well, and we know where our interests lie."

"Mr. Premier," said Shefferton. "The question requires a simple yes or no. Will you admit the grain surpluses we know you have, and join us to prevent world famine, or will you continue to lie? If the latter, then the sanctions will be carried out. You will be denied all trade from Europe. You will be denied use of American facilities in space. We will blockade your space bases. And we will make our information public, particularly to the Ruling Families."

"You come very near to bringing war, Mr. President," growled Brasnikov.

"Between the Unified Soviet State and the world. That's what it would boil down to, Mr. Premier."

"It's blackmail, blackmail!"

"I never claimed otherwise. Now, I'm sure we'd all like to settle this before we return to the auditorium. Will you answer, yes or no?"

Peter Brasnikov almost choked. "Yes."

4

Lights flashed and holovision cameras whirred as the president stepped up to the rostrum.

"I have no announcements this morning. This is an informational news conference about the Food Treaty. So we'll proceed directly to questions. Yes, you sir?" He pointed to the first man to raise his hand.

"Abernathy of the L.A. *Times*. Mr. President, is that what you're officially calling it, the Food Treaty?"

"Yes, I believe that's to the point. Yes?"

"Craig Jones of NBC. Do you anticipate opposition in the Senate to the treaty, Mr. President. If so, from what quarters?"

"Mr. Jones, I have great respect for the Senate, so I take great pleasure in educating it and the American people about every facet of this treaty and its sister legislation dealing with the PH station. Perhaps I'm not answering your question the way you would like, so let me say I don't expect much opposition. I won't be presumptuous enough to guess who will support the treaty and who will oppose it." He pointed to the back of the room. "Yes sir?"

"James Burbank, Miami *Herald*. Rumor has it that the Soviets didn't want to sign the document. Were they reluctant to do so?"

"If you read your history books, Mr. Burbank, you'll find that the Russians have always been tough bargainers. You can rest assured that they wouldn't have signed the treaty unless they felt it was in their best interests. I suggest you address any follow-ups on that to Mr. Brasnikov."

"Is it also in their best interests to distribute food to Greater Asia, their enemy of many years?"

"All relief supplies will be turned over to an independent international distribution commission. Individual nations will not have a hand in that."

"Haley of the Seattle *Sun*, Mr. President."

"Mr. Haley."

"Sir, paragraph sixteen of the document says that relief will continue until the crisis ends. Does that mean the United States will continue to contribute food if crops fail next year or the year after?"

"Yes. Without such a provision it would be analogous to a fireman arriving at a fire, but under the stipulation that he fight it for only thirty minutes. We must be prepared to continue aid if there are unforeseen circumstances."

"What if we run out of grain surpluses?"

"I don't foresee that happening, Mr. Haley, Yes ma'am?"

"Janet Grantham, Atlanta *Constitution*. Mr. President, when do you expect the PH station to become operational?"

"Two years, give or take six months. We won't know for sure until we choose the contractor."

"Have you chosen a project head?"

"That comes under the jurisdiction of the Department of Space Exploration and Development. I'm leaving that choice to Mr. Mayfield, although I expect that whatever company we pick to build the station may have some say in who heads the project."

"Eric Gold, Sacramento *Bee*."

"Ah, Mr. Gold, I noticed your column gracing my parrot's cage this morning. Not intentional, I assure you."

"I'm flattered, sir. Could you give us a hint which company might get the contract?"

"Mr. Mayfield and I have some ideas, but we'll keep them to ourselves for now. You're welcome to ask him, of course, and see if you have any better luck."

A good deal of laughter accompanied this sally. Sheridan Mayfield had the worst public relations reputation of any federal official in Washington.

"You sir, in the front row."

"I'm Jeremy Crest, the Kansas City *Star*. Mr. President, both the Grover and Hastings polls show you with an approval rating of seventy-five percent last week. What, if anything, do you attribute your sudden popularity to?"

"You're giving me an almost irresistible opportunity to be coy, but I'll resist. I believe the poll shows that the American people support my efforts to end our long period of isolation. I believe they support the concept of a powerful, responsible America that bears its share of the burden in the struggle against darkness, tyranny, and starvation. Not only an America that stands against evil, but one that stands for progress, enlightenment, and political freedom all over the world. Lest anyone claim that I support a global welfare program, I do not. I do think America should use its great power to encourage other nations to discover within themselves the great things we have found in ourselves: industriousness, compassion, a love of knowledge for its own sake, and a desire that all men have the opportunity to fulfill their goals as individuals, not as servants of all-powerful states. I think you'll find, Mr. Crest, that our nation was at its moral pinnacle when we believed we were tending the light of freedom that would one day spread over the globe. The world has never needed that little light more than it does today. I believe the people know that, and that is why they support me. I'm sorry, I didn't plan to give a speech, but I have decided to make an announcement now instead of next week. After the Senate makes its decision about the food treaty, I shall ask Congress to repeal the Thirty-First Amendment."

"Newton Shaker, *Washington Post*. Sir, does that mean you'll campaign for its repeal?"

"I'll do what I can within the limits of my office to ensure its repeal. This is, I believe, the most important foreign policy decision of our time, and long overdue. I think the people will agree with me. Thanks for your attention, ladies and gentlemen."

"Thank you, Mr. President."

Chapter

* 25 *

1

The FBI director's office air was so hermetically clean and dust-free that it was the only place Roger Ferdinand ever visited where he didn't immediately brush off his clothes upon exiting.

It was furnished in high anachronism, an increasingly popular style with the great moneyed classes, whom Director Houston Pollux took great pains to cultivate. High anachronism was typified by decorative objects that had once been useful, but now had no earthly use, like fountain pens, television sets, hard-bound books, typewriters, swords and armor, cash registers, and the like.

When Ferdinand entered with a flourish of the imperial purple cape he wore over his white worsted wool suit, he noted the obvious bugs. Two, of course, were his. One of these Pollux knew about, the other was probably still a secret. Of course the FBI director had Ferdinand's office bugged too. It went without saying that Pollux's office was also bugged by the CIA, DIA, NSA, and Secret Service, and possibly by some foreign agencies too.

Pollux, at his desk, signaled to communicate in code. Ferdinand wasn't surprised. Upper echelon FBI officials used a code of guttural noises, hand gestures, and body movements that had been developed in a POW camp. The bureau's code master, formerly of His Holiness's Secret Service, was developing a variation of the famous Sistine Chapel code used so successfully by papal guerrillas in Italy. Other agencies had their own codes, of course. The CIA used a Wall Street investment code from shortly before the Great Depression; the DIA used a pygmy hunting language; the NSA was experimenting with telepathy.

Ferdinand sensed the director's unease. Pollux was not the best FBI director in history, nor the worst, but he was an Allen administration holdover. That made his position uncertain. His name was at the bottom of Shefferton's list of heads to chop, but the president had reason to dislike the FBI, so sooner or later he would probably reach the bottom. Ferdinand, the ultimate survivor, hadn't made up his mind yet whether Pollux would survive. When he did, he would either help the director, or else join the other sharks in the water in rending him to pieces.

Pollux's message was short and bitter. The president had ordered a funding cut. Naturally the knife would fall on field agents, not administrators, so some investigations would be cut off at the knees.

He told Ferdinand to wrap up the Nye investigation, which was moot anyway. What annoyed Ferdinand was that Pollux lumped that investigation with those of the deaths of Dr. Xerxes and Karl Chapin.

When Ferdinand reached his office, he took out his diary, and gold pen and made a furious entry:

"Pollux 'welcomed' me back to the bureau with open arms. Does he suspect me of 'going native' when I worked for Mayfield? In his place I would. He told me to kill my current investigations. I pointed out that if my interest in Hunning led to solving Adam Scott's murder and the deaths of people connected with it, it could get us on good terms with Shefferton. A graph of the deaths associated with Scott shows that the bell curve reached its zenith this year. I think the attempted assassination of Nye was an isolated event of Lloyd Hunning's diseased mind. The only connection was Hunning. Perhaps whoever is behind the other murders arranged Hunning's escape; even programed him to commit an act that got him killed. Pollux said if I could convince the stockman program that this is somehow related to our investigation of the Bengal spy ring I could keep on it. He's covering his ass. If I'm ever caught by the stockman program he'll deny knowledge. Unimaginative fool. If he doesn't see the opportunity for advancement, I do."

Ferdinand smiled grimly. For the rest of the day and part of the night he worked at his terminal. The stockman program was maddeningly persistent but he knew ways around it. For instance, he was able to maintain his spy near Mel Hardrim by paying him from funds used to investigate internal corruption in the D.C. police force. When he finished he had covered his trail—for a while. That left Pollux. Yes, he would definitely have to think of a way to neutralize Pollux.

Meantime he marshaled his limited resources to try to second-guess his Drang assassin. The computer still listed over forty possible victims: those high enough in Scott's organization or the TEA to have knowledge that made them dangerous to someone.

He assigned agents to the most likely victims, and enlisted local law enforcement to help him with the rest. Even so, if he caught his fish, it was going to be with a net that had quite a few holes in it.

What he needed was for luck to break his way.

2

Henry "Hank" DesCopia was a cowboy, but John Wayne wouldn't have recognized him.

DesCopia didn't wear a crushed Stetson. He didn't roll his own, or even smoke. He didn't drawl, or squint, or carry six-guns to blow away rattlers. Fish and Game would have given him hell for that, so when he ran across one he zapped the slithery bastard with a taser.

He did drink a lot of tequila from a silver flask kept on the seat of his chopper. Under her whirling blades he rode herd on three thousand head of cattle of the Imperious Ranch, about twenty miles out of San Antonio.

The helicopter's equipment monitored every member of the herd, each one "branded" with a homing device when it was born. The immense ranch was crisscrossed with sensory devices that could read heat, hear, and otherwise sniff out coyotes, including the two-legged variety.

So foolproof was the system that when Hank DesCopia was out on the range he felt totally confident that he was alone and that no one could sneak up on him.

But he'd never broken himself of imagining that someone was trying. The job was a good one. It reminded him slightly of the work he'd done for Adam Scott as his chauffeur and man Friday. At least he was able to work in a chopper. But he never could rid himself of those feelings of being pursued.

He poured some tequila on his quivering guts and managed to anesthetize them for a while.

He climbed out of the teardrop, crushing Texas scrub under his anaconda-skin boots, his one concession to the cowboy mythos. The Milky Way whirled above him. On the horizon was the foggy white of San Antonio. Clustered shapes of cattle a few dozen yards off shifted nervously. Strange—they knew him and accepted him as part of life. He had turned to check the monitors when a hand clamped over his mouth and an icy cold stabbed under his sternum.

He fell to the ground. The Milky Way whirled faster and faster until it was a pinwheel. Then the white whirlpool swallowed him up.

The man who had been known as Fain to Karl Chapin stepped over the body and wiped his stiletto clean with a white handkerchief.

He stretched and flexed his arms. It was quite a ride under the helicopter's fuselage from San Antonio airport. But it was the only way to get a moment alone with Hank DesCopia. He knew that at this moment he was being filmed by any number of spying eyes hidden in the scrub. That was why he wore a black hood.

He took out his camera and the flash burned several times as he photographed DesCopia. Then he climbed into the teardrop and roared off into the Texas night.

3

The helicopters rode on legs of light as they passed slowly back and forth over the knot of Texas Rangers and other homicide investigators who were stamping around in the night.

Roger Ferdinand watched and gloated. Luck had finally turned his way. The murder victim, one Hank DesCopia, had been five minutes away from a scheduled call-in when he died. Since he was on the list of possible victims, his failure to call sparked an immediate investigation. Fortuitously, Ferdinand was in Dallas, cleaning up after an incompetent former local administrator, when he got the call. They were on the scene within the hour of death, although not soon enough to catch the helicopter, which was found abandoned a few miles outside Odessa. The killer could easily lose himself in that uninhabited wilderness of derelict oil rigs.

"Mistuh Ferdinand!" The ranger captain made a wide run around the glowing blue inertia field that preserved DesCopia's body exactly as it had been discovered. The light attracted myriad insects, who, when they ventured into the field, plunged to earth, captives of a single moment in time.

The ranger captain clutched the recording from the nearest infrared sensor. "That's an affirmative on this, Inspectah. We ran it and it definitely shows a figure."

"Excellent, Captain. Let's go have a look at it."

Four men carefully loaded the inertia field and the body inside it into a police hovercar. Nobody would chance an inertia field in the air. If it came loose it could touch an engine—which would mean nasty wreckage to clean up, for someone.

When the field moved, a thick cloud of insects, suddenly free, rose into the night sky like a thick fog.

4

The grainy, indistinct figure bent over the dead man and snapped flash pictures.

"Ah'll be gawdahmed!" snorted one of the rangers.

"Lookit that! Bassard moves like a cat or some kinda jungle animal."

"Drang training." said Roger Ferdinand smugly. The film showed the murderer sneak up on DesCopia, cup a hand over his mouth, and slip a blade under his breastbone. It was quite obvious that the killer was male and was aroused sexually by the act of killing. Ferdinand shifted uncomfortably in his chair while the rangers around him guffawed in awe.

The film didn't show much else, but it was Ferdinand's first unimpeachable data for his ever growing list. There was incontrovertible proof that the assassin was male, and his size and build were known. It was a start, thought Ferdinand, feeling a satisfied warmth circulate through his body.

Chapter

* 26 *

The road, six lanes wide, had been cut into the Himalayas by Soviet army engineers with a characteristic lack of subtlety or concern for the environment. In clear weather it gave a tremendous view of the roof of the world. But now, along the entire length of the convoy, it was socked in.

At the end of that highway, almost straddling the mountains, was the Institute for Magnetic Propulsion at Tingri Dzong. So near the border, security was heavy. Around the institute were stationed three tank divisions, a motor laser regiment, a motor rifle division, one rocket army, and an airborne assault brigade.

The road inclined a steady fifteen degrees, which meant low gears all the way. The fog made it even slower.

The driver of the lead truck, Sergeant Kirov, shared the cabin with an old major hitching a ride up to the installation. Like most of the best army sergeants, Kirov was a Tatar.

Kirov had been about to lead off the convoy when its commander, Captain Vaya, who was riding in one of the middle trucks, brought the old gentlemen to Kirov's truck.

"Sergeant, this officer will ride with you," said the captain brusquely. "His credentials are in order. That is all you need to know."

I'm to be a mushroom again, thought Kirov, kept in darkness and fed shit.

The major, immense and bearlike, with a ready smile, looked like a reserve officer. His visit to a high security area smelled like week-old fish. Kirov had driven a dozen loads on the long stretch of highway from district HQ at Alma Ata in the past two months. He had shivered under hard-eyed CosMarine officers who all looked as if they hoped for the chance to open you up with those big knives hanging from their belts. If the old officer's business wasn't official enough, it would probably be the last Kirov (or anybody else) would ever see of him.

He was a nice old gentlemen. He shared his bread and cheese and told amusing peasant tales. He contributed to the warmth in the truck, a significant item since the heater didn't work. He took his turn at driving. Most important, he shared his vodka.

They got as chummy as was possible in the stratified Unified Soviet Army, where fraternization was discouraged.

Kirov had his own ideas about the mysterious installation, all based on ignorance. He had never been farther inside than the gate. There his truck was always unloaded by CosMarines who made him stay inside the cab while they glared at him and waved their Kalashnikov assault rifles about.

He didn't share his speculations with the major. Pleasant as he was, it was always possible he was a K officer in disguise.

Huge garish warning signs, coupled with a gradual leveling of the highway, announced the installation miles before they actually arrived.

A semicircular tunnel entrance loomed in the mist and they were swallowed up into a black maw.

They emerged from the tunnel and ground to a halt in front of a guard station. The gate bristled with armed men in the natty red and black uniform of the elite CosMarine Division. Above them two MI-59 armored helicopters poised with spotlights probing the mist, deadly cannons at the ready.

A sneering young captain emerged from a comfortable, warm guard-house and strutted over to the truck. Kirov resigned himself to a long session of red tape. No doubt throwing their weight around was one of the few amusements allowed officers in this desolate place.

"Papers!" he snapped. Kirov had them ready. The captain read them, casting suspicious glances at the major. Kirov's stomach tightened. The major looked around, not paying attention to the CosMarine officer, just taking in the scenery.

"Your papers too, Major!" snarled the captain. CosMarines seemingly had nothing but contempt for any of the other services.

The major reached into his tunic and casually handed a clump of papers to the young officer. He opened the cab door and heaved himself out onto the road. He was immense, more polar bear than man.

He removed his massive overcoat and tossed it into the cab. Underneath was the uniform of a marshal of the Unified Soviet State.

The blood drained from the captain's face. He opened the packet of papers and ran his eyes over them. It was unnecessary. He had instantly recognized the massive figure: Antonine Tiomkin, commander-in-chief of the Strategic Spaceborne Forces.

Tiomkin looked over his shoulder. "Get the convoy moving again, Captain. I require transportation to headquarters. You may tell your commander that I am here." He turned to Sergeant Kirov. "It was a pleasant ride, Sergeant."

Kirov tucked his head down. "Thank you, sir!"

As intended, Marshal Tiomkin's arrival was a complete surprise. But by the time his car arrived and whisked him to the underground headquarters, the commandant Colonel General Wolff, had had time to turn out a CosMarine honor guard.

Most of the Institute for Magnetic Propulsion was underground, invisible from the air. A spy satellite would show only an ordinary military base for a division of mountain troops stationed along the frontier with India. That same satellite would note—indeed, U.S. satellites *had* noted—the immense volume of traffic along the highway that Red Army engineers had built two years before. But military traffic along a disputed border was commonplace. And disputed this border certainly was.

It must be admitted that the Himalayan Military District did not encompass all the Himalayas. Armistice lines followed the fortunes of the last war, bogging down at the high water mark of the last Soviet offensive, which, after crushing the Asian invasion, had pushed from Afghanistan to the Indus River. Airborne assault troops and marine infantry had pushed across the Karakorams, down the Indus into Tibet, while two tank armies wheeled north to cut off a half-moon slice of Sinkiang.

At the signing of the truce, which settled nothing except to stop the shooting, two Soviet armies straddled the Himalayas with the Brahmaputra River at their backs, gazing across the mountains at the Valley of the Ganges, while in the hereafter Czar Nicholas I probably raised a glass of vodka at the fulfillment of his ancient dream. They occupied much of Nepal, while on their left shoulder was Mount Everest and the Kingdom of Sikkim.

Half a mile under the living mountains was carved an unbelievably huge cavern, ten miles long and three miles wide, with a ceiling three hundred feet high. Such a task would have taken a decade without several excavation fission bombs.

The cavern was lit like day with hydrogen lamps. On the road that wound up a rise to the installation headquarters, Tiomkin could see the entire setup. Dominating its length was a wormlike structure a hundred feet high, built of bulging rings of a black glossy material: Collapsium, molecularly collapsed metal, incredibly dense, incredibly strong. At one end the black worm burrowed into the rock face of the cavern. At the other end sprouted large tracks on which squatted a torpedo shape, about as tall as the worm and three quarters of a mile in length. It was also made of Collapsium.

Six domed fusion power generators were spaced in a semicircle at the nearer end of the worm and connected to it by large pipes that, at that distance, looked almost like tendrils. Men and vehicles swarmed over the installation, making it look like a disturbed anthill.

Marshal Tiomkin had never seen the installation, although he helped plan it. His car stopped in front of the installation headquarters. The CosMarines presented arms. He returned their salute briskly and buried the outstretched hand of Colonel General Wolff inside his own.

"An unexpected pleasure, Your Excellency." Colonel General Erwin Wolff was small, pale, and sickly, yet straight and unyielding as a steel rod. He was in his early forties, the son of an East German army officer who had remained loyal to the Soviets during the Civil War and the European invasion that had taken East Germany from Russia. The father had chosen to live in Russia; so had Erwin, who had lost his left leg to a land mine. He still had traces of a German accent.

"No reflection on you, General," said Tiomkin amiably. "I sometimes like to inspect a base without informing the commander first, but this is an informal visit to prepare you for the arrival of someone much more important than I am."

"Premier Brasnikov?"

"Yes. Let's go inside."

In the colonel general's office they tossed off shot glasses of vodka. Tiomkin loosened his collar. Wolff, who sat ramrod straight behind his desk, didn't touch his.

"General, how soon can you launch your first payload?"

"Sir, in my report—"

"I've read the report. How soon can you launch if you are ordered to do it immediately?"

"Immediately?"

"Virtually. In three to four weeks' time."

"We must test the inert payload first, sir, before we commit the X vehicle."

"That timetable has changed. It is necessary to launch as soon as possible, without a test. The premier has decided, and I agree whole-heartedly, that the moral effect of launching the X vehicle into space without warning will be stunning."

Wolff's pencil-thin pale lips pressed together; his left eye, blind from a piece of shrapnel, became a slit. His good eye, an icy blue, showed no emotion. He took a long, thin cigarette from a silver holder in his blouse.

"It's stuffy in here, comrade. Why don't we take a stroll outside?" suggested Marshal Tiomkin.

"Outside" was several hundred feet below the actual outside. But it was likely to be free of bugs, unlike the colonel general's office. As their boots crunched on the lifeless red dirt, Wolff regarded Tiomkin intently.

"Speak your thoughts, comrade." Tiomkin gazed at the immense Collapsium torpedo resting on its tracks and smiled faintly.

"It will take many days to remove the test vehicle and put the X vehicle in its place."

"And what else?"

"You agree with this decision?"

"I agree that the moral effect will be tremendous."

"We haven't tested the Collapsium shield under actual conditions before. The X vehicle cost as much to build as—"

"As an aircraft carrier. It is a risk. But the first secretary is fond of risks."

"And you, sir?" Wolff was treading on dangerous ground, and he knew it.

"I do what you do, my friend—what I'm ordered."

"This could destroy the entire program, Your Excellency. I protest strenuously. I must have this order in writing. You are eliminating an entire series of tests just to achieve a propaganda victory. Will you let me speak to Premier Brasnikov?"

Tiomkin frowned darkly. "Colonel General, I admire your dedication. I will give you the order in writing if that is your request. I will not take your objections to the premier. He has made up his mind. It would only hurt your career. I order you not to bring up the subject when he arrives. Clear?"

"Like glass."

Tiomkin softened his expression. He had a creed for dealing with subordinates: Never promise anything, never threaten, and respect your men. He decided the last was the most important in this instance. "My friend, be charitable in your judgment of me. Remember, I was the force behind this project. My devotion to the railgun brought my throat close to the knife several times when the old premier was in his cups." He never referred to the dead Kurtzov as anything but "the old premier."

Wolff looked contrite, an unusual expression on such a Prussian countenance. "My gravest apologies, sir. I am a fool to criticize you. I hold you in the highest regard. We all do."

The "we" he referred to was a select group of young Red Army officers who had fallen under Tiomkin's influence through a series of lectures he gave as commandant at the Frunze military academy and later at the general staff academy on the strategic value of space. Tiomkin's rise to the Politburo had its origins in a book of his lectures: *The New Strategicon: Our Military Future in the Cosmos*. Kurtzov had read it and promoted Tiomkin over the heads of senior officers to be the top-ranking officer in the planning of Russia's comeback in space. He had developed the plan to end the monopoly of American power on the moon and in space.

"Is there nothing we can do?"

"Any suggestions that don't involve treason I would be happy to hear," said Tiomkin mildly. He laid a bearlike paw on Wolff's narrow back. "Be patient, comrade. Brasnikov is young and headstrong. He needs a propaganda victory to bolster his power base. He is intimidated by the memory of the old premier—"

"Intimidated? After he throttled him to death?"

"Don't believe everything you hear. Yes, our young premier is intimidated by the old, and by our American friends. He feels constricted when he thinks that Soviet spaceships travel the void between planets at the sufferance of the U.S. lunar fleet." Tiomkin's open palm slapped loudly against his own chest. "I intend that Soviet ships will never again have to ask anyone's permission to travel in the cosmos."

"What happens if the X vehicle burns up because of a premature test?"

"You and I will probably take our ease commanding small garrisons in Mongolia," Tiomkin chuckled. He took out a list on a crumpled piece of paper.

"You'll need accommodations for the first secretary and these officers. You know General Chin, commander of the Himalaya Military District. Colonel Orlov is my aide, but he has just been appointed to command the CosMarine Division on my recommendation. He will jump two grades."

"Chin and Orlov, the two brightest stars in your firmament, Comrade Marshal." Then Wolff sneered. "I hope Chin rots in hell!"

"Wolff, you make trouble for yourself. Is it not enough that you belong to a hated race? Must you also despise your superiors and criticize your premier? You do not demonstrate superior genetics." His smile was ironic.

"I will be happy to see Pavel Orlov, though. How is he?"

"Ambitious. Like you. Like Chin. Like the others."

"Not like Chin. No one is like Chin. He would make soup out of his grandmother." His good eye fixed on the older man. "Worse, he would make soup out of *you*."

"I am ever mindful of Chin, Comrade, never fear. Particularly since the premier placed him at my back."

"Your back?"

"I've been made minister of defense. Chin will be my deputy. It's not a position I relish. I prefer to directly control the spaceborne forces. But I have no choice right now. The young premier admires me greatly. He has said so."

"If he admires you, persuade him to cancel this asinine test until we're ready!"

"I said he admires me. I didn't say he takes my advice."

"This is a small list. No members of the Politburo?"

"The premier sees that while there is a chance to score a propaganda victory, there could also be a failure. He prefers not to advertise those.

Am I correct in supposing that if the X vehicle doesn't clear the atmosphere it will burn up?"

"It is probable."

"Good. Then we won't have to proclaim our defeat to the world, if it comes to that."

PART

* 5 *

DREAMERS
OF
THE DAY . . .

Chapter
* 27 *

Wherein in time past ye walked according to the course of this world, according to the prince of the power of the air, the spirit that now worketh in the children of disobedience.

—*Ephesians 2:2*

1

Secretary Mayfield was unhappy. It was, he had decided, a definite disadvantage to be one of the president's best friends. Besides running the Department of Space Exploration and Development he also oversaw the food distribution program at its American end. He particularly hated testifying before various committees for supportive legislation for the PH station.

Mayfield rested his head in his hands and stared at his model of the solar system. What he really hated to admit was that, in a masochistic sort of way, he was enjoying himself.

His holocube buzzed imperiously.

"Yes Ruth."

"Sir, I have that list of companies that bid on the PH station project."

"Fax them up for me, would you? You know how I dislike reading things from the boobcube."

She appeared in the flesh and gave him two plastic sheets.

He ran his eyes over the list. An impressive array of prestigious engineering firms. But only one, Python, had ever built a zero-gravity facility. The others had built structures on the moon or Mars, and bases to resist the corrosive atmosphere of the Jovian moons, and some undersea bases. But only Python, owned by billionaire Horatius Krebs, had experience, earned from constructing Midway, the unimaginatively named space station orbiting between the earth and the moon. The other qualified outer space construction companies didn't seem interested.

Mayfield hated having one choice. Why weren't the others interested in the most challenging space engineering project of recent years? He decided to find out.

Several phone calls later he succeeded in reaching Alban Tupper, whose Minerva Enterprises had built L-5.

Tupper wasn't happy to see him. His image looked down at Mayfield uneasily.

"Hello, Mayfield. What do you want?"

"I'm overwhelmed by your greeting."

"Skip the pyrotechnics and get to the point."

Mayfield choked down a stinging reply. "I called to ask why you didn't bid on the PH station? It's right up your alley."

"We're contracted to the hilt," said Tupper with a weasellike smile. "We're building several undersea domes in the Atlantic Trench. We're partners with Rockwell on the extension work at Tycho Base. We're quite booked up—"

"I'd think with the way you were burned on the Challenger tap, you would have set your sights higher than the Atlantic Trench." Mayfield couldn't resist throwing the barb at the smug face.

"How amusing. Now, if you'll excuse me—"

"Would you explain something very puzzling to me, Alban?"

"I'm very busy—"

"Cut the crap! Believe me, your business is your business, but why will no qualified company except Python work for us?"

Tupper's expression softened. "Leave it alone. Let Krebs have his way. He'll do a good job, and everyone will be happy."

"That's not my way, Alban. I'm getting middle-aged and set in my ways, so I'm going to find out what the devil is going on!"

"We're all just letting Krebs have his way, that's all."

"We?"

"All of us. The space engineering firms. Krebs let it be known that he wanted the job, so we all backed off."

"This is insane!"

"It's called power. Horatius Krebs is very powerful and used to having his way. He doesn't ask favors often, but when he does, it's wise to grant them. It's bad to be on his bad side."

"I've heard that said about you, Alban."

"We all have those we fear. I don't want his kind of trouble. None of us do. It's that simple."

"It's criminal."

"You'll never catch Krebs doing anything demonstrably criminal, any more than you'll catch me. He doesn't have to."

"What do you mean?"

"I've already talked too much. Good-bye, Sheridan."

"Goddammit!" Mayfield exploded. He looked around for something to break when his holocube buzzed again.

"What?"

"There's a young man outside with an engraved invitation to deliver to you, sir."

"I don't have time to waste on that nonsense."

"It's from Horatius Krebs."

"What the—? Bring it in, I'm curious." Nobody sent invitations anymore, engraved or otherwise. What for, when you could flash into a home by holocube and deliver a personal invite?

The invitation came in a crimson-bordered royal blue envelope with the Python seal in the upper left-hand corner, and smelled faintly of wintergreen. It was printed in raised Spencerian script on silk paper. It said:

The Honorable Sheridan J. Mayfield is invited to a most
unusual party beginning at midnight July 3 aboard
the Flying Ballroom on the airship *Olympic* to celebrate our
nation's birthday. The event will last 24 hours.

RSVP

Mr. Horatius Krebs

Mayfield reread it several times. He looked at Ruth.

"I'm impressed."

"Sir, the young man outside is waiting for your answer."

"My answer to what?"

"If you'll attend. He'll return to his employer with your reply."

Mayfield grinned. "Much as I'm tempted to dislike Mr. Krebs, he does have style. Panache seems the exclusive property of scoundrels these days. Yes, I'll go. Oh, be sure to slip that young man something, a five milligram perhaps. I'm not without style myself!"

"A ten might be better."

"To hell with that much style!"

He went back to work, and reviewed many documents before Ruth buzzed him to say good night.

"I'm going to escape this rat's nest myself soon," he said. "There is, uh, one more thing."

"Yes sir?"

"Did you think that invitation sounded interesting?"

"Oh yes! I've heard of Krebs's airship. It's a giant helium zeppelin ballroom floating a mile in the air. It's simply marvelous! I envy you."

"Come along, then."

"Do you really mean it?"

"Yes I do. I may need you to take notes."

She laughed. "You won't be dictating aboard that marvelous airship, will you?"

"I'm not going for fun. I have serious things to say to Mr. Krebs. But I must admit I'm intrigued by the idea of a party aboard an airship. You will go, then?"

"Try and stop me!" She blew him a kiss and terminated the picture. Through the door he heard her whistling. Then the outer door open and shut.

He sat at his desk, wondering what ailment had so afflicted him that he hadn't noticed before how remarkably pretty Ruth was.

2

The aircar rode two thousand feet above the white Alaskan wilderness. Below, a glacier crawled like an endless serpent, looping between the mountains, grinding to the sea.

Mayfield and Ruth boarded Krebs's private jet in Washington. They disembarked at Anchorage Airport, where an aircar waited to whisk them to Krebs's floating ballroom, the airship *Olympic*.

It was near midnight and the moon poured its whiteness onto the panorama of small lakes and colonies of trees stabbing the sky, moving below like a child's play kingdom. It was hard to believe that Alaska was the Union's most populous state, although easy to believe that it was the richest.

In the distance a silver salami shape lazed above the ice, outlined against a domineering mountain range, a promontory of savage peaks leading the eye like a magnet to the central peak—Mount McKinley. Could there be a more magnificent setting for a Fourth of July celebration?

The zeppelin grew until it blotted out the mountains. Its silver skin, latticed with delicate lines, caught the moonlight and magicked it into a coronet to adorn itself. A gondola the size of a yacht bulged from the airship's belly.

The aircar crept toward the opening in the bottom of the gondola. From a distance it looked like a tiny spacecraft landing on a silver planetoid.

They were engulfed by the landing bay and blinded to tears by bright lights. A uniformed attendant opened the hatch.

"Mr. Krebs is waiting to greet you, sir."

"Uh, thank you." Mayfield was unsure whether to tip him. He decided against it. He took Ruth's arm, admiring her new elegance: a pink chiffon dress, and her hair coifed into a swirling blond maelstrom. His own attire was typical Mayfield, conservative and unimaginative. He slipped a finger under the black bow tie and tugged at the collar as they climbed the stairs.

Horatius Krebs was one of those uncommon men who convey size and great strength without being either very big or very strong. His face was round and pink, his nose a strawberry. Flinty chips formed his eyeballs. His arctic stormcloud brows poised, ready to descend in anger at the slightest denial of a whim. Curly gray hair twisted around his shiny skull like a Roman victory wreath. He watched guests cavort in his ballroom as a condor might survey the sky from its high nest.

"Sheridan Mayfield, I've waited a long time to meet you." As they shook hands, Mayfield noticed that Krebs's were as rough as sandpaper.

"I find that hard to believe."

"It's true. We'll find time to talk later. We do have twenty-four hours. But now I'd like you to mingle and enjoy my hospitality. Drink?"

"Milk, if you have it." Mayfield turned to Ruth. "You like rum and cola, right?" She nodded.

Krebs snapped his fingers. A waiter appeared with a tray of drinks, including a glass of milk. "Never let it be said that I am not the perfect host." Krebs smiled. "You're surprised I know your preference. I confess I've done some research on you."

"I'm not sure I like that." Mayfield frowned. He noticed a man a few feet away who seemed to be following the conversation intently. He was out of place, like a bobcat in a herd of sheep.

"I could apologize for invading your privacy," said Krebs, "But you would know it for hypocrisy. Besides, I don't like to apologize—for anything."

"By all means don't." Mayfield returned his gaze steadily.

Krebs patted him on the shoulder. "We'll talk later."

"I'll count on it."

Krebs moved away and the man who had been observing them followed. He moved with animallike grace, never straying far from Krebs's side.

"What on earth was that about?" said Ruth.

"A testing of the blades, my dear."

"You called me 'dear.' "

"Did I? I'm sorry, I didn't mean to be familiar."

"I'm not sorry."

In the center of the ballroom was a large blue circular area. As the orchestra played it pulsated, and the people standing on it found themselves floating a foot in the air. Several couples familiar with the effect twisted and writhed in ways impossible in a gravity field. Soon virtually everyone was moving in wild abandon to the throbbing beat.

"Looks divine!" breathed Ruth.

"Krebs must have money to throw away. It takes tremendous energy to power a Michlanski antigravity field." He absent-mindedly caressed Ruth's back. "Why don't you find somebody who wants to do that while I check out the rest of this party?"

"Yes sir."

Mayfield wandered about like flotsam in a strong current. He recognized many government employees, celebrities, holo actors, writers, and millionaires.

One man seemed as alien and rudderless as Mayfield. He looked in his mid-thirties. He had red hair cut by a band of white. He returned Mayfield's look calmly, and slowly maneuvered through the surging bodies to his side.

"Hello, my name is Jason Scott."

"Pleased to meet you, I'm Sheridan Mayfield."

"I recognize you from your picture."

"Oh, are you one of the people Krebs assigned to find out everything about me?"

Scott threw back his head and laughed.

"I don't think it's amusing."

"I'm sorry, Mr. Mayfield. I'm laughing at Krebs. He never ceases to amaze me. He always maps his territory out before launching an attack. I hope you're prepared to withstand a siege."

"I take it you don't work for Krebs."

"No, I don't."

"Your view of him is unique. I don't know anyone who knows him who isn't afraid of him. You seem contemptuous."

"You misread me, Secretary Mayfield. I am amused by him. He is dangerous: powerful, crafty, immoral, ruthless, vengeful. Name a bad quality and he possesses it. I respect his ability to win and bend others. But I don't fear him, any more than I fear a mountain lion or cobra, even though I approach them with caution. The only difference is that they don't yet build zoos for the Horatius Krebses of our time."

"Now that's an appealing notion!" Mayfield glanced at Krebs, who was laughing with a charming young woman.

"Do you have a grudge against him?"

"I object to his business practices."

"So do I."

A voice called across the room. Mayfield turned to see a man plowing through the guests. He arrived and looked at Scott with a hybrid of a sneer and a grin.

"Jason, how pleasant to run into you."

"Is it, Jacob?"

"Oh yes. Very! Especially when I think of the irritation your presence will cause Horatius. Does he know you're here?"

"Maybe he invited me."

"The thought is too ridiculous to entertain," said Jacob Kane with a raspy laugh.

"Secretary Mayfield, let me introduce Jacob Kane, Horatius Krebs's right hand."

"I dislike being introduced as someone's this or that. Being Jacob Kane is distinction enough for me, thank you." Kane's immaculate scarlet evening jacket contrasted sharply with his thin, hungry-looking face and jet black hair.

"Then it's simply Jacob Kane. And much improved by the dissociation from your boss," said Mayfield.

"Ah, another admirer. Perhaps you were led to believe this was his wake tonight?"

"Hope springs eternal."

Kane laughed. "I've looked forward to meeting you. We were in the same room before, at Sherlock Michlanski's speech at the physicists' convention. I saw you but you didn't see me."

"I recall the speech vividly, but most of the people are a blur. I have heard of you. Aren't you the engineer who humiliated Alan Randall in front of several hundred people after he attacked Michlanski's speech?"

"Yes, I take credit for making a fool out of one of the great educated asses of our time."

"Good for you."

Kane smirked at Scott. "Secretary Mayfield is a fine judge of character."

"He doesn't know you like I do."

"Secretary Mayfield," said Kane. "I look forward to working with you on the PH station. A fascinating challenge. A great scientific breakthrough, if successful."

Mayfield looked uncomfortable. "It's not certain that you will be working on the project, Mr. Kane."

Kane's eyebrows rose. "Really? Horatius indicated that the deal was virtually settled."

"We've signed nothing."

"That's only a formality."

"You don't know me, Mr. Kane. It is more than a formality. I don't like your employer or his methods."

"You don't have to. He's selling an excellent reputation, and my first-rate services. And they are first-rate, as anyone in the field can tell you."

"I don't doubt it. Too bad you work for such an unscrupulous man."

Kane laughed again. "I wouldn't give a wax farthing for his scruples. I work for him because I make the highest salary in the business and work on the most fascinating projects. He could have a harem of donkeys and burn little babies and I wouldn't care. I mind my own business."

"You would leave him if the price was right?"

"Of course. Do you think I'm loyal to that old tyrant? He doesn't expect it. Surely you've noticed Emil, who follows Krebs around like a dog?"

"You mean that creepy-looking character who has been bending silverware with one hand all evening?"

"Yes. He's a mercenary. He fought in Lao Tse's army in the Drang war. Drang training made him a killing machine. Then he betrayed Lao and joined the Greater Asians. Now it's too hot for him in Eurasia, so he serves Krebs. His code is that of the mercenary. I am an economic mercenary. I have no personal loyalty to Krebs. If someone makes a better offer, I'll snap it up."

Suddenly Krebs and his omnipresent thug Emil joined them.

"Remind me to raise your salary, Kane."

"My pleasure, Horatius," said Kane insolently. He offered a languid wave. "Excuse me for leaving, but I feel a 'night of the long knives' coming on."

Krebs followed Kane with his eyes, then turned and raked Scott with them.

"I don't remember inviting you to my party, Jason."

"You once told me I was welcome at any of your gatherings."

"That was a long time ago. You're taking advantage of my generous nature. But I won't make a fuss. It makes me look good to have the competition as my guest." He indicated Mayfield. "What foul lies have you been feeding Mr. Mayfield about me?"

"He has far too many good honest conceptions of you for me to pollute them with additions of mine."

Krebs's face darkened.

"Why don't you take a long walk?"

"It's dangerous outside. Cold and dark and a long way down."

"You'd be surprised how dangerous it is inside." He bit the words viciously.

"I'll oblige you, Horatius. I have plenty of time. It's a long party."

"Be careful, Jason. I wouldn't want you to fall off the observation deck." His look was of such distilled malevolence that Mayfield feared for Scott's life. When Scott left, Krebs favored Mayfield with a brilliant smile.

"Merely a personal grievance, Mr. Mayfield. Nothing to concern yourself with."

"You do have some interesting people here tonight."

"Yes. Could I persuade you to visit my office? We have business to discuss."

"Now, if you like."

"Good. Fol—" Krebs was suddenly thrown off balance as the floor tipped. Mayfield held onto a table. The floor righted itself.

The ballroom buzzed with surprised and frightened voices. No one was hurt, but the party atmosphere had been spoiled. Krebs reached under his lapel and talked into a microphone.

"Friends!" his voice was amplified. "There's nothing to be alarmed about. We ran into an updraft. Please return to your pleasures. Eat! Drink! Dance!" The crowd cheered lustily and almost immediately the noise level returned to normal. Krebs adjusted the microphone and spoke into it angrily.

"Captain Gains! Report to me at once!"

A moment later the captain appeared and began to apologize.

"Enough!" Krebs snarled. "Who was piloting the airship?"

"Mr. Roper, the second officer—"

"Fire him immediately. You will personally pilot the *Olympic* until the guests leave tomorrow night. When the cruise is over you will deduct half your salary. Clear?"

"Yes, Mr. Krebs." Gains glanced nervously at Emil. "Is that all?"

"Yes. Don't let it happen again, or it's your job."

The captain left, apparently relieved that the ordeal was over.

"You were hard on him, Mr. Krebs."

"I don't tolerate incompetence. That's why I'm successful, and why I should build your PH station."

"How can he remain at the wheel for twenty-four hours?"

"He is under the influence of the same insomnia rays playing over the ballroom."

Mayfield eyed the ceiling. "We're being bathed by radiation?"

"Harmless radiation. I'm not wearing lead clothing. Insomnia rays switch off that part of the brain that mandates sleep. It's the opposite of the Somnus ray. There are no ill effects if it is used less than thirty hours at a time. That way my guests can enjoy the party and Gains can work for twenty-four hours straight. Do you approve?"

"Not really."

"Of course I provide beds, equipped with every aid imaginable, for guests who wish privacy. If you and your lady friend feel the need, by all means feel free."

"No, thank you." Mayfield felt himself reddening.

Krebs shrugged. "Your choice. We were interrupted as we were going to my office. If you'll follow me—"

His office glowed with polished redwood and pine paneling. An intimate yellow light hung over a huge black desk that dominated the room. Krebs sat at the desk, leaving Mayfield a lower, less regal chair. Mayfield mentally saluted him.

"Secretary Mayfield, you know why I want to see you. I know no reason for us to hold hidden cards. I want to be frank with you about anything that disturbs you."

Mayfield folded his hands. "I'm glad you feel that way. Since we're displaying our cards, I'll tell you at the outset I'm prejudiced against you and your company. My prejudice is entirely emotional and based solely on my personal reactions to you. But I think I can make an objective decision."

Krebs laughed deep in his throat. He sat forward and put his palms squarely on the desk. "That's fine, because I think you're a stuffed shirt, an outdated prig, and a sanctimonious puritan. But that shouldn't prevent us from working together. Drink?"

"Tea."

Krebs grinned and ordered the drink. The servant bringing it was let in by Emil, who stood outside like a stone gargoyle.

At the touch of a button a large holocube sank from the ceiling. The image of a space station appeared, floating in the black vacuum dusted with stars.

"Midway," said Krebs with pride. "The finest space station ever built. Python put her there. We created the plans and carried them out." The image enlarged and shifted to show different views. Krebs commented on each. The station faded to columns of figures. Krebs discussed them, their relationship to stress and heat factors, and an analysis showing that Midway had twice the theoretical life of any other station. "Midway has no equal. She's operated five years without a major complaint. We can do the same job with the PH station."

"Very impressive," said Mayfield "But if you're certain you can build it better than anyone, why edge out the competition?"

"Simple greed. I didn't want to meet someone else's low offer. I have one offer, which you can take or leave. So I suggested to my competitors that it would be wise to drop out this time, and they did."

"You don't like the concept of competition, do you?"

"I don't bother with ideologies. I'm in business to make money."

"What is your offer, which I can take or leave?"

"Five million ounces of gold."

Mayfield stood. "That's ridiculous, and you know it!"

Krebs was amused. "Do you reject it?"

"Yes!" said Mayfield furiously. He started for the door.

"Keep this in mind. Python is the only firm that can do the job. The others are second-raters. When you consider that, five million ounces is a bargain. Enjoy the rest of the party."

Mayfield slammed the door and walked past the impassive Emil with a cold feeling at the base of his spine. He breathed deeply and exhaled. The ballroom was dark except for an oscillating strobe. In the weird blue light twisted a snake of naked human bodies, dancing with abandon to the low, almost subliminal beat.

He went to the observation deck. The air was piercing but he reveled in its freshness, flushing his lungs with deep breaths. He rested on the railing.

A shape emerged from the shadows. Mayfield stepped back, his heart pounding.

The ashen moonlight fell on Jason Scott's face, mixing with the blue white glow of the mountains to make it appear like a porcelain lamp, glowing from within. His fiery hair tossed in the wind.

"I'm sorry I startled you, Mr. Mayfield. We both seem to need fresh air tonight."

"There's something about corrupt people that drains all the breathable oxygen from the air."

"Are you referring to the party?" Scott glanced at the snake dance.

"No! I don't give a damn about that. It's Krebs himself who makes me sick!"

"Do you intend to award him the contract?" Scott leaned on the rails and gazed at the mountain.

"He's got me in a corner, and he knows it. I'd rather cut my throat than give him the job, but the PH station must be built. That's more important than honor or honesty or my life. And it must be built right!" He balled his fists at his side. He looked at Scott. "Why are you so interested?"

"Professional interest. I'm in the same business."

"Wait a minute!" said Mayfield. "Now I recognize you! Adam Scott's son. You saved the Challenger core tap. Aren't you building the highway across the Andes?"

"Yes, I'm building the highway."

"Now that's a worthy undertaking! To carve a road through a wilderness once thought impassable."

"Ah, you understand the thrill, the challenge to human ingenuity. It's also a personal challenge, since I convinced the governments involved that it could be done." He looked out. "It's a great land, very much like that. Rugged and untamable."

"But you're taming it."

"To tame it would be to kill it. I'm trying to build a highway to enhance that beauty, the way the Golden Gate Bridge enhances San Francisco Bay." He was drawn back to the moonlit tableau. "That old mountain doesn't need enhancing."

"Mount McKinley is spectacular."

"Around here they call it Denali, the Great One. Even if we spread over every inch of the earth's surface, still we should leave places for the Great Ones to be alone."

"We'll kill ourselves off before then, or else spread to the stars." Mayfield watched an aurora undulate drunkenly.

"You feel that way too?"

"A few weeks ago I heard Professor Sherlock Michlanski compare humanity to an unborn baby, and call our existence here and in the solar system a prelude to a future among the stars. I believe him. Someday soon we will spread from this solar system."

"The president chose the right man to head the space program, Mr. Mayfield." Scott stood back from the railing and clasped his hands together as if to warm them. "I wish you luck finding someone to build your space station. As for me, I've more than outstayed my 'welcome' here." He smiled mischievously, then became serious. "Meeting you was the high point of the evening."

"Before you go—why does Krebs hate you?"

"He has many reasons. The main one is that I left him after working for him, and set up my own business. I learned from him, then became his rival. He doesn't like his servants to leave him. He prefers to cast them aside.

"Also, I am a living reproach to his way of living and thinking. I do projects because I want to, because they're worth doing, not for prestige or money. Not that I lack either, but they aren't the yardsticks of my existence. It rankles Krebs that I look on him with disdain instead of envy."

"Why does he care? I don't mean to insult you, but what is one man compared to his immense power?"

"The answer to that is . . . everything."

Mayfield looked away thoughtfully. When he looked back Scott was gone. He wandered into the ballroom, almost colliding with Kane.

"Are you all right?"

"Kane?"

"You look stunned, or frozen." Kane forced a glass into his hand. "Drink this."

Mayfield automatically swallowed. Hot alcoholic fumes made him gag.

"Forgot you don't drink," Kane said, frowning.

"I'm fine!" He shook him off.

"What were you doing out there? Much too cold for civilized people."

"Kane," said Mayfield with such intensity that Kane was taken aback. "Will you answer a question honestly?"

"Probably not."

"Who built Midway?"

"Python." Kane smiled easily.

"Who designed it? Whose brain was responsible? Who did the work?"

"That's three questions. With three answers."

"Not if it's the same man in each case."

"I'm going to hate myself tomorrow. You are right. Jason Scott is the man."

"Krebs hates him because he's the better man."

"I'm not Freud."

"You know it's true!"

Kane took a drink and looked uncomfortable. Then he gulped the drink down. "Actually, it's about time I back-stabbed Krebs."

"You can't fool me. You're not the self-centered bastard you pretend to be."

"Yes I am, Mr. Secretary. I may do you a good turn, but I'm helping myself. I know you want me to work on the project, but you don't want to give Krebs the contract. By steering you to Jason Scott, I assure myself employment." He looked self-satisfied, and surveyed the ballroom like a prowling cat. "Be seeing you. I've got things to do." He ambled off toward a very pretty woman in a clinging blue gown.

Mayfield smiled. It was going to be a pleasant evening after all.

Chapter

* 28 *

Marshal Tiomkin sat at his ease in front of a sumptuous nineteenth century desk once owned by Czar Nicholas II, now owned by Premier Peter Brasnikov, who was in uncommonly good humor.

The marshal guessed that a half-empty bottle of vodka on the desk was the reason. For Brasnikov, vodka was a two-faced muse, provoking good cheer one day, and blind, black fury the next. Tiomkin sometimes thought it frightening to contemplate the shade of the old premier, struggling to be reborn in the new.

"We will be able to launch the *Aurora* into space on schedule then, Comrade Marshal?"

"Ahead of schedule, First Secretary. Yes, we can launch, although I still advise against it. It entails grave risks—"

Brasnikov waved his hand as though brushing away an insect. "Your insecurities about this project are known to me, my friend, and I say again that you're infected by the pessimism of those who are too close to the project. Wolff, for example. Obviously, he has lost his nerve."

"No man has sacrificed more for his country, First Secretary."

"Adopted country, Marshal. Always remember that whatever else the man is, Colonel General Wolff is a German, whose race once in this century and twice in the last turned with rending teeth on Russia. Perhaps the project could use some fresh blood at the helm—"

"He said he would meet your deadline, First Secretary."

"Very well, Antonine Mikhailovich," said Brasnikov with false joviality, "I'll take that as your *personal* guarantee that *Aurora* will launch on schedule and be operational when needed."

"Yes, Comrade."

"When the *Aurora* becomes operational, the Unified Soviet State will enter a new era: the age of the new Soviet man." Brasnikov rested his slim, aristocratic hands on the mirrorlike wood surface and steepled his fingers. "The new 'genetic man,' Comrade. Already plans are being completed for a program to breed Soviet citizens who are at home in space, who can outthink and outperform their Yankee counterparts."

"That is some years in the future, is it not?"

"Yes!" Brasnikov let a breath out explosively. "But I'll show you something beyond the planning stage—something that may someday put us at a great advantage over our capitalist friends in computer technology." The premier lurched to his feet and belchingly called for his limousine.

Computer technology! thought Tiomkin, who sat next to Brasnikov in the back of a large black Volga as it whisked through icy streets cleared of traffic by detachments of the K. The Unified Soviet State, and its predecessor, had always been pathetically behind the capitalists in cybernetics technology. Any giant leap in that field would be worth a hundred motor laser divisions in terms of the global and solar balance of power.

Brasnikov refused steadfastly to talk about what he was about to show Tiomkin, who, as a member of the Politburo, felt somewhat chagrined that he had never even had a glimmering that such a project existed. It particularly galled him because his own branch of the service was so dependent on new technology.

Instead, the premier regaled Tiomkin with sentimental accounts of his days as a young party member before the Civil War. How he was hunted like a rat by Orthodox police during the short reign of the Theocrat. (Tiomkin knew for a fact that Brasnikov, like most young party members, had been kept in a very comfortable prison by the theocratists, whose hands were full fighting czarists, neofascists, and a German army moving on Leningrad in concert with a French and Balkan attack on the Ukraine. Rumors had it that Brasnikov recanted communism and was baptized during that time.) Tiomkin remembered that era quite well. He had been a captain in the militia of the Maritime Peoples Republic, a rump Communist state resisting the Theocrat and fighting an invasion of Vladivostok by a mercenary Samurai corps.

They reached the outskirts of Moscow, then drove east for more than two hours, and the conversation moved to Brasnikov's courageous wartime career. By then Tiomkin guessed where they were headed: Lysenkograd. The ultrasecret science city was named for the formerly discredited but now resurrected Stalinist "scientist" who had taught that acquired characteristics, such as a grafted limb, could be passed on to succeeding generations. Lysenko's theories, bought wholesale by the madman Stalin, caused much hilarity in the Western press. But these theories acquired new respectability under the Genetic Communists.

But then, Tiomkin thought with wry humor, the Genetic Communists don't believe in quantum physics either. Although Tiomkin didn't consider himself particularly knowledgeable in physics, he read as many layman-oriented articles on the subject as he could get his hands on— some of them from the West. He had been amused lately by a diatribe in a party organ attacking quantum mechanics as counter to dialectical materialism. Nature was expected to conform to dialectical laws, therefore quantum mechanics, where subatomic particles behaved pretty much as they pleased, ran counter to accepted theory. Tiomkin shrugged and wondered how many members of the Unified Soviet Academy of Sciences actually accepted that judgment.

The premier's car was passed through heavily guarded gates into the city. They drove on for several more miles, then pulled into what appeared to be a former czarist estate, preserved for almost a century and a half.

Gates opened as if by necromancy and the limousine deposited them at the staired entrance to an imposing stone edifice. They chatted on the stairs while Brasnikov's K escorts swept into the building, securing all entrances and windows.

"Prepare yourself for something wonderful and revolutionary, comrade marshal," exulted Brasnikov. "Consider yourself honored. Barely half a dozen Politburo members know of the monumental nature of this research."

Tiomkin's curiosity was roused even more when the director of the institute greeted them, dressed in a doctor's white suit. Trailing a white-clad retinue of obsequious personnel, they moved through the corridors, finally stopping at a double door where Brasnikov motioned the others to stay outside while he and Tiomkin entered.

.They closed the doors behind them. It was dark except for a reddish half-light and the illumination provided by a wall of holocubes.

Tiomkin became aware of something that made the white, close-cropped hairs on his skull try to stand on end. A low, mewling sound seemed to emanate from many different sources in the room.

As his eyes adjusted he could make out small shapes in front of the holocubes: pale, squirming, indistinct, doughy shapes that mewled and complained. In the back of his mind, Tiomkin was reminded of the months shortly after his wife gave bi—

"What!?"

"You're familiar, of course, with computer interfaces?"

"Yes, Comrade First Secretary. The Americans have done operations on a large number of persons lately, transforming them into human conduits between computers and the world of humans."

"Being operated on to be an interface is one thing, being *born* an interface is quite another." Brasnikov sounded smug. "The last decision made by my illustrious predecessor, before he became an overwhelming burden to the State, was to order this research, which has now borne fruit. Look! Behold the future, Antonine Mikhailovich!"

Unwillingly, Marshal Tiomkin moved forward until he saw several quivering shapes in the lurid light. They seemed almost formless. He saw no eyes, or ears, or other orifices. "What—what are they?"

"Infants. You will note that they are without sight or hearing. Those orifices have been eliminated. They have rudimentary mouths, but with more efficient intravenous feeding methods we will soon dispense with those also."

I have no mouth and I must scream! thought Tiomkin, irrationally remembering some ridiculous Western trash he had read during a liberalized period.

"Their nerves are disconnected. They cannot smell. They cannot taste. All they can do is react to the computer implants in their brains. They sit, and are fed, and excrete, and they think, and lacking any senses, they develop sensual connections to the computers that are totally beyond the understanding of normal humans—even beyond the understanding of those who have had interfaces surgically implanted as adults."

"But . . . why?"

"Someday, when they are older, they will monitor the large computer networks of the Unified Soviet State. They are constantly indoctrinated with the truth and unpolluted by random thoughts. They are perfect custodians for our computers. And they are but the vanguard of an endless army of genetically engineered men designed to do their jobs—manufactured to be content, and efficient at the job for which they were born."

The pathetic complaining that was a constant undercurrent became louder, as if the infants sensed their presence through a heretofore undiscovered sensory perception.

"What do you have to say, Marshal Tiomkin?" demanded Brasnikov exultantly.

"I'm speechless, First Secretary."

And so he was, though Tiomkin was such an old hand at survival that he was able to keep his true feelings hidden until he returned to the flat where he lived when he was in Moscow. He stumbled up the stairs, threw open the door, and vomited the remnants of a lamb and borscht dinner into his bathtub, which didn't work anyway.

Chapter
* **29** *

1

"**F**erman," said Hardrim, "Your story is nuts, but I believe it."

Ferman looked up from the cell bunk like a man reprieved from death. He grasped the bars. "You wouldn't kid me?"

"I don't kid," said Hardrim gruffly. He was touched. He told Ferman his discovery that Chambless and the Argus Society were linked. "When I found that picture I started to believe you, and myself. Now I know the Argus Society is up to something. It started with Dorian Nye's disappearance. Your man-made famine came in the middle. God knows what knots and twists lie between, but they are tied together somehow."

"When am I getting out?"

"Soon. Take a room at this hotel." He gave him a slip of paper. "Wait; I'll contact you. Talk to no one. These people are incredible! Every holocube is their spy, every computer terminal an informant. Don't take chances. Keep down. Keep quiet."

On his way out Hardrim passed a janitor mopping. The man took pains to conceal the fact he had listened to the exchange. Hardrim had fallen victim to an old pitfall of his profession; missing the obvious. How could he know the janitor was a spy for Roger Ferdinand?

Later Hardrim ignored his own advice with the one person who mattered to him now.

They had finished dressing after a stormy bout of lovemaking that was almost as much a combat as an expression of passion. He stood in the doorway. Lenny held his wrists, digging her nails into him. "Why'd you quit your job?"

"I asked for two more weeks' leave to pursue this thing. Flaherty gave me an ultimatum. A Hobson's choice actually. Either stay at my desk or don't bother coming back. I hate ultimatums, so I told him to shove it. What the hell? I can get other jobs."

"Yeah, maybe so. You're bright and intelligent. But there aren't many job openings for dead people. And that's what I'm afraid of. Why must it be you, Mel?"

"Because I'm all there is."

"Like hell! Take it to the FBI! You're just a D.C. cop, why not act like one?"

"For all I know they may *be* the FBI."

"Mel," Her voice was low. "If it's that kind of conspiracy you might as well stay with me. One man, even you, can't fight an organization like that."

He smiled down at her. "My evidence is pretty convincing."

"I still can't visualize an organization capable of tapping every computer system in the country. But I can't deny that someone has such a tap. I must warn you that with such a mole in the network, they probably know someone's digging out information on them." She pressed close. "They'll be waiting for you."

"I'll have to be careful."

"No one can be that careful."

"You'll just have to trust me."

"Dammit, Mel! Grow up! You're not John Galt, or King Arthur or Sherlock Holmes."

"Certainly not Sherlock Holmes. He didn't like women." He pulled her against him.

"That won't work, damn you!" She pulled away. "You're letting your stupid macho prejudices blind you to the fact that you're doing something that could hurt us both. I am part of you now. When you're cut, I bleed."

"If you are part of me, then you know that I am part of the world. I can't ignore this."

"Ignore it! Live your life. Our life. Grow up, or I may do something that forces you to grow up!" She held him desperately.

He gently disentangled himself and kissed her forehead, then looked at her face. "Good-bye, dear."

2

Hardrim stepped to an automated booth and opaqued it for privacy.

He punched his ID code and a list of his stocks appeared. At birth each citizen started with fifty shares of United States common stock, worth one ounce of gold per share, paying an annual dividend of three percent by law. The government also issued U.S. Commodities stock, U.S. Aerospace, U.S. Computer, U.S. Agriculture, and so on. These were the "gambling" stocks. Their worth was the average of the stocks of industry they represented. If an investor thought cybernetics were going to boom, he could invest in U.S. Computer and put his money where his mouth was. Likewise maritime stocks. If the investor was wrong, the government was that much richer.

United States common stock, on the other hand, wasn't a gamble. You couldn't reap big bucks or take a dive either. That was why the government gave it gratis to newborn babies. It replaced welfare; you could hang onto it your whole life and be taken care of if you were disabled or old. If you gave in to temptation and sold it, as many did, that was your hard luck. You wouldn't starve; there were always the "public troughs." Government-issue stocks had replaced income tax, and people lost money to the government through gambling instead of by being taxed. These reforms had come at the height of the taxpayers' revolution, when the dollar was abolished and the gold standard adopted, just after the great crash.

Hardrim's portfolio wasn't impressive. He hadn't touched his fifty original shares of U.S. common, but he'd skimmed the interest. A few years before he'd bought 100 shares of U.S. Aerospace. A mistake. The industry was a snail crawling up a dusty window. Later he'd bought 200 shares of U.S. Funeral just before several medical breakthroughs raised average life expectancy ten years. He then sold his shares right before the last epidemic outbreak of rogue cancer.

Like most amateur investors he avoided the old stock market, and let others make the real money. His portfolio, not counting the fifty shares of U.S. common, netted thirty ounces of gold.

He left the booth feeling cold. Without his job and pension all he had was thirty ounces. It was not all that much. He put the coins in his money belt, almost weighing it down to his ankles.

3

Hardrim dipped his brush in brown paint, made a wide stroke on the canvas, then examined it critically, although not with the care he had used earlier to make himself look old. He had sprayed on jowls and bags and scored his face with deep lines. He even walked with a limp and a stoop.

He sat under a tree in a small park, painting the home across the street. It had been Dorian Nye's when the scientist had lived in Hillcrest, Michigan and taught a few miles away at Harriet Beecher Stowe College in Detroit.

Hardrim had questioned the neighbors, and found old-timers who remembered Nye, and remembered that there once was a private school in the same neighborhood, in the vicinity of the park. One of them suggested talking to an old man who came to the park nearly every day. Apparently he had worked at the school.

Hardrim decided he would be less conspicuous if he looked occupied. He added the disguise because he had made himself pretty visible with his questioning of the neighbors. He hadn't painted a stroke since the third grade, but he was starting to get into it when . . .

"Hi!" Hardrim looked up at an old man, skinny and wrinkled but hale, who was comparing his work to the original. Hardrim nodded and continued painting.

"Been painting very long?"

"Not long."

"I could tell."

"You could do better?" Hardrim did his best querulous old codger, although he didn't care what the other thought of his technique.

"I dunno. I never tried. I haven't seen you here before." .

"Good reason for that. I haven't been here."

"That's the old Nye house. You know, the scientist who disappeared. Well, that's his house all right. Yep. I know him."

"Know who?"

"Nye! Aren't you listening to me?"

"Sometimes I don't hear so good." Hardrim tapped his right ear. "How did you know him?"

"I was a janitor in the Argus School." His wrinkled features beamed. "Best damn janitor they ever had! That's what Dr. Strubeck told me. Told me himself, he did."

"So?" Hardrim sat back indifferently, painting wide, crude strokes. His heart was pounding so hard he feared the old man could hear it.

"Where you been? Don't you know who Alfred Strubeck was?"

"I thought you were talking about this Nye fella."

"I'm talking about both!"

"Go on!" Hardrim sneered. "Everybody knows that Dr. Strubeck was a college perfesser."

"Well, he ran the Argus School. It was right over there!"

"Those are houses."

"They tore it down years ago. But it was there. I was the janitor; the head janitor. Dr. Strubeck was there, and Dr. Nye, and lots of famous people. They used to make terrible messes!"

"If that's so, why didn't I read about it in the papers?"

"I don't know," he said doubtfully. "They weren't noisy about it or anything. It was just there. But not anymore. It was a nice place, easy to keep clean, except when those darn kids dreamed up ways to make everything filthy. Smart people aren't so nice sometimes."

"I guess I believe you."

"Good!" He stuck out a withered hand. "My name's Jack Small. Who are you?"

"Nobody special."

4

"I knew," said Hardrim with a deeply satisfied smile, "that if I hung around there long enough, I would find someone who knew something. But I never expected anything like this!"

Ralph Ferman turned from the hotel window with great agitation. "Yes, and you may have hung around long enough to attract someone's attention to *us*."

"You don't sound too happy, Ralph."

"This may excite you, but it frightens the hell out of me. I feel like I just found out I have a deadly disease, only it's the whole country that's infected!"

"It's scary, but fascinating. After sitting out there every afternoon for three days I was ready to chuck it—"

"Quit congratulating yourself, would you?"

"Let's add what we now know and see what we come up with."

"We keep coming up with nothing."

"Humor me." Hardrim put an edge in his voice. For all Ferman's griping, the man was easy to intimidate. "All right, we know that twenty-five years ago, Dorian Nye and Alfred Strubeck ran a private school for very intelligent children. Several old-timers remember the Argus School, though it's not in Hillcrest city records. There are no records of Alfred Strubeck having lived in Hillcrest at that time. They were suppressed by our Argus Society friends, as they tried to suppress all information about themselves. We know one of those students was Sherlock Michlanski, one of the teachers was Dorian Nye, that Noah Chambless was connected with the enterprise, that every one of them kept his membership in the society a secret, and that Noah Chambless is covering up the fact that the Santa Bella blight is man-made. What have we got?"

"The most sinister conspiracy every conceived on this planet."

"Sax Rohmer and Ian Fleming would gag at such a line," said Hardrim with a wince. "Unfortunately, you may be right."

"May be?"

"Circumstantial evidence points to your conclusion, but others are possible. That's why it's imperative for me to get inside the Argus Society building."

"You may get us killed." Ferman looked unhappy.

"I may get me killed," corrected Hardrim. "I'm going alone. You're a nice guy, Ralph, but in a fight you'd be worthless. As for sneaking around, I'd rather have a main battle tank. Besides, if I'm caught, you'll be left. You convinced me. You might convince someone else."

"Thank you. It's wonderful to be told you're incompetent."

Hardrim shrugged. "You can't be good at everything."

"What if you don't return?"

"Wait here twenty-four hours." Hardrim slipped on a black sweat shirt. "Then hightail it out of here. I won't say where, because I might be forced to reveal it if I'm caught. Contact Lenore Lippman at the

Department of Justice in Washington. Don't go in person. Call her. Tell her what happened. She may be able to help. Anyway, I'd like her to know."

Ferman shuddered. "If you're caught will you commit suicide?"

"Are you crazy? No! I'll try and find out as much about those jokers as I can, in case I escape. Suicide!"

"Isn't that what secret agents do when they're caught?"

"I'm no secret agent. I'm a cop with a terminal case of curiosity." Hardrim checked his revolver and slipped it in the holster. Handguns were noisy, but they killed faster than lasers. When you got kicked by a .44 you stayed down. In the right situation, however, a hand laser could preserve the element of surprise for a few vital seconds, so he also carried one of those.

Hardrim paused at the door. "Lock this. See you later."

Several hours later Hardrim parked the hovercar across the street from the brown stone building.

Finding it had taken longer than anticipated. The street address wasn't on the city map tile he bought for his auto navigational computer. That block showed as an empty lot. He was getting used to such coincidences.

He smiled. Someone was going to a lot of trouble to make his job entertaining. He rested his arm with the elbow sticking out the hovercar window, enjoying the haphazard explosion of rain drops against his skin. The ancient car's windscreen field was broke and the drops made little kitten paw prints on the glass as the rain clouds retreated.

The building was dark against the cantaloupe sky. Its solid, twentieth century unornamented dignity befitted a former courthouse. Now, with only ten human judges in the entire state, the building was in the backwaters of Detroit; respectable but not very active; the ideal neighborhood for the Argus Society.

Hardrim watched and rehearsed his plans. No one entered or left. He smoked several cigarettes. A strange piece of music played in his head; he had heard it a week ago on a culture network. It was a recently uncovered work from a civilization contemporary with the Babylonians, which had a musical notation that musicologists had just deciphered.

A big red street cruiser slowly passed on the street. It was adorned with garish oriental holographic detailing of a dragon in combat with a unicorn. Hardrim perked up. Two hoodlums, in formal night wear, with yellow top hats, gave him the eye. Their dress was so similar to that of two who had walked by twenty minutes before that he would have bet a gold coin that they had patches cut from their formals right at the crotch. He longed wistfully to bash their heads together. But instead of matching gazes with them, he looked down. They laughed derisively. The driver gunned the monster to the intersection, running a stop sign.

He waited until sunset, then he left the hovercar, crossed the street, and strolled down the sidewalk. Alongside the Argus Society building he ran his eyes over windows, door, and masonry. No obvious security devices. No alarms. Whatever security devices existed were well hidden. He quickly walked past and around the block to an alley that ran behind the building.

He examined the back door. He was familiar with most antiburglary devices and had instruments to detect them. He ran a thin wafer an inch from the door's surface, following the outline. No electronic devices. He turned his laser on the lock. When it was melted he pushed the door open.

It looked like a dark storage room. He sprayed luminous powder in the air to detect lasers. None appeared.

The next room was larger, but just as dark. It had a stairway. Hardrim took each step after elaborate examination and infinite care. He was sweating. This was too easy. Nobody left buildings without alarm systems! No sound. No smell. Nothing disturbed the deadness.

At the top of the stairs he waited, all senses turned on full. Nothing.

At the end of the hall under the door was a barely visible bar of light.

He padded to the door and opened it. Immediately a light came on. He was in a library or study. Standing in the center of the room was a man Hardrim recognized from his picture.

Chambless looked Hardrim over carefully while training a laser on his chest. He looked weary, with dark patches under his eyes. He was leaning on a stuffed chair for support.

"I was wondering when you would show up."

Chapter

* 30 *

1

"**Y**ou were expecting me?" said Hardrim.

"Yes," said Chambless. "Please remove your handguns, one at a time, and throw them away from you. Now sit down, Mr. Whoever-you-are." He moved away from the stuffed chair and faced Hardrim.

"How did you know?"

"We became aware that someone was showing an inordinate interest in our affairs a few days ago. As you probably know, we have sensors in the national computer network. Your scrutiny of Argus Society records alerted us. Yesterday, your search of Hillcrest city records alerted us again. We guessed you'd try tomorrow night, but we were prepared tonight just in case."

"Prepared!" Hardrim's laugh was an outlet for his seething emotions. "I walked in here like the door was unlocked."

"It was. Mr.—ah, I wish you'd tell me your name. I hate addressing people without names!" Chambless took a pipe from his coat and put it in his mouth, but didn't light it. "We didn't want you killed by our security devices." He pointed his pipe. "I recognize you! The policeman who guarded Dorian Nye." He smiled as if to himself. "No wonder you pursued us with such tenacity. Revenge is a powerful motivation. You were fired from your job?"

Hardrim nodded.

"Naturally you wanted to track us down. I speculated that it would take a highly motivated mind to connect the disparate elements of our activities and get the correct answer."

"What is the correct answer?"

"You tell me."

"Stop playing games, Chambless!"

"You know my name. Very good. How? From my books?"

"If you intend to interrogate me, get on with it!"

Chambless looked shocked. "You expect to be tortured? Why? You have no information I want. We know the leaks in our security, thanks to you. We will eliminate them. There's no need to extract information, except what you reveal voluntarily."

"Don't hold your breath."

"I'm not sure I understand your hostility. Surely it's not based entirely on your lost position with the Washington police."

"You're trying to starve the world and you ask what I have against you!"

Chambless nodded with dawning comprehension.

"I underestimated you. Tell me, have you had dealings with a man named Ralph Ferman?" Hardrim glared as an answer. "I'm surprised you believe his story. Did it occur to you that it might be the product of an extremely active imagination?"

Hardrim saw no harm in answering. "At first, but information I later discovered supported him. Do you deny it?"

"I don't bother to deny anything," said Chambless calmly.

Another man entered. He was very stocky, with thick hands. What looked like a bad case of sunburn was just starting to peel.

"Hello Sebastian." Chambless didn't take his eyes off Hardrim.

"Who we got here?"

"He's not inclined to say, but he's the policeman who guarded Dorian Nye's facsimile, and lost his job because of it. He's also a friend of Ralph Ferman."

Sebastian's face lit up. "Where is he?" He rested the knuckles of his right hand against the palm of his left.

"He's pulled out of town by now. I told him to beat it. I didn't tell him where."

"That was clever of you, Inspector Whatever," said Chambless. "It doesn't matter. Ferman knows nothing harmful. His word is worthless without you to back him. By the time he persuades the authorities to listen, you won't be here, nor will any information damaging to us."

"I'll be dead."

"No, you fool! If you're anything like the man I think you are, with anything like the brains you've shown deducing our operations, you'll be on our side."

2

Hardrim was in a projection room. It was dark, but he saw a glimmer in the corner from where a voice came.

"Certainly you are familiar with the Surroundee, Mr. Hardrim. Yes, we found out your name. It's always pleasant to be on a name relationship, don't you agree?"

"Go to hell!" Hardrim strained against straps holding him firmly to a chair. He felt sticky electrodes like sucking insects on various sensitive parts of his body.

"As I was saying. Your experience will be similar to attending a Surroundee, except you'll be more emotionally involved, thanks to new techniques that heighten the subject's receptivity. They were developed by a distinguished Academy Award winner, and member of the Argus Society."

"You bastard! You're going to wash me!"

"Not at all. You're going to be given certain valuable information. It's not complete, but later, when we move from this building, you'll stay in a room with journals and notes of a number of people and other documents that may interest you."

"But why?"

"You're valuable: stubborn, tenacious, intelligent. We need those qualities. There are limits to what intellect alone can do. We need your strength. We want you on our side, but not by brainwashing you. If you join us, it must be because you believe in what we stand for."

"I doubt that will happen."

"I hope you're wrong. Let us begin."

3

It was dark. Then a bright light appeared in the dark and coalesced itself into a person . . .

A frail yet healthy-looking gentleman aged anywhere from his late sixties to early century-teens walked into Hardrim's restricted field of vision. Under a frayed laboratory smock he was natty in a three-piece tweed suit so ancient that it was in style again. His frizzy white hair, over keen, yet humorous blue eyes, was totally uncontrollable. He smiled at Hardrim, whose own eyes came near to bugging out.

"You're—"

"Hello, I'm Alfred Strubeck," said the old man.

"But you're dead! Even the Argus Society isn't big enough to successfully fake *your* death."

"You're right, of course, Mr. Hardrim. Although I have no other evidence, I assume I'm dead or I wouldn't be talking to you." Strubeck put his hands in his pockets and looked up, and then back at Hardrim. "I suppose that sounds rather confusing."

"You're not only dead, you're quick!"

Strubeck smiled, apparently tickled. "One can't be both. Surely, you know that."

Hardrim strained against his bonds, feeling a charley horse building in his calves and thighs. "If we're going to continue this decorous badinage, I'd like to be let loose. I promise I won't try to hurt you."

"That's unnecessary. You couldn't if you tried."

"What the hell are you, a holo projection?"

"Not exactly. I'm a computer reconstruction of Strubeck. Since his body is dead, I am, for many intents and purposes—he."

Hardrim, despite his discomfort, was fascinated. Suddenly his bonds freed him and he was rubbing circulation back into them—but he was still fascinated. "Reconstruction. You're a computer program made to stimulate Strubeck?"

"More than that—I am the result of an Argus Society project that was very successful." Strubeck looked about as though searching for a place to sit, then shrugged and faced Hardrim again with a sheepish smile. "How familiar are you with research into artificial intelligence?"

"Since I dropped my membership in the Software of the Month Club my education in that area has been dreadfully deficient."

"That was a joke, I believe?" said Strubeck, cocking his head sideways. "One argument against artificial intelligence has been that one has never been created that could recognize humor."

"That's all right. My former boss, Commissioner Flaherty, managed to run the Greater Washington D.C. police department without a sense of humor; and it could be argued that he is intelligent."

"You *are* somewhat familiar with the arguments pro and con concerning artificial intelligence?"

Hardrim sighed tiredly. "Somewhat."

"Do you know the term 'helix chord string of numbers'?"

"Some sort of eleventh generation computer technology, wasn't it?"

"Yes, a type of logic wherein molecule chip-generated particle streams dip in and out of the fourth and fifth dimensions. It was a direct result of Teddiwitz's zero-resistance generator, although poor Sam never had a chance to see that."

"I'm almost completely in the dark—skip the college prep lecture and give me the bottom line on this process."

"Artificial intelligence yeasted with something resembling, if not actually, nonlinear, intuitive logic jumps. Quantum leaps of intelligence, so to speak."

"Does that actually work?"

"No, of course not. What it actually does is create a computer program that slowly becomes insane. Sort of a self-induced virus. Without being creative, which at least would be some small consolation for being stark, raving mad."

"Then what are you?"

"The next best thing. You've seen rudimentary forms of the type of technology I represent: the 'An Evening with FDR' show at the Epcot Center. Where the Roosevelt simulation answers questions from the audience. Maybe you've seen the 'Altered Classics' film series, with computerized simulations of famous movie stars recast in familiar films they weren't originally in."

"Like *Gone with the Wind* with Groucho Marx as Rhett Butler, and *Casablanca* with Dick Powell playing Rick and Ronald Reagan in Paul Henreid's part?"

"I remember now that you are a film classic buff."

"You're not being strictly truthful, Dr. Strubeck. How could a computer just 'remember' something?"

"Because I'm not a computer, I'm a program, of a human. Programmed to be close as possible to the real me, and to possess, for instance, my famously fallible memory."

"You're more than a Disney World exhibit, Dr. Strubeck."

"My program is backed up by actual memory tapes of myself, last taken shortly before—well, my last memory of current events was when President Allen got his divorce in Las Vegas."

"That's a few weeks at most before your, ah, demise."

Strubeck rubbed nonexistent hands together briskly. "Let's dispense with euphemisms, shall we? I'm obviously dead, and making references to it won't discomfit me at all."

"What's—it—like?"

"That's like explaining a blind spot. I have a spot of humanity missing I can't quite focus on. While it's not truly uncomfortable, I won't be sad when someone pulls the plug on this form of existence. I certainly hope my shade is enjoying death a bit more than I am."

"You're just temporary?"

"Of course, to turn off and on like a light bulb."

"You're not actually running the Argus Society?"

"No, small flaws in my program would become enormous holes if I operate for an extended time. I am, for instance, about one hundred percent effective at remembering and explaining events and motivations of the past. My effectiveness takes a nosedive when I speculate about the future. I wouldn't be able to make any kind of sound plan, for example. I would be a dismal leader."

"You seem to know your own faults extremely well, doctor."

"This program was developed more than two years ago by my reckoning, and I've run it through its paces several times. For instance, I know that after a few weeks my 'personality' will grow increasingly despondent and depressed—the more I grapple with the reality of my own death and the stone wall that dictates that no matter how long I linger, or how much I try, I will never grow, or learn, or—" The scientist seemed to take a deep breath. Then he looked Hardrim in the eyes. "Enough of this nonsense. Since my time is short, let's make the best of it."

"What are you supposed to do, convince me that the Argus Society isn't an organization of criminal minds?"

"I'm to be your guide through a series of mind tapes, such as the ones that make up my persona. You will live some of my life. Hopefully, your mind is open enough and you are intelligent enough that you *can* be convinced."

"Don't bet the farm on it."

"Must Dr. Chambless and his people use physical persuasion to make you sit through this? If so, you disappoint me."

"No, I won't rip off this paraphernalia they went to such lengths to attach to every goddamn nerve on my body."

"Good, I could ask no more. Now relax."

Chapter

* 31 *

I was on the beach. A long way off I saw Cape Kennedy Space Center. I imagined unused gantries, falling into disrepair, concrete walks cracking with age, and in my mind's eye I saw the control room, with none moving in it but old dreams, and I cried to. myself. . . .

—From the journal of Alfred Strubeck

1

The wind called Santana by the Indians raged out of the Anza Borrego Desert. It coiled through Laguna mountain passes and overflowed into the valley of Santa Maria, California, toppling fences, wrecking roofs, and filling the air with grit.

Alfred Strubeck struggled down the street, perpendicular to the wind. The sky was gray paper with filthy cotton pasted on. Near the horizon was the uniform brown of airborne dust.

He crept past store windows. Across the street a tavern's neon sign fell, casting milky shards onto the pavement. The stationery store's wooden sign up ahead flapped dangerously. Strubeck ducked through the nearest door.

The gloom disoriented him. When his eyes adjusted he recognized the Mercantile Emporium, Jay Waller proprietor. Strubeck drew up to his full six feet and brushed tangled brown hair from his eyes.

The emporium stocked stereo equipment, wood-burning stoves, kerosene lamps, water beds, water pipes, incense, kooky art, and pinball machines. It reflected the life-style of its owner, an amiable aging hippie, a remnant of the Now generation.

Waller's bearded face reflected the flame of a kerosene lantern. He acknowledged Strubeck's presence, then hunched forward to listen to his transistor radio.

"Why the lamps? Are you regressing to pioneer days?"

"Haven't you heard? County's out of power. Wind's destroying power lines faster'n they can string 'em. What a blast!"

"Does this sort of thing happen here often?"

"Man, it doesn't happen often anywhere or else we'd all be eating off stone plates in caves."

"Sounds like what's in store if you Earth First and Small is Beautiful people take charge."

"Oh you college boys!" said Waller impishly. "Radio says it'll blow over in the morning, maybe the next day."

"Oh, fine."

"I'll sit it out in comfort. I've got wood and kerosene."

"You can stuff your lamps up your nose! How much for one?"

"Going to live like one of the people of the soil, eh? Twenty dollars for our cheapest model."

Strubeck put the bills on the counter.

"You need a gallon of kerosene and an extra mantle."

He plunked down two more bills.

The door opened violently and a small woman rushed in. She struggled with the door until Strubeck gallantly went to her aid, and, with an effort, got it closed.

"Thank you," she said. About twenty, tall, slim, with long ash blond hair, she wore a flowered dress and sandals.

"Hello, Mrs. Bennett," said Waller.

"Hello, Jay. I'd like a quart of kerosene for my lamp."

"Storm's not likely to be over today. A quart won't last."

"A quart will do."

"Well, what do you think about the wind?" asked Waller as he rummaged for a funnel to draw off the kerosene.

"It certainly puts us in our place! We think man is master of the universe. It takes a big wind, a flood, an earthquake to show us how puny we really are. I wish an earthquake would wreck one of those nuclear plants, or that the sun would flare and burn out the space lab. We need to be put in our place."

"If we had more thinking people like you, Mrs. Bennett," said Waller, "the world would be a better place."

"Why thank you, Jay." She took the quart container, struggled again with the door, and left.

"She probably cheered when the space shuttle blew up," Strubeck said.

"She's one of the people."

Strubeck picked up his lamp and fuel. "This is a tactical retreat. In ten years this kind of blackout will be impossible."

"Why?"

"Power broadcasting. Even Santa Maria will have it. No lines to foul up, ergo, no blackouts."

"Oh, the SunSat."

"Right!" He grinned. "You can't beat progress."

"Maybe we can hold it up a bit."

"What's wrong with convenience? Why do you hate the modern age?"

"It's dehumanizing. It chains humanity to the tyranny of machines."

"Only if we let it. We're also freed to pursue things that make us men, like art, books and music, and religion."

"Okay man!" Waller smiled. "But you're prejudiced. Your whole career is built around science."

"That gives me perspective to see opportunities we let pass us by. We're becoming antitechnology. For example, you've heard of the White Point probe?"

"Can't say I have—"

"Not surprising. It's on the back pages of the newspapers." One of his favorite subjects was the tendency of the media to play down scientific achievements, and play up their risks.

White Point probe was an interstellar robot craft launched secretly fifteen years earlier to explore the Tau Ceti system. Its existence had come to light recently. The president, to draw attention from a domestic policy blunder, had leaked information on the probe, playing it up as an abortive scheme by a past administration to get a military edge in space.

Now it was interesting only to amateur astronomers and science enthusiasts. White Point probe was an orphan. Her signals, the first from another star, would be officially ignored.

And all but ignored by the press, which instead gave front-page coverage to a demonstration to ban core taps. The adverse public reaction was working: A judge in Alaska had last week killed an experimental version with an injunction.

"Man, that's important!" said Waller, when Strubeck brought it up. "We can't let them sink wells to the center of the earth. How'll it affect the environment? It could start an earthquake."

"We're into my field, Jay! I'll be working to develop core tap technology. It's superior to nuclear power. No radioactivity. No environmental danger if taps are made in geologically stable areas. Taps drain tectonic energy, and may prevent quakes."

"You don't know that. You haven't done it yet."

"And possibly never will." Strubeck's voice was bitter. "We're gradually eliminating all our options until the only one left will be to do without."

"I haven't gotten worked up over anything since the sixties. Space? That's all Captain Kirk and bogus! No one will ever make that trip unless they discover faster-than-light travel, and according to experts that's impossible."

"Most scientists believe so. But experts have been wrong."

Outside the wind rose to a shriek.

"I'd better leave."

"Hang loose, Al. Watch yourself in that gale."

"I will." He opened the door and braced himself. Once outside, he took a short cut behind a store and through a bank parking lot.

He was peppered with dust and pebbles. He stepped over a broken tree to get to his parking lot. A persistent clatter, like tin cannons, came from the disintegrating corrugated roof of a storage building in the next lot. Several sheets had blown off. Some had attached to the sides of cars, others were rampaging around the lot. His aging Triumph looked safe for the moment.

A man struggled to pull a sheet of metal from his car.

"I'll help you!" Strubeck put down his package, hoped it wouldn't blow away, and ran to his side. Each grabbed an end.

The other looked gratefully at Strubeck. He was small, in blue jeans, a turtleneck sweater, and highly polished wire rim glasses. His blond hair was cut almost in a crew cut.

They dragged the aluminum from the car, but it was alarmingly difficult. The man examined his paint job.

"Doesn't look too bad. Let's get inside before one of those things decapitates one of us!"

"You live here? I haven't seen you before."

"This is my first day." He pointed toward the mountains. "I've been up there. I'm an astronomer at Palomar Observatory. The moon is up so I must wait two weeks to resume my work. Actually I'm not an astronomer yet. I'm a graduate student. I'd like to work at Keck Observatory at Mauna Loa, but it's booked up with Cal Tech students. Palomar's director, Dr. Hayland, lets me do work even though I'm not at Cal Tech. You a student?"

"Yes. Physics. San Diego University, La Jolla."

"Ah, we're neighbors, sort of. San Diego State."

"We're neighbors anyway, since you live next door."

"Neighbor, how about something to take the chill off? I'm Philip Norrison."

"Alfred Strubeck. I'd be glad to—wait! I left something in the parking lot."

When he returned with his package, Norrison was heating water on a kerosene camp stove. The apartment was obviously inhabited by someone interested in things celestial. A poster of the Andromeda galaxy covered one living room wall. One of the moon hung over the sofa. A bookshelf occupied the third wall. Physics and astronomy books predominated, although he also seemed to have a subsidiary interest in art and tennis.

They spent a pleasant hour over tea discussing the large problems of college, and of making money in their chosen professions. Of course they talked a lot about women. Strubeck was glad for a new friend, his first since moving to California.

The conversation drifted to the world situation. Like all young men, both had definite ideas on the subject. They discussed the United States's deteriorating position in Europe and whether the European states would form a confederation. Strubeck believed they would. Norrison thought the Soviets would gobble them up piecemeal. Strubeck thought America's new weakness was a manifestation of a national mood against technology and progress.

Norrison leaned forward in his seat. "That's exactly what I mean! People talk as if living in tents and grubbing for food is not only inevitable, but desirable. Maybe for them—I want no part of it. Man isn't man without new horizons and problems. Progress is man's beating heart. If it stops, he's dead."

Strubeck nodded. "But today even professors teaching the sciences are against them. I told my dean of physics I want to help develop efficient

reaction drives for the space program. He laughed in that damned condescending way of college professors and said that in five years there
won't be a space program, so I'd better think about problems here on
earth.''

Norrison sipped his tea thoughtfully. "It makes you wonder how he
got that position in the first place.''

"If he was any good he would be working in his field instead of trying
to discourage others. Shaw was right: 'He who can, does. He who cannot,
teaches.' ''

"I used to infuriate my teachers with that line!" Norrison looked at
the Andromeda galaxy. "You know, there must be lots like us; physics,
astronomy, and engineering students who want to make a contribution.
But we're influenced by an older generation of scientists. A lot of them
actually hate science. I sometimes wonder how many young people they'll
derail with their cynicism. What inventions won't be discovered because
students were discouraged from creating them?" He set his mug down
decisively. "Al, what are you doing this weekend?"

"Not much. I don't have finals for a few weeks. Take in a movie
maybe—"

"Why not come up to Palomar and witness a moment in history?"

"I missed last month's *Sky and Telescope*, so I don't know what you're
talking about.''

"Sure you do! You must know about the White Point probe. It's
sending this weekend.''

"Since when has Palomar been a radio telescope? The White Point
probe won't send up smoke signals.''

"In a way it will. Most information will arrive on a high-frequency
radio signal, but a failsafe was built into the probe in case of radio
malfunction, or solar flare-up. It will send a laser message, several thousand pulses a second, that can be picked up by mirror. The orbiting
telescope will undoubtedly pick it up. So will the Keck ten meter. Some
of us persuaded Dr. Hayland to turn the Big Eye in that direction.
Thousands of amateurs will try to pick up the pulse message, but nothing
on earth of less than a hundred and fifty inches will be able to capture
it well enough to get a message.

"Why not come? Hayland won't mind. I work my butt off for him
on special projects, so he owes me. He'll like you. He's an old-fashioned
astronomer, a sucker for idealists. He gets teary and prosaic on man's
destiny in space. He's a great old guy!''

"Sounds terrific. But how will we decipher the message? It was a big secret at the time."

"Hayland worked on the project. That's why we were able to persuade him to do this. He knows the basis for the code. Since it's no longer a matter of national security, he's willing to feed the code into the computer. We'll be able to read a message from another solar system as it arrives. You'll come, of course."

"You couldn't pay me to stay away!"

2

It was cold on Palomar Mountain. Although it was spring, snowdrifts lined South Grade that wound up through long stretches of silent forest, broken occasionally by a home stuck back in the pines, and, near the summit, a general store and restaurant.

The night turned out as clear as a flawless diamond. The stars were so brilliant it hurt to look at them.

The waxing lunar crescent had sunk into the gauzy haze that was mostly Los Angeles and San Diego smog.

The massive motor hummed as it moved the telescope to catch the concentrated glint of ruby red that had traveled between the stars for seven years. A light sensor—in the cage where, in former times, astronomers had exposed photographic plates—was linked to a decoding computer in the monitoring room.

As the telescope moved, so did the dome. Strubeck stood on the walkway that encircled the inside of the dome. So smooth was the mechanism it was difficult to tell that the dome was moving and not the inside of the observatory. It was, as Dr. Hayland remarked, an example of relativity in action.

Although the decoding computer was in a toasty control room, for some reason the young technicians and students had collected in the dome. Strubeck and Norrison had ridden an ancient, slow, tiny elevator that once saw the likes of Herbert Hoover and Albert Einstein, from ground level to an outside catwalk that circled the dome. Here they watched the stars until the cold chased them into the only somewhat warmer interior. The air around the 200-inch mirror had to be kept the same temperature as outside to prevent even a slight distortion of air passing in front of the mirror.

Alfred Strubeck felt very much at home.

An excited Dr. Hayland bustled about like a grandmother, serving hot chocolate to the forty or so people present. He had an angular face, froggy eyes, and a moustache that looked as if a firecracker had exploded on his face. He told anyone who listened that he had been with the probe project at the beginning.

As the hour approached, there was really only one job—monitoring the decoding computer. Everyone else stood around like Strubeck, who held his hot chocolate in one hand and kept the other in his coat pocket.

Everyone grew quiet. They filed into the small control room and crowded around a computer. A clock ticked loudly. From now until early morning the message could arrive. No one knew exactly when.

The quiet was broken by an occasional low mutter. The available chairs were occupied; those without them sat cross-legged on the cold floor, or stood.

Suddenly the computer's printer rattled. Philip Norrison tore the sheet off and read it.

"It's the identifying code for the White Point probe. It gives its location, origin, distance from earth, angle from the plane of the galaxy, and how long it's been in space."

Minutes passed. The printer fired off again without stopping for a long time. Norrison scanned the contents, then read them aloud almost reverently. "Much of this is technical. The probe is telling NASA how it functioned during the journey. It is badly pitted by interstellar dust. Its propulsion system is shot. Without a functioning drive, it will soon fall into Tau Ceti. Here it comes:

ELEVEN (11) PLANETARY BODIES IN SYSTEM, FIRST BODY LO-CATED .24 ASTRONOMICAL UNITS. 20,000 KILOMETERS DIAME-TER. NO ATMOSPHERE. SECOND BODY LOCATED .68 A.U. 8,000 KILOMETERS DIAMETER. ASTEROIDAL SHELL OCCUPIES AREA OF APPROXIMATELY .9 A.U. THIRD PLANET AT 1.2 A.U. 12,000 KIL-OMETERS DIAMETER. ATMOSPHERE 50 PERCENT OXYGEN, 28 PERCENT NITROGEN, 18 PERCENT CARBON DIOXIDE, 4 PERCENT TRACE GASES. SURFACE GRAVITY .88 EARTH, INDICATING LOW DENSITY. FOURTH PLANET 2,000 KILOMETER DIAMETER. AT 3.4 A.U. NO ATMOSPHERE—"

"Skip the rest for a moment, Phil," said Dr. Hayland. "Is there any more information on the earthlike planet?"

"More data's coming in. Don't you want to hear about the gas giants?" he said almost plaintively.

"The hell with them!" said somebody. "We've got us an earthlike world. That's what they sent it to find."

"This may be old-fashioned of me," said Dr. Hayland. "But may I propose a toast to those who launched the White Point probe, whose work has been vindicated tonight? Now we know that habitable worlds wait for us around other stars, planets where man can shake himself free of Mother Earth."

"You making a speech, Dr. Hayland, or proposing a toast?" said a voice.

Hayland joined the laughter. "Both! Prosit!" He drained his chocolate. The young people followed suit with a cheer.

Strubeck licked chocolate from his lips as his mouth stretched into a grin. His face warmed with rushing blood. He felt as he had as a child, watching the Apollo astronauts step onto the surface of the moon. He knew he would never experience a moment more moving. Perhaps science had meaning after all. Man's future wasn't on the earth, where teeming billions blundered toward destruction. It waited on Tau Ceti, Alpha Centauri, Betelgeuse, and Sirius. It waited behind clouds that hid the Galactic Core. It waited on Andromeda and beyond those mysteries of creation, the quasars. It waited at the threshold of the universe. It would always wait, just beyond grasping, but well within dreaming. He was glad to be at its beginning.

Chapter

✳ 32 ✳

It is impossible for someone not living then to imagine our frustration at being rejected at every turn. The nation was no longer interested in space. Congressmen glanced over reports of habitable worlds on other solar systems, and said "So what?" After hearing "so what?" enough times, we decided to show them what!

—*From the journal of Alfred Strubeck*

Astronaut morale fell to an all-time low. Drug use and sexual experimentation, even in space, became commonplace, although you won't find any NASA or SED officials who will admit to it. For an unconventional account of this phenomenon, the reader is directed to Fear and Loathing: On the Space Shuttle *by . . .*

—*From* A Centennial History of NASA,
by Nathan Kilhock

1

Transcript of testimony of Alfred Strubeck before the Senate Appropriations Committee, Senator Franklin Nune, chairman:

SENATOR NUNE: For the record, state your name and occupation.
STRUBECK: Alfred Strubeck, a physicist, presently employed by Global Dynamics.
SENATOR NUNE: It was in this capacity that you developed the

fusion drive that Global Dynamics has been contracted to provide NASA?

STRUBECK: Yes sir.

SENATOR NUNE: May I ask your age?

STRUBECK: Thirty-two.

SENATOR NUNE: That's a young age to win the Nobel Prize for physics. My congratulations, Dr. Strubeck.

SENATOR HOLLINGSWORTH: Mr. Chairman, it's very close to lunch time. I'm sure we all admire Dr. Strubeck for his work, but could we get to the point?

SENATOR NUNE: In deference to the senator's lunch, we will proceed. Dr. Strubeck, I understand that you advocate replacing NASA with a department of space. Could you elaborate?

STRUBECK: Mr. Chairman, the importance of space exploration has reached a level requiring more attention, funding, and planning than ever before. The future is in space, and ultimately the stars. Someday this or some other nation will develop interstellar travel. It will require a national effort dwarfing all previous efforts—

SENATOR NUNE: Excuse me, are you proposing a department of space bigger than all other departments, including defense, education, energy, and the rest?

STRUBECK: Yes sir.

SENATOR NUNE: You're saying that someday, perhaps fifty or sixty years from now, we'll need to expand our space program to the size you mentioned, and we should plan for that today?

STRUBECK: No sir. At the present rate of global population increases, that would probably be too late. I was speaking of the immediate future. We must begin soon or not at all.

SENATOR PALEY: I'm confused. Why such a large program to develop interstellar travel? Haven't you done that very thing, and won a Nobel Prize for it? My understanding is that that fusion drive could easily reach ninety-nine percent of the speed of light.

STRUBECK: Senator, that is not an interstellar drive, although it could certainly transport limited numbers of people to the closer stars. It would be impractical for large numbers, and unless interstellar travel is practical, it is really no solution.

SENATOR NUNE: You are proposing that the United States

fund a faster-than-light drive? That's impossible. Faster-than-light travel cannot exist in the Einsteinian universe.

STRUBECK: That is correct. I propose research to uncover the universes where Einsteinian physics do not apply, where interstellar travel may be possible.

SENATOR NUNE: But this is all mere theoretical dreaming. You can't ask a great nation to commit a large part of its resources to something that may be possible.

SENATOR PALEY: Mr. Chairman, it's a minute until noon—

SENATOR NUNE: You're quite right, Senator. Dr. Strubeck, I'm sorry, our time has run out this morning. Unfortunately we have several other matters scheduled this afternoon. Could you speak to us some other day in a couple of months?

2

"It sounds like a conspiracy," said the biologist.

"Of course it's a conspiracy; of reason against unreason, of mind against entropy. We are forming this organization to advance the cause of intelligence in the world," said Strubeck.

"Why be so secretive?" asked the chemist.

"There's no other way," said Philip Norrison, seated next to Strubeck at the long conference table. "And, damn it, they've got their own conspiracy. How else do you explain the systematic cover-up that data about an earthlike planet was ever received from the White Point probe? They forced the early retirement of Palomar Observatory's director to keep him quiet. He's in an old folks' home, and nobody can see him. How would they would treat an organization like ours?"

"He's right!" said Strubeck, throwing himself in like a wedge. "Alert them that scientists are forming an organization to advance technology, to fight governmental and institutional Luddism, and they'll round us up. If they thought the great minds of our time were uniting to fight them, they'd try to outlaw IQ's of over one twenty-five. We must keep our intentions secret. We can't keep the Argus Society a secret, but we can make it seem so innocuous that it won't be worth a second glance. Our actions must seem innocent, yet serve our ends. For instance, our intelligence test should be introduced as a test without cultural bias. It's that, too. But its main purpose is to identify individuals we need. We hope to introduce it worldwide in a few years. Call it conspiracy if you like, but it's a conspiracy for mankind, against stupidity and ignorance. Can we bring this to a vote?"

He counted the votes and sat down, satisfied.

"Thank you, gentlemen, and ladies. That is a beginning."

3

"Sit down, Dr. Strubeck," said Adam Scott.

They were in Scott's executive suite in downtown Hollywood. From the window Strubeck saw the old Pantages Theatre, now a mosque whose minarets thrust into the smog. Five times a day a muezzin took an elevator to the top and called to a population of the faithful larger than any outside Africa.

The two men regarded each other with frank interest.

"I'm flattered you invited me this afternoon, Mr. Scott."

"Dr. Strubeck, did you tell anyone that you were coming?"

"No, I followed your instructions to the letter. I came right over after I received your message."

"Excellent. My secretary is at lunch. As far as this organization is concerned, your visit today never took place. All records of this afternoon will be destroyed."

"Seems pretty cloak and dagger, Mr. Scott, although I'm not as familiar with the world of industrial espionage as you."

"That's amusing, coming from the head of the Argus Society."

Strubeck sat quietly.

"You don't need to pretend, Dr. Strubeck. I've known of your organization for some time, and I approve of it and its aims."

"Excuse me if I sound skeptical. But what exactly are our aims?"

Strubeck noticed that Scott seemed almost impatient with the limitations of ordinary human communication; as if his mind worked faster than he could speak. "To fool a misguided country into not committing suicide. To hoodwink a nation into not selling itself to the kind of charlatanism characterized by our friend Senator McClaren."

"Favoring technology is certainly not a crime. This is still a free country. Why do you think we have secret activities?"

"There are varying degrees of freedom, Dr. Strubeck. The freedom to make a discovery doesn't always include the freedom to use it. The freedom to hold a belief doesn't always include the freedom to give it a tongue. You know that as well as I do."

"Lately the atmosphere created by McClaren has stifled scientific research. Universities that once enthusiastically funded research in faster-than-light travel have been threatened with cuts if they don't channel their resources elsewhere. I'm sure you know that data from a deep space probe about habitable worlds on nearby star systems was suppressed. How much worse will it be if the Archer McClarens get control of the government?"

"I don't believe the people are stupid enough to give power to a man like McClaren."

"If you don't believe that most people are stupid, why did you form the Argus Society?"

"The American people are good at heart even when they are occasionally victims of demagoguery."

"This is a world of marvels, Dr. Strubeck." Scott shifted his piercing gaze to the window. "Look at the radioactive cloud over San Diego, or the square miles of incinerated farmland in the Midwest from a rogue power broadcasting satellite. Cast your memory a few years back, when paratroopers fired on crowds to keep them from burning down Atlanta to bring about the millennium." From his expression, he seemed to see what he described.

"And that's just America. I haven't mentioned the Moslems who cut their own throats by the millions, or the Europeans, who are demonstrating that two thousand years of civilization can be snuffed out in a single season, or the so-called civilized Asians—little wonder there's a movement in Congress to institutionalize the isolationism that's always been a native American trait.

"In such a world, I have no trouble imagining power being handed over to Archer McClaren to protect us from ourselves. If that happens, men like us will be forced to take action. Progress must continue, even if most of the world is asleep—research and development can't stop. Have you heard of Osirium?"

"I know quite a bit about your metal. It could cut years off the development for a prototype of my fusion drive."

"It's technology that must be in the hands of people who will use it. You agree?"

"Obviously you know something about our organization. I grant that we are more than the face we present to the world."

" 'Dreamers of the day are dangerous men,' Dr. Strubeck."

"I beg your pardon?"

"Lawrence of Arabia wrote that in *The Seven Pillars of Wisdom.* 'All men dream, but not equally. Those who dream by night in the dusty recesses of their minds wake in the day to find that it was vanity; but the dreamers of the day are dangerous men, for they may act their dreams with open eyes, to make it possible.' "

"But we have nothing like the scope you envision. We don't have the resources—"

"What if you did?"

"Are you offering a contribution to the Argus Society?"

"Yes. Would a billion dollars help?"

The obvious reply was, "You're joking," but he didn't say that. The next most obvious was, "That's a lot of money." He didn't say that either. Instead, he said the third most obvious:

"How?"

"If and when I see an irreversible trend in this country toward smothering research and development, I will begin liquidating Scott Enterprises. Books will be juggled, frauds perpetrated, careers ruined. People will go to jail. When I'm done I'll have a billion dollars in gold bullion. Untraceable to me or anyone. It will be yours."

"Why?"

"An insurance policy. Use the money as you see fit. You are an honorable man; I know you'll use it as I would if I could."

"You're talking as though you expect to die."

"This insurance policy only pays off if I die."

"In that case, how shall I collect the gold?"

Scott frowned. "I pondered that for some time. My problem is to keep this secret between us. I cannot trust anyone totally, except you, and that because I have no choice.

"So I have built a vault at a certain location. I used workers who did not know whom they were working for. They were blindfolded each time they traveled to and from the vault and were told they were working on a government secret.

"I have the combination to the vault. I'll give it to you now. If I die, an envelope will be delivered to you from my attorney. Inside will be written the vault's location.

"One more precaution. The combination will only work if used by you or me. Go to an address I will give you to have a hologram taken and programmed into the vault computer. If you grow a beard, or significantly alter your appearance, contact me. Otherwise, it's safer if we never communicate again."

A light on Scott's desk began to blink. "A very close associate, one of my closest friends, is headed up to this office. To be on the safe side, please leave by my private entrance."

"Are there no other conditions?" said Strubeck.

"Just one. This intelligence test—yes, I know about that. If I were you I'd use that money to develop some airtight security. You can't have others finding out as much as I did.—This intelligence test. When my son, Jason, is old enough, I want you to give it to him."

"I can't guarantee that he'll do well on it."

"Just guarantee that you'll give it to him."

"That's all?"

"That's all. Oh, and one more thing."

"What?"

"I expect you to save the world."

Strubeck left; seconds later, he heard a knock on the door. A closed venetian blind covered the window that looked into Scott's office. Uncharacteristic nosiness made Strubeck peek as Scott greeted his best friend: Horatius Krebs. Strubeck promptly forgot the face until years later— and went on his way.

4

Take the Argus School Test. If your child qualifies, he or she might be awarded a special scholarship for deserving youngsters by the Argus School Educational Fund. Your bright child deserves this chance. For free information write: Argus School, 8651 Tennebile Ave., Hillcrest, Michigan.

"There are thousands—literally—of test results high enough to merit our attention, Dr. Strubeck. But I call your attention to these three. Extraordinary even by our standards."

Strubeck fit glasses on his face. At forty-three he was discovering, to his dismay, that he needed them more and more. He ran thin fingers through even thinner gray hair.

"Three boys. Interesting. Are they available?"

"The two American boys won't be a problem. The youngest, the Polish boy, will be trouble. I don't know how we'll get him out of the country. It's only a matter of time before the Communists discover him, even if they don't know his full potential."

"How did he take the test? Iron Curtain countries have resisted introduction of our tests."

"His father is a pro-West scientist. He obtained a smuggled copy of the test."

"Is there any way to contact him, offer our help?"

"I'm way ahead of you, sir. I sent an agent. The father told our agent that if we can get the child out of Poland, he'll agree."

"That could be dangerous for the father."

"I think he knows, Dr. Strubeck."

"Continue on that course. Get the other two boys and hope that we get the third!"

Sometime later it clicked in Strubeck's mind. Perhaps he was getting prematurely old, but he had just now recognized the name of one of the boys: Jason Scott.

Adam Scott would have been pleased.

Chapter
* 33 *

Strubeck stepped back into Hardrim's sight again. It was so dark, except for Strubeck, that the figure had a peculiar, cartoonlike quality.

"Is this part of the mind tape, or is that really you I see?" demanded Hardrim.

"That's an academic question, all things considered."

"Can you give me a straight answer?"

"Yes, well, actually you are under the mind tape at this moment. Your eyes are closed. Your breathing is deep and regular. You are not even really speaking to me."

"The three small boys. They're the boys in the picture, aren't they? The one with Chambless and the Argus symbol."

"Possibly. Remember, I can't see into your mind, I can only receive thoughts you send me as though you were speaking them."

"What is the significance of the three boys?"

"You'll discover that when you can better assimilate the knowledge."

"You mean when you decide that I can be trusted?"

"Yes," said Strubeck with a trace of a smile. "Do I detect a desire on your part to be trusted?"

"Let's just say that you have my attention, Dr. Strubeck. But you and Chambless have to provide answers to some very tough questions before you even come close to winning me to your side—if that's your goal."

"Let me wax reflective about those youngsters. I *can* discuss an interesting philosophical point about them without giving away the game. Have you ever given serious thought to the strange pattern that nature has shown upon occasion in blessing a particular nation or era in history with a large crop of geniuses at a time when they were particularly needed or useful?"

"Yeah, it keeps me awake at night."

"For instance, infant, rural America, with a population of three million, produced, in a single generation, or two, Benjamin Franklin, Thomas Jefferson, James Madison, John Adams, George Washington, Alexander Hamilton, and a dozen or so scarcely less brilliant minds and dispositions of greatness. Any of them would rank head and shoulders above the 'great' men the United States produced in the twentieth century, with fifty times the population.

"During a period of about a century, a tiny corner of Europe, the patchwork nation of Italy, was the source of a virtual explosion of creative energy from a dozen great statesmen and artists who made the inhabitants of the rest of the continent at that time look like midgets, and who make most of their subsequent successors in modern Europe look like insects.

"Even more amazing was the minuscule state of Athens, with never more than thirty thousand citizens. During the generation of its Golden Age, it produced Socrates, Plato, Aristotle, Pericles, Euripides, and was the fount of Western philosophy, political thought, and drama. Today what town of thirty thousand, anywhere in the world, could produce such a crop of men?"

"Until now. Is that what you're saying?"

"I think that evolution, which normally works as a quiet, steady rain, sometimes throws in a thunderbolt."

"Those three boys were that special?"

"You met one: Michlanski. Possibly you saw another, since he was at the hotel where you heard Michlanski's speech. His name is Jacob Kane. The third man you've never met. He's a brilliant engineer: Jason Scott."

"After meeting Sherlock Michlanski, I could almost believe he represents a forward step in evolution. I did some research on Kane, too. He's not a man I would like to have to fight. I know nothing about Scott."

"Take my word for it. He is as special in his way as the other two."

"Are you going to satisfy my curiosity further?"

"Yes, if you're ready."

"Fire away."

PART

* 6 *

. . . ARE DANGEROUS MEN

Chapter

∗ 34 ∗

1

Below, the stark, rugged mountains formed the vertebrae of a continent. The granite giants seemed to regard the jet's passage with malevolence. When it flew close to a peak with a swirling girdle of angry clouds, Mayfield easily imagined the mountain waiting for the right moment to swat the aircraft down.

How could civilization exist here? The air was gaspingly thin. It was no place for man, yet for centuries an empire flourished in the rarefied heights of the Andes, and vast empty cities testified to its greatness.

The Incas had succumbed to European barbarians, but men descended from that noble race were once more building a marvel: a highway to unite the Andes and connect two halves of a continent.

The airplane nosed up, the great peak dropped, and they were over the top. Below was a small, incredibly green valley, like a gem between the summits. Of such do men dream when they pen tales of Shangri-la, Eden, and lands that time has forgotten.

Then he saw the highway.

It was blue—not sky blue, but dark cobalt. It topped the far peaks and unwound into the valley like a ball of yarn. The jet descended and it grew. It was immense. Mayfield searched for adjectives. But what words can describe a paramount creation of human genius? What superlative describes the pyramids? The answer is that they supply their own. They are there and they are unanswerable. So it was with the highway.

The airfield barely accommodated the jet. Mayfield descended the steps, and the cold, thin air hit him. His vision clouded and his breath came fast. His heart flopped painfully against his ribs and his head roared. He willed his system to calm, but he felt like a car whose accelerator has broken off in high gear.

Far away he heard a voice and felt pressure on his lips. He swallowed. Slowly his vision cleared and he breathed normally. He was on a cot. The man who gave him the liquid was Jason Scott.

"Feeling better, Mr. Mayfield?"

"I think so," croaked Mayfield.

"You just encountered anoxemia. It hits most Europeans, or anyone unused to high altitudes. We don't suffer here because we use almost all native labor. That medicine should fix you up."

"Permanently?"

Scott laughed. "Only the Indians have permanent immunity. Your children will if you decide to live here. One lifetime isn't enough to adjust. That medicine will last a couple of hours. If you're still here then we'll fix you up with an oxygen mask."

"How do you get along, Mr. Scott?" Mayfield sat up and took an experimental deep breath.

"I thrive on cold weather. I don't experience anoxemia as long as I keep exertions under control. When I do hard work, I wear a mask. It wouldn't do for the boss to collapse in front of the crew, would it?"

He sat on a flimsy-looking canvas camp chair. He wore green khakis and rugged hiking boots. He sported a red beard bisected by the same white streak so prominent on his head.

He noticed Mayfield's scrutiny. "I dress and live as comfortably as possible on a job. I spoil myself. I eat my favorite foods. Keeps me in the right state of mind, because for me, work is a vacation. Creation fulfills me. It's natural to extend my spiritual joy to the physical."

"So how do you live when you're not working?"

"On a Spartan diet, with few luxuries. It makes me look forward to work."

"I wonder if we can talk?"

"I thought we were talking."

"Privately." Mayfield glanced toward the others in the room, who included the camp doctor.

"Of course." When they left: "What can I do for the president's trusted aide?"

"Mr. Scott, I want you to organize the Sunside Project."

"Sunside Project?"

"You're not familiar with the term?"

"I'm somewhat isolated here. I rarely read the news. The workings of society don't interest me, I'm afraid."

"Sunside Project is the name for the construction of the PH station. I want you to organize it. Do the hiring, arrange contracts, monitor purchasing of materials, and their transport to orbit. In short, boss the entire effort, from bottom to top."

"I'll be available in two months, when the highway is complete. Before I accept, I must ask: How much control will I have?"

"I know your reputation, Mr. Scott. I promise you as total a control as any government official can have in a democracy. You'll answer only to me and the president. I promise to back any decisions you make."

"I see. What was your decision regarding Python and the PH station?"

"If you accept my offer, that decision will be yours. You're the engineer. I expect you to pick the best people for the job."

"Knowing the animosity between Krebs and myself, can you expect me to be objective? I don't want to be your catspaw."

"I know I can't make a logical decision about Krebs. I dislike him too much. From what I've seen, you can, despite the bad blood between you."

"Does the president know about this?"

"He will shortly."

"Will he approve?"

"Yes."

"How can you be sure?"

"I feel very strongly about this, Mr. Scott. He will either approve the appointment, or I will resign."

"Why does my participation mean that much to you?"

"Mr. Scott, I don't believe we met by chance. Call it fate, kismet, the Wizard of Oz, or God. Something answered my call for help. I don't understand it. I sure as hell don't question it. I'm just going to take advantage of it. If you're willing."

"You're putting your career on the line out of faith in me. I have no choice but to accept your offer."

"The salary won't be anything like you're used to."

"I'm honored to serve my country, Secretary Mayfield. Besides, I was given some shares of the Tectonics Corporation when I helped Rita Duce out, and when she hit the mother lode, I made out very well. I'm quite wealthy at the moment."

"At the moment?"

"I've been a millionaire several times and broke just as many times. I like long shots. Some didn't pay off. Sometimes I've had nothing left but clothes on my back and my reputation."

"What a disconcerting existence."

"Nothing is so conducive to a good night's sleep as knowing you're completely broke and that your life depends entirely on your ability. But I've never failed to pay a debt or finish a job. Do my stormy fortunes affect your offer, Mr. Mayfield?"

"Not in the slightest."

2

Senator Percy Shelley Manners, majority leader of the Senate, was from a wealthy family, but he was unprepared for the barbaric opulence of Horatius Krebs's Yucatan estate.

Manners vaguely knew its location, in the hot, humid jungle of east Yucatan, called Quintana Roo, near Belize.

The meeting began strangely when Krebs's private jump-jet brought the senator to his estate in the dead of night. Manners had choked down his indignation. Krebs was so incredibly rich that his support in Manners's upcoming reelection could be vital.

The jump-jet landed in front of a modest-two story Spanish colonial gabled house. A short, squat servant in white cotton trousers and blouse appeared. He looked to be of almost pure Indian blood. He led Manners to the downstairs library.

"This is the guest cottage, señor. Mr. Krebs will be here within the hour."

"Where does Mr. Krebs live?"

The servant pointed out the window east toward a wall of jungle that seemed to go on forever. Manners had the beginnings of a chill at the back of his neck.

Although past midnight, it was chokingly hot. Inhaling was like trying to breathe underwater.

His state of mind was not improved when an animal began howling and slavering near the house. He looked out the window. A servant wearing leather guards around his arms, legs, and throat vanished into the jungle. He heard the servant curse and reproach something. Straining his eyes, he thought he saw some sort of dog, but with an enormous bulge in its skull.

Manners shivered and turned away.

Ninety minutes later Krebs still had not arrived. Manners was leafing through a book on tropical fruits when the servant entered.

"Señor Krebs apologizes, but he cannot meet you. But if you please, we have a motorcar outside to take you there."

"How far is it?"

"A few kilometers, señor."

Manners's slow burn began to sizzle, but he swallowed an indignant reply.

An astonishingly good road had been cut through the jungle at what must have been tremendous cost and labor. It was dark, and Manners imagined he saw and heard all sorts of exotic creatures, although they never actually ventured into the jeep's headlights.

The trees formed a thick, impenetrable canopy overhead, woven of cedars, hevea, palms, mahogany, and sapodilla. Some soared hundreds of feet, their tops lost in the gloom. Creepers, ferns, and shrubs of all kinds grew in profusion near the ground.

A dim glow grew into a floodlit opening.

A vast shape reared up three hundred feet, cutting off the stars. It looked like an ancient Mayan pyramid. That seemed impossible. Archaeological discoveries were turned over to the government . . . yet Krebs was almost a government unto himself.

That didn't bother Manners. He didn't really believe in democracy or redistributing wealth, although those were cornerstones of his political dogma. He opposed the present system of raising funds because it was hard to use it to his advantage. With taxes you could bribe people with their own money.

More of the Mayan buildings were tantalizingly revealed by the swerving lights.

Manners was led to a building near the pyramid, which was one part of an ancient acropolis. It rose on several levels, each connected to the others by steep stone steps. In the center was a plaza whose borders were guarded by sculptures shaped vaguely like tombstones, apparently carved in relief.

He went through the doorway of what seemed a temple. Its entrance was ringed by a bizarre sculptural decoration of Promethean figures kneeling on death's-heads and between them supporting a giant double-headed serpent.

They entered a chamber lit by gas-powered torches. A great monolithic stone head had been carved from volcanic rock, a flat-nosed warrior staring sightlessly out of the rock. Every detail was painstakingly restored. He gasped at the perfectly preserved mosaics, at the rich engraved stone floors. If this wasn't the real thing, it was so close . . .

"My dear Senator Manners," said Horatius Krebs, entering the room at something approaching a gallop. "I'm happy to see you!"

"Mr. Krebs—all this. Is it—?"

"It's real. An archaeological team I financed discovered it. I decided I could make better use of it than as a museum for wide-eyed tourists."

"But how? The laws."

"Are flexible. Yucatan officials have children to send to college or apartments they've always wanted in Mexico City; there are archaeologists who want pie-in-the-sky projects funded; and college presidents and professors with tastes beyond their means. I take care of them all." Krebs guided Manners down a long hall to a wall. On it was a magnificent carving, a fantasy of gods, winged serpents, and something else that was quite unbelievable.

"What does that look like to you, Senator?" Krebs pointed toward a representation of a strange ship crewed by very un-Mayan warriors.

"That's a galley. They look like Romans!" whispered Manners. "It must be fake!"

"I assure you, it's not." A superior smile spread across Kreb's face.

"But how can you keep such a find to yourself? It would turn history upside down. They'd have to rewrite the books—"

"That's why it pleases me not to. This way I'm the only one who knows the truth."

"I wonder what John Q. Public would think of all this."

"Senator, down here it's Jose Q. Public, a peon. And nobody, least of all me, gives the slightest damn what he thinks."

Manners started to reply, thought better of it, and sat down.

"Don't sputter, Senator. Have a drink. Anything that's legal, and down here that's everything. I recommend the Cinderella Bombshell Sunrise."

"What's that?"

"A marriage of illicit, highly potent drugs and alcohol. Or perhaps you would simply like a margarita?"

"That sounds fine."

Krebs signaled a silent, nearly invisible person. "I'm sorry if I put you off with my opulent little playground. But I like to impress visitors. I've got used to being *patrón* down here."

Manners was handed his drink. He took a sip and was astonished. It was the most delicious margarita he had ever tasted, and he thought he was accustomed to the best.

"The ingredients are specially prepared. I'll send you a supply if you like."

Manners nodded.

"Senator, a man can have anything if he applies the power at the proper place and moment. You almost won the nomination of the Progressive Nationalists a year ago, but you lacked the power, in this case the money. You agree?"

"I lost the nomination for several reasons, Mr. Krebs," said Manners painfully. "I didn't identify Shefferton early on as the formidable candidate that he was. I didn't enter enough primaries. I couldn't maintain momentum, so I appeared weak. My enemies kept the nomination from me. A deadlocked convention turned to Shefferton. I was unlucky and badly served. No proper convention would have rejected me for that idealist. But it did."

"People make their own luck, Senator. With unlimited capital, you could have entered all the primaries. You could have influenced the undecided delegates when there was still time."

"What you say is true, but it's also past history."

"It could be future history. We learn from our mistakes, but few get the chance to replay them. You could. You could replay the nomination. You can have a chance at the presidency."

"I already do, Mr. Krebs," snapped Manners. "No one in the party, apart from Shefferton, can stand against me. When he serves his two terms, I'll be available. With the Republicans and Democrats in disarray I shall prevail. I'm young. I can wait."

"Why wait? It's best to be prepared to grab any opportunity. Shefferton is vulnerable. He is embarking on a risky course. If disaster strikes, you should be waiting to rescue party and nation, in that order, of course."

"Of course," Manners folded his hands in his lap and regarded Krebs with raised eyebrows. The billionaire returned the look unblinkingly. Each reappraised his initial measure of the other. Manners knew that to continue would steer them into a channel that would be hard to back out of. He decided to risk it.

"What exactly are you offering?" His voice was almost inaudible. "And what is your price?"

"I'm offering to do all in my power to ensure that you become the next president of the United States. As you know, my power is not inconsiderable."

"Why do I feel like Faust?"

Krebs sipped from his glass. "Your soul is in no danger. Not that I think for a moment that you possess one, or an ounce of honest principles. I won't ask you to do anything you'll feel uncomfortable doing. Judging from your record of 'support' for Shefferton, you'll probably derive some pleasure from this."

"Oh? Now I'm interested."

"You were interested ten minutes ago. Now you've swallowed the hook and it's caught in your gut."

"Charming."

"Nothing I ask of you will be repugnant to your nature." Krebs paced silently for a moment. "It has come to my attention that Python won't be chosen to build the PH station."

"How did it come to your attention?"

"I talked to Sheridan Mayfield," snapped Krebs, who didn't like interruptions. "He'll fight giving Python the contract. He's another idealistic idiot like Shefferton—he can't separate reality from emotion. I offended his sensitivity when I put pressure on my competitors so I wouldn't have to bid low." Krebs shattered his whiskey glass against the far wall. The door opened and a servant stole in to clean it up.

Manners was shocked. He cleared his throat. "Some people just don't understand business."

"It angers me that such a pipsqueak is in charge of a government agency, and in a position to make decisions and moral judgments about men like myself."

"I wouldn't call Mayfield a pipsqueak. He has a very strong will. That's probably why you and he didn't get along."

"I don't want your opinions. I want your power! As Senate majority leader you have power and influence." He clenched his fist until the veins stood out from the white skin.

"Ah, the price. I must tell you I can't influence Mayfield's choice. I can criticize it, and suggest your company is more suitable than the one he picks. But I can't come out dead against it. It's years before the presidential election; I can't sound like a challenger to Shefferton. Not yet. That would be suicide."

"Fool! I know little can be done once Mayfield awards the contract. But Congress has final approval on the budget. I want you to work quietly to undermine Shefferton. I will help with under-the-table funds, and information."

"I don't understand. I thought you wanted the PH contract?"

"I do."

"But what you're outlining is nothing less than a systematic scheme to destroy the president."

"Have you always been this quick?"

"To what end? You must have a motive besides simple spite."

"If Python doesn't get the project. I want to discredit the administration and ensure that the PH station is not finished on time. If you replace Shefferton, I expect you to make the Strubeck equations available to private enterprise with the capital and expertise to exploit them properly. Namely Python."

"That's how you acquired the rights to Osirium."

"Yes."

"You're talking about a monopoly of the world's new food supply. No wonder you're angry with Mayfield. If he caught wind of your plans—"

"He won't. Unless you tell him. If you do, I'll know it, and you'll be dead within the hour."

Percy Shelley Manners was a brave man who had served in the Cuban war with distinction. But he was chilled to the marrow. "Are you threatening to assassinate me if I refuse your offer?"

"The word is *kill*. And no, I don't threaten you if you refuse my aid. But you would be wise to keep this conversation forever sealed between us."

Manners took a deep breath. "I'd like time to give your offer proper attention. Can I give you my reply in a week?"

"Whatever. But the longer you take to decide, the more time we lose in undermining Shefferton." He noticed the angry flush that the president's name brought to Manners's cheeks.

Krebs drove Manners back to his jump-jet. Manners didn't know it yet, but he had accepted Krebs's offer. It was only a matter of time until he realized it.

Chapter
* 35 *

Just past midnight, when Senator Manners's jump-jet vanished into the Yucatan darkness, Krebs drove his jeep back to his palace. Franco, his head housekeeper, met him.

"Señor, it is almost feeding time for Kali."

"So?"

"Do you wish me to give her another baby goat?"

"It seemed to last her several days. Why not?"

"Señor Emil has taken to feeding Kali and I didn't know—"

Krebs deliberately made his question casual. "How long has Emil been doing that?"

"Several weeks."

"What has he been giving her?"

"I do not know." The Indian's normally stoic countenance betrayed him slightly.

"I think you do know."

"No! But Señor Emil has a reputation in the village. They think him a demon. They say he is in league with Satan and takes their young men away—"

"We know that's silly, don't we, Franco?"

"Sí, but La Asquerosa—I mean Kali, she could eat a young—a young—"

"Don't be ridiculous, Franco." said Krebs harshly.

"Yes, Señor."

"A goat will do." He brushed past Franco and entered the pyramid's main chamber.

He entered his bedroom, which was literally that and nothing more. A hardwood slab was his bed. Krebs had never been able to sleep in a normal bed, or for more than a couple of hours at a time.

When he awoke it was several hours from dawn. Wearing a silk robe, he left his bedroom and walked to the pyramid's main chamber, where an elevator shaft was sunk into the green stone blocks. He took the elevator down.

The doors opened to a vast chamber under the pyramid. Glass cases lined the walls under the illumination of hydrogen lamps.

In his private museum he hoarded the results of thousands of hours of paleontological labors. Besides illegally owning a pre-Mayan temple, he also possessed a large collection of rare and unknown fossils. Whenever he financed a dig, he got first crack at the findings. He had collected enough fossils to fill the gaps in a hundred textbooks.

Krebs wanted things no one else could have. To know things no one else knew. He wanted space. He wanted it all.

Once he had considered himself an idealist. His greatest friend was Adam Scott. But he came to see that even Scott was just a twig in the flood of human folly. Scott was doomed, so Krebs joined his friend's destroyers and saved himself. He sold his friend out to Senator McClaren (but had revenge by arranging for Scott's death to backfire on the senator) and later used his connections to steal vital patents of Scott Enterprises.

He had decided humanity was too petty and foolish to exist: a decadent pig's trough foul beyond redemption. Lacking compassion to weep for the world, he chose to mock it. He vowed vengeance on a world intolerant of greatness. He would rape it because that was all it respected. He would dominate and own all that he could. And laugh because it would beg for more.

He wanted to possess the high ground and deny it to the plague-ridden mass of corruption below. Mankind was nearing a critical mass, like a giant virus ready to spread. Unless stopped, it would infect the universe with weak, inferior men incapable of meeting the universe on its own terms. It would be Horatius Krebs's pleasure to deny them the opportunity.

Meantime Krebs played many parts, and all ends against the middle. For years he had sold United States space secrets to the Service Europeene d'Intelligence. It gave him connections he needed to circumvent U.S. antitrade laws. Two years ago he had gained a dividend by becoming the control for Europe's pitifully tiny intelligence-gathering operation in the United States. As Puvain he sold his European friends a scheme to expand operations. He had plans for the sleeper, Bengal, and his associates.

He walked past the cases, his shoes echoing on the hard floor. At the far end of the chamber another door led into what looked like a medical laboratory.

A medium-sized man was measuring liquid in a beaker.

"Dr. Dollfuss. You're keeping late hours."

The doctor absently passed his hand in front of his face. "Yes, I've worked thirty hours straight, but I've been nervous lately. Can't sleep."

"Did those papers I purchased for you prove of any use?"

"They only proved that Dr. Mengele was a very sick man."

"Doctor, I paid a king's ransom for Mengele's lost notes."

"You were cheated. Mengele knew nothing about genetics."

"It was worth a try."

"We've taken the science of genetic engineering beyond what anyone imagined even five years ago. To suppose a Nazi war criminal could have discovered anything we don't know—"

"He did experiment with thousands of human subjects."

"Without learning anything important. That's the true tragedy of Mengele's idiotic research."

"A true scientist, aren't you, Dollfuss?"

"Don't be patronizing."

"Produce a walking, breathing *Tyrannosaurus rex* in this cage, and name your price."

"Do you appreciate the difference between breeding a hybrid of different species and reconstructing genetic material by tracing genetic ancestry, reverse breeding, and examination of fossils?" He turned away. "I'm not interested in money."

"I've only met one man who couldn't be bought. But even if you can't, you are interested in performing experiments that violate certain intolerant laws."

Dollfuss's skin paled. "I've done everything you've asked."

"True. I just like to remind you now and then why that is." He patted him on the shoulder. "Don't be depressed."

"Does a man like you really know the meaning of depression?"

"Oh yes. But I have my little remedy. I go shopping . . . for a life. I pick a valuable man and study him. I discover his weaknesses and vulnerabilities. I find out everything. I take advantage of all his failings to bring him down. And when he is totally helpless, I buy him. Remember, Doctor?"

Dollfuss clenched his fist so tightly a drop of blood appeared in his palm.

Krebs ignored it. "When do you go to San Diego again?"

"Several days," croaked the scientist.

"Any progress with your colony?"

"Very promising. I will be able to apply my findings to some practical matters very soon, I think."

"I'll send some men to keep you company, Doctor Dollfuss."

"I'd rather *not* have your goons tagging along."

"I'm protecting my interests, not just you," said Krebs. "I think I'll visit your latest creation."

"She has diarrhea. What has that giggling psychopath been feeding my snake?"

"Don't concern yourself with trivia, doctor."

Krebs took the elevator back to ground level. He was anxious about Emil, who had vanished since that night on the dirigible. He had heard of his servant's handiwork, however. Emil was stepping up the pace of his murders, which was as Krebs wished it, but drawing more and more attention to them, which Krebs didn't want at all.

Jeremiah Xerxes, director of the federal sanitarium, had had to be killed because he would eventually have figured out that his orders to release Lloyd Hunning hadn't come from his CIA superiors. Hunning, who could link Krebs with Adam Scott's death, was released because he had developed a fixation for killing the new president's adviser. He was safer as a dead assassin than as a sanitarium patient some curious person might interview someday. His death, like the deaths of those once close to Scott, eradicated paths connecting Krebs with Scott's death. Archer McClaren had known those connections, but he and Krebs had too much on each other for either ever to reveal anything about the other. But that one secret could now destroy Krebs, and in his determination to make himself secure, there was no room for anything less than total commitment. So he had chosen Emil: mercenary without a conscience. Emil cared less for the whys and wherefores of execution than does a layered blade of Damascus steel as it cuts through flesh and sinew.

Yet he was more than a killer. He was a trainer and leader of fighting men. When Krebs managed to gain control of the European sleeper spy, becoming middleman between Bengal and Europe, Emil was the obvious choice to train Bengal's force. It was elegant. The terrorist organization would do Krebs's bidding, yet the blame would fall on its European control.

Krebs went to the control room, whose holocubes let him monitor his domain. He fast-forwarded through the day's recordings, but found no sign of Emil, although he ran across the man's personal cadre. For want of a better term, Krebs thought of them as Emil's suicide squad.

Emil called them Cradle, Jaff, and Smack. Not their real names, but they'd long since stopped using those.

Smack, a former hacker, was in his early twenties, emaciated, with stringy yellow hair, an unhealthy pallor, a rasping cough, and bad knees. He was hooked on "Jack" heroin. Injected into the thymus, it slowed subjective time, letting hackers integrate completely into a computer network. It gave the user an orgasmic feeling of intense power—but only during interface. Smack had dug himself too deep a hole. His supplier had got him by the gonads, then sold him to Emil.

Cradle was addicted to Love Fudge, a Sohi derivative that induced an intense feeling of being in love. He was tall and thin with a bald pate, a poor man's lounge lizard. His line of patter had grown less and less successful and he had turned to Love Fudge more often. Then he met Emil, who turned him on to the good stuff.

Jaff, a little creep, hung out in bars, picked fights, and liked to hit people very hard, sometimes until they died. He had so far escaped punishment for his hobby. His weakness was that he was also a pervert. Emil introduced him to a woman trained in the Drang techniques of sexual pleasure—the "silk" part of the infamous needle and silk treatment. Jaff was his—body, soul, and genitals.

They were an odious trinity—even Emil, whose standards were not high, found their perversions tiresome. But they were entirely his creatures, even more than he was Krebs's creature.

They would, quite literally, die for him. Unlike Moslem fanatics, they didn't court death; for them death didn't exist.

They were in a garden near the jungle. Smack was hooked into a computer, eyes closed in ecstasy. Cradle was looking at a cube that presumably contained pornography. Jaff was shadow-boxing.

Emil's creatures, but no Emil. Krebs left the monitoring room and walked out to visit his pet snake.

At the edge of the raw jungle, Krebs had built a giant maze on a similar scale to the classic Victorian topiary hedge mazes. The maze material was not living plant, however, but stone.

Over the maze Krebs had put a roof of a glasslike substance so transparent it was practically invisible. It was exhilarating to walk on. It gave the distinct illusion of walking on air twenty feet over the twists, turns, angles, and dead ends.

Through trap doors in the transparent roof food was dropped directly into the maze. The trap doors were also quite invisible.

It was dark but Krebs knew his pet was down there. He could almost feel her hatred. And who could blame her? To have a chimpanzee's brain imprisoned in the armless, legless body of an impossibly large South American anaconda . . .

Kali was without doubt a bad-tempered creature. The bulging skull hid a nasty little mentality capable of ingenious cruelties toward those unfortunate enough to be caught in the maze with her. Of course they were faster than she, but sooner or later, with unrelenting, implacable, sleepless tenacity, she wore them down until they were trapped. Then she had her fun.

A few more like Kali, prowling the jungle around the estate, and the village Indians would stop their nuisance raids. They already feared the chimpines, Dr. Dollfuss's first creations, mating the brain of a chimp with the body of a dog. But they would be terrified half to death by Kali. In her, Dollfuss had taken the fears from the back of men's minds and made them flesh.

Krebs heard a sound. He turned.

Emil walked toward him. Krebs knew Emil had deliberately made the noise. You couldn't hear him coming if he didn't want you to.

"You botched that last job, didn't you?" said Krebs.

Emil feigned misunderstanding. "I don't know what you mean. He's the deadest cowboy I ever saw."

"You know what I mean. When I saw you last I hadn't seen a copy of that tape. It was broadcast on the police stations a dozen times. Even the newsspools picked it up."

"There was no other way." The tone was that of an aggrieved child unfairly accused. Then his mood changed and he laughed.

Krebs handled Emil like a vial of nitro. He was a classic sociopath, useful, but with a strain of unpredictability that made him dangerous —to everyone.

"You heard of an FBI man named Roger Ferdinand?"

"No."

"Remember the name. My sources say he was in charge of the investigation in Texas the other night. A murder on a cow ranch would not normally interest the FBI. True?"

"Do you want me to kill him?"

"I want you to behave rationally, if possible. Mainly I want you to quit *taking those goddamned pictures* of your victims!" Krebs breathed heavily. "Do you still keep that photo album?"

"It's my portfolio."

"It's a death sentence for both of us. Remember that, Emil."

"Maybe that's why I've got it. It's insurance that you'll never betray me, because the album can be traced to you." Emil smiled again. That smile would have terrified anyone else, but Krebs merely noted and filed it for future reference.

"What if you die through your own stupidity, which seems a distinct possibility?"

"Better hope I don't."

"Get rid of the album." Krebs looked down into the blackness of the maze. "What have you been feeding Kali?"

"Maybe I'll let the air out of that squealing kraut, Dollfuss."

"You know you can't hide anything from me." He looked at Emil implacably. Fear replaced the assassin's swagger. Fear of disapproval. Emil was a child in many ways. "I know you like your games. What do you do? Kidnap villagers and run them into the maze?"

"You've done it," accused Emil.

"To instill terror, to whip the rest into line. Not for fun."

"It's fun to sneak into the village, past their guards, avoiding their traps. They're getting good at traps." He held his hands out. "I have to reward myself some way, don't I?"

"Well, stop it. You're making her ill. She's no use to me moping around with indigestion."

"Sure you don't want me to kill Ferdinand?" A conversation with Emil was like a tennis match with a very erratic player. You never knew where the ball was coming from.

"If he becomes a big enough nuisance, you may have to. But I don't want the FBI down on us without a very good reason. Keep your itchy fingers in your pockets. Stop exposing us both to risks, or I'll quit trusting you. I will replace you."

"I'll kill anyone who tries to replace me." His voice was a child's again. "You know you can trust me."

"Do I? Then destroy the album. Stop taking pictures."

"Yes, Horatius."

"You've been away a lot. Are you working with Bengal?"

"I've been training him and his men to be water, to be air, to be all-seeing."

"You forget to whom you are speaking. I 'perceive that which cannot be seen with the eye.' I know it takes half a lifetime to produce a true Drang adept. Although, from your example, I also perceive it only takes a season to warp and corrupt all that. Which is to my advantage. 'To win against one opponent is the same thing as winning against thousands or tens of thousands of opponents.' "

"You know Musashi's *Gorin No Sho?*"

"Don't try to plumb the depths of my knowledge, Emil. Suffice it to say that I know enough about your craft to know when you lie."

Emil bowed his head like a child who had been discovered raiding the cookie jar. "I'm sorry, I didn't wish to bore you with details. I have trained Bengal's men in standard terrorist techniques, with some Drang philosophy and methods thrown in. Enough to give them confidence. Not enough to make them Drangs. They believe, of course. They always believe."

"Of course," mused Krebs. "All young men think that they, like Luke Skywalker, can learn the wisdom of the ancients without working or suffering. And people like you—and me—use such men to our own ends."

"They are vessels, nothing more. They are ready."

"I hope you didn't overdo it. We want them to hurt the Sunside Project and my competitors, but also to fall into the hands of the FBI, so Europe's government will be blamed for everything they do."

"Bengal's no fool. I think he suspects. He may contact his control."

"That's all right. Puvain is I and I am Puvain. By the time Bengal figures out what is going on, he should be dead."

"So much trouble—I could have thrown Jason Scott from the dirigible and no one would have suspected."

"Your solution to everything is death. It does have an elegant finality, but too much will draw unwanted attention. Your assignment becomes riskier as you leave more clues for people like Ferdinand to find."

"That is why I have Cradle, Jaff, and Smack. The only clues they leave will be themselves."

"An added dividend is that the world will be rid of them."

"Have I done well? You only tell me when I fail you."

"Carry out the next assignments without flaw and you can bring *that* subject up. These are places I want Bengal's men to hit and people I want eliminated." Krebs showed him a list.

Emil's eyes gleamed at each target: links in the chain of aerospace technology, culminating in the Gigatex aerospace factory in Detroit, home of the Gilgamesh scramjet project and site of the nation's largest store of rocket fuel.

"Succeed and I may reward you. I may let you create a plan to destroy the Sunside Project, particularly if Senator Manners proves unreliable."

"Yes, Horatius."

"Now go inside and get some rest."

"Don't you want me to get you something to eat or drink?"

"We're home. My servants care for my needs. Go to bed."

Emil turned abruptly and left the platform. When he had gone Krebs spoke into a small microphone in his lapel. "Franco—put surveillance on Emil tonight. Tell me if he gets up again."

Emil's promise would bind him about as much as would a four-year-old child's. He might be more cautious, for he truly believed Krebs was almost omnipotent, but Krebs doubted Emil would actually destroy the album. If only he knew where Emil had hidden it!

Krebs found it fascinating that Emil thought of his henchmen as worthless vessels, to be thrown away after use. For that was precisely how Krebs thought of Emil. He was reminded of another oriental work of literature, *The Tao Te Ching*, which made the point that the uses of a wheel, a house, and a bowl all derive from the parts of them that are empty. So it was with Emil, whose usefulness derived from his lack of humanity, of the void where he soul might have been.

Nevertheless, it was becoming more and more obvious that someday something would have to be done about Emil.

Chapter
* 36 *

Washington *Times*—A Baltimore manufacturer of molecule chip components for the U.S. Space Navy and Gilgamesh space shuttle has been damaged by an explosion.

Police say an estimated two hundred thousand ounces of gold damage to the Megatech factory was the latest in a series of strikes against aerospace industries by a group of terrorists. . . .

Roger Ferdinand dimmed the holocube until the floating letters were ghostly glows, and rubbed his strained eyes.

He was in the Washington bureau headquarters. He loved the capital. Power, intrigue, and corruption were like meat to him. He thought of himself as a quintessential policeman; Washington was his favorite sinkhole of evil, even more than New York City. He recognized his symbiotic relationship with crime.

He was close to exhaustion, but the heady wine of near exaltation ran in his veins, and he felt nearer than ever before to the great success of his career.

There were terrorists, all right! The Megatech explosion and four others in the last few weeks bore identical hallmarks: same ultramodern triggering devices, same species of high energy release explosives, same techniques for breaching high security establishments, same brutally efficient way of dealing with security guards who got in the way.

These terrorists were professionals, or their leader was. Evidence pointed to Bengal. Just as Ferdinand had warned months before.

Not only were the terrorists blowing up labs and damaging factories, they were also committing assassinations that fit the pattern of deaths committed by the Drang assassin.

The inescapable conclusion was that the Drang either was working for Bengal, or was Bengal.

This puzzled Ferdinand. He saw the Drang as a loner. Nor could he fathom a connection between European spies and deaths of people associated with Adam Scott years before. Unless the spy ring was older and ran deeper than anyone imagined.

Ferdinand expected to find those answers very soon. He had recently received a tip on where the terrorists would strike next. Of course, the FBI took dozens of calls from people claiming responsibility for the crimes, but only the most recent one had an authentic ring. It precisely described methods used in the attacks. Such knowledge could only be possessed by an insider.

The next target was big: the Gigatex aerospace factory in Detroit, linchpin of President Shefferton's push into space, and manufacturer of the Gilgamesh and several vital components for the Sunside Project. Significant damage to it could stop the space program in its tracks for months.

Ferdinand was in overall command of the effort to stop Bengal, with hundreds of agents and thousands of local law enforcement officers at his disposal. This was his opportunity to give his career a megakick in the pants, or to fail dismally, as he was sure Director Houston Pollux was hoping for.

Pollux was just down the hall, plotting plots, weaving webs.

But Ferdinand felt very good. He hadn't been so confident about his future since the Nye shooting incident, when he'd lit on Inspector Mel

Hardrim as his suspect. That his suspicions were misplaced had shaken his confidence in his own intuition, but he'd never lost the feeling that Hardrim wasn't quite right. That intuition, and his dislike of Hardrim's independent attitude, had made Ferdinand defy orders and keep a spy in the Washington police to watch Hardrim.

This day it had finally paid off.

Ferdinand had been intrigued, but not surprised, to learn that Hardrim was too unstable to stay on his job. And he was amused when Hardrim had sprung a crackpot from jail and began some sort of silly investigation.

But everything clicked when his agent tailing Hardrim informed him that the former inspector was now in Detroit.

That was too much of a coincidence. Hardrim was mixed up with Bengal somehow. If Bengal had planned and executed the fake assassination of Dorian Nye to embarrass the United States government, it made perfect sense that Hardrim had been his accomplice all along.

To be right about Hardrim was as delicious as going to his private tailor's and trying on a well-made, expensive suit for the first time.

Ferdinand set about to net Hardrim in the same basket in which he planned to catch Bengal and possibly even the Drang. He would give Hardrim more rope to hang himself with, then take him in.

Chapter
37

1

It wasn't like awakening. It was like reentering his body after a long absence. Hardrim seemed to flow back into himself. Arms and feet came on like circuits being reconnected. It was an electric feeling, warm and cold. A Niagara of sensations pouring into his brain until . . .

He sat up and pulled the deep-connectors from his ears. He was completely alert, without the sleepy-grumpy-stagnated-cotton-candy-cobwebs-looking-through-a-dirty-window feeling that normally accompanied waking. He breathed deep and it felt fine. He bounced to his feet. Sitting in front of him, complacently chewing an empty pipe, was Chambless.

"Interesting experience, wasn't it?"

Hardrim sat on the cot. Everything came back at once, like a rubber band snapping in his face.

"Yes." He pronounced the word with care. "It was."

"You're all right?"

. "Fine," said Hardrim absently. "You must excuse me. It's not every day I live another man's life."

"Bits and pieces of it, anyway. You ready to do some reading? Strubeck's journals and papers are in a library nearby."

"I thought it was all confiscated by the government."

"Only what he wanted to fall into their hands. Toward the end of his life, he wrote a new set of journals and papers. The Strubeck program is also available to consult. But remember, it becomes less useful with time. Eventually it will become insane."

"I have many questions. What happened to Jason Scott, and Kane? Are they and Sherlock Michlanski part of some great scheme of Strubeck's? The mind tape leaves so many blanks."

"The Strubeck library will fill them."

"Incredible. I was ready to destroy the Argus Society. Now I know I can't. Too much is at stake. You must finish your work."

"The question is, will you help us?"

Hardrim's mouth fixed in a grim line. "I don't know—yet. I don't approve of your methods, particularly loosing the Santa Bella blight on mankind. And from Ferman's description of you, I'd bet the farm it was your idea—not Strubeck's."

An exhalation of air sent smoke in the shape of a tiny mushroom cloud floating above Chambless's pipe. "You'll find in further readings that you're correct. Dr. Strubeck desperately wanted to find another way to implement the plan. In the end he let the majority have its way. The Argus Society adopted my method by a sizable margin."

"I don't know enough to condemn you. Perhaps this is a case of the ends actually justifying the means."

"A textbook case."

"But I'm glad Strubeck disagreed with you."

"He was a visionary. A creator. I'm more practical."

Hardrim smiled wanly. "You are right. My mind tells me to help you, even as my heart condemns you as a criminal. My God, though! Do you realize what a great man Strubeck was? Have you any comprehension of his dreams and visions?"

"I daresay. Otherwise I've been wasting much of my life."

"Sorry. That was stupid of me."

"The mind tape creates deep personal identification with its persona. Fortunately, it wears off with time. In the wrong hands it would be a grim weapon. You could brainwash entire companies of men to idolize their enemies."

"You've taken the same tape?"

Chambless nodded. "Not in the same vivid form." He stood and pocketed his pipe. "But I have sympathized with Strubeck's goals for most of my adult life." He glanced at a clock on the wall. "We haven't much time." A Hardrim's questioning look he said, "We're evacuating this building in an hour. It's no longer safe. What you discovered others may also.

"The Detroit Fire Department is in for some work tonight. In ninety minutes a fire will erupt in the records room. The automatic fire extinguisher will malfunction. Fire will devour every printed and computerized record. When firemen arrive there won't be much of the Argus Society building to save. Pity." He shook his head tragically. "Sadly, the ashes will yield the body of Mel Hardrim, formerly of the Greater Washington Police."

A chill mounted Hardrim's spine and he automatically tensed. But Chambless was grinning broadly.

"Good reflexes, Inspector. Let's hope they're useful to us. The body I described will be a surgically altered corpse, indistinguishable from yours. When you were under the mind tape, we took data. Dental configurations, internal, external scars, blood type, the whole spectrum. We have access to several morgues. Our specialists will prepare a suitable cadaver. It should be indistinguishable, from, ah, the original."

"I think I've experienced your technology before."

"That's before we were friends."

"Why fake my death? Why can't I retain my identity?"

"Are you so attached to it?"

"My parents are dead. I was never close to my relatives. I have few friends outside my profession. Only one person matters. She's the only one I won't abandon, fool, or play games with."

"Who is she?"

"Lenore Lippman."

"The woman who helped you dig out information on us?"

"Yes."

"The one person you can't contact if you work for us."

"I haven't said I will."

"You said you won't betray us. I know of Miss Lippman. She's very able. What if she doesn't share your opinions about us? What if she believes you were brainwashed?"

"She'll believe me."

"I don't share your confidence. The Argus Society has learned that secrets are best kept by an exclusive group."

"There's a problem with that."

"What?"

"How long was I under the mind tape?"

"Twenty hours."

"The problem is Ralph Ferman. If I don't return to the hotel twenty-four hours after I left him, he's supposed to run and contact Lenny. She'll find out all the bad things I know about the Argus Society. She'll do her best to get the Justice Department interested—"

"They won't believe her any more than your superiors believed you."

"Can you afford to take that chance?"

"Damnable hell, Inspector! You are a very infuriating young man. One thing I insist on is finding the ubiquitous Mr. Ferman and putting him in cold storage. I thought him harmless. But his information combined with yours could wreck everything!"

"Why are we talking when maybe I can catch him before he leaves the hotel room?"

"It seems you're working for us after all."

"Don't let it go to your head. It's just for the moment."

"I make it a habit to live moment by moment."

2

Ralph Ferman didn't wait a second past the deadline. He was packed. He was already sweating, his panicky mind conjuring up horrible possibilities for Hardrim's fate.

He started to hyperventilate. Looking wildly around the motel room, he rushed to the bed, grabbed his bags, and almost ran to the door. He wrenched it open.

In the doorway were two men dressed in dark, conservative business suits and wearing dark glasses: one had a clipped little mustache, the other was clean-shaven; one was short, the other tall. The tall one was smoking a cigarette. Both pointed laser pistols at him.

"Good morning. Come with us, please." said the short one in an almost pleasant voice.

Ferman fainted in their arms.

3

"I'm going with you, Inspector," said Sebastian. His face was still peeling from when Ferman had thrown hot water on him.

Hardrim didn't turn a hair. "Don't trust me yet?"

"Oh, I suppose. But you can't tell what rough customers you might run into out there."

"Like Ferman?"

"Yeah, like him." Sebastian's eyes had a nasty gleam. Hardrim laughed and patted Sebastian on the back. "Little bastard almost provoked me into laying him out once or twice. I understand your emotion. Let's go."

They jumped into Hardrim's car, still parked out front of the Argus Society headquarters. It was early evening. The drive to the broken-down motel took about half an hour.

They entered from the back. Eight doors were visible in the corridor. Ferman's room was the third on the left.

Hardrim took out his key card, but the door was unlocked.

"He's gone. No sign of a struggle."

Sebastian frantically searched under his coat.

"Looking for this?" Hardrim held out a laser pistol, butt first.

"What?"

"Don't hold your mouth open. It makes you look stupid." Hardrim smiled slightly. "I took it from you back at the Argus Society. I didn't want you wasting Ferman. He's a friend."

"I'm more concerned with how than why." Sebastian looked embarrassed.

"Let's just say that I'm a professional at this and you're not, and leave it at that."

"Nevertheless, you must show me how you did that some time."

They searched the room on the chance Ferman had hidden in a closet, bathroom, or under the bed, but he was gone.

Hardrim sniffed the air. "Ferman doesn't smoke. Yet there is a definite tobacco smell."

They left the room to see if anyone had seen or heard Ferman leave. At the entrance to the door, in a cylindrical ashtray filled with sand, was a burning cigarette.

They looked at each other.

"Let's separate," said Hardrim. "Maybe they're still close by."

Hardrim ran right and Sebastian left.

Hardrim was halfway around the building when he heard a yell and footsteps. He turned the corner cautiously. Lying near the half-open window was Sebastian. His laser was next to his hand. He was groaning as if in his sleep. He stirred at Hardrim's footsteps and propped himself on his elbows.

"What happened?" asked Hardrim.

"Can't move my legs. Somebody zapped me with a taser. I saw a guy loading Ferman like a sack into a red Nazgul convertible. Then I smelled a cigarette and—then it's all woozy."

Hardrim helped him to his feet.

"Damn! It's like my legs went to sleep!"

As Sebastian stamped blood back into his legs, Hardrim examined the scuff marks in the dirt.

"Nice shoes," he commented.

"How do you know?"

Hardrim knelt in the dirt. His fingers traced an imperfectly formed footprint. "This shoe is two sizes too small for Ferman."

"You remember Ferman's shoe size?"

"I wish you'd quit impugning my abilities as a detective."

"Then suppose you tell me who attacked us, and why?"

"A papal agent, sent to keep us from discovering that the crucifixion was a hoax and that Christ was actually electrocuted."

"Somehow, I'm comforted that you *don't* know, Inspector."

"Do you remember anything else about the men?"

"Yes! The license number! I'm usually terrible with numbers, but that one stuck in my mind."

"Write it down before you forget it. Then we'd better go," said Hardrim. They pulled away in Hardrim's car just as a police car arrived with sirens screaming and lights pulsating. A neighbor had called the cops.

4

For a week FBI Inspector Alexis Moran had operated his forward headquarters in an abandoned warehouse two city blocks from the abandoned auto factory where Bengal had been located.

Moran had never really looked right for his job. He was short, muscular, with a heavy jaw shaded by an ubiquitous five o'clock shadow. From across a room, facing a holocube with his shirtsleeves rolled up, the shirt stained under the arms and random black hairs glued to his retreating hairline, Moran most closely resembled a stevedore foreman or a teamster boss. Early in his career, in fact, after a bum knee forced him out of college football, he had infiltrated a crooked union as his first assignment for the bureau.

Talking to Roger Ferdinand always turned Moran's armpits into the headwaters of the Nile in a way that murderous union bosses could never do. Besides being legendary as a prime bastard, and a man with an unerasable memory for slights and trivial offenses, Ferdinand was also the one man most likely to screw up Moran's career.

Moran was in what he regarded as a no-win situation: a pawn in a power struggle between Ferdinand and Director Houston Pollux. He was loyal to Pollux, who had made it clear that anything he could do to embarrass Ferdinand would be appreciated. The problem was that Ferdinand was obviously a comer, and might end up toppling Pollux, in which case Moran would be cut off at the knees.

"I have over a hundred agents watching the terrorists in the old auto factory," said Moran. "When one leaves, we glue a team of tails onto him. They don't know yet that we're onto them."

Ferdinand smiled slightly. "I think you have things in hand, inspector, but I have some modifications of your plans." Moran shuddered. Ferdinand well deserved the appellation some colleague had given him: Black Velvet, after the mixture of Guinness stout and champagne that went down smooth, but could knock you on your ass if you didn't watch out. "See that no one catches on that we're watching them. That's vital to our—my plan. I intend something quite historic in the annals of domestic counterespionage. We are going to capture Bengal's entire spy ring intact."

"That's certainly a great idea, if it can be done."

"Oh, it can. It just requires people who can follow orders."

Ferdinand's plan was to wait until most of Bengal's men were assembled in the plant, right before their strike against the Gigatex factory. Then a helicopter would fly over the auto factory and fire an armor-piercing missile through the roof. The missile's nose would broadcast Somnus rays so intense that anyone within range would fall into a deep sleep within seconds.

"I'm sending one of my people, Kirsten Fale, to be liaison between your office and mine, and with the Detroit police."

Damn, thought Moran, a spy. He tried to ploy: "I could use a good second in command. I've heard impressive things about Miss Fale. How about transferring her to my unit?" If she was serving under him, it would be hard for her to be Ferdinand's snitch.

"Sorry, Moran, I appreciate your good opinion of Kirsten, but she's too valuable as my eyes and ears. Besides, somebody's got to keep an eye on the local constabulary."

Moran hadn't really expected Ferdinand to fall for it. "We will make her welcome, then."

"What about Inspector Hardrim?"

"I just sent two agents to pick him up. They'll escort him back to Washington for safekeeping."

"My plan may be too obtuse for you," said Ferdinand silkily. "I want you to bring Hardrim to your field headquarters and when you capture Bengal, arrange for them to meet. Trideecord that meeting. I have a feeling it may be quite historic someday."

"Yes sir."

"You understand that under no circumstances are you to order any assault on the terrorists without my go-ahead?"

"That's clear also."

"Well, if it's clear, let's see if you can carry out your orders. Goodbye!"

Moran watched Ferdinand fade into the pink dial tone. He wiped his shiny forehead with a handkerchief.

His pocket communicator buzzed. Moran listened a minute. His round stevedore's face creased with pleasure. "Bring Hardrim here," he said. "Is he all right?"

"They are carrying the prisoner between them, sir."

"He must have put up a fight!"

The two agents manhandled the limp man into a chair, holding his head up under the chin.

"Who is this?" asked Moran, frowning.

"The man you sent us to get."

"No, it's not."

"But it was the right room—"

"It must have been one of those men—"

"What are you talking about?" demanded Moran.

"We knocked, pointed our guns at this man, and he fainted. As we put him in our car, two men entered the motel and went into the room. One came after me and I disabled him with my taser."

"I don't like this," said Moran miserably. "Describe the men." He held up a holocube of Hardrim. "Is this one of them?"

"It's not a very clear picture, sir."

"Unhappily, my picture of how this day is going to turn out is becoming crystal clear. This man fainting should have been a clue. Hardrim is by all accounts a tough man. He took a slug in the shoulder and still brought down the guy who drilled the Nye impostor. You people should consider yourselves lucky I'm not Al Capone. This city's filled with people who messed with him and ended up wearing cement pinstripes or something."

"That was in Chicago, sir. And I think it was cement overshoes."

"Thank you."

Moran rifled Ralph Ferman's pockets and examined his wallet. A groan escaped Ferman, who opened his eyes. As the circle of rather sinister-looking FBI agents closed in he almost shrieked.

"Okay, you've got me. This time I suppose, you'll kill me to keep me from talking."

"Ferman, is it?"

"You went through my pockets!" accused Ferman.

"Never mind. Where's Inspector Hardrim?"

"You're playing with my mind. I know you've got Hardrim. What do you want? Why not just kill me? I can't tell you anything you don't know."

"Or probably anything I want to know." Moran folded his hamlike arms wearily. "Ferman, what are we going to do with you?"

Chapter
* 38 *

November 13—Galveston *Sun*—Drilling began today on Wildcat I, twin to the Tectonics Corporation's very successful Challenger tap. This is years ahead of schedule because of the recent
discovery of rich deposits of platinum group metals. Almost over-
night the Challenger drill site began producing the world's richest
gold ore. This, in addition to vast amounts of electricity generated
by the tap, makes Tectonics Corporation the newest international
giant. . . .

The Tectonics Corporation jump-jet, piloted by Rita Holcombe Duce,
hovered over an empty Atlantic Ocean twenty miles east of the Challenger
tap. Seated next to her was Jason Scott.

"It's down there somewhere." She brought the aircraft lower. "By God, I never thought it would happen so soon."

"Nobody did. Fate certainly smiled on you, Rita," said Scott. "But those who take big chances deserve big rewards."

"Did you know I paid off that bastard Krebs in gold bullion? Four years ahead of schedule. I wish I could have seen his face."

"That rumor has made the rounds. I wondered if it was true."

The jump-jet swept down in an alarming arc. Scott found himself gripping his seat.

"Whoa! Is this a demonstration of your skill with this thing?"

She grinned. "Actually, no. I just got my solo license."

"Then what am I doing in the aircraft with you? Solo license means just that, solo. No passengers."

"You know how I feel about stupid rules."

"Well, that happens to be a smart one. Since I am a certified pilot, I'll take the controls." He leveled the jump-jet at 2000 feet.

"You don't know how much I wish you *were* taking the controls—of this operation." She looked at him piercingly. "You're the man to run this project. I'm uncomfortable without you on Wildcat."

"That won't be possible, Rita."

"Then why did you call this meeting? Just to sightsee?"

"This time I need your help."

"What? You gone bust again? You know I'd float you a loan before I'd feed myself—but I insist you boss my Wildcat tap."

"It's bigger than my personal finances. It could be the biggest venture in history. What's more, I want you to make an investment that probably won't produce a profit and may lose you a lot of that gold you're taking from the earth's mantle."

"I hate to sound crudely capitalistic, but what's the point in backing a venture if there's no chance of making a profit?"

"For you, perhaps the best reason of all. To keep it out of the hands of Horatius Krebs."

A speck appeared in the sparkling blue and resolved into the floating command post for the new tap: Wild-Surf One. Scott approached the landing circle and began to set the jump-jet down.

"Jason, I'm not quite the knee-jerk Horatius Krebs hater I once was. I learned my lesson. I don't automatically hire old Python alumni, just to irritate Krebs, and I don't jump into ventures just to spite him. Besides, why would I want to keep Krebs out of a project where *he* might lose his shirt?"

"Because he wouldn't lose his shirt: He'd make a fortune, and achieve a monopoly over a vital part of the world's economy."

They jumped from the cockpit to the mildly rocking deck and headed for the control room. Rita stopped in her tracks and poked his chest, looking up at him triumphantly.

"This has something to do with the Strubeck equations!"

"Yes."

"You're an idealist, Jason. That's your weakness—and your glory. God help me, it's mine too. Let me guess: You promised to create a consortium to do the project at cost. Am I right?"

"I promised to beat any offer Krebs makes. Doing it at cost will guarantee that Prometheus Enterprises gets the project."

Rita Duce looked pensive. "I don't know if Tectonics Corporation has that much liquid capital. Although I can make a big dent in providing your requirements."

"You don't know it, Rita, but right now you've got the Midas touch. Your name alone could persuade investors to sign on."

"Maybe. And maybe if I decide to come on board it will be to provide the lion's share of the financing. Because you're not telling me everything, are you?"

"There is one more thing. The agreement I made with Sheridan Mayfield forbids me or anyone in the consortium to profit from the technology or application of the Strubeck equations. But we are not forbidden to use any scientific spin-offs from the project."

"That sounds like 'Dig me a gold mine and you can keep any pieces of coal that you run across.' "

"Or diamonds."

"But you can't guarantee anything like that."

"All I can guarantee is that your money will get a workout."

"I'd love to take some of this gold I've been digging up and throw it in the faces of those throwback Neanderthal McClarenites who tried to murder the Challenger tap. I'd also like to deep-six Horatius Krebs's aspirations for becoming a global slumlord."

"You've always been a good hater, Rita."

"You misconstrue, my dear friend. This is for you. You're the only one I'd risk my fortune for, because you're the only one with any claim on it."

"Thank you," said Scott simply.

"You once told me not to thank you for doing your job. Well, don't thank me for doing what's right. I don't have any choice."

"I understand."

"We both do."

They stood looking at each other for a long moment, which was broken when they were drenched by a cloud of spray.

"Let's get inside," said Rita gruffly. "Not only have I not gained a manager on this deal, but I've probably caught my death. Thank God I've still got Matt Taylor."

"Sorry, Rita." Scott grinned again. "I'm taking Matt too."

"Well, after the Challenger episode I knew he'd desert to you someday. You going to steal any more of my vital personnel?"

"No, but I am going to raid every major engineering firm in the country. And they'll come, too, because I offer a once-in-a-lifetime chance."

She reached up and ruffled his hair in a motherly way. "You've damaged me enough for one day, Jason. Besides, I've got to get ready for an intimate dinner with an old friend who's flying out in a couple of hours."

Scott arched an eyebrow slightly. "Senator Macadew?"

"Yes, and you don't have to say what you're thinking. He *is* just an old friend. Of course, he's still in love with me, and as for me: Who could resist a charming old warrior like that? But that's all. He'll stay married. It's sad, how things turn out. When he loved me, I was married to my work. Now that I can love him, he's married to a woman he doesn't love. Sometimes two lives never quite mesh." She took a deep breath and smiled. "Anyway, I intend to enjoy dinner. I'm confident I can recruit Charles. He's got a lot of clout in the business world himself."

"Then I'll go. I'll fly that same jump-jet back to the mainland when it's refueled. Good-bye, Rita."

Chapter

⋆ 39 ⋆

1

When Hardrim and Sebastian returned to the Argus Society, their expressions told Chambless they had failed.

"This is very minor or very serious, depending on whom you encountered tonight," said Chambless under a halo of pipe smoke.

"We must treat it as very serious," said Hardrim.

"Agreed. It's now imperative to destroy this building tonight. A new safe house is already prepared."

"Let's even our odds a bit. Sebastian memorized the license number of the car carrying Ferman. Dr. Chambless, how thoroughly have you infiltrated the national computer network? Can we access sensors in the city to keep an eye out for Ferman and that car?"

"I'm not sure we should discuss that yet," said Sebastian.

"We must trust Mr. Hardrim. We had to trust someone from outside with the complete truth, Sebastian, and Hardrim is the man. He's in too deep for us not to trust him now. His approval by the council is really a formality."

"The way you operate, it is."

"To answer you, Inspector, we can access both national and city networks. What exactly do you want done?"

"What I have in mind is to alert the locals to watch for Ferman, but route any inquiries back to us."

"When you deal with human agencies you risk discovery. We've kept our profile low by making inquiries only of computers. They have no curiosity to be roused."

"This may be the time to be reckless. We must get a line on what happened to Ralph Ferman."

"I agree. But at this moment the single most important thing is for us to leave here. Sebastian, prepare the fire bombs."

2

Two days later Chambless entered the study in the new safe house where Hardrim had isolated himself with the works of Alfred Strubeck.

"What news on Ferman?" asked Hardrim.

"None." Chambless frowned. "It's very annoying. We can't identify that license plate, either. I hope Sebastian's memory is not at fault, but he was unconscious for several seconds—"

"Yet if he's right, then if anybody can trace the number, it's you."

"Just so."

"What about Lenny? Have you found out if she returned home?"

"She is not home and has not been for several days."

Hardrim slammed his fist into his left hand. "Damn! That's not like her! She's a homebody. I've got to go look for her."

"Under no circumstances—"

Hardrim matched stares with him. "Chambless," he said in a low voice, "Don't try to stop me."

"It won't come to that, my boy. But please postpone your decision until after the meeting of the governing council of the Argus Society."

"I don't have time—"

"This is serious!" fumed Chambless. "Indulge me. How many people do you think are fully knowledgeable about our activities?"

"You mean, how many know as much as I do?"

"Correct."

"Thousands?"

"Less than a hundred. So few that we communicate by closed circuit holovision, as we will do in a few minutes."

"How can so few people be responsible for so much?"

"I said 'fully knowledgeable.' Thousands belong to the society. Most think they're working for higher standards of education, expanded scientific research. Some view it as a club for the cream of the science world, or a think tank of super minds. They're all right. We do all those things. We've been able to hide our true activities because ninety-nine percent of the members are ignorant of them too." He looked at Hardrim piercingly. "So why do you insist on telling your lady friend about our activities?"

"I see your point. But I won't work for you if I can't tell Lenore."

Chambless ground his teeth. This discussion had gone on for two days. Hardrim had proved immovable. "I must bring this before the full committee."

"Who has the authority to decide?"

"We've had no executive since Strubeck's death. Senior members have the most voice. Dr. Norrison is our most influential member. He helped found the society and was Strubeck's best friend. Soon, however, the workings of the society will change."

"What do you mean?"

"I'll wait until the committee convenes before I explain. We are making the hookups now. Follow me."

Upstairs in the library, Chambless sat at a console. His fingers glided over the light board. He nodded. "Everything's complete. Make yourself comfortable."

"Where's Sebastian?"

"Even he does not attend our most secret meetings."

Without warning, the room was full of people. Hardrim knew they were holographic images, but that didn't detract from the sheer drama of the moment.

Chambless nodded to the 'assemblage.' "Glad to see you all."

Hardrim recognized several famous scientists. All returned Chambless's greeting cordially except one, an old man who stared, apparently unseeing. Then he became animated.

"Hello, Chambless. Hello, everyone!" His vibrant voice contrasted with his frail appearance. "Sorry about the transmission delay. Damned nuisance, but better than being on earth with a faulty ticker." He laughed thinly. Hardrim realized that his image originated from the moon.

"Quite all right, Dr. Norrison," said Chambless deferentially. "In view of that delay, I suggest that someone else chair the meeting."

"Good idea, Chambless. No need to hobble the rest of you with my heart condition. Why don't you do the honors?"

"If no one objects?"

"Who's the young man?" said someone.

"Mel Hardrim." Chambless waited for this to sink in.

"I presume you know what you're doing, Chambless," said a middle-aged woman Hardrim recognized as a leading authority on oceanography. "Please explain why Inspector Hardrim, who has caused us so many problems, is at our most secret meeting?"

"He has been persuaded to join us," said Chambless slowly. "He knew much about us when he entered our headquarters. He knows even more since he took Strubeck's mind tape—"

"You took it upon yourself to do that?"

"I take full responsibility. He's also had extensive conversations with the Strubeck program. I felt it was time we had someone in this organization equipped to act, not just think. Inspector Hardrim's tenacity and ingenuity was demonstrated against us. Fortunately he has been persuaded by the pure light of reason to join us."

"We have other strong-arms in our employ," said someone.

"I don't suggest that his specialty is physical. In his work he uses brains more than brawn. He is talented in an area where many of us are lacking: translation of thought into action."

"Bushwah!"

"Your arrogance has reached new bounds, Chambless!"

"I think it's a good idea," said Norrison after the delay imposed by distance. "A first-rate idea!"

"Ah, there is one more thing—" Chambless looked uncomfortable. He threw an irritated look at Hardrim. "He insists he can't work for us without consulting his lady friend—"

"Fiancée!" said Hardrim sharply.

"Just so." Chambless tapped his pipe against his desk. "That means two additions to our inner circle, if Miss Lippman is persuaded." He lit his pipe. Someone started to protest the smoke, until he realized it couldn't possibly affect him.

Norrison's voice penetrated the angry murmur. "You're all being a little thick-headed tonight. Perhaps low gravity aids clear thinking. Or maybe I've just been at this longer." The hostile voices ceased and all faces turned to the old man. "You forget that soon this committee will be no more. Our project will be launched with all our blessings, but it must reach its ultimate destination without us."

"I'm totally in the dark," said Hardrim. "I've been told the ultimate goal of your activities. But I still don't understand exactly how you hope to achieve it."

"Young man," said Norrison, "most of Alfred Strubeck's life was devoted to raising and teaching three exceptional boys chosen by aptitude tests. They are now grown, ready to fulfill the purpose for which they were educated. Through our actions we set in motion the Sunside Project, whose purpose you know. But we can no longer guide events. Soon the fulfillment of Strubeck's plan will fall on the three. They bear this burden in ignorance. They don't know they were raised for this purpose, although every fiber of their beings was trained for it."

"Surely Sherlock Michlanski knows of the plan. Didn't he go to the president along with Dorian Nye and persuade him to initiate the Sunside Project?"

"Sherlock knows the plan, but not that it has existed since he was a child. He is unaware that his upbringing had a purpose beyond mere education."

"And Nye?" How responsible had Nye been for Hardrim's troubles? The question had plagued him since he had made the connection between the scientist and the Argus Society.

"One of our inner circle. He would be with us tonight, but he is heavily tied up with the Sunside Project."

"Is it moral to precondition individuals as you did the three boys?"

"Not if they were actually 'conditioned.' But they were picked because they scored perfectly mentally and psychologically on our tests. They were born that way. Such genius can't be created, only searched for, and if found, polished to perfection. That we did. We caused the present world crisis and brought it to a head. Now their time has come. They will control events. We can only watch and hope they succeed, and perhaps offer an unseen hand without calling attention to ourselves."

"Is it fair for them not to know their heritage? You took them when they were young and trained them toward one end. Where is free will? Do you think you are gods?"

Chambless choked on his smoke. He tossed the pipe on the desk as if he had been bitten. "That tears it," he said to no one in particular.

Norrison remained placid throughout a barrage of angry comments directed at Hardrim. "The questions are reasonable. If he's sincere enough to question the morality of our actions, I'm more inclined to trust him."

He nodded at Hardrim. "Your question has been asked many times. And you must realize it applies even more to the nation and the world, who are also victims of our manipulation."

"More than manipulation!" said Hardrim sharply. "You people loosed a plague that could have killed billions."

"Could have, but didn't," said Chambless. "No evidence exists that anyone actually starved because of the blight. Famine relief efforts were very efficient."

"What if the president hadn't responded as he did? What if the 'have' nations hadn't joined the famine relief efforts?"

"We would have released a bioengineered serum that would have destroyed the blight virus in days," said Norrison. "No one wanted a catastrophe, except perhaps Chambless." He looked at the biologist with a mischievous twinkle in his eyes.

"I didn't want one either! But I was willing to go a good deal farther than my colleagues were before we released the countervirus. I was willing to accept some deaths if it took that to mobilize the scientific effort we needed."

"We wanted a catalyst," said Norrison, "to force action, primarily by the United States government."

"These questions were resolved years ago?" asked Hardrim.

"Alfred and I discussed them at length, but never resolved them. We reached a compromise, although it was no easier to 'play God.'

"Strictly speaking, you're right. The boys had a right to know, to make their own decisions. On the other hand, they *did* make the decisions. They had complete educations, with emphasis on sciences, and even more emphasis on enhancing each one's special talent. We did not suggest they were obliged to the Argus Society. We tried to persuade them they were young men of destiny, that it would be wise for them to discover what their destinies might be. But coercion was impossible with such strong individuals. They would have resisted, and since they are so remarkable, they would have prevailed," said Norrison.

"What we did was analogous to taking a seed, giving it fertilizer, a perfect climate, and care. Is it manipulation if that seed grows to be what its genes intend? Is it fairer to deny the seed nutrients? Is that free will? I don't think so. I don't think it would have been wise to tell the boys about themselves.

"Genius is a factor of ego. I believe it springs from the ego, that self-esteem is tied directly to it. If they had been told that they learned and matured by a set plan, their egos might have been irreparably damaged, and with their egos their genius.

"Talk about playing God! Think how we contemplated the possible results. Do we tell them? Let them decide for themselves? And risk annihilating their egos, perhaps their talents? Or do we deny them free will, but ensure that their genius develops unimpaired, without the added weight of self-doubt?"

Chambless, who had been nodding vigorously, spoke up, using his pipe to emphasize his points. "Furthermore, do we go before the world court of opinion to present our scientific ideas? Do we ask for a vote? Yes, if you want stagnation. No, if you want advancement. In the present climate, they'd put us all in prison. We've always known that. Subterfuge was our last resort."

"I suppose," said Hardrim slowly, "all your actions are filled with moral pitfalls. I apologize for assuming you did not consider them. I don't know if I would make the same decisions. I'm glad I didn't have to. What's done is done."

"Amen," said Norrison. "I see no reason not to admit you to our circle. I think we can trust you not to endanger us if your fiancée doesn't see things our way." He looked about the room, and such was his influence that no one disagreed.

"One thing," said Hardrim. "You said we've reached a point where the Argus Society no longer guides events. But can it still carry out damage control?"

"What do you mean?" said Norrison.

"When Hardrim infiltrated us, he had an accomplice." Chambless didn't hide his distaste. "You've read my reports about Ralph Ferman. Hardrim penetrated our defenses because of Ferman's information. When he broke into our building, he left Ferman at a motel. When he and Sebastian returned there, Ferman was gone. Evidence suggests Ferman is in the hands of a third party. If you watch your screens, I'll pass this information on to you."

The silence deepened as each member read the report.

"This could be disastrous!" said a zoologist.

"We have one more item to discuss," said Chambless, smoothly regaining control. Hardrim found himself admiring the Texan's ability to shape the meeting. "I was forced to abandon the old headquarters. I destroyed our records by fire. We can set up a new headquarters here, or in a smaller location, and continue to function innocuously in public."

Chambless smiled. "In case you don't read the obituaries, Inspector Hardrim died in that fire. I believe I acted within my authority. If you disagree I'd like to know."

"Ye gods! What can we do if we disagree? Pull the ashes back together?" said a woman physicist.

"Your arrogance is unbounded, Chambless!" said a mathematician.

Chambless was cool. "A decision had to be made. We don't need a headquarters any more. Record centralization is dangerous, particularly since Ferman is an unknown, possibly explosive quantity. With our main work accomplished I thought it wise to disperse the records, or destroy them. We can't afford discovery this late in the game. The public must *never* learn that we were behind the famine."

"I think you acted within your authority," said a particle physicist. "Since we can't undo it, I move that we endorse it."

"In favor," said Chambless. The show of hands supported him.

"Inspector, you spoke of damage control" said Norrison. "Are you volunteering to stop Ferman from destroying our work?"

"I feel responsible for him. I think I should find him. But I can't promise until I talk to Lenny."

"Your mission has become a vital element of our work," mused Norrison. "Perhaps the most vital. The Santa Bella blight has died out. Our headquarters is gone and the records destroyed. The Argus Society has done its job. The only positive contribution we can make is to be the Sunside Project's guardian angel. We must be as 'wily as serpents, and as harmless as doves.' Our strength lies in our hidden access to the world's computers. We know, but are not known. That advantage may help us find Ralph Ferman and keep him from using his information against us. All departments of the society that can't be used for damage control should be deactivated. And I so move." He fixed his gaze on Hardrim. "I hope you make the right decision, young man."

"All in favor," said Chambless. This time the vote took longer, but the results were the same. "Very well." He consulted his timepiece. "I have things to do. I suggest we adjourn. Thank you, and good luck to us and our endeavors."

The next day Hardrim sent a message to Lenny Lippman's computer at the Department of Justice. Only she could access to it. He hoped to God it would reach her. It read:

Report of my death was exaggerated. You have a heart-shaped birthmark under your right nipple. I'll see you soon. Love, Mel.

Chapter
✳ **40** ✳

1

Horatius Krebs left his limousine at the curb in front of the Python building.

Krebs entered the lobby and was dutifully ignored by every employee. Instead of being fussed over, he preferred an imperial control in which each employee is trained to know his employer's whim, and to provide it before he asks. If Krebs fumbled for a cigarette lighter, or looked as if he were going to sneeze, a lighter or handkerchief would be produced. That was more satisfying than a dozen sycophants yapping at his heels.

He was almost at the elevator when someone approached. He turned with irritation slightly mitigated when he recognized his financial aide, Lewis Cocker, who never interrupted unless it was important. Even so, Krebs turned on him with a snarl that almost cowed him into the fibers of the heavy shag carpet.

"What do you want, Cocker?" He left toothmarks on every syllable. He knew everyone called the man Krebs's cocker spaniel, and he knew Cocker knew it too. "Don't you have enough work?"

"I'm sorry, sir." Krebs noted with approval that Cocker's spirit was almost broken; a combination of a high-powered salary and humiliation. When he first hired the brilliant young college graduate, he had applied his own brand of psychology to warp Cocker's will. Krebs's record of judging men was almost perfect. He had only been wrong once, when he had misjudged Jason Scott. Now, as if to torment him, his enemy's name escaped Cocker's lips.

"I thought you'd want to hear this news about Jason Scott."

Krebs lips drew back over his teeth. He felt an urge to strike Cocker. He let out a hissing breath.

"What about him?" Krebs never watched the news, relying on aides to keep him abreast of news that affected his interests.

"Prometheus Enterprises, Scott's company, will do the contract work for the PH station. His news conference was on the cube five minutes ago."

Krebs snapped his jaws shut and narrowed his eyes. "There must be more. Scott could never get away with giving the contract to his own company unless there's something else—what is it?"

"Prometheus Enterprises and a consortium backing him will do the work at cost, under the condition that technological spin-offs are fair game for them. They will take losses out of their own pockets." Cocker watched Krebs for signs of an explosion.

"Who's his main backer?"

"Tectonics Corporation."

"Of course!" Krebs chuckled gratingly. "I knew there was a catch. Smart bastard! He'll look like a hero to the world, and gain control of the Strubeck equations. With Rita Duce's gold! What a magnificent idea! Why didn't my high-priced geniuses think that one up for me?"

They boarded Krebs's stomach-twisting private elevator. He noticed Cocker's knees bending with the acceleration and grinned.

"There's more, sir." They got out on the top floor. Cocker struggled to keep up with his employer.

"Hurry. I don't have all day!"

"Scott is already raiding the big engineering firms for people. He snapped up three topflight employees of Transnational minutes after he left the air."

"He works fast. I'm not surprised he got some of Transnational's brains. Henry Nab could be outwitted by the pope. Has he made a grab for any of our people?"

"Not that I know of."

"Cretin! Make sure you do know!" Krebs burst through the outer door of his office. He poked Cocker's solar plexis. "I want a report every hour. I want to know who Scott gets, when, from where, and for how much. Get our lawyers cracking on ways to delay him, trip him up."

"Won't that look like we're opposing the public good? It's very bad public relations."

"Idiot! I want them to be subtle. Let them find reasons why Scott giving the contract to his own company is bad for free enterprise, competition, the American way, all that crap. They're lawyers; I pay them plenty to lie and cheat. One more thing—"

"Sir?"

"I want to know the instant he tries to recruit my people. Offer whatever is necessary to keep them working for me. Anybody who helps Scott, unless he's the kind of specialist Scott is trying to pirate, is to be fired. I will make it hell on earth for anyone who traitorizes me! Tell 'em that! You'd be surprised what fear can accomplish. Then again, maybe you wouldn't." He turned away with a sneer and entered his inner office.

His secretary flagged him down.

"What?"

"Jacob Kane's waiting in your office."

"Man's a mind reader!"

Kane sat slumped carelessly with his right foot resting on Krebs's desk. He acknowledged Krebs's arrival with a languid wave.

"I take it you've heard the news," said Krebs.

"What news is that?" Kane's expression was innocently blank.

"Don't play games. I'm not in the mood."

"I presume you're talking about Jason Scott's announcement."

"Damn right!" Kane fell into his chair. "He's raiding all the engineering companies for their best people. Bastard's a fast worker, I'll give him that. But that's all I'll give him. I'm especially not going to roll over while he grabs my people!"

"What do you intend to do about it?"

"Discredit Scott and Mayfield with the public. I'll offer more money and work incentives to anyone approached by Scott."

"How will you know when they're approached?"

"That's your job. Prepare portfolios on those likely to be contacted. Have them watched, homes bugged. Start immediately."

"Do you think it'll work?"

Krebs hit his desk top with his palm. "Why am I getting these stupid questions, Kane? Are you drunk, or just trying to irritate me? Of course it will work! I don't intend to lose a single technician to Jason Scott."

"You've already lost one."

"*What?*" Krebs sprang to his feet with such force that his chair rolled back into the wall. "Who? Why didn't you say something? Dammit! He won't get away with it!"

"Too late, Horatius. It's me."

"I don't like your jokes!" He glared, comprehension dawning. "This isn't one of your jokes, is it?"

"No. I'm quitting, as of now, this morning."

"You won't quit." He grinned widely. "I know you too well. You're virtually second in command here. Okay, how much do I have to shell out this time? Mercenary son of a bitch—I just doubled your pay. But I admit, you know what you're worth. How much?"

"More than you can pay."

"Absurd! Name your cost. I'll pay it."

"I want to work on the PH station. You aren't in a position to give me that."

Krebs's strawberry nose turned deep red. His voice was deadly calm. "The Sunside Project won't get started, much less finished, because I'm going to scuttle it. When it's destroyed, I'll get control of the Strubeck equations."

"That's aiming high, even for you."

Krebs grunted. "I always aim high. Stick with me and you'll share the spoils. Don't worry, I don't begrudge you making me pay through the nose, as long as I can work your ass off." He folded his hands over his stomach. "Then we have a deal."

"No," said Kane. "We don't."

"You're stretching my patience with this mercenary routine."

"It's difficult to communicate with you." Kane picked up the digital clock on Krebs's desk and smashed it. Pieces scattered over the desk. Krebs thumbed the switch on his holocube.

"Tell Emil to bring in a broom." He looked at Kane. "I have my answer. Now get out. Before you go, know this: I'm going to ruin you. I'll not only destroy Jason Scott, but you too."

"You may be taking on more than you can handle."

Emil entered with a whisk broom. Kane smiled at his incongruous appearance. Emil returned his look stonily, but beneath the stone, Kane sensed a seething fire.

"Clean this up," said Krebs. His catastrophic eyes drilled into Kane like twin lasers.

"I'll be seeing you, Horatius."

"Count on it."

Kane left. Emil dumped the clock into a flash disposal unit.

Krebs sat for several minutes. Then he looked up. "I'm upping the stakes. Return to Detroit. Be prepared to take delivery of a small industrial-type atomic bomb with enough explosive power to destroy the Gigatex plant."

"You're a man of vision, Horatius."

"I knew you'd be happy. But it's not quite what you think. You will also be getting a type Y-Zenith detonator."

"That's a European make."

"It will identify the bomb as having come from Europe."

"When the bomb explodes, the detonator will be vaporized. No identification will be possible."

"I don't intend for it to go off. It will be discovered by the authorities after Bengal and his men finish their raid on the Gigatex plant. When the FBI finds the bomb, they will wipe out Bengal's force to the last man."

2

The air force helicopter, flanked by three escorts, settled on the lawn in front of Space Exploration and Development headquarters (formerly NASA), sending leaves and dirt swirling.

Reporters and scientists alike rushed to the windows and jostled to see as several men emerged from the helicopter and ranged themselves protectively around a tall, older man.

Jason Scott, who was about to begin a press briefing, was left alone at the podium. Sheridan Mayfield, a few chairs away, looked out the window.

"The president is paying you a visit, Jason."

"An unannounced visit."

"He has a flair for the dramatic. You must learn to enjoy these little moments in the sun."

"The Gilgamesh Scramjet should shift their attention pretty quickly. Reporters are fascinated by hardware."

"Not too quickly, I hope. We want to use the Sunside Project as a fulcrum to justify deploying Gilgamesh. That's why he's here, to drum up interest." Mayfield stood with a groan. "And to check up on his investment. Trust comes slowly with him, but once he does trust you, he'll give you the world. You do realize you hold his political future in your hands? If the Sunside Project fails, Shefferton will get a place in the history books next to Warren Harding—that is, if there are any history books."

"I'm not interested in his future. The country and world have far more at stake. I'm working with that disaster in mind, not the minor one that he might lose the next election."

"You don't think much of Shefferton, do you?"

"I don't think much of politicians. That's why I like you."

"He's put it all on the line, Jason. Not just a political career. Everything. Not one in a million would have risked what he has. I thank God we have him." Mayfield didn't hear footsteps enter the auditorium.

"Thank you, Sheridan," said the president softly. Mayfield looked up, his face red. "I like to think any president will do what's best for his country, even if his own interests are threatened." Shefferton turned. "And you're Dr. Scott?"

"Just Jason Scott, Mr. President. I never finished college."

The president nodded and stepped up onto the platform into an electrical storm of holovision and camera lights.

"I'm not here to make a speech. I came to hear Mr. Scott. If you folks don't mind, I'll take a seat up here, and listen."

"Mr. President, question!" yelled a reporter a microsecond ahead of every other journalist in the room.

Shefferton looked apologetically toward Mayfield and Scott.

"Okay, but make it brief. No questions about subjects not pertaining to this project."

"Mr. President, is this your first briefing?"

"I've had lots of information from Secretary Mayfield. but I've never had the pleasure of meeting Jason Scott. I decided this was a good time for that, and to talk to him about the project."

"Are you satisfied with the progress so far?"

"Yes. The real delays came from the congressional hearings. But now they're cleared up, I think we'll have smooth sailing."

Several voices called in unison, but Shefferton declined firmly. "Later.

I'm anxious to hear Secretary Mayfield and Mr. Scott, just as I'm sure you are."

Mayfield stood before the microphone, looking disheveled and uncomfortable, as usual. He awkwardly adjusted his tie.

"Secretary Mayfield?" said the Boston *Globe* reporter.

"Yes. Sure."

"What's your comment about Horatius Krebs's charge that choosing Jason Scott's company is unethical?"

Mayfield took a deep breath for a furious counterattack and then he saw the president raise his eyebrows almost imperceptibly. He let the breath out again.

"Slander laws make it impossible to reply as completely as I'd like. But it's a matter of public record that Krebs was angling for the contract for Python Corporation. He used a lot of influence around Washington but didn't get it. So he's mad.

"I don't see how awarding the contract to Scott can be called corrupt, since he's offered his services free. That's more than Krebs ever did. We took the cheapest offer. We also picked the best company for the job!" He paused, surprised at himself for keeping his temper. "Now let me introduce Jason Scott, who'll answer your questions after an initial presentation."

Scott had shaved his beard. Even his hair, normally uncombable, had been brought to heel. His confidence communicated itself to the audience in an almost electric way.

To those who had known Adam Scott, his son seemed almost a reincarnation. One reporter, who had been at Adam Scott's last news conference, wiped tears from his eyes at the memory.

"Ladies and gentlemen, the purpose of the Sunside Project is to construct the first experimental PH station, where the Strubeck equations will be tested. If we succeed, for the first time in history food will be made from sunlight without the intervening step of an oxygen-producing plant.

"The PH Station will be built twenty million miles from the surface of the sun, to take advantage of concentrated energy. In the past, space stations were engineered piece by piece, like L-5 and Midway, or like Skylab, shot into space complete. The PH station will be built from three space ships constructed in the shipping yards at Luna's Tycho Brahe base. They will journey toward the sun and be joined to form the hub and spokes of the station. At the hub will be a zero-gravity docking area and laboratories.

"After the ships are cannibalized, the station will be partially functional. More materials will arrive in the form of similar ships and raw materials shot by mass-driver from Mercury. New sections will be added to the existing structure.

"The station's outer skin will consist of sun cells. Very soon after the joining we hope to have a self-sufficient community, beginning with about one hundred scientists, and growing to one thousand when we finish in eighteen months.

"Experimentation to produce simple sugar molecules will begin when the lab sections are habitable." Scott pointed to a large blueprint drawn on an electric blackboard. He indicated where the crew would sleep, work, and sometimes play, as in the small area that could be used for zero-gravity tennis.

"Mr. Scott," asked the Spokane *Mirror* reporter, "When will construction of the ships begin?"

"As soon as I arrive on Luna. I'll supervise their construction. Most of the crew (including myself) are leaving for the moon this month."

Scott introduced his staff.

"Chief of staff will be Dr. Dorian Nye, assisted by Sherlock Michlanski, who will also be in charge of several subsidiary research projects. A base so close to the sun will offer numerous opportunities for study, and we will take advantage of them."

There was a murmur of disbelief that Michlanski was to be junior to Dorian Nye. It seemed inconceivable that he would consent to take orders from anyone, even his old college professor. Michlanski mounted the podium and laughingly but deftly navigated through the cross-examination.

"I want to stop these rumors that I'm not easy to get along with." He held his hands out palm up in an imitation of Jack Benny. "Really! I don't mind a subsidiary position when my superior is as qualified as Dr. Nye. Nor do I think my creativity will be stunted." He grinned mischievously "Actually, a junior position will leave me more time to pursue my main object; seducing all the young ladies on the PH station."

Michlanski returned to his seat. Later it dawned on most of the reporters that he had avoided answering any real questions.

Scott stood again. "Until recently Jacob Kane was an executive for the Python Corporation. He will be chief design architect and engineer for the PH station."

"Mr. Kane," said the *Washington Post* reporter. "Rumor has it that

Horatius Krebs was furious at you for quitting. Did he threaten to ruin you?"

Kane grinned sardonically. "The very idea that Horatius Krebs could be vindictive is ridiculous. We parted under most cordial circumstances. He even offered me a position in one of his natural history museums, as an exhibit."

Nervous laughter greeted this remark. Kane was blatantly rubbing his former employer's nose in his resignation.

After the press conference, Michlanski, Kane, and Scott joined President Shefferton. Mayfield watched from across the room. He wasn't asked to join the conclave. The Sunside Project was slipping from his grasp. It belonged to Scott, his picked men—and the president.

Mayfield knew he was being left out. Shefferton wasn't telling him something. He'd known since that night at the White House when the president met privately with Michlanski and Nye. He felt a twinge of something lost. Scott, Kane, and Michlanski belonged together, like brothers, or something more. A wild thought lingered: What if Scott had maneuvered *Mayfield* into picking him to head the Sunside Project, instead of the other way around?

One of the president's aides handed him a note. Shefferton called Mayfield over from across the room.

"Sheridan," he said. "Something has come up. You and I need to get back to the White House immediately."

Chapter
* 41 *

. . . Thou art as a whale in the seas; and thou camest forth with thy rivers, and troubledst the waters with thy feet, and foulest their rivers.

—*Ezekiel 32:2*

1

Several days after the meeting of the Argus Society's ruling council, Sherlock Michlanski paid a visit to the new safe house.

Chambless and Hardrim were in the Strubeck library when he was announced. His gleaming curls and beard fell like jewels onto his black silk waistcoat as he swept in, trailing a red-lined velvet cape. He was eating miniature marshmallows from a bag.

Chambless's smile of welcome was forced. Hardrim surmised it was the tension of an intellect of the second class in the presence of an intellect of the first class.

The first time Hardrim had observed Michlanski, he had been amused by the scientist, and a bit contemptuous. Now he knew better. He saw that Chambless viewed Michlanski with awe, fear, and more than a shade of pride, as J. Robert Oppenheimer must have regarded his child, the atom bomb. He sensed that Michlanski was almost an elemental force. He projected an aura of intense energy hinted at by his constant pacing and inability to remain motionless, as a cut power cable throwing sparks only hints at its potential.

It had to be discomfiting for Chambless to know that the youth he had helped educate was a stellar genius far beyond him. That it was impossible to know what Michlanski *was* capable of.

"You really shouldn't be here, Sherlock."

"Wherefore not, Dr. Chambless? Marshmallow?"

"No thank you. Someone might recognize you. You should be at Deseret—"

"Fussiness is your least endearing feature, old friend."

"Nevertheless."

Michlanski held up his hand. "You're right. But I *am* here."

"But why? You must be extremely busy at this time."

"Curiously, I'm not. I've waited for this all my life. I'm as prepared as I'll ever be."

Hardrim glanced at Chambless and wondered how much Michlanski had figured out about his own past and that of his two boyhood friends.

"But why here?"

"I don't know. Loose ends I need to tie up, perhaps." Michlanski wandered about the room, idly picking up books and looking at covers without apparent interest.

His eyes fell on Hardrim. His cherubic smile became fluorescent. He leaped forward as if to embrace an old friend, "My dear Inspector, I'm happy to see you!"

"I'm happy to be seen," said Hardrim wryly.

"Perhaps you're the reason I'm here. Marshmallow?"

Hardrim shook his head. "I don't understand."

"The day we met, we underestimated each other." Hardrim was taken aback by Michlanski's almost telepathic reading of his own feelings. "You did some remarkable detective work on us. I've wanted to talk to you again."

"I'm flattered."

"No you're not," said Michlanski impatiently. "You're curious, as I am." He whirled in a black cyclone of silk and announced dramatically: "Come on, gentlemen, we're going out to dinner and music. My treat!"

"This is ridiculous, Sherlock," said Chambless.

"What's ridiculous about an afternoon on the town with friends before I leave for an extended tour of space? Come along, old teacher, don't be a stick in the mud!" He started for the door, then turned. "You don't have a previous engagement, I hope?"

"No—" said Chambless unenthusiastically.

"I'd be delighted." Hardrim felt himself the vicarious recipient of some of Michlanski's enthusiastic energy.

"But—where are we going?" They had folded themselves into Michlanski's stripped down red custom sports car (Chambless was virtually resting his chin on his knees) and were approaching the turnoff to Detroit's airport.

"California."

Michlanski's jump-jet was small but luxurious, even to a robot arm that served canapes as they prepared to leap into the sky. "I'll only have a few." Michlanski nibbled on Gruyere cheese and apples. "The marshmallows took the edge off my appetite."

"What's in California?" said Hardrim, munching on a cracker spread with cream cheese, caviar, and truffles.

"The suicidal whale, naturally."

2

Looking down on Southern California, a suborbital traveler would see the southernmost tentacles of the Los Angeles megalopolis (between Camp Pendleton and San Diego) engaging in a game of footsie with the northernmost tentacles of the Mexican megalopolis, which included Tijuana and Ensenada and originated in the ancient Aztec Tenochtitlan (Mexico City). The tentacles avoided what had been San Diego, now a latter-day Coventry and Cherokee strip.

Also separating the super cities was a bluish strip that zigzagged like a lightning bolt from San Clemente across deserts and mountains for several hundred miles. To see its terminus, the air traveler would have to become a space traveler and rise about 150 miles over the earth. The bluish lightning bolt seemed to blast through the mountains, reenter the great deserts, and end in a man-made inland sea upon whose shores plants turned sea water into fresh, and factories made hydrogen fuel. The sea, called Lake Deseret or the Sea of Cibola, embraced parts of Arizona, Nevada, and Utah. It had turned Phoenix and Tucson into seaports and spawned the nation's newest metropolis, Deseret, to service the national spaceport.

The waterway connecting the Pacific Ocean and the Sea of Cibola was the American Transterrain Canal. It was linked with California's inner waterways, so one could take a riverboat from the Sacramento River to the San Jauquin River, join the northern link of the canal and continue on to Deseret.

Somehow or other, a forty-ton humpback male had gotten turned around during the mating season and was swimming placidly up the American Transterrain Canal toward destruction.

Along his route a carnival atmosphere prevailed. His swim toward doom had acquired a mythic quality. Hundreds of thousands lined the mile-wide canal to watch him approach the locks that would carry him over the mountains. If the thin air didn't kill him, he would undoubtedly be destroyed by less salty water beyond.

"Why are we here, Sherlock?" asked Chambless plaintively. "You're about embark on what may be the most important mission of mankind, and we've come to watch a whale commit seppuku."

They stood on the shore of the canal. Michlanski's cape flapped in the Santa Ana winds, which, although Chambless didn't realize it, contributed to his frustration and vague unease. Hardrim, on the other hand, was fascinated.

"Old teacher, I can't think of a more important thing we could do." Michlanski smiled a gentle, sad smile. "Whales and porpoises are the closest thing to brothers man has on this planet. Our friend in the Interuterine Canal may be closer to Homo sapiens than we suspect, judging from his behavior."

"We're here to see how close?" said Hardrim softly.

"Perhaps." His voice was almost tossed away by the wind.

"Why must the whale die?" said Chambless. "For him to go beyond this point, the operators of the locks must let him through."

"Our treaty with the Cetacean herds is complex. They are vital to our deep-sea mining and to maintenance of our floating cities. They travel the earth-Saturn routes, maintaining the tankers alone, without ill effects. We can't offend them."

"How does preventing one of their number from committing suicide cause offense?"

"When we sang our treaties with the herds, we felt residual guilt over our treatment of the American Indians. Nobody wanted a treaty like that with the Cetaceans. We were very accommodating. The treaties forbid us from interfering with any legitimate Cetacean activity. And suicide is definitely a legitimate activity among the great whales."

"The locksmen will not prevent the whale from coming through?" said Hardrim.

"No."

"How long before it arrives here?"

"Within the hour, I think."

On the plain overlooking the canal, jojoba plants gave way to brown Southern California grass. The land formed a natural amphitheater. As the crowds grew, a large helicopter landed and regurgitated a full-sized orchestra, in tuxedos and tails.

"That's the Los Angeles Philharmonic," said Hardrim.

"Some millionaire has financed the 'Divine Intervention' concert. Sort of a musical prayer," said Michlanski.

"I wish I'd brought my sitar."

"I learned to play a symphony orchestra in my youth. I too will be intrigued," said Michlanski with that infuriating mix of placid condescension that he held virtually under a patent.

"I wished I'd stayed home." Chambless's mucus membranes cried out for moisture in the dry wind. He fumbled in his coat, now folded over his arm, for a pipe he had left in Detroit.

The musicians sat in portable chairs and tuned their instruments. Some enterprising fellow set up a sidewalk bistro near the orchestra. Soon Michlanski, Hardrim, and Chambless were seated. The Polish scientist examined the menu's offering of escargots. "As I promised, dinner and music. Although I consider it in poor taste to offer mahimahi as part of the menu."

Dinner arrived. Michlanski plucked mollusks from shells and dipped them in garlic butter while, a few feet away, a holovision arts critic breathlessly interviewed the maestro of the orchestra, a world-renowned composer.

Chambless squirmed. "If they turn their camera this way, the world will see the startling sight of a national celebrity, Sherlock Michlanski, dining with the well-known Noah Chambless and Inspector Mel Hardrim, who the world knows is *dead*."

"They won't do that." Michlanski's calm was better suited to St. Francis of Assisi in a den of cobras. He gestured with his fork toward the holovision critic and his interviewee. "These sorts of people are tiresome. The interviewer will ask inane questions that add up to: How do you do it? Of course the poor fool doesn't know. People assume creative people understand the creative process—that they can somehow explain it. They can't. That's why artists sound like asses when they describe the act of creation. I have a writer friend who describes writing a novel as being like peeling an onion, in reverse."

"You mean you can't understand how you formulate your scientific creations?" asked Hardrim. Chambless looked decidedly green around the gills, whether from the proximity of the cooked mollusks or from the turn the conversation was taking.

"Of course not!" snapped Michlanski. "It's my nemesis. Often my best ideas occur in the tub. It's uncontrollable. Somehow the right side of the brain sets up a relay with the left, and *kaboom!*"

The interview with the composer ended and the orchestra began, in a clash of violins and a vibrato quivering of cymbals, with Thanos's *Mass for the Undead*, continued with the inevitable Hovhaness piece, then entered into Balboa's *Concerto for Orchestra and Low-Flying Airplane*.

During the cadenza Michlanski pointed west, where the mottled green, living island could be seen amidst the sapphire waves of the canal. "Look."

"I can't hear you!" yelled Hardrim.

"The *whale!*"

As if on cue, the music stopped. There was a strange hush, which abruptly ceased with a sudden inrush of air down a multitude of gullets, a sound like a gigantic *whoosh*.

A Coast Guard cutter cruised alongside the whale, playing the haunting whale song familiar to those who know the Cetaceans.

Air and water spewed from the whale's blowhole. It dived. For a moment its tail was visible, then it too, disappeared.

Tears coursed down Michlanski's cheeks. "Old friend," he whispered.

"Do you know this creature?" said Chambless.

"For several months 'this creature' and I sang together off the reefs of Hawaii. I found him a far more congenial friend and companion than many humans."

"Why does he want to die?" asked Hardrim.

"Whales, like people, races, and societies, sometimes reach a crisis of the soul. They wrestle with themselves to decide if life is really worth living. Sometimes the answer is no. Our species is in the process of deciding that question, I think."

"You're saying he didn't make a mistake? He didn't make a wrong turn at San Clemente?" said Chambless.

"What could be more absurd?" said Michlanski between elephantine sobs. "That beautiful creature is at least your equal in intellect, and ten times the philosopher. Can you see yourself making a wrong turn on the way to the Argus Society and driving into the Detroit River without knowing what you were doing?"

"I did not request to be insulted—"

"Why not sing to him? Ask him to go home," asked Hardrim.

"He knows I'm here. Just as I knew it was he when I saw his tail, which is like a fingerprint on a human."

"Are you suggesting whales are telepathic?" snapped Chambless.

"I wouldn't think of suggesting anything that would snap your credulity, old teacher. He knows I'm here and he knows how I feel. To sing the obvious would be a true insult. If he does decide to live, it will be his own decision."

The great mammal steadily swam toward the first in a series of locks that would carry it several thousand feet up and over the mountains. Two helicopters appeared over the water. They wore the logos of local holovision stations.

A groan escaped the crowd as the whale dived again. Then a spout of water appeared downstream of where he had submerged and his mottled green shape surfaced again. He was swimming away from the locks.

"And the answer is *yes*," said Sherlock Michlanski.

3

Night had descended. Once more they were airborne and approaching a small private airport in the Detroit suburbs.

"I suppose you both realize I kidnapped you on false pretenses." Michlanski cast an occasional unconcerned eye at the automatic pilot as it made its approach to the landing field.

"I supposed something like that, Sherlock," said Chambless coolly. "I know you too well. When you said you were as ready as you would ever be for the mission, I knew that was untrue. You're worried because you don't understand how you create."

"I understand quite well how I think. Linear thinking is no mystery. If there's a clear road to an objective, no matter how winding, I'll find it. But intuitive thinking is unpredictable. Yet it is my genius. Any computer can follow a road; it takes intuition and genius to leap a chasm."

"Yet you are, without doubt, a genius. Why worry about what so obviously works for you?"

"I can't control it. And in the coming days and months I must *learn* to. My work's too important to rely on chance." The jump-jet landed and they scrambled down the ladder to the tarmac.

"The other day I was working on a formula. I reached a dead end, the sort that no matter how you worry it, doesn't work. Totally frustrated, I sat down and read an article about penguins. For some reason that created a rend in my consciousness, and I saw the image of an article I had read in *Scientific American*, not on the subject of penguins or even birds. Suddenly the solution to my problem sprang into my mind, complete to the last decimal place. Now that worries me."

"Is that how geniuses work out their problems?" asked Hardrim.

"God knows. Einstein said he got his ideas shaving in front of a mirror. Some mathematicians can see the symmetry and subtle pattern of a complex formula completely hidden to equally intelligent colleagues. I am such a person. I also detect flaws in other theories. That makes me extremely unpopular, for example recently when I published a paper attacking current interpretations of the prevalent model of the 'neosuperstring' theory of physics, which, by the way, is full of horsefeathers."

"That's a unified field theory, isn't it?" said Hardrim.

Michlanski raised his eyebrows. "You do impress me, particularly for a former police person."

"That's swell."

"If you want true food for thought as to how the creative part of the mind works, I suggest a visit to our friend Mr. Slim, at the Issland lab."

"My dear Dr. Chambless, now that is an inspired suggestion!"

"Another cross-country flight?" asked Hardrim.

"More like a crosstown jaunt," said Michlanski.

It was raining when Michlanski's roadster screeched to a halt before the massive cinderblock foundation of a tiered hydroponics farm that drew water from the nearby Detroit River. It occupied a full city block and was twenty stories tall.

Chambless inserted a plastic card key into a steel-faced door, which slid open without a sound. They stepped inside.

The light was dim, but Hardrim saw they were at the end of a corridor between two rows of plants that stretched as far as he could see. Beyond the two rows on either side the scene was repeated, as if two mirrors faced each other, until they were lost to sight. Plants dangled over a porous corklike material. Roots, like webs, were connected to the material by tiny capillaries. A constant sound of dripping water provided background noise. Hanging from the plants were round shapes the size of baseballs. The overwhelming smell of strawberries clung to every breath; Hardrim was allergic to strawberries. He buried his hands in his coat pockets and groaned inwardly.

"Did you say something, Inspector?" asked Michlanski. He fondled one of the Goliath strawberries.

"I thought they kept lights on these things all the time."

"They are turned off periodically to let the plants rest."

They followed the row of plants to a cement column that contained an elevator. They boarded it. Hardrim sighed with relief when the smell of strawberries faded in the whine of air-conditioning.

"This is another Argus Society establishment," said Chambless. "We maintain a rather extensive laboratory under the farm, which is entirely legitimate. The Issland Laboratory."

The elevator door opened to a well-lit corridor that looked like the inside of a hospital. There were no people to be seen.

"Spooky." said Hardrim. "But, thank God, no strawberries."

"It's almost entirely automated," said Chambless.

He led the way, but it was obvious that Michlanski had been in the building before. They walked down about halfway, then entered a doorway.

The lab held the usual computer cubes, beakers, and glass tubing associated with biochemical work. Hardrim saw something that might be an electron microscope. With a rising probability for error he recognized an X-ray machine, a centrifuge, an electron spin resonance spectrometer, and a gas chromatograph.

In the corner, hunched over a high-powered microscope, was a tall man with thinning white hair. He looked up. His eyes were ice blue, childlike. His skin was smooth, yet he seemed very old.

"Hello, Mr. Slim. No need to be alarmed. I brought someone to meet you," said Chambless as if speaking to a child.

Slim bobbed his head up and down and a shy smile crept onto his face, then he turned abruptly back to the microscope.

"People frighten Mr. Slim. Why don't you go over to him and shake his hand?" said Chambless.

"How do you do?" Hardrim offered his hand. Slim reached around and took it. He looked sideways at Hardrim.

"Did you know the president is running for reelection?" Slim's voice was raspy, as though he seldom used it.

"No, I didn't. Are you going to vote for him?"

"You want to look at Lucy D.?" Slim indicated the microscope.

"I'd be honored." Hardrim looked into the eyepiece. A colony of bullet-shaped viruses swam in his field of vision.

"Lucy D.," said Slim. His eyes looked sad.

"Very interesting, Mr. Slim."

Chambless stepped forward. "Inspector, you may be interested to learn that Mr. Slim perfected the Santa Bella blight."

They left and closed the door behind them after Mr. Slim reminded them to vote for the president.

"He developed the Santa Bella blight?" said Hardrim. "How?"

"He's an idiot savant," said Michlanski. "He was one of the finest biologists in the country. He became morose over a love affair. We think her name was Lucy. He gave himself an experimental drug that acted like a lobotomy. All that remains is his brilliant scientific ability. He has a child's emotions, but his mind can still concentrate on things biological. Ask him to tie his shoes, and he'll burst into tears."

"He also developed the antidote to the blight. We keep him here working just in case something like a mutation goes wrong with the blight," said Chambless.

"Who was the president he was talking about?"

"Reagan. The 1984 election made a big impression when he was a kid. It's the only historical event he remembers," said Michlanski.

"That is mind-boggling. A man with the mental maturity of a child created the Santa Bella blight."

"Kind of makes you wonder about creativity," said Michlanski with a troubled smile.

They returned to ground level. Michlanski asked Chambless to go on ahead. "I'd like to speak privately with Mel, old teacher."

"Do what you want." Chambless vanished into the dark.

Michlanski looked at Hardrim. "There's something you've wanted to say to me. I've sensed it all evening. What is it?"

Hardrim was astonished. "Amazing! I have wanted to ask you something." He looked at Michlanski intently. "You *do* know, don't you?"

"Oh, you mean the Plan." Michlanski chuckled. "Strubeck told me about the scheme to hoodwink the government and everybody else when I was twenty-two, but he never trusted Jason or Jacob or me with the truth about ourselves. I figured it out when I was twelve. I was a bit of a scamp. I hacked into Strubeck's secret files. I found references to tests and psychology. Some had my name on them. Over the years I put the clues together. Occasionally I hear things."

He took a trideecorder from voluminous pockets. A three-inch cube materialized in the air between them. Hardrim recognized the room where the last meeting of the Argus Society had taken place and Philip Norrison's voice: "What we did was analogous to taking a seed, giving it fertilizer, a perfect climate, and care. Is it manipulation if that seed grows to be what its genes intend? Is it fairer to deny the seed nutrients?

Is that free will? I don't think so. I don't think it would have been wise to tell the boys about themselves."

Michlanski touched a button. The scene fled back into the recorder. "From little acorns mighty oak trees grow. This particular oak didn't agree with his teachers about that."

"You don't hold it against them?"

"Not a bit of it. I'm grateful. If they'd left me in Poland God knows what my life would have been like."

"Kane and Scott. Do they know?"

"They never figured it out. And I've never told them."

"You two coming?" called Chambless irritably from the car.

Hardrim followed Michlanski to the car and they drove off.

PART
* 7 *

RETURN
OF THE
GUMSHOE

Chapter

∗ 42 ∗

I looked in the cracked glass. My bristle-faced mug snarled back at me. The bastards had done it! I was the enemy now. I stared at interface cables growing out of my neck. My hand crept toward my automatic. I brought the muzzle to my forehead . . .
—*Rocky Dillon,* 'Face in the Mirror

1

"**I**'m going to go find Lenny," said Hardrim.

Chambless puffed on his pipe furiously. "We've gone over this! Sooner or later we'll find Ferman. Then we'll need you."

They were at the entrance to the Argus Society safe house. Coming in, Chambless had met Hardrim, who was dressed for travel.

"Then send for me. I can do more good by finding out what's happened to Lenore than by waiting for your computers to spot that license number or Ferman's face! Lenny doesn't know what happened to me except that I'm not dead."

"Logic cannot sway you?"

"The other night I realized that geniuses like you and Michlanski are no more ruled by logic than anyone else. If the greatest physicist on earth gives in to intuition, who am I to resist mine?"

Sebastian had slipped into the foyer. He placed himself in the doorway in front of Hardrim.

"If Dr. Chambless doesn't want you to go, I don't think you'd better go, Hardrim."

"Sebastian, I like you," growled Hardrim. "And I think you like me. You probably think that because I'm bigger than you, and don't want to hurt you, that your being in the way will stop me. But if you don't move, I'll stuff you into Chambless's pipe!"

Sebastian tensed and narrowed his eyes and looked as if he might make a fight of it. Then he shrugged and stepped aside.

"Have a good trip."

2

Hardrim went to Lenny's office at the Department of Justice, and learned she was on a medical leave.

She wasn't home, but had left a message on the door recorder, dated before he sent his message. He held his thumb up to the scanner and it played. Lenny sounded tired:

"I don't know if I'll ever see you again, Mel. I worry so much. You've acted like a child in many ways. I've tried dealing with your prejudices about my career. I've decided you must make the adjustment. I told you I might do something to make you grow up. If you hear this, look for me at Capitol Private Hospital, on Jameson Street. Remember, no matter what, I love you. Lenny."

Hardrim raced through reasons why Lenny might have checked into a hospital: corrective surgery, rogue cancer. That disease, unknown in the twentieth century, was hallmarked by swiftness. You could be healthy one month and die of rogue cancer the next.

It was all he could do to keep his foot from depressing the accelerator pedal of his hovercar to the floor.

Capitol Private Hospital was just inside Maryland. Its unassuming two-story building was set in a parklike area. He entered through tinted double doors that opened silently.

"I want to see Lenore Lippman," he told the lobby receptionist. "I'm her fiancée." He didn't think it necessary to maintain the charade of being dead in this place, which had probably never heard of him or his fiery death.

The receptionist punched a number. "Dr. Brace will be down in a minute, Mr. Hardrim."

That threw him. She knew his name. Then he relaxed. Lenny had undoubtedly left his name with the desk.

Dr. Brace resembled a supreme court justice. His heroic forehead was right off Mount Rushmore (if it had been carved from black onyx). He had a full head of kinky white hair and a booming voice born in a barrel chest.

"Mr. Hardrim, Miss Lippman's doing fine! She's responding to postoperative therapy faster than any patient I've ever had."

He led Hardrim down a well-lit corridor. Through thick glass he saw Lenny in a chair in front of horseshoe-shaped controls, apparently meditating. What he saw next made the blood drain from his face. Wires sprouted from the back of her head and ran to the computer.

"She's learning her new skill very quickly."

"I—I—"

"She said you'd be shocked. I assure you, Lenore is changed for the better. She's the same woman you love—with an added dimension—" he stopped. He saw murder in Hardrim's eyes. Hardrim's fists clenched at his sides and a forehead vein throbbed.

Sensing his presence, Lenny opened her eyes. They stared at each other a long moment, then he tore himself from the sight of her and stalked down the corridor toward the exit.

"Mr. Hardrim!" Brace called.

Hardrim turned.

"She needs you. She told me your problem—how distasteful it is for you. Frankly, I don't know why the two of you didn't opt for some sort of joint therapy first."

"Because she wants me to grow up," said Hardrim sarcastically. "She thinks I'm the same sort that used to string up your forebears during Reconstruction."

Brace stiffened. "And are you?"

"What do you think, Doctor?"

"I think if you love this woman, the fact that she had an operation to become a computer interface will be unimportant."

"To you, maybe. To me, it's like she's renounced her humanity. She'll think like a machine eventually. I've known computer interfaces—they're cold, cold!"

"Mr. Hardrim, do you think it is unnatural to communicate with a computer by means of a keyboard? Or by talking to it?"

"It's not the same, damn it, and you know it!"

"Are you going to leave her like this?"

"She's punched me in the gut! I've got to catch my breath. I have to think. She has to give me time—to grow up."

"Then you'll be back?"

"I can't honestly say. Good-bye."

His belly churned and his eyes burned with tears he couldn't allow himself to shed as he drove east out of the D.C. complex.

He drove nonstop for two days, sleeping when the automatic pilot drove. When he did take the wheel it was more therapy then anything else. He brooded, cursed, and called Lenny's name over and over as he drove; he saw her face, and the snakelike tendrils growing out of her neck, a new Medusa, when he dreamed.

3

The midnight wail of a saxophone.

Hardrim pulled his coat tight against the fog and looked up at the fifth-story window whence the mournful music originated.

He didn't see the player, just a shadow in yellow light that spilled onto the street. As the brassy chords lifted on the mist, Hardrim saw a scrawny cat, one-eyed and three-legged. It limped around a corner and vanished into a trash bin. That fit, he thought bitterly. Sad music, a dying cat, and pain—all created an almost unbearable synergy.

He was on some street in Detroit. He had walked aimlessly since early afternoon. He hadn't told Chambless he was back yet.

The sax music faded like a radio smothered by a pillow. He passed another window and heard another bit of music: Berlioz's *Symphony Fantastique*. Now, that was appropriate counterpoint to his thoughts: drug-crazed ravings of a lovesick swain.

He stood under the window. "Enough!" he whispered. "Enough feeling sorry for myself. I've behaved like a child. I abandoned the Argus Society for Lenny, then abandoned Lenny. Enough!"

An elderly man put his head out the window. "If you don't like the music, why not hang around another bedroom window?"

Hardrim looked up at him and laughed. That broke the spell.

"I'm glad you're back," said Chambless when Hardrim stepped into his study. "We've located Ferman."

"The FBI has him," said Sebastian. "That's why it took so long to trace him. That license number was classified. Apparently an FBI assistant director named Ferdinand—"

"Roger Ferdinand, the man of a thousand business suits."

"You know him? Well, he wanted you and got Ferman by mistake. They still have him. Now, of course, Ferdinand may think you're dead since your 'body' was discovered burnt to a crisp."

"Has Ferman told them anything?"

"Our intelligence is good, but not *that* good."

"Then we have to get him out," said Hardrim.

4

Boris Baptiste, aka Bengal, was fencing. He was swashbuckling in a white blouse and black leotards. He faced a tyro. The foils' snicking echoed in the old warehouse near the abandoned General Motors plant, used to store thick metal sheets and huge laser-cutting machines. They had leased it for a month.

Bengal had taught his agents to fence with the outlawed lunar-style electric foils. It was good exercise, but boring after he had scored off his opponent for the twentieth time.

He waved him away, throwing his foil onto a wooden table, next to a bottle of aquavit and a tall glass. He tossed off a glass, pushed greasy locks from his face, sat, and lit a marijuana cigarette.

His twenty-five men and four women had their own amusements: chess, cards, reading. Two kept hand weapons ready and watched at the windows.

He had built a fine organization of pickpockets (they made brilliant spies because they were already trained to be inconspicuous), muggers, and assorted scum. True Quebec patriots were in short supply.

Emil had seen to their training. He knew more ways to kill a man than Bengal knew ways to make love to a woman.

No matter how marvelously lethal Emil was, Bengal's stomach churned when he was near. Emil repulsed everyone. But he was obeyed without question. He was not someone to piss off.

Bengal had had unbelievable success following Emil, but he had begun to doubt that blowing up aerospace factories benefited United Europe.

He finished his joint and gave lieutenants Tourmaline and LeFebre a tongue-lashing for sloppy security. A shipment of explosives was due, and they couldn't afford mistakes.

But his heart wasn't in it. Something was very wrong about this new raid on the Gigatex factory. It smelled rancid.

He finished the liquor and stood unsteadily to get another bottle. Suddenly Emil was standing before him, like a wraith in night colors.

"Are you ready?"

Bengal amazed himself with how fast he was able to sober up. "Ready for what?"

"Idiot," Emil said in his dry voice. "You're discovered. U.S. agents have you surrounded. They can invest it at any time."

"Then we're done for."

Emil frowned. "I told you, weapons are to be used. But the game is now more challenging. The explosives are here, right under their noses—in a truck that's been collecting garbage on this street for the past half hour."

Bengal couldn't help laughing. "Merde! You do have balls!"

"I hope you do." Emil suddenly grabbed Bengal by his manhood so hard Bengal choked down a groan. "Because it's up to you and me."

Emil's plan was to infiltrate the nearby forward FBI base and create a diversion to let Bengal's men escape. Later they would meet at the garbage truck, drive to the Gigatex factory, set a timer, and leave the truck to blow up.

"That must be a powerful explosive," said Bengal.

"It is."

Emil explained his plan to Bengal's people. At the first explosion from the FBI base, they were to attack the western perimeter, which Emil judged the weakest point. When they punched through, they were to split up and meet at a prearranged spot outside the city.

Bengal and Emil donned the uniforms of city sanitation workers and left the warehouse through a service entrance that led to a manhole out of sight of the observing federal agents.

They approached the garbage truck as though they had been on foot for blocks. The truck appeared to be down with a broken fan and they looked like repairmen. They "fixed" the fan, boarded the truck, and rumbled off, all in plain sight.

Inside a false exterior were living quarters for three men. Emil introduced them by their last names. The driver was Barbas, the others Romaine and Early.

In a corner were foil-wrapped loaves of plastique, unattended while Romaine and Early worked at a table on "the package." Twice the size of a suitcase, it was shaped like a barbell with a fat middle. Romaine, who looked like a tall, blond, youngish Hitler, slid a canister into a metal cylinder at one end of the contraption. Early, a small middle-aged man with a half-moon of black hair on his forehead, squinted through wire-rim glasses as he obliterated a saucer-sized insignia with a power sander. While he worked he sang a Verdi aria in a passable tenor.

Bengal looked closer at the emblem. He had seen it before: the coiled snake, logo of one of the big American conglomerates.

He knew what "the package" was, although the nuclear warning symbols were filed off it too. Ice crawled on his spine. He was working for a madman. Puvain, if he existed, was a traitor to Europe. Only a mad dog would plant an atomic bomb in a city.

Emil told Early he didn't have to finish sanding.

"I have my instructions," said Early.

"You have new instructions."

"Mr. Krebs was very clear. He wanted the logo filed off."

Emil flushed and lashed out with the back of his hand, leaving Early's mouth bleeding.

Romaine whipped out a laser. His little blond Hitler moustache twitched with fright. "We don't want trouble. We know who you are. But the boss made it clear what he wanted."

Bengal knew Emil could easily disarm Romaine. Instead, Emil relaxed and laughed his whispery laugh.

"I lost my temper. Go ahead, finish. We all work for the same guy, right? But it is wasted effort."

Romaine put his laser away but kept a watchful eye on Emil, who entertained himself as they worked by tying and untying knots in a short length of rope, and humming.

Bengal went by him to sit down. He heard Emil's whispery voice singing low, "And I think to myself, what a wonderful world!"

When Early finished destroying the logo, he armed the bomb.

Barbas drove several blocks east of the FBI base and parked. Emil sent Bengal up ahead while he gave final instructions.

The sun dipped behind a nearby highrise. Bengal could see the FBI building. He lit a joint and caressed the comforting warmth of his flechette gun, which shot streams of razor-sharp metal darts. He also had a knife and a laser pistol.

Emil emerged from the shadows carrying a small flash camera in his right hand.

"Merde!" said Bengal, startled. "Why the camera?"

"I'm a shutterbug. Any more questions?"

"Did you cut yourself? That smear on your arm—"

"Caught myself on one of the edges of the truck."
"Is everything all right?"
"Perfect. It is time to rattle their cage."
"Will the men in the truck wait for us?"
"They'll wait for us until doomsday. Let's go."

Chapter
✳ 43 ✳

1

The trap was about to be sprung.

Inspector Alexis Moran's deputy, Priskorn, had just reported by holocube that most of Bengal's people were inside the warehouse.

Moran rested his generous rear on his desk and pushed his hands together, flexing his biceps. "Then we can order in the helicopter whenever we please," he told Priskorn's image, which originated atop a building across the street from the warehouse.

"We were waiting for the garbage truck to get clear."

"What's that?"

"It broke a fan in front of the plant. Took most of an hour to get going."

"Why didn't you flag it down before it got there?"

"Bengal's people were out. We didn't want to give the game away."

"Okay, as long as it's out of our hair. We'll hit the warehouse in sixty minutes, mark now!"

"Roger."

Moran winced at the word, and turned to find Ferdinand's deputy, Kirsten Fale, facing him with a smile that would have set his blood running hot under almost any other circumstances.

Five-foot-four, with fiery red hair cascading over the shoulders of a business suit that covered but concealed none of her devastating body, Fale stood with her hands primly behind her back, mocking and inviting. Moran had to remind himself she was the enemy.

"Are you ready to do it?" she breathed.

"Yes, I anticipate a successful operation. Better alert Ferdinand, so he can get here in time to grab the credit."

"Don't be bitter, Alexis. There's enough to go around. If the operation's a success."

" 'Inspector' will do, Miss Fale."

"Don't let us be enemies. It doesn't have to be that way." She walked past, managing to brush his beefy arm as she went to a faucet and drew a glass of water. "I'm going to change and observe how you go about bagging a spy ring. I'm pretty sexy in fatigues."

"You're sexy in just about anything."

"You know, if I write my report up right, you could get a lot of credit for this operation."

"My problem is that I'm loyal."

"An admirable quality. Roger Ferdinand prizes it highly. But try being loyal to yourself first."

"Yeah? Just how loyal are you to yourself?"

"You want to explain what you mean by that?" Her stance shifted slightly, from inviting to almost threatening.

Moran studied one of his fingernails. "Your meteoric rise in the bureau has more than one tongue wagging, Miss Fale. Everybody knows how Ferdinand behaves around you, like he's Daddy Warbucks and you're Little Annie Fanny. Frankly, I find it unprofessional, and just a little bit disgusting."

She flushed furiously. "Listen, Moran, Roger is definitely a prick, but I've never seen evidence that he has one. And I won't. He's a swine. You know it. I know it. I think even Roger knows it. But he stays on his side of the fence. I'm where I am in the bureau because I'm good at what I do. Now, tell me how you rose up through the ranks without kissing a little ass!"

Moran grunted unintelligibly and left. He didn't like the turn the conversation was taking, and it was almost time to supervise the operation. He passed the room where Ferman was being kept. He decided to tell him that he was being released.

Hardrim's burned body had been found and Ferdinand had ordered Ferman questioned as a material witness. Ferman proved a dry hole; he could link Hardrim to nothing but his own hare-brained conspiracy quest. Moran liked Ferman, and had convinced Ferdinand to order his release.

Ferman was lying on a cot with his arms behind his head. He nodded at Moran. Moran couldn't resist needling him.

"How are you? Discover any more threats to global security?"

"I feel like Don Quixote, or, more accurately, Sancho Panza."

Moran wasn't much of a reader; the literary allusion flew past him. He sat on his haunches near Ferman. "Let's talk."

2

Emil was right. FBI security was lax this time. It was partially the unfamiliar building, but mainly it was overconfidence. Everyone expected the spies to be bagged without a shot.

Emil and Bengal entered through the air ducts. "I am air, I am water," whispered the Drang as he wormed through the tight passage. Bengal was athletic, but he marveled at Emil's serpentine agility. Emil planted explosives at fifty-foot intervals, to isolate the bottom floor from the upper levels by disabling elevators and wrecking stairwells.

As they crawled through the air ducts, Mel Hardrim came in the front door with ID prepared by the Argus Society. It identified him as an inspector from the General Accounting Office. He'd added twenty years of makeup and a stoop to his appearance.

His credentials gave him carte blanche to explore the corridors. He found an unattended computer and took out his old trideecorder, modified by Argus technology to be a computer security cracker. He inserted a recording tile and jacked into the first security level. He called up RALPH FERMAN, and got his current location in the building.

He penetrated several levels of security codes to get the right directory. He saw files he wanted: HARDRIM; NYE; ADAMS SCOTT, ASSASSIN. Other titles caught his fancy too. He downloaded them all onto the tile. He spied a filename that made him pause: ROGER FERDINAND. It contained an itinerary for the FBI chief, who was due in town the next day, plus several reports written by him. He toyed with the idea of screwing up Ferdinand's schedule, but decided such pettiness was beneath him. But he did download the file.

The terminal's owner arrived and gave Hardrim a suspicious look, but Hardrim pointed at his badge, smiled, and swept past.

Emil and Bengal dropped into an empty corridor just outside Ferman's room, a few yards from an emergency exit. As they crept by the open door, Emil heard something that made him stop.

3

"Don't play games with me, please," said Ferman.

"I don't want to do that," said Moran. "I want to help."

"Let me ask you something," said Ferman desperately. "Have you thought about what evil men you're working for? Men willing to starve half the world. They've got the president of the United States fooled into backing them. They're diabolical!"

"There's two sides to every argument," said Moran, trying to draw Ferman into spelling out what he was talking about. "You ever looked at it from their, I mean our, point of view?"

Ferman narrowed his eyes. "Just *who* are you people?"

"Obviously not who you think. I'm beginning to get a glimmer of who you are. You're a man who's been through many dangerous adventures. Like to tell me about them?"

Ferman began talking about the Santa Bella blight, the Argus Society, and he mentioned the words "Sunside Project" several times.

Outside Emil and Bengal listened. Emil understood little of what Ferman was discussing, but he knew Krebs was interested in anything that could harm the Sunside Project. He signaled Bengal and they positioned themselves on either side of the door, waiting for the first explosion.

"Ferman, I can't keep this from you any longer. You're going to walk. We're not holding you."

"If this is not a trick I want to walk right this minute."

Moran thought about that, eyebrows knit, then he chuckled. "Why not? I'll take care of the fingerwork. You'll have to stay a few minutes more. Okay?"

"I suppose so."

Hardrim was almost thrown off his feet by the first blast. He regained his balance and had his slug-throwing .44 out before the next hit, this time closer. He ran toward Ferman's room.

The first explosion was still echoing when Moran staggered through the doorway. Emil clapped his right hand over Moran's mouth, cupped his left hand over the back of Moran's neck, and twisted. Moran kicked feebly and died.

Emil released the man and reached into his own jacket for his camera. He snapped two quick photos of Moran.

Inside, Ferman was petrified. Moran was dead and obviously he was next. Chambless had managed to tie up the last loose end. When Emil stepped into doorway, Ferman fell to his knees.

"I'll never say anything. I promise! Just let me live!"

Emil smiled, and another bomb exploded. Ferman's fright was an aphrodisiac; Emil felt himself responding. The lust to kill was over-powering his reason for keeping Ferman alive.

For Bengal, watching Emil take snapshots of his victim was the last straw. He felt compelled to end Emil's career with a glittering mist of whirling saw-edged darts. His hand tightened on the weapon, then loosened as agony radiated from the back of his head. Suddenly he was on his knees, then his cheek was resting on the floor.

Hardrim had laid him out with a blow from his .44. He leveled it at Emil as he turned at the sound of Bengal falling.

Each recognized the other for what he was. Hardrim knew an assassin when he saw one, and Emil could spot a professional cop across a crowded room, even under a pound of makeup.

"This is interesting," said Emil with his killer's grin.

Hardrim didn't reply; he was concentrating. He could tell from Emil's stance that the man was a Lao Tse psychodynamic combat adept, a Drang. "Ralph, get the hell out of here!"

Ferman came to the door. "Inspector Hardrim, you're alive."

"Obviously. Now, run!"

"He'll kill me!"

"If he turns to fire at you, I'll kill him."

Ferman turned to run, and almost stepped on the body of Alexis Moran. He found he couldn't move another step.

"Go, goddammit, or I'll shoot you myself!"

Ferman believed him. He inched past the body and started hesitantly up the corridor, away from the emergency exit.

"How will you get away, Mel?" asked Ferman. Then he was gone.

"Cowardly little shit," commented Emil. "But he raised an interesting question. How will you get away?"

"Mexican standoff."

"I know when the bombs will blow. When one explodes close enough, you'll flinch."

"Conversely, an agent may come around that corner, and you'll flinch."

Another explosion. Hardrim's eyes didn't leave Emil.

"Very good!" said Emil.

Hardrim knew the slightest physical mistake could open him up to a devastating Drang attack. He was at a terrible disadvantage, never having formally studied the discipline.

Bengal staggered to his feet.

Hardrim was sweating. "Move a muscle, I kill your boss."

"That's an empty threat," sneered Bengal. "Blow a hole through the filthy pig!"

"You don't seem very popular with your employee."

"Bengal, you have one chance," said Emil, his eyes fixed on Hardrim. "Point your gun at him. Otherwise, you're dead."

"Wrong! You're dead. I know Python Corporation is my control. Do you think Paris will like your plan to explode an atomic bomb in Detroit? You're lucky I don't help this man kill you." He stumbled toward the emergency exit.

Another explosion. This time Hardrim almost lost it.

"You *will* lose it next time!" whispered Emil.

"Before that happens I'll blow you away."

"And die also."

"It occurs to me that our reason for killing each other walked away." said Hardrim.

"Yours, perhaps. I never need a reason."

"Do you need a reason for dying?"

"You have a point. What do you propose?"

"We back away from each other, slowly, until we reach opposite ends of the corridor."

"Fair enough. One foot follows the other," said Emil, who capered back several steps on his points, like a dancer.

"Funny! You almost bought it that time, pal," said Hardrim, shaking with fury. He backed up, slowly, deliberately.

They simultaneously reached the ends of the corridor.

Emil's left hand caressed his cheek. "Next time, my friend, I'd like to take your picture!" He brought his gun up to fire.

Hardrim dived for cover as Emil let fly a stream of flechettes. He twisted in mid-dive and hit the floor with his head. In the spot where he had stood a moment before, the wall had sprouted quills like a porcupine.

He heard Emil's footsteps as the assassin vanished through the emergency exit, and then he began to black out. Goddamnit, I've lost him again, he thought.

4

If it was chaos in the FBI office, outside it was pandemonium.

Cued by the explosions from several blocks away, Bengal's people poured from the warehouse and attacked the FBI position.

Kirsten Fale was with the forward unit across the street from the warehouse, waiting for reinforcements.

Over her jumpsuit she wore a flak jacket. She carried a special issue Dan Wesson "Mamba" .45 magnum automatic laser/slug combo with a fifteen-shot magazine. Moran had laughed himself silly the first time he saw it, and called her Dirty Harriet. That was before he saw her use it on the firing range.

Her instincts told her a fiasco was brewing. The ops officer, Priskorn, who was on the roof overlooking the street, was totally ineffectual. He had been foisted on Moran by FBI Director Pollux, who wanted to advance Priskorn's career with field experience. Priskorn had a hundred men, but from what Kirsten was hearing on the radio, most were trapped on the upper floors of their base building.

The eight agents left to cover the warehouse were in a ragged defensive line, with minimal cover, about to be rushed by thirty of Bengal's people from the other end of the street.

Nobody was ready for this. Bengal's men didn't know enough basic combat tactics to spread out, or to use fire and movement to cover an advancing group. They didn't know massed "infantry" attacks down a street were suicide, exposing them to enfilade. So they walked in like children, firing wildly, shouting and even enjoying themselves until they realized what they'd walked into.

On Kirsten's side, most of the agents had fired weapons in life-and-death situations—against SoHi smugglers or gangsters—but never against what was practically a frontal assault.

Priskorn babbled over the radio. "I need reinforcements here. Is anybody listening? I need people! Is anybody there?"

"Priskorn," said Kirsten on her own radio. "Where's Moran?"

"I honestly don't know. I didn't expect this. Tell him I wasn't trained for this! I'm an administrator."

"Of course you are," said Kirsten reasonably. "Look, we don't have time to get reinforcements. This is now. If you want to be useful, get that helicopter here!" As if validating her statement, a bullet whanged off the wall inches above her head.

An agent Kirsten recognized as Basie sidled up to her. He was graying and cautious. "Crowd control isn't my strong point, but these guys are working up to charge," he said. "Where the hell is the chopper with the Somnus missile?"

"Not due for half an hour. Priskorn's trying to get it here earlier. Otherwise this'll be over."

"What do we do?"

"Ask Priskorn."

"I hope you don't mean that. Do we stop 'em or let 'em through?"

"They're terrorists. First priority is stopping their escape. Our lives are expendable in that purpose."

"Do you realize we have no cover here?" asked Basie, kneeling and holding his service revolver with two hands.

"I'd noticed that, yes," said Kirsten, who preferred to stand. For a moment it was silent. She looked around. Some agents were kneeling, two were stretched out, one had taken cover behind a hydrant. Several stood in doorways.

"Uh-oh, incoming!" said Basie.

Then the eye of the storm passed.

For Kirsten the battle was a series of freeze frames taking place in a wind tunnel of noise.

She fired steadily, not aiming, as if firing was its own purpose. Each time it was like a hammer against her palms.

The enemy was half a block away, screaming, gesticulating, some running, some walking, some firing. They seemed like a solid wall of people, although Kirsten's rational mind whispered that there couldn't be that many.

There was a flash and a loud bang right before her eyes. Someone had thrown a grenade.

She couldn't see through the painful afterimage. She aimed blindly and fired, emptied the clip, automatically loaded another and fired again.

A man ran toward her, right arm up, grasping a dueling rod. (Frame.) His mouth was open. Kirsten fired but he kept coming, and passed the way a bull passes a toreador whirling in a veronica. His foil brushed her left elbow and sent a shock up her arm, which went limp. (Frame.) Another man. She saw every black tip of his whiskers, the light in his eyes. (Frame.) She felt the impact as she smashed the butt of her gun into his teeth with her good hand. She cut her hand on broken teeth. (Frame.) Someone aimed a pistol at her. He pulled the trigger but nothing happened. She raised her gun and pulled the trigger, but it too was empty. He sidestepped out of her sight. (Frame.) Flash of light. Momentary shock to her ribs, like being hit with a fist. (Frame.) Darkness.

As in a dream she saw a stand of corn shaped like people. A flame touched the stalks and they withered, until they were black husks that became the dead and dying.

"You can stop firing now." Basie sat on the pavement in a pool of blood, holding his stomach with one hand as if he expected the contents to fall out if he let go.

A helicopter hovered over the carnage, directing beams of light onto the bodies scattered through the street, up to the point where they had clashed with the FBI agents. That was the greatest concentration of corpses.

Kirsten laughed with the sheer joy of surviving. She had never felt so exhilarated. Sharp pain made her pull her jumpsuit where it stuck to her ribs. A bloody furrow ran along her torso.

She probed the throbbing slash; no bones broken.

"You'll live," said Basie, who huddled forward as if he had indigestion. Then he relaxed and fell in a grotesque imitation of an exerciser touching his toes.

"Basie?" called Kirsten, knowing there would be no answer.

Chapter

∗ 44 ∗

1

The garbage truck sat in a pool of light from a street lamp.

Bengal approached from its blind side. He didn't know what he could do against three armed men, but he intended to try something. He didn't want an atomic explosion on his conscience.

He slipped up on the driver's side. Barbas looked as if he was taking a nap. Sloppy!

He swung up, flechette gun drawn, and opened the cab. He froze. Barbas was dead, gray eyes bulging from strangulation. Bengal swallowed rapidly. Barbas's throat was cut, and his tongue had been pulled through the slit in an imitation of a necktie.

With a sinking feeling, Bengal stepped down, opened the truck's false exterior, and saw the others. Romaine had been opened up like a game bird dressed for roasting. Early would never sing again. He didn't have the equipment any more; and from the bloody patch on the front of his pants, Bengal guessed that even if he could have carried a tune, he would have sung in a higher voice. Bengal found the evidence in a wastepaper basket, along with the bloody shears that had done the job.

He examined the bomb. It was not armed. All he had to do was dispose of the bodies, drive away, then alert the authorities.

He left the truck cautiously, looking both ways. He neglected to look up. Emil leaped on him from the roof, wrestled him to the ground, and jammed the muzzle of his flechette gun painfully up his left nostril.

"Do you know what it's like to feel a hundred razor-edged darts play hide and go seek in your brain? No? Well, I have something more creative in mind."

He made Bengal hunch forward, hugging his knees, and tied his arms and feet together. Then Emil busied himself attaching a detonator to the loaves of plastique. Most puzzling of all, he put the nuclear bomb back in its original carrying case.

"Not quite what you envisioned?" taunted Emil. He opened a crate and removed a dozen flash and concussion grenades. He stuffed wads of wax in his ears, then put on a protective helmet.

He pulled Barbas from the driver's seat and put him back with his companions. Then, hoisting Bengal into the passenger's side, he leaped into the cab and fired up the Hazelton fans. The massive vehicle lumbered off on a cushion of air.

Bengal had lost feeling in his extremities, and was barely conscious, but saw which way Emil was driving, and his eyes widened in alarm.

"That's right," said Emil, "We're headed for the Gigatex factory. For your edification, because it's the last thing you'll ever know, I'll explain how your death will bring my plans to a conclusion. But first a few adjustments."

He parked on the side of the road. Up ahead was one of the four entrances to the factory.

Emil wired plastique to the acceleration pedal. When it was depressed, it would activate the detonator. When it was released, the plastique would blow. It was, literally, a dead man's switch.

He moved Bengal into the driver's seat and sat next to him, with the atomic bomb at his feet.

"We're going to drive through the main gate. The security people will take a few moments to react. We'll drive by the six Gilgamesh scramjets in a row inside an area cordoned off by electrified barbed wire and innumerable booby traps. We'll smash the fence, miss the scramjets, and continue toward the factory. By then security should be on to us. At that point, my bomb and I will leave and things will get interesting for you, Bengal."

He moved Bengal's nearly inert leg until the foot was poised over the accelerator. Bengal tried to resist depressing the pedal and Emil rapped him brutally under the right knee. His foot jerked and the truck lurched ahead.

Emil held his flechette gun to Bengal's cheek with his right hand, and steered with the other. It was an awkward arrangement, but Bengal wasn't capable of taking advantage of it.

The truck accelerated until it howled like a typhoon. They approached the gate. Security guards opened fire. The truck reached sixty mph and smashed through the guardhouse and gate like pie crust.

Inside the cab they experienced a shock comparable to an old-style automobile running over a deep chuckhole.

They roared across a field, gathering speed. Searchlights came on and Bengal saw lights of vehicles crossing the field to intercept them.

Emil pulled out a knife and Bengal closed his eyes. He felt a tugging behind his back and his hands were free.

The fence around the Gilgamesh scramjets was suddenly before them. Bengal saw the sleek white scramjets, each as large as a medium passenger jet, placidly lined up like a museum exhibit.

They bounced as the truck triggered an explosion. Electricity cascaded around them as they broke through the fence. Emil wrenched open the cab door on the passenger's side, grabbed the carrying case, and dived out. A moment later the air was split by several intense explosions. The thick glassteel cab windshield crazed like the floor of a desert.

Bengal tried to restore circulation to his limbs, but there was no time. His extremities exploded with a thousand pinpricks as the four-story blockhouse form of the Gigatex factory loomed. He was traveling better than ninety miles an hour. He looked down and by force of will ordered his foot to relax. The truck decelerated for a split second, then an explosion blossomed out of the cab, tearing it and Boris Baptiste, aka Bengal, asunder.

2

Mel Hardrim awoke as a dust-covered young man with a scratch over his right eye helped him to his feet.

"Are you all right, sir?" he asked.

"Yes, I think so. Hell of a headache, though."

"We're evacuating the building. If you'll come this way."

Hardrim followed him outside, where dozens of agents were milling about. He decided he had just about used up his luck at FBI headquarters. First chance he got he ducked around a corner.

When he returned to the Argus Society safe house, before he answered any questions from an anxious Chambless, he found a terminal, inserted his tile containing the pirated FBI files, and read.

3

Nov. 13—Deseret *Gantry*—The first experimental versions of the Gilgamesh scramjet, the controversial proposed replacement for the shuttle fleet, have left Detroit, for Deseret Space Center. The first tests will begin in about a week.

Funding for the prototype passed during the first weeks of the Shefferton presidency. The scramjet, a hypersonic vehicle that can fly into low earth orbit, is a descendant of the X-30, the aerospace plane tested extensively during the 1990s and abandoned. Once more it is at the center of controversy.

Yesterday the prototypes narrowly avoided damage in a suicide attack on the Gigatex factory where they were stored.

Proponents of the traditional space shuttle fleet have mounted an effort to stop funding for a new fleet of a dozen Gilgamesh scramjets, to be built by a consortium of Rockwell, Harley-Davidson, and Gigatex. . . .

Roger Ferdinand was in his limousine being driven into Seattle when news of the Detroit disaster began to trickle in.

He was listening to the weather report; he wasn't about to have his three-piece raw silk suit, made from fibers secreted by weightless silkworms in Greater Asia's "wheel" space factory, marred by rain.

"—thick morning fog on all freeways leading into Seattle. USTRANS will clear that up within the hour. The U.S. Weather Bureau promises two hours of rain beginning at 4 A.M. tomorrow. . ."

An imperative beeping told him someone was trying to call. He used his masked holocube and got a description of the disaster. He hung up and ordered his flight to Detroit moved up.

Hours later Ferdinand was staring out the window of the executive jump-jet as it left Seattle-Tacoma airport. His hands formed a tense inverted V on the tray before him. He ignored a glass of iced mineral water the flight attendant had brought.

The situation was pregnant with potential for advancement—and disaster. "I have always felt that in the greatest disasters are the greatest potential for victory," he wrote in his diary.

Alexis Moran had been entirely the creature of FBI Director Houston Pollux, who was fighting for his professional life. The president wanted to fire him, but he had powerful friends. Pollux's strategy had been to give potential rivals difficult assignments. Ferdinand was in overall charge of the Bengal spy ring operation. Any botching of it made Ferdinand look bad.

How much of the fiasco was Moran's fault he would find out when he talked to Kirsten. Kirsten Fale! His pulse quickened.

He pictured her in his mind. Kirsten Fale was Ferdinand's pride, his finest handiwork. Her body exemplified every delicious sin. She had a mind like a razor. In her loins no man's secrets were safe. Ferdinand himself had never dared sleep with her. She had more than a touch of lamia. But she was his loyal ally, as much as she was anyone's.

Ferdinand continued to let his fantasies play as his jet glided into Detroit on a blanket of oily air. The city still suffered from Michigan's declaration, years ago, of a nuclear-free zone. That states' rights conceit was imitated by several midwest states, and tolerated by the jelly-backed government. Most of the state's power still came from shale.

Kirsten Fale met him at the airport. Her bronze hair cascaded onto a well-tailored suit. One reason he was so fond of her was her exquisite taste in clothes. He was also pleased that she had arranged to have a chauffeur at the wheel of a low, sleek limo.

He rushed to it, eyes squinting at the grimy Detroit air. His suit would probably be ruined.

"Moran was dead before the assault began." Kirsten's eyes reflected more emotion than he approved of under the circumstances. "Two witnesses will testify that Priskorn broke down and gave impossible, contradictory orders."

"Where was my brave Kirsten during all this?"

"I kept myself occupied." Kirsten knew Ferdinand always traveled unarmed. She wondered what reaction she would get if she pulled out her monster handgun and gave him a demonstration.

"Secure the witnesses before Pollux transfers them to Neptune. Administer full-spectrum lie detector tests, before cameras."

"They're under guard, although they don't know it. They think they're part of a surveillance of a neo-Nazi terrorist gang."

Ferdinand inspected the devastated field division base, walked the bloodstained scene of battle, and finally was driven to the Gigatex aerospace factory. It was crawling with police, but Ferdinand banished them from his sight with a curt command.

Eyes shaded against grimy daylight, he stood in the field between where the Gilgamesh scramjets had been parked the day before and the pockmarked facade of the Gigatex factory, where the terrorists had died in a suicide run.

It was impossible to say exactly what had occurred in those final seconds: flash and concussion grenades had disabled the nearest holovision cameras.

Kirsten excused herself to go to the nearest ladies' room while Ferdinand contemplated the ruin and marveled that the terrorists had somehow missed the real prize, the scramjets.

"Got a light, Mr. Ferdinand?" asked the chauffeur.

Ferdinand scowled. "I don't allow my employees to smoke."

"It's okay—I've got it." The chauffeur reached into the glove compartment for a Zippo lighter. When he straightened, Ferdinand's eyes widened.

"Hardrim! Alive! So this is how it ends. I'm unarmed."

Hardrim took a puff and looked at Ferdinand with amusement. "Even at bay, you're a pompous ass. I'm not here to kill you. I have information you want, to trade for information."

"I don't treat with terrorists."

"Use common sense. I wasn't connected with Bengal, although I'm sure any proof I offer won't sway you. But you thought I was dead. Why would I show myself, if I were really a criminal?"

"I don't pretend to understand you, Hardrim. I've tried to fathom your motivations since the day Dorian Nye's stand-in was shot."

"I'm simple to figure, Ferdinand. I've always wanted to find out who set me up. And maybe there's a part of me that wants to avenge poor old Arthur Vinius."

"Vinius?"

"The poor schmuck who got snuffed in Dorian Nye's place. Maybe I'm the only one who cares why he had to die."

"Don't ask me to join your crusade. I'm interested in the big picture."

"Okay." Hardrim took a drag. "I'll paint you one. How's your investigation of the Drang coming along?"

"What?" Ferdinand's face clouded.

"Who is the Drang? Start with a pool of suspects that includes every man, woman, and child in the United States. Eliminate females, because we know the Drang is male. That was evident from the video of DesCopia's murder. And from an analysis of a strand of black hair found on the body."

Hardrim was enjoying himself. "Eliminate males under age seventeen and over fifty. Eliminate those in wheelchairs, in prison, those known to have been five hundred miles away from the DesCopia murder that night, those in the armed forces, those who weigh more than one hundred and eighty pounds and are two inches more or less than five foot nine and who don't have B positive blood.

"That leaves fifty thousand suspects to work with. You should have your man in no time."

"You should be in criminal investigation," said Ferdinand drily.

"You write very good reports. But I have information to add: A man trained in psychodynamic combat entered your office, blew up the first floor, and broke Alexis Moran's neck."

"The Drang!"

"The same man may have also killed the Dorian Nye impostor in Armstrong International Airport."

"Go on."

"The Drang has an atomic device."

Ferdinand paled.

"You know I'm right, don't you?"

"Radioactivity was found in the garbage truck wreckage. Fissionables may have been stored there." Ferdinand turned away angrily. "I don't know why I'm talking to you! I should arrest you."

"I still have one missing piece of the puzzle. I know who the Drang is working for. I know who provided the bomb."

"He worked for Bengal, and indirectly for United Europe."

"Wrong. Bengal worked for him."

"All right. Who is it?"

"A trade, Ferdinand. Information for information."

"What do you want?"

"My friend, Ralph Ferman. You held him for a time. What happened to him?" Hardrim decided to leave out his own role in Ferman's escape from Emil.

"Inspector Moran interrogated him shortly before his own death, and prepared papers ordering his release. Ferman was discovered hiding in a janitor's closet after the terrorist bomb attack on our temporary base. We gave him his possessions, a voucher for two night's stay in a hotel, and cab fare. I can give you the name of the hotel. What else?"

Hardrim smiled inwardly, amazed at the occasional denseness displayed by bureaucracies. Apparently no one had connected Moran's death with the man whose cell he had been standing near when he was murdered. "Nothing else."

"You don't wish to be exonerated? Restored to rank?"

"No. I'd be obliged if your computers record that I'm dead."

"If you wish, I can record that you never existed."

"That's not necessary."

"Very well, who is the Drang's master?"

"A very rich man named Horatius Krebs."

Ferdinand sagged. "Krebs! If you had a hundred eye witnesses that he'd done something illegal, he'd buy them off. I'm not surprised he's behind this. I'd almost give up my career to nail that bastard! But in the Yucatan, and up here with his powerful friends, he's invulnerable."

"You can do nothing about his hired assassin?"

"Try and catch him in the act, and blow him away. That's about all. Your information makes that easier."

"What about the atomic bomb? You going to let him set it off because you can't touch his employer?"

"I need proof! I'm bound by legality."

"Isn't it obvious where he's going to strike with the bomb?"

"Yes it is."

"And what will you do?"

"Alert the authorities at Deseret."

"You *can* do something else. Loan me a dozen agents."

"Kiss my ass! You have no authority to command federal agents. I couldn't justify it. It would be strictly—"

"I think out of a hundred agents who lost comrades in that attack we can find a dozen volunteers. What do you think?"

"I think you're insubordinate, a poor excuse for a police officer, that I wish I'd hanged the rap for the Dorian Nye shooting on you when I had the chance."

"Can I take that as a qualified yes?"

Chapter

* 45 *

1

Horatius Krebs owned a lake in Manitoba near the Churchill River. He had been there since dawn, piloting his cabin cruiser.

He sat at the wheel, eyes raking the shore. He owned it all. And if a gnat came unannounced within two miles of him, it was because his army of employees was slacking.

Krebs was restless. Too many birds were coming home to roost simultaneously. He had hoped to eliminate evidence of his collaboration with McClaren to destroy Adam Scott, but instead he'd focused unwanted interest in the case.

Now Jason Scott had access to secret government files. He might eventually deduce that Krebs had helped destroy his father.

He needed more time to develop a plan against the Sunside Project, and to completely enlist Senator Manners. Now, to top things off, he had heard nothing from Emil about the atomic device the Drang was supposed to plant to drive a wedge between America and her new ally, United Europe.

Around noon a feathery V of swirling water propelled a speedboat toward him from the shore.

"Why haven't I heard news of an atomic bomb abandoned by the European terrorists?" rasped Krebs as Emil climbed aboard.

"There's been a change of plans, Horatius. I have the atomic bomb. That is, I know where it is."

"You betrayed me and set yourself up in business, eh?"

"I knew you would never agree. Now you have no choice."

"Is that so? Where is the bomb?"

"Aboard one of the scramjets just moved to Deseret."

"How?" Krebs was excited, in spite of himself.

"When the truck crashed through the Gigatex gate, I jumped. I set off grenades that disabled the local cameras. I hid the bomb aboard one of the scramjets."

"It will be detected."

"If you want to hide an atomic bomb, hide it in a nuclear reactor. Gilgamesh is nuclear, you know."

"Fool! I'll simply tell the Department of Space they have a bomb aboard one of their scramjets."

"How? By calling them up and saying 'I'm Horatius Krebs and I know there's an atomic bomb on one of your ships'?"

"An anonymous tip. The way we told the FBI about Bengal."

"How will you explain a bomb that has Python's logo on it?"

"That's why I haven't heard from the men I sent to you," he mused. "What are you going to do, Emil?"

"Explode the bomb. That's the only way to deliver a telling blow to the Sunside Project. People must die."

"You do enjoy your work, Emil."

"This way you will never betray me. Even a peripheral association with such a disaster would destroy you."

"All right, what is your plan?"

"Create a diversion, using my operatives. They expect a sabotage attempt. We'll give them one. While they're occupied, I'll enter the space center and arm the bomb."

2

Emil had one more element to his plan: Bethany Williams.

Rita Duce's former executive secretary was in Denver in a home for derelicts. It was across the street from a "public trough" that served unappetizing food three times a day. To earn a place to sleep, the women did public chores.

Bethany had fallen as far as a person can: She no longer respected herself. Ever since being released in Miami by Rita Duce's security officers, she had drifted.

She discovered that with her lover Harold Peron dead it was impossible for her to get to the money he had been given as a down payment for trying to wreck the Challenger tap. She went through her own funds quickly.

It was true Duce hadn't prosecuted her, but her activities were entered on her personnel file, without which it was impossible for someone in her profession to apply for a job. She had used her considerable computer skills to fabricate a fake job history, but each time she was found out. It was as if she was being hounded.

At first she suspected Duce or even Jason Scott, but she soon dismissed that notion. Neither was petty enough to seek vengeance in that fashion. Bethany was stunned when Scott didn't prosecute her for sabotage, but if you understood his philosophy, his actions were entirely logical. Vengeance was outside his consideration. Obstacles were to go around or to be overcome. They were not objects of hate.

She had admired Rita Duce more than any person she had ever met, up until the day she met Scott. Despite her admiration for Duce, she had been willing to betray her, but after a few days with Scott, it took all her passion for Harold Peron, and the wealth he represented, to make her continue to work for Python.

Scott was unlike anyone she had known. His strength was not physical, but strength of character and will. He was a natural force, like a hurricane, an earthquake, or the sea. Such a man might be killed but not defeated. She was drawn to him because she aspired to be that kind of person, and his final words to her had hurt like a knife cut, because they undermined her view of herself. "I'm gravely disappointed in you, Bethany. You were meant for great things."

In the months that followed she tortured herself a thousand times with that image, and worked up what she imagined to be a hatred for Jason Scott and all he stood for.

She worked west, hitchhiking and sometimes selling herself for a few miles. She sank until she was no better than the lowest derelicts. Strangely, that was a comfort.

Subconsciously, her target was the national Deseret Space Center. At least that was Emil's thought.

He kept track of her wanderings. It was he who made sure that all her prospective employers knew her history. As he became more familiar with her, he realized she might be very useful.

He found her skewering leaves in a park. Her once stunning helmet hairdo had long since collapsed into a mass of greasy curls. He bought her real coffee. She thought he was a potential john. Lately the pain and emaciation in her face had turned off all but the most perverted or desperate.

Emil's Drang training served him well. With casual questions he deeply probed her wounded psyche. He preferred less subtle methods, but restraint was called for—he would reward himself with an Indian boy when he returned to the Quintana Roo.

Although she bitterly denounced him, it was apparent she was in love with Jason Scott. Emil tried a bold, oblique approach.

"I'd like you to work for me." That penetrated her self-induced haze and she became alert.

"Who will I be working for, really?"

"The same man I work for: Horatius Krebs."

A kaleidoscope of emotions passed across her face. The last emotion, the one that settled, was guile.

"What do you want me to do?"

"Pose as a systems inspector for the shuttle *Sally Ride*. You were a systems engineer for Tectonics Corporation. You can fake it. Find out what's going on the shuttle, and the passenger list.

"You'll disguise yourself and be smuggled into the space center with a new ground crew. You'll have impeccable ID: Python developed the supposedly counterfeit-proof ID for SED."

He could almost see the wheels turning in her head as she asked: "Are there others in the space center working for Krebs?"

"If it is necessary for one to contact you, he will."

"Who does Jacob Kane work for? He's been all over the cube, supposed to be part of Scott's team. Does he really work for Krebs?"

Emil kept his voice neutral. "Of course."

3

The Sea of Cibola gleamed like a polished bronze shield as dawn became day 'at the Deseret Space Center.

Before dawn, Bethany Williams and fifty other maintenance personnel boarded the SED bus in Deseret City for the twenty-mile drive to the space center.

Someone who looked like Emil talked to three men just as they boarded the bus.

She watched them. They looked like the sorts who had been her constant companions the last six months. They acted odd for three apparent acquaintances: Once on the bus they sat as far away from each other as possible.

She decided to watch them. Their uniforms indicated they were in her division: last-minute maintenance of the shuttles' fuel and electrical components.

Morning sunlight caught the shuttle gantries from miles away. It was still awe-inspiring to see the three great ships, each as tall as a skyscraper, poised for launch.

Bethany had decided this time to prove to Jason Scott that he had been right about her: She was meant for great things.

Chapter
* 46 *

First Secretary Peter Brasnikov arrived at the railgun facility like a whirlwind. He enjoyed playing the dashing young premier, full of vitality and ideas.

New things fascinated him. He had commandeered one of the ten working prototypes of a helicopter gunship, the MI-70—really a flying tank—so he could fly in with a maximum of drama.

He had several senior officers in tow, including Colonel General Wen Chin and Colonel Pavel Orlov, deadly rivals for years.

Orlov was tall and Nordic, blue-eyed, open, strong, with curly reddish hair, and blinding teeth. Chin was as short and formidable as a warrior of the fabled Golden Horde. His muscles were stretched cords of wire covered with tanned horsehide.

The remarkably agile Chin leaped from the helicopter and climbed the steep hill to Wolff's headquarters. Dark, brooding, hawkish eyes in sunburnt folds of skin took in everything.

While Orlov took professional delight in examining the soldiers of the CosMarine Division he would soon command, Chin gained the heights overlooking the X vehicle, which was in the last stages of being loaded onto the railgun. He regarded the vehicle with fierce joy.

Chin was joined by Marshal Tiomkin, Colonel General Wolff, and, after much grinning and playing the man of the people to the hilt, Premier Brasnikov.

"You'll find this launch interesting, General Chin," said Tiomkin, with a smile for the man who was his greatest threat.

"Pity I won't get to see it in person."

"Eh? Do you have to get back to Alma Ata then?"

Brasnikov, who was chatting with Wolff, interjected: "There's been a change in plan. As a reward for his excellent work, I'm detaching Chin for a temporary assignment before he surrenders to high command. He'll command the *Aurora* on her maiden voyage!" He looked enormously pleased with himself. "With special instructions from me."

"What a surprise," said Tiomkin. It was not unheard of for Strategic Spaceborne Forces officers to command warships but it was unusual to make an appointment without consulting the commander in chief. Commissions for the spaceborne forces routinely crossed his desk even when awarded by the Politburo.

"Yes, it will be." Brasnikov's face darkened. "Chin will have some amusement with the shuttle carrying the project head of the Sunside Project, which we were blackmailed into backing. This will send a message that we will never again be bullied."

"I anticipate the assignment," said Chin. "If I'm to ride the shuttle and rendezvous with *Aurora* I must leave immediately."

The premier grasped Tiomkin's elbow. "Walk with me, Antonine Mikhailovich."

They strolled onto the promontory that overlooked the rail.

"It amuses me that the Americans have so effectively tied their own hands with the food treaty, my friend."

"First Secretary?"

"Entering a public pact, I achieved what we have tried to do for many years. They won't risk war to stop us from deploying our new warship. They have stopped us from building battleships in space and threatened facilities we began in orbit. They monopolized the cosmos—and they were right to do so. But now their president cares more about his food treaty than about keeping us down."

"A propaganda coup, Comrade First Secretary," said Tiomkin.

"We won't announce our technical triumph to the world. Since America operates under the glare of publicity, we have an advantage if they increase their space fleet. They will face a dilemma, tempted to denounce our building program, but also wanting to keep quiet to avoid hurting the 'cooperation' between us."

"Do you think the president is so dedicated to his treaty that he will let us threaten his nation's security?" asked Tiomkin.

"He's an idealist. Although he bested me in our first round together, this is, as the Americans say, a fight to the finish."

2

The railgun track stretched a hundred miles underground. The tunnel's mouth opened nearly five miles above sea level, overlooking rocky tundra surrounded on three sides by the world's highest mountains.

The railgun was a Lorentz force mass accelerator. Its force was generated within an expanding current circuit, acting in association with a magnetic field. The current circuit was closed at one end by the power source and at the other end by a moving armature of dense plasma.

The armature would accelerate a projectile through a hundred miles of bore pumped to a near vacuum, and theoretically achieve speeds far superior to anything ever reached by a rocket drive.

The main problem was frictional stress on the projectile when it shot into the atmosphere. The Soviets had solved that with the Collapsium shield, built to burn away from the hull.

Collapsium shielding was expensive, but the projectile would only be launched through an atmosphere once during its lifetime.

Twelve hours after the premier's arrival, the sun rose, casting red fingers into Greater Asia. The closest human habitation was a Buddhist lamasery just inside the Asian frontier.

What happened next convinced the monks that the end of the world had come. The mountains trembled under a vibration similar to that of an approaching train but magnified a thousand times. It grew in intensity until every mountain within miles began to shake loose its garment of ice into cascading avalanches.

With violence comparable to a volcano, fire and smoke belched from the side of the mountain. Glaciers melted under heat unknown in the region since the last ice age.

A fiery ball arced across the sky. It lingered on the dazed retinas of those who looked toward the mountain when it erupted. It was visible over much of India, Tibet, Afghanistan, and the Indian Ocean.

It left the atmosphere faster than any missile ever had before. Intense heat burned away much of the Collapsium shielding, as was intended.

The missile shot away from the earth in an extremely elongated trajectory that took it almost to the orbit of Luna. With constant firing, by remote control, of its forward rockets, the missile slowed its trajectory on the return trip.

Twenty thousand miles over the territorial waters of Australia, long ago withdrawn into its own, smaller, version of Fortress America, the missile entered a stable parking orbit.

Nearby, in geosynchronous orbit between Asia and Hawaii, floated the space city Cosmograd. Grown from the first permanent Soviet space station, Mir, it was the only major Soviet base near earth. It was home port of the fleet, such as it was. The size of the warships berthed in the five-mile-long tube of latticework was limited by the materials that could be brought from earth.

America's Tycho Base fleet did not permit others to build military craft on Luna. It also monitored the small warships built at Cosmograd. No one doubted that if work began on anything threatening, the fleet would take action.

Both sides lacked a powerful enough space drive to build a massive warship on earth and boost it into orbit.

Until now.

Most of the Collapsium had burned off. Three Cosmograd shuttles approached. Onboard computers came on and the remaining shielding was released. The shuttles rendezvoused with the missile and spacesuited figures detached the segments.

Hours later, the mirror-surfaced battleship liberated from Collapsium, the cosmonauts entered to take up duties as its crew.

Chapter

* 47 *

1

Sherlock Michlanski was in his lab in the Deseret Space Center inspecting a package of instruments when he got the call.

Mel Hardrim's video image, in camouflage fatigues, materialized. For once, Michlanski was at a loss for words. How did he address Hardrim, since the inspector was probably on an unmasked line?

"This call is secure," said Hardrim. "Chambless felt circumstances warranted brute force. The Deseret communications system will be disrupted for exactly three minutes."

Michlanski was quite familiar with the technology that had temporarily knocked out Deseret. "Then you'd better talk quickly."

"Someone has smuggled an atomic bomb into the space center."

"Well, that's certainly interesting. How?"

"Unknown. We know it's connected with the terrorist spy ring in

Detroit and one of Horatius Krebs's people is involved. I'll send a hyperspeed transmission of our data. Can you accept it?"

Michlanski keyed in a sequence. "Go ahead. The federal authorities warned that someone might try sabotage. I hadn't heard the words *atomic bomb* used, though." He squinted at Hardrim. "You off to the wars? You look awfully martial for a former police person."

"I'm leaving shortly on a trip I hope may provide me with more data. I hope you can do something about this."

"Several things occur to me. I have an idea how an atomic device might be smuggled onto the preserve. I seem to remember that Python designed our ID system. Fascinating!" Deep in thought, he forgot Hardrim was on the line. He looked up again and dismissed him with a wave. "Leave it to me, young man."

2

At minus six hours to *Sally Ride*'s launch, Bethany Williams was nervous. She had watched her three coworkers for days and had seen nothing suspicious. She couldn't turn them in without proof. The chances of anyone believing anything she said were nil.

She took part in a final inspection of the *Sally Ride* from top to bottom. Half the passengers had already boarded.

It was easy spying for Emil. No one monitored her assignment: detecting oxygen leaks and electrical shorts in the labyrinth of crawl spaces and corridors enclosing the fuel storage tanks of the shuttle booster.

The crew of *Sally Ride* were sitting on top of an armed bomb of liquid oxygen. LOX, one of the most volatile substances in existence. It was the inspectors' job to help see that their trip was not a suicide mission.

In the booster's starboard bay, she knelt in the narrow corridor and unfastened a maintenance shaft grill. She slithered inside to check an electric cable. When she came out three men gathered around her in a semicircle.

"You've been watching us," said Smack. Cradle's eyes were glued to Bethany's backside; he caressed his bald head lasciviously. Jaff rubbed his hands together. His smile was unpleasant.

"I—I, watching you?"

Smack moved closer. "We were told to contact you."

She let out a breath. "You work for Emil?"

Smack nodded slowly. "Yes. You will help us?"

"What do you want me to do?"

"Help us get to where liquid oxygen is pumped into the booster's main fuel tank."

"That's a slim space, intended to be serviced by robots."

"You're small enough to fit." Smack held up a package the size of a freeze-dried meal. It was wrapped several times with black tape. Wire from the top ran to a digital finger watch. "Tape it under the pipe where the fuel is pumped in."

She took a deep breath. Only by cooperating would she be able to do something against them. "All right."

They climbed to the booster's forward bay, which housed the main tank. They passed several maintenance workers. Bethany longed to call for help.

The crawl space was accessible from a hatch sealed by an easily removed panel. She was wrong about the size. Narrow as it was, Smack, who was thin, could have slithered through it. It was low, but wide enough for two people to crawl side by side.

Bethany squirmed into the hole. Fortunately the crawl space was lit by glowing strips or she would have felt claustrophobic. The sides were lined with molecule chip boards and wiring. She pulled herself along until she came to a raised area where several fuel conduits joined and bulged up. The liquid pulse was very strong, like a giant's heartbeat. Although insulated by several inches of glassteel wool, the metal was quite cold.

She crawled over the bulge. She was under the conduit leading into the booster. The pulse was almost overpowering.

She examined the bomb. She knew nothing about explosives. If she tried to disarm it, she would blow up herself and the hundred people who had boarded the shuttle in the last hour.

She taped the bomb to the pipe. She assumed it was armed, although the watch gave no clue how much time remained.

They were waiting outside. She described what she had done. Smack nodded. "You have a little while. Find an excuse to leave."

"No excuses, except medical, are accepted today."

"You must arrange to have an accident then," said Smack.

"I could help." Jaff smiled nastily.

"Thank you. I'll think of something," said Bethany quickly.

"Just a friendly offer," said Jaff.

"Leave her alone, Jaff." Smack almost sounded like a human being. "Good-bye, Miss Williams."

After she had left them, she realized something was very strange about the last hour's events. Something was even stranger about her employment by Emil and Horatius Krebs.

Emil had asked odd questions about her attitude toward her betrayal of Jason Scott and Rita Duce. How much had she revealed of herself?

Was this a trap set for her—and Scott? Why did Smack, Jaff, and Cradle need her help to plant the bomb? For that matter, why were there three of them, when one could have done the job?

Was she supposed to warn Jason Scott? Being who he was, he wouldn't trust defusing the bomb to anyone else. He would probably walk into a trap. They wanted him on the ship when it blew. And they were willing to give up their lives. Bethany had noticed signs of drug use by Smack. She guessed he was a Jack heroin addict; he had interface marks.

Bethany left the booster via the access arm, emerging onto the gantry. She took the elevator down and walked out the only gate from the launch area. She crossed the tarmac to the box-shaped administration center for the Sunside Project at Deseret. Until now she had avoided it, fearing that Jason Scott, Jacob Kane, or Matt Taylor might recognize her. Now she walked boldly inside.

"I'd like to see Jacob Kane."

3

"How wonderful to see you again, Bethany, particularly under such interesting circumstances." Kane sprawled, like a spider, at his desk, casual and insolent. His dark eyes seemed to pick through Bethany's jumpsuit to fondle the flesh beneath.

"Did your secretary tell you what I told her?" she demanded.

"Yes, that's why you're not on your way to prison for trespassing on federal land with fake ID." He laughed raspingly. "I told them to change their security procedures, to issue new IDs. God, I love to be right!"

"You're wasting time, Jacob."

"Time spent talking to a beautiful woman is never wasted."

"No? Time spent talking to a pompous ass sure as hell is!"

"All right. Where's the bomb? I'll take care of it myself."

She told him.

"And how long do I have to defuse it?"

"I don't know. That's why I want you to get off your ass!"

"Point taken." Kane sprang to his feet in a single fluid motion. "Rest that magnificent fanny right there, love. In case you're tempted to stray, I have a guard just outside. 'Bye!"

When he was gone she rushed to his holocube. She entered a code: "Get me Jason Scott's extension, please!"

3

"What's your game, Bethany?" demanded Jason Scott fifteen minutes later in his office.

"No game. I'm just trying to save a few hundred lives."

"But why didn't you go to Jacob first?"

"Because I don't trust him."

"Surely the irony of that statement must amuse you, Bethany. Don't trust *him*? Why should I trust you, of all people?"

"What I did against the Challenger tap—nothing I did endangered anyone's life."

"Unless you count me."

"I didn't know Harold would try to kill you."

"This conversation is pointless."

"Remember, Jacob Kane was my control on the Challenger and Emil told me he still works for Krebs."

"If you don't trust him, why tell him about the bomb?"

She told how she had been recruited by Emil. "A few minutes ago I realized Emil has been setting me up—to trap you."

"Why you?"

"Because I—I think very highly of you," she said lamely. "He knew that when I found out a bomb was on the shuttle I would warn you and thus lure you into a trap. I decided to turn the trap on its head. You must see the validity of this test! If Kane defuses the bomb, he's loyal. But if he fails to report it—"

"You've missed a vital point. You're right that Emil probably figured I would defuse the bomb—I have had extensive training with explosives. But the point is, with three saboteurs inside the perimeter, we've probably got more than one bomb. Emil intended you to think that Kane was a traitor so you would send him to a trap especially set for him."

"I only saw the one bomb."

"*You* only saw one. Yet you admit they were using you as a Judas goat."

She nodded grimly. "Yes."

Scott sat at his holocube, fingers flying over the keyboard. Three busts appeared in the cube. "Are these the three men?"

"Absolutely."

"The computer says they have impeccable backgrounds." His blue eyes blazed. "Give me a reason to believe you. You may be trying to disrupt this launch."

"Are you aware that the system that makes the counterfeit-proof ID cards and badges for the center was manufactured by a subsidiary of the Python Corporation several years ago?" As Scott quickly double-checked this fact, Bethany added, "You have no choice. You *must* evacuate the ship."

"No time. The bomb must be found and defused." He stood up. "I ordered a bomb squad to meet me at the launch gate. Come along." He started down the hall.

She struggled to keep up. "I want something from this!"

"What? Money?"

"No, damn you! I want a place on your team. I've earned it!"

"Correction, the slate's clean. When this is over, we'll talk."

"That's all I ask."

Matt Taylor met them at the gate. The wind was tossing his white hair. His mahogany complexion was shiny from sweat. He was cradling a submachine gun.

"Every time I see you, we have to shoot somebody," said Scott.

"I got two dozen armed men."

"Post half of them outside. They know the dangers of firing near liquid oxygen?"

"Nobody's trigger-happy. Especially not me."

"Search the booster in teams of two. The passenger bay is sealed. There's no way between the bays, so they can't get among civilians."

"Did you notify space center security?"

"Yes, but this is our show." Scott looked at Taylor grimly. "You told the men we don't know when the bomb will go off?"

"Right."

"Any word from Jacob?"

"Doesn't answer his personal communicator."

"Then we must assume he's inside the ship and in trouble."

"Yeah. There's one or two other possibilities, too."

Scott knew that Matt Taylor had never entirely trusted Kane since the Challenger tap incident. Scott had known Kane since they were boys, and still he could not say that he entirely understood Kane's motives. Kane's actions were suspicious, although Scott wanted more than anything not to think about the implications of that fact.

"We'll keep all the possibilities in mind, Matt," he said, banishing his doubts for the moment. "Ready? Then, let's go."

Chapter

* 48 *

As the new Soviet battleship was approached by shuttles from Cosmograd, President Shefferton and his advisers watched on a large holocube in the White House situation room.

Shefferton towered over his subordinates, except for Secretary of State Randolph Harmon. Sitting nearest the president was Colonel Jim Farley, the CIA director, recently returned from a painful implantation of new teeth. A former colonel in the Mississippi National Guard, he liked white suits and black string ties, and sported a silky white goatee.

Senator Charles Macadew sucked on an unlit Cuban maduro and leaned against the situation room's mahogany table.

Sheridan Mayfield watched with fascination and revulsion.

The chairman of the joint chiefs of staff, General Abraham Ball, flanked by aides, watched impassively. He was totally bald and built like a tree stump. His tan, weathered face was impossible to read.

The vice-president and the national security adviser were absent. Mayfield knew the NSA was fishing in Canada but he wondered about Teresa St. Clair. Like his predecessors, Shefferton often overlooked his vice-president, whose views differed so sharply from his.

Cosmonauts stripped away the shielding to reveal a mirror surface emblazoned with the red sickle and golden helix of the Genetic Communists. Shefferton turned to Farley.

"I can't say you didn't warn me, colonel."

"Not soon enough, I'm afraid, sir."

"I can't hold you responsible for what the CIA wasn't allowed to do under my illustrious predecessor."

"There is some good news, sir. We never actually knew where the Russians were taking railgun research. We hypothesized they were developing an ICBM system to swamp our ABMs. But a railgun massive enough to launch this monster must have taken such an effort that they can't have gotten far in adapting it for launching warheads. Our ABM defense is safe for now."

An aide interrupted. "Mr. President. The chief of space naval operations is on line if you wish to speak to him now."

Shefferton nodded. "Please." The grizzled, energetic face of Admiral Hanley Davis materialized in a second cube lowered from the ceiling. "Admiral, good of you to respond so promptly."

Davis nodded. "Sir, we've been observing the new craft and made a pretty good thumbnail analysis of her capabilities. She's something completely new for the Soviets: a fully armored battleship with ship-melting lasers, a full complement of antiship weapons, and a Collapsium ceramic 'sandwich' hull that can withstand a small nuclear warhead if it's not a direct hit. We only have five ships as powerful."

"What do you mean?"

"That ship is possibly on a par with any of ours. It's actually much larger than ours, but I doubt in this case that size translates into fire power. Whatever its capabilities it will be operational in minutes, or hours at most."

"Do you suggest any course of action?"

"I've ordered Commodore Hastings's squadron with the *Thunderer*, the *MacArthur* and the *Tecumseh* to intercept the Russian battleship."

"To what end?"

"Why, to destroy her. At least you have that option if you choose to exercise it."

"What!?" Secretary of State Harmon virtually shrieked.

"Or, if you prefer, we could use our new railgun ABM platforms to take her out."

"Didn't you just say this battleship is as good as any of ours, Admiral?" said Shefferton calmly.

"She *will* be. Right now she is a powerless hulk. A sitting duck, in orbit without a crew and or sensitive electronics. Any living thing aboard would have been killed by the tremendous acceleration. She's vulnerable for a short time.

"Hastings's squadron is an hour away. One warhead will do it. We'll evacuate the crew. No one will be hurt."

"What about the force at Cosmograd?"

"We can reach the battleship first."

"They could still make a fight of it, couldn't they?"

"They'd lose. One battleship can deal with Cosmograd."

"I'd like you to countermand that order to Commodore Hastings, Admiral," said Shefferton coolly.

Davis's reaction was as cool. "Yes sir. I remind you that a Soviet warship this powerful will undo our strategy. In one stroke the Soviets become a major military player in space."

"We knew our monopoly couldn't last. Such a one-sided balance of power leads to resentment, and arms races, and wars."

"As you say, sir. Personally, I prefer unequal contests that are over in an afternoon."

"You're a dangerous man, Admiral Davis!" said Harmon.

"I certainly hope so, Mr. Secretary."

"I do think you're exaggerating the danger from this one ship, Admiral," said Shefferton.

"I submit the Soviets didn't build an expensive railgun to launch *one* ship," said Davis. "Even so, at this juncture this first battleship can be dealt with relatively bloodlessly—"

"Admiral," exclaimed Harmon, "you military types are always willing to spill the blood of subordinates!" Davis remained impassive, but General Ball turned slowly, a red spot on his bald pate, and regarded Harmon with undisguised hostility.

"Mr. Secretary," said Davis, although his eyes were on the president, "we can destroy the ship now. But once you have a functioning battle-wagon up here, it will take a war to end it. And the problem will grow each time they launch another."

"They want parity, Admiral," said Harmon reasonably. "We've bullied them for decades. Their pride won't let them grant us domination of the cosmos. We must swallow our pride and let them catch up. Or we'll have another arms race. Nobody wants that!"

"Wal, then, by God, let's do 'er easy and blow the goddamned thing into a ball of radioactive gas right now, while we can!" said Macadew.

"You've been drinking, Senator."

"So I have. But that's beside the point."

"So is this discussion," said the president. "You all miss the point. Hostile acts toward the Russians will make it impossible to carry out the food treaty. It will endanger the Sunside Project and leave her open to reprisals. The project and food treaty are cornerstones of this administration. I won't do anything to threaten the spirit of cooperation."

"Jeff, let's at least publicize what the Soviets have done." There was a note of pleading in the senator's tone.

"Absolutely not! I hope the usual Russian love of secrecy keeps them from announcing this. The press would have a field day. We'll do nothing to rekindle the distrust that helped establish Fortress America."

Mayfield had kept quiet. Now he spoke up. "Mr. President, the shuttle *Sally Ride*, with Jason Scott and senior members of the Sunside Project aboard, will launch from Deseret in a few hours, followed by the *Glion Bluford* and *Fra Mauro*. They'll rendezvous at LEO-4 and the passengers will board the lunar shuttle. Only the *Sally Ride*'s flight can be intercepted by the Russian battleship. If there is a danger, we should abort the mission."

"No!" said Shefferton. "We're not going to cancel a mission that has been scheduled for weeks. I'll not buffalo the Soviets, but I certainly won't let them buffalo us—not from performing a legitimate function of a treaty they signed."

"Sir," said Mayfield. "This development is all the more reason to push to develop the Gilgamesh fleet with all speed."

"I fully agree." The president sighed heavily. "Well, this has caused enough excitement. Let's get back to work."

2

"I need a drink," croaked Macadew as he and Mayfield entered his sanctum sanctorum: a library, bar, and card room. Here he often hosted marathon poker games. "Hell, I need the whole bar!"

Macadew fumbled under the wetbar for a bottle, and threw peeved expressions at Mayfield.

"Okay, Charley, what's on your mind?" snapped Mayfield.

"Uh, nuthin'."

"Bull! Spill your guts, *if* the room can hold that much."

Macadew's coat was off, his hair was skewed. His necktie was in ruins.
He lifted his tumbler, winked, and gave his killer smile. "You're always
abusive, son, when you feel guilty."

"I'm abusive all the time. But I can tell when you're trying to shift
your own guilt onto my shoulders. Yes, I can!"

"Okay, we're both guilty."

"Of what?"

"Lettin' Jeff make the wrong decision."

"He's the president. He can do any damned thing he wants." But he
looked deflated and Macadew knew he had scored a point.

"Yes, but you and I were the only ones there who could've stood up
to him with th' possibility of changin' his mind."

"So, when do you blast the president from the chambers of the Senate,
Charley?" Mayfield looked sardonic.

"Same time you issue a statement deploring his decision."

"It would be a security breach of enormous magnitude."

"Security breach my ass! Whose security would be compromised if we
let the public know the Russkies put a battleship into space?"

"We'd end up in a political wilderness. You've been through it before;
I'd be out of a job. We'd both lose our friend."

Macadew was gloomy. "I 'spose we could toss our political fortunes
an' do the right thing because it's for our country."

"But we won't do that, right?"

"Right."

The holocube chimed. "We have a call for Mr. Mayfield."

"Dammit! The bastards always know where to find me."

"We'll take the call, darlin'."

"Secretary Mayfield?" The woman was director of Deseret Space Center.
"We have an emergency at the launch site."

3

CLASSIFIED HOLOVIDEOTAPE RECORDING
BY ORDER OF THE PRESIDENT OF THE UNITED STATES
TO BE OPENED BY MY SUCCESSOR UPON MY DEATH
OR INCAPACITATION

[President Shefferton is seated at his Oval Office desk]

I assume the person viewing this is Vice-president St. Clair.

A grave responsibility is now yours. I have been custodian of a secret for many months. I now reveal it to you. You must decide what to do with it.

I deliberately kept you in the dark about certain decisions I made, not from distrust but for your own protection.

My actions leave me open to impeachment. I want you to be able to prove you had no knowledge of my actions. I wish to state also that Secretary of Space Exploration and Development Sheridan Mayfield was ignorant of any illegal acts. It is my wish that this recording be available as evidence in court, or in an impeachment trial of any members of my administration before the United States Senate.

When Dorian Nye came out of hiding, I met privately with him and Sherlock Michlanski. The subject we discussed and our resulting agreement was the basis for the Sunside Project.

The Sunside Project, as we have announced it, is a hoax. The Strubeck equations are not what we told the world.

Alfred Strubeck did discover a formula to create complex sugar molecules from sunlight. But the process is not efficient enough to feed more than a tiny percentage of the world's population. The equations could feed a space station, not a world.

They cannot, by the most optimistic calculations, end the inevitable cataclysm of world famine, only forestall it.

The world was pushed toward catastrophe by the Santa Bella blight, but it was already going that way. In the last war the combatants nearly wrecked their industry and agriculture, but populations remained high. Infrastructures are now so flimsy that another war would cause their collapse and push the world into barbarism. The United States herself could fall.

When Michlanski and Nye brought me this news about the Strubeck equations I felt like a man who has just been told he has rogue cancer.

I grasped at the tiny ray of hope they offered.

The equations for creating food are part of Strubeck's larger schemata of time and space, energy and probability.

Call it part of a grand unification theory, or unified field theory. Think of it as one of the pillars holding up Mount Olympus. Strubeck's equations harness the process of creation of matter and energy. They can take man to the stars.

I don't pretend to understand the math, although Michlanski and Nye took pains to explain to me what they were talking about. The equations would enslave the laws of probability, to move matter (perhaps re-create is a better word) from one point in the universe to another, without occupying the space in between.

Strubeck predicted that islands of perturbed probability will be found orbiting large masses, like our sun. The purpose of the Sunside Project is to verify that prediction, and to use an island of improbability to perfect a star drive.

Will a star drive solve our problems? Perhaps not. But we will be in an enormously better position.

Years ago the White Point probe found an earthlike planet orbiting Tau Ceti. That data was suppressed.

At this point in history, our world has energy left for one last hurrah. Whether for the final conflagration, or a possibly futile effort to fight starvation, or to push out of the womb and grab for the universe—that is the choice.

Perhaps I didn't have the right to make that choice for America, for the world. Does any government? Does any man?

Sometimes democracy breaks down. Sometimes the people can't make a rational decision. The majority is not always right. In today's political climate, no popular government could gamble on FTL to save our race. Popular governments always pursue the low-risk course. Democratic peoples can produce great cultures, freedoms, and prosperity. But when it comes to defending themselves, they are handicapped by the necessity of consensus.

We had no time for consensus.

I asked my countrymen and the world to unite to save humanity.

To sacrifice, and ration resources until salvation arrives. They responded. Our relief program has been a replay of Christ and the loaves and fishes. The great powers, even Russia, are sharing resources. We have averted a war, for now.

What is the worst case? We fail to discover a star drive, war happens and we say good-bye to civilization for a thousand years. If we do discover FTL, we have a chance to move part of our population to Tau Ceti and beyond. This will relieve some of the aggressive pressures, and even if the cataclysm occurs, we will have transferred some eggs out of our fragile basket.

The best that can happen is that we move enough of our people to provide substantial relief and prevent war, and that the new colony can not only feed itself, but send back surpluses.

I gambled with lives not mine to gamble with, I made decisions not mine to make, and I carry the weight of the universe on my shoulders, which I never asked for.

Tonight, I saw my friends doubt my judgment because I let the Soviets put a superbattleship into orbit. I understand their concern, but nothing can stand in the way of the Sunside Project.

Whether history will judge me a criminal or a hero is not for me to say. Let history at least give me the benefit of the doubt when it hands down its verdict.

Good luck, Teresa.

END

Chapter

* 49 *

"Ladies and gentlemen, this is the National Science Network, bringing you live the launch of the *Sally Ride* . . ."

The camera panned across Lake Deseret, where hundreds of pleasure hydrofoils and sailboats gamboled. It moved to take in the dramatic sight of three spacecraft, each as tall as a skyscraper.

"To the right are the first experimental prototypes of the Gilgamesh scramjet, due to be tested next spring . . ."

Senator Percy Shelley Manners watched the broadcast from his office. He glared moodily at the image.

He had tried banishing Krebs's offer from his mind, but it always crept back. Now, watching Shefferton's triumph, Manners felt overwhelming jealousy, like flames, licking up his guts.

"Goddamn him!" he muttered.

* * *

"One hundred thousand people are here to watch the triple launch. That's the largest turnout for a space launch since Colonel Tarketon's Uranus expedition in the *Achilles*, fifteen years ago."

Ralph Ferman sat at the foot of the bed in a small cabin in Michigan's Upper Peninsula. He had switched the tiny holocube to the science channel to watch the launch of the Sunside Project shuttles. He ate a stale granola bar slowly, to make it last.

This was the last time he would have a roof over his head, at least for the foreseeable future.

That didn't frighten him as it once had. He had been alone for some time now. Once he was free of the FBI he had headed for the sparsely inhabited Upper Peninsula.

Hardrim was alive, but Ferman didn't know how to contact him. He had tried to call Hardrim's friend Lenore Lippman, but had been told she was in the hospital. That meant he was alone. As he saw it, the only way to survive was to avoid people as much as possible. He had given up on convincing anyone in authority about the Argus Society conspiracy. At least for now.

He had done a lot of backpacking as a student, including a hike to the summit of Olympus Mons on Mars. He knew it would take weeks of seasoning to get in tone to where he could hike into the mountains. He would begin with the least traveled byways, where there were still dirt roads and towns the world had forgotten. Later he would go into the wild. His compass setting was west.

He finished the granola bar and decided to watch the end of the launch before he set out.

"It is T minus two hours, and for an explanation of what crew members of the *Sally Ride, Glion Bluford*, and *Fra Mauro* will do on the moon, we switch you to our lunar editor . . ."

The Gilgamesh scramjets were lined up a mile from the gantries. Perfect range for the baby nuke, thought Emil as he walked toward the end ship, identifiable by its serial number.

From here he saw the gantries, oil derrick shapes. Resting on top of them were the cranes. A quarter of the way down each one was the shuttle access arm, where passengers boarded. Below that was the booster access arm where liquid oxygen was pumped to the booster.

His papers identified him as a high-level technician for the Gilgamesh project, as did his immaculately pressed sky blue uniform. Under mirror sunglasses his eyes were restless, tiny tracking antennae. So far he had had no difficulty going anywhere on the base, even though security had been tripled and everyone who stopped him ran his ID through a computer.

He wondered about Cradle, Jaff, and Smack. He expected momentarily to see evidence of their activities. He had noticed security's heightened state of readiness around the gantries and guessed they had already been detected. If so, his plan was working perfectly.

He was passed through one more checkpoint and then he was inside the scramjet preserve. He walked to one of the vast white structures, wheeled a portable stair to it, and gave a friendly wave to the guard who had passed him through. He climbed the stairs and went inside.

Horatius Krebs stopped in front of a sapodilla tree to let his two fine male chimpines leave their marks.

Quintana Roo was hot and muggy. Sweat beaded on his upper lip and crawled down his open-neck safari shirt. The air was spicy with the smells of the Yucatan jungle, the buzzing of insects, and avian calls.

When the chimpines finished with the tree, they twisted their large heads to look at Krebs with remarkably intelligent eyes, eyes that could almost speak.

"Sher! Kang! We're going to the house." He meant the small guest house where he often stayed. He was not immune to the anticipation surrounding the shuttle launch. He wanted to watch the drama.

The chimpines' ears perked up over bulging craniums at the mention of the word *house*. Meat! They opened their jaws and white saliva drooled onto the spongy soil.

Suddenly their ears pressed back against their skulls. Krebs swung around, frowning. He could hear no birds, no insects. Everything was quiet, except for the low keening growls of Sher and Kang.

A tall, big man in army fatigues, carrying a full kit, stepped into the clearing.

The chimpines went for him, and died in midleap, torn to bloody shreds, as an astonishing beautiful redhead appeared next to the man and emptied a flechette gun at point-blank range.

Bandits! thought Krebs. In the distance he heard automatic arms fire.

Short bursts. Some shouting. Then what looked like one of the army's new gunships skimmed overhead.

"My guards?" rasped Krebs, unafraid. Whatever these people wanted, it couldn't conceivably end in his death. He was too valuable.

"Surrendered or dead," said the redhead. She talked into a communicator. "A little bit of both."

Mel Hardrim walked over to Krebs, covering him with a .44 automatic. He clucked with false sympathy. "It's so hard to get good help these days."

"Who are you?" said Krebs.

"You don't know me."

"That's why I asked the goddamned question!"

"I'm asking the questions." He put the muzzle of his gun against Krebs's forehead. "Mr. Krebs, to me you are the lowest, stinking, ratbag pile of garbage I have ever met."

"So?"

"So, I ache to terminate you. I want to kill you!"

"How much?"

"A lot."

"I mean, how much money do you want? A million ounces of gold? Everyone can be bought. I deal in the human commodities market, and I've never gone wrong by selling short."

"I'm afraid a recession just hit." Hardrim jammed the .44 harder against Krebs's head just as a small explosion mushroomed a mile away. "Other people don't like you either. If you keep making offers, you'll approach my price, in which case I'd have to blow you out. So let's not discuss deals. Let's discuss shoes and ships and sealing wax, and where the atomic bomb is planted and where your Drang is."

Krebs clenched his jaw so hard it hurt. Emil! The swine had screwed them both. "It's on one of the scramjets at Deseret."

"Which one?"

"I don't know. It's not my doing! It's too late anyway—one of my men has run amok. I've tried to stop him. You can't prove otherwise."

"I don't have to. I'm not the government. I'm just the man who can put a forty-four slug in your brain. I know about your Drang assassin, who systematically wiped out people connected with Adam Scott; and about your funding of European spies. I'm prepared to release that information to the public."

"You'd have done so if you thought it could hurt me. The government can't hang anything on me." He laughed harshly.

"Krebs, it's all right to dabble in politics. But you're going to have to give up extracurricular activities. It's time for the Drang to shuffle off this mortal coil."

"Damn you! Why doesn't anybody talk English?" raged Krebs. "The word is kill. And nobody wants Emil dead more than I do."

"That almost rings true." Hardrim tapped the .44 against Krebs's forehead again. "Tell you what. I'll give you the chance to deal with Emil, if that's his name. I'm going to check your information about the atomic bomb. If you lied, or you don't take care of Emil, I'll come back and kill you. You can't trace me. Double or triple your guards, and I'll get through. I hope you believe me."

"I believe you," said Horatius Krebs.

"We interrupt for a special report at the launch site: There seems to be trouble. Security has cordoned off the launch area and a dozen armed men have taken up covered positions near the shuttle.—Wait! A shot! I can't tell where it came from . . ."

Technicians had cleared out of the booster when Kane got there. He took the elevator up to the booster access arm, then climbed a ladder to the forward bay.

He carried a case of bomb defusing equipment and a .38 automatic pistol.

He had considered calling Scott. It would have been like old times when they were both young engineers working for Krebs.

It never entered his mind to call the space center's bomb specialists. It would be too much fun to do it himself. He had told his secretary to call security after he got on board, so those near the launch pad could take shelter. It was useless to try to evacuate the shuttle.

He reached the forward bay. His communicator, part of his lightpad, started to beep. He turned it off. Probably Jason trying to spoil his fun.

He found the hatch Bethany had crawled through to plant the bomb. The panel was leaning on the bulkhead. He stuck his head in the hatch. He saw nothing but glowing strips. It would be a tight fit. He pulled his head out and opened the case.

He heard a sound, dropped the case, and sprang to his feet. Two men in SED overalls rounded the corner. One was tall and bald, and hefted a nasty-looking spanner. The other was little, but with the look of a small dog that gets its jaws around your wrist and never lets go. He had a knife. Both were like zombies, with leaden, unfocused eyes.

"Horatius's standards are slipping. You guys join the team during one of those 'hire the handicapped' programs?"

"You laugh it up. We'll have some fun," said the short one with a grin that displayed brown broken teeth.

"I don't think so." Kane leveled his .38 at them.

"Fun." He came toward Kane, oblivious to the gun. He swung the knife. Kane fired. The little man whirled like a piñata struck by a stick, then came on again, with a dark stain on his shoulder.

"Shit!" Kane fired again. The man whirled back a step, righted himself and came on, this time with a ragged tear and a spreading stain in his chest.

Over his attacker's shoulder Kane saw the other on his knees entering the hatch. He sidestepped a knife aimed for his stomach, twisted, and fired point-blank into the little man's right knee.

His scalp crawled when the man went down—without a sound. A knee shot should have made him scream. As it was, he flopped around and tried to stand.

Kane holstered his gun and dived into the hatch. The other was a few yards ahead, moving arms and legs in a curious crablike motion that ate up distance.

It's like being inside of a coffin, thought Kane as he imitated the other's movements, moving joints and muscles he hadn't known existed. He put on a burst of speed and his hand closed on an ankle. He pulled with all his strength.

He ducked kicks from the other foot and held on. His left hand reached for his gun. Another kick caught him on the knuckles and turned his whole hand to numb ice. The gun flew away.

Kane scratched and gouged with his numb hand while his adversary tried to turn in the narrow space. Feeling returned to Kane's hand and he closed it around the man's crotch. There was a sharp intake of breath and a spray of saliva as he thrashed; his foot smashed into Kane's mouth and he squirmed loose.

They grappled in a clumsy, silent wrestling match, pummeling each other ineffectually because there was no room for leverage. Kane concentrated on punching the man's midsection, but took painful blows to his own face and chest.

For the first time Kane felt fear. His own strength was ebbing, but his adversary had a superhuman, drug-induced endurance. The man knew it, too; blood dripped down his face from a gouge over his eye, but he was grinning.

Kane's fingers closed on the two arteries on either side of the man's neck, the only supply of oxygen to the brain. No matter what drugs he was on, he needed oxygen.

Kane absorbed three powerful blows to his chest without loosening his grip. He began to beat the other's head against the floor. The man's answering blows were lighter and lighter until his eyes rolled up in his head and he went limp. Kane continued to bash his adversary's head until he was sure the man would never move again.

For a moment he lay, breathing heavily, nerves on fire. Then he pushed the body out of his way and continued crawling.

The bomb was a simple affair, as befitted its artificers. He didn't have to be particularly careful to disarm it. That frightened him. Maybe this bomb was just a decoy.

He retrieved his gun, returned to the hatch, and slithered out, every joint on fire.

The short man was still trying to stand. He saw Kane and tried to throw his knife, but Kane pinned the man's hand with his foot. Then he very deliberately put his gun to the man's head and fired.

2

Smack had left Jaff and Cradle to deal with whomever Bethany Williams sent to defuse the bomb. He fully expected them to die. Just as he expected to. But it didn't matter. Nothing mattered except getting more Jack heroin.

His backpack was filled with explosives set to go off in thirty minutes. He could also set it off manually. Until it went off he would stay out of sight inside the booster.

3

Kane stumbled onto the booster access arm and took the elevator down. When he stepped out several guns pointed at him.

"What's this?" he demanded, as Jason Scott and Matt Taylor sprinted over to him.

"We were expecting the mad bomber," said Scott.

"What do you mean? I just killed a couple of guys up there."

"Sensory equipment aboard shows one other in the booster. He's in the starboard bay now. Everyone else is cleared out. It has to be the third man."

"Third man. I didn't know there was more than one! Where is that bitch?" He looked around for Bethany.

"We have her to thank that we had any warning, Jacob."

"*You* may have her to thank, but she set *me* up."

"Quit bitching. I need a way to deal with this third person."

"Simple. Flood the booster with fire-retardant gas. It sucks up oxygen. He'll suffocate or be forced outside."

"What if he brought an oxygen mask?"

"Then we'll be up the Great Manure River."

"It's worth trying." Scott gave instructions to Taylor, who spoke into a communicator, then looked at Scott and nodded.

They waited.

"There he is!" A man appeared on the booster access arm.

"Don't fire," said Scott. "A shot can set off the LOX."

"Then what do we do? He's got a bomb on his back."

"Somehow," said Kane, "I get the feeling that trying to reason with these people is a futile gesture."

"Cut power to the gantry," said Scott into his communicator. "If he wants to get around, let him climb."

Smack started up the gantry, toward the shuttle access arm.

"He wants to be next to the passenger bay when he blows up!" said Taylor.

"I thought it might come to this." Scott took a climbing harness from his bag and slipped it on.

"You gonna climb up after him?"

"No time to try anything else."

"The hell we don't," muttered Kane, out of earshot. He stalked toward the gate.

Moments later Scott was on the gantry, attaching a line to each beam as he scaled it. He worked fast, with no time for safety. As he climbed Smack watched him intently.

Scott redoubled his efforts. He stopped taking time to attach a safety line between each girder.

Smack aimed something at him. He smelt burnt paint and saw a dimple on the steel a few feet from his foot. A laser.

He used girders to shield his body as he continued climbing.

Halfway up, several levels under the shuttle access arm, was a metal ladder. Scott decided to chance Smack hitting him for the added speed. He put his foot on the first rung.

His legs moved like pistons. He felt the heat from a laser beam near his ear. He looked up. Smack fired again. Luckily, laser pistols were very inaccurate at almost any distance.

He climbed. Breaths were gasps of fire and his heart pumped in his ears. He grabbed the next rung and pulled his right hand back in agony. The rung was melting and as Scott watched, it came loose. The ladder swung away from its mooring and Scott was suspended in space, unable to reach the girder or to climb up.

A black shape blotted out the sun over Scott. A single-seat helicopter seemed headed directly for him. At the controls was Kane, a look of fury on his face.

Scott's heart froze. Bethany was right. Kane was a traitor.

He looked into Kane's face and realized, as the chopper flew by him, that Kane wasn't looking at him, but at Smack.

Too late Smack saw the helicopter. For an instant a strange tableau was enacted on the shuttle access arm as the man seemed to battle a giant insect.

Scott swung like an acrobat and cleared the space between ladder and girder. He fastened his safety line and hung on.

The helicopter pulled closer to Smack, who fired wildly at the canopy. The whirlybird swung its tail and Smack lost his balance and fell in a long arc.

About fifty feet above the ground he blew up.

The shock wave hit Scott and knocked the wind out of him. The hot updraft caught the chopper and Kane fought the controls to keep away from the gantry. Up and up, the helicopter turned rapidly in a clockwise direction.

Gradually the controls responded and the helicopter descended until it was level with Scott. Kane opened the cockpit door. A sardonic grin played on his lips.

His words were lost in the chopper's roar. He motioned to Scott to pick up his communicator, which dangled at his belt. Kane's raspy laugh grated in his ear.

"I said, if you're tired of hanging around, I'll give you a ride down."

"When we get down, some apologies are in order."

"What the hell?"

"You need to apologize to Bethany for misjudging her, and I need to apologize to you—for the same reason."

Chapter

✳ 50 ✳

1

Emil turned on the inside lights in the scramjet. He moved apt along a corridor lit by blue overhead globes.

In a locker room he donned a yellow radiation suit and proceeded until he came to a heavy metal door with large red signs warning of radiation. This separated the reactor from the rest of the ship. It opened with a satisfying metallic clank.

He stepped through. The bomb was where he had left it days before: hidden behind a panel, surrounded by multicolored wires.

He inserted a key in the bomb's housing and tried to turn it. It didn't turn. He put weight behind it, but it didn't budge.

He examined the bomb closely. It was not the same one he had left aboard the ship! He kicked it savagely. Only one thought occurred to him: flight. He ran out of the reactor room.

He reached the exit hatch. It wouldn't open.

The lights flickered once, then came on full force, changing from blue to white incandescence. He shielded his eyes.

"Attention, intruder. This is Sherlock Michlanski. I'm afraid you're caught. You'll find none of the exit hatches work. You're no doubt asking yourself how we figured out where you hid the bomb. While it is fruitless to try to plumb the depths of genius, analyzing the process of ratiocination is a valuable exercise."

Emil took a gun he had smuggled onto the base and fired at the voice. "Shut up! Shut up! Shut up!"

"I asked myself how would I smuggle an atomic bomb onto a base. The obvious answer was, to let SED do it for me. My father didn't give me the name Sherlock for nothing—"

Emil's last shot ended Michlanski's sentence.

He went to the cockpit. He had given himself a Surroundee-conditioned learning session on the plane's controls; it was in many ways like a jet aircraft, with added capabilities. It had some fuel. Not much, but enough for some test firings. Enough to get airborne.

He sat at the controls.

"Zerrk!" exclaimed Michlanski in dismay. He was seated in front of a console in Mission Control. Scott and Kane, still bruised and bleeding, stood behind him.

"What's he doing?" demanded Kane.

"Taxiing for takeoff. My word, you can't fault him for a lack of initiative."

Scott picked up a handphone. "The intruder is taking off," he said into it. "He can't have much fuel, only enough for a test firing tomorrow. Yes, I'd say alert the Pentagon. You may have to shoot it down."

The scramjet took off and screamed over the Mission Control blockhouse.

"It's headed southeast," said Scott, giving the exact bearing. Already a squadron of fighters had scrambled to intercept the stolen scramjet.

Moments later it left radar, although it was still picked up by satellite and plotted on a big map on the far wall.

"It's over Mexico," said Scott, listening to the transmissions from the fighter squadron. "They've fired a missile." He listened. "A hit! It's breaking up over the Yucatan Peninsula." He smiled tiredly. "That seems to be that."

2

The survival pod came to rest ten kilometers west of Horatius Krebs's estate. Emil emerged from the pod, bruised and weary, and with a badly fractured leg.

He dosed himself with the drugs in the pod's first aid kit, and cut a serviceable splint. He could endure the pain. Pain was nothing to him. He began limping east. He kept up his spirits imagining how he would run one of the village boys into the maze that contained Krebs's monster snake, Kali.

His enemies thought he was dead, as he had intended. After a few weeks' rest at Krebs's estate, he would be ready for revenge.

His almost superhuman constitution kept him going until he reached the clearing that marked Krebs's property. The great Mayan pyramid rose over the jungle. It all faded into green as he collapsed onto the ground.

He awoke in a clean bed. Krebs was standing over him, conferring with a physician. It was that filthy Kraut, Dollfuss! Emil masked his contempt.

"Ah, you're awake," said Krebs nodding. "I'm glad you're safe and sound. Dollfuss says you'll be up and on crutches in a few days. Mend quickly, Emil. I have plans for you."

Emil closed his eyes, contented, and slept.

Krebs walked onto the clear substance that covered Kali's maze. Down below, he saw her immense coiled shape, with the unnatural-looking bulge over cold, never-closing eyes.

Yes, he wanted Emil on his feet again. Otherwise he would be no sport at all.

For the next few weeks, the great snake was afflicted with a most extreme case of diarrhea.

3

In the dying fire of afternoon, *Sally Ride* stood poised to return home—to space.

Secretary Mayfield's helicopter brought him to the space center in time to see Smack's long fall and explosion, and to see Emil's escape in the scramjet.

Near the launch site he held an impromptu news conference and answered as many questions as he could. He was joined by Scott, Kane, and Michlanski.

Mel Hardrim watched the show from a bed in a small motor inn. Kirsten Fale was in the other bed, asleep. They were returning to Detroit together, not from any physical attraction between them, but because they enjoyed each other's company. He had spent hours telling her about his relationship with Lenny. She had just about convinced him to go back to her, if she would have him.

But first, he was going back to the Argus Society, to follow up on the information Ferdinand had given him about Ralph Ferman. Hardrim had a lot of work ahead of him.

4

"It's been a hell of a day!" said Mayfield irritably.

"It's going to end better than it began," said Scott.

"You're going to continue with the launch?"

"I'd be a fool not to. We've used up our bad luck for the day."

"I won't allow it," said Mayfield, although he knew President Shefferton wanted the takeoff to happen as planned.

"Take it up with a higher authority, like Kismet, God, or the Wizard of Oz," said Scott with a mischievous grin. "We've got work to do."

Mayfield decided not to spoil it by telling Scott about the Russian railgun launch. He could give Scott a few minutes of triumph before the bad news.

Today was a time for triumph—or at least hope. The world was truly in a mess. The Soviets were becoming an international menace again. Famine threatened Africa and Asia. Juba Aman Dana, the Leopard, was making warlike noises toward his neighbors. And Mayfield was beginning to doubt the wisdom of his president.

But if anyone could make a difference—Mayfield believed Scott, Kane, and Michlanski were the ones. They were dreamers, yes, but with a vital difference. They could turn their dreams upon lathes of reason and dedication and make them real. Such men are dangerous—and wonderful.